The
Metropolis
Case

The
Metropolis
Case

A NOVEL

MATTHEW GALLAWAY

CROWN PUBLISHERS

NEW YORK

Copyright © 2010 by Matthew Gallaway

Published in the United States by Crown Publishers,
an imprint of the Crown Publishing Group,
a division of Random House, Inc., New York.
www.crownpublishing.com

CROWN is a trademark and the Crown colophon is a registered trademark of Random House, Inc.

Translation of the *Liebestod* from *Tristan and Isolde* used with kind permission of Christopher Bergen.

Library of Congress Cataloging-in-Publication Data
Gallaway, Matthew.
   The Metropolis case : a novel / Matthew Gallaway. — 1st ed.
     p. cm.
  1. Opera—Fiction.   2. Immortality—Fiction.   3. Wagner, Richard,
1813–1883. *Tristan und Isolde*—Fiction.   I. Title.
   PS3607.A415515M48   2010
   813'.6—dc22   2010013576

ISBN 978-0-307-46342-5

Printed in the United States of America

DESIGN BY BARBARA STURMAN

10 9 8 7 6 5 4 3 2 1

First Edition

FOR STEPHEN

First Act

Contingency

1 . . . .

The Tristan Chord

NEW YORK CITY, 2003 *(via e-mail)*

S—news!—your elder brother has procured four tickets to
the opera on the Saturday night of your visit next month
AND invitations to the after-party at Demoiselles, an
old and rather exquisite French restaurant not far from
Lincoln Center. There will be champagne; there WILL be
chocolate soufflés. (Obviously M had a big hand in making
this happen: you'll be able to thank HER in person.) We're
seeing Tristan and Isolde by Richard Wagner, which
means I should fill you in on a few things starting now, to
prepare you. You'll be happy to note (as I read somewhere,
or possibly imagined) that certain listeners who attended
the opera's premiere 130-something years ago did in
fact GO INSANE and were shipped off to asylums in
the Bavarian Alps with a diagnosis of "Tristania." I can
hear you muttering "apocryphal" in your Ph.D. voice, and
while I'm not inclined to disagree, insanity IS perhaps
an understandable reaction if we put ourselves in the
shoes of 19th-century listeners (always an interesting
exercise at the opera, or at least the old ones) and
consider the unprecedented volume of the orchestra (one
of the largest ever assembled) combined with a complete
absence of recorded sound to that point in history—i.e.,
NO WALKMEN?!—and an equally unprecedented musical
dissonance (except for perhaps a few "tone poems" by the

supremely gorgeous and talented Franz Liszt—who by the way was Wagner's father-in-law and whom he shamelessly ripped off both financially and artistically, in the way things were done back then)—I DIGRESS.

First the easy stuff: on its most superficial level, Tristan and Isolde is about an affair—surprise!—between T and I that unfolds as she's about to be married to his uncle ("uh-oh" is right), after which scandal and tragedy ensue, THE END. What's more interesting is that their love, in addition to being illicit, is very much entwined with an unceasing torment and longing (represented by "the day" or more broadly "life"), not just for each other but for a more permanent form of relief (otherwise known as "the night" or "death"). BEAR WITH ME—IT'S NOT AS DEPRESSING AS IT SOUNDS! Or even if it is, it doesn't matter because the music—despite possessing very little that might be considered a "tune"—is lush and restless and revolutionary to the extent that, like so many great works of art (leaving aside the question of exactly which ones), it encapsulates much of what came before and predicts much of what followed. Or to put it in more musico-historical terms (whatever, I know it's not a word), it's essentially—and perhaps shockingly, for those of us who get excited to find traces of ourselves in such things—"modern" for its failure to ever quite resolve, or at least until the very end, by which point—if it's a good performance, which I expect given the parties involved— you'll be reduced to a spoonful of quivering jelly. The piece is in a state of constant flux, with one atonal chord giving way to the next and then to the next and so on and so on and so on, like you're listening to the aural equivalent of one of those time-lapse photography projects of an endlessly mutating landscape. My own theory (by which I mean I may or may not have also read this somewhere) is that Tristan contains the seeds of modern "abstraction" and "psychology" that ultimately defined so much of the twentieth century, i.e., it's no accident that in the wake of

Tristan (1865) you have impressionism (Elstir!), cubism, Duchamp (specifically Nude Descending a Staircase, No. 2), Freud and Jung and V. Woolf and Einstein (that's for you, Professor Vallence), and eventually, I don't know, the Smiths? (Hey, I never claimed to be an academic!)

Which is not to say Tristan will hammer you over the head—for most "contemporary" (such a horrible word, ruined by furniture catalogs and bad radio stations) listeners, it's a more subtle form of annihilation. (Speaking of which, I ordered you a copy: listen to it, ideally more than once—SEE ABOVE, REGARDING RISK OF INSANITY.) Take note of the instrumental section at the beginning (the famous first-act prelude), the quiet call-and-response of the cellos and winds, the pizzicato burst of strings that will (after you've acclimated) strangely dictate the beat of your heart to match the languid tempo of the piece. And once you've listened a few times, I guarantee the music will start to "infect" you (but in a good way), so that—if you'll allow me to play "rock critic" for a few seconds—you'll start to hear Tristan echoed everywhere, in the beautiful, angry chaos of our beloved Velvet Underground, in the ethereal, tremulant white noise of My Bloody Valentine, or even—and perhaps more to the point, given where you'll be staying—in the endless tides of traffic moving into and out of Manhattan along the West Side Highway, five hundred feet below my balcony in Washington Heights. You should also note that however "difficult" it may be for listeners to digest, it's even MORE dangerous to sing; Tristan is the super-double marathon of operas, and its history, like that of Mt. Everest, is littered with the corpses (both literal and figurative) of those singers who made the mistake of attempting it too early in their careers, or lacked the proper training, didn't have the right kind of voice, or—saddest of all—simply expired under the weight of so much dissonant longing.

In practical terms, what all of this means is that you and C should absolutely, positively resist the temptation to plan anything on Saturday afternoon that doesn't involve napping, or at most lounging, because curtain is at 7:00 p.m., the opera is five hours long (I KNOW), and dinner won't be served until 1:00 a.m. or thereabouts. (I've learned that most denizens of the opera house, like those of the seediest East Village punk-rock venues, are truly nocturnal, which perhaps explains some of my affinity for both?) Plan to wear whatever you'd like as long as it's "fabulous" (I offer in a half-ironic tone), but there's really no such thing as overdressing for the opera—especially on opening night—so when in doubt, DO NOT HOLD BACK. (By the way, I'm also imposing a similar regimen on P, who is equally uninitiated and who will be joining us as MY date.) So brace yourself, little S, it's going to be an evening you won't forget too soon; the curtain will rise to lead us to new lands from which we—like so many before us—will return both destroyed and cleansed, knowing we'll never be the same! xoxo M

2

Through Its Street Names, the City Is a Mystic Cosmos

NEW YORK CITY, 1960. Anna Prus stepped out of her apartment building onto Seventy-fourth Street, where she paused to glance back at Central Park, which looked opaque and grainy like an old newsreel. It had been snowing for days, but a sallow, expectant glow emanating from the crenellated perimeter of the park told her the storm was nearing an end. While she did not relish the idea of negotiating a trip downtown, the transformation of the city into a tundra, with squalls of powder and amorphous mounds where there had once been cars, mailboxes, and shrubs, struck her as the perfect accompaniment to the magic, improbable turn the day had taken, now that she was about to make her Isolde debut at the Metropolitan Opera.

Though Anna was not an unknown, she had to this point in her career been relegated to smaller houses and (except for some minor roles) hired by the Met as an alternate to the type of leading soprano she had always wanted to be. But as sometimes happened with singers her age—Anna was forty—her voice, after six years at the conservatory and over fifteen more of training, auditioning, and performing, had at last blossomed, giving her reason to believe that she had found her calling in the Wagnerian repertory. Which is not to say her future had been unfurled like a red carpet; if anything, her reputation as a dependable but hardly breathtaking talent still preceded her, and for this current production, she had been brought in only to "cover" the Isolde and so had expected—as she had always done in the past—to spend her nights in the wings, anxiously hoping and not hoping (because she was not one to wish ill health or misfortune on anyone) that she would finally get her chance.

This time her luck was better; from the start, the lead struggled with the role and after much gossip and speculation had finally canceled, which meant Anna was going on tonight and possibly for the entire run if she could deliver the type of performance the Met general manager, Rudolf Bing (having made a point of attending one of her cover rehearsals in the event of just this contingency), expected of her. Anna buried her scarf-wrapped chin deep into the neck of her fur coat and wrapped her arms around her bag, which held a carefully folded dress, shoes, and jewelry for the opening-night party scheduled for after the show. She walked forward into the wind, nimbly tracing a line through a group of men digging out with picks and shovels, and forced herself to review a mental list of exactly what she needed to attend to—wig, costume, makeup, voice—and whom she needed to see at the theater—Mr. Bing, the maestro, the director, the Tristan—before her seven o'clock curtain.

Reaching the corner at Broadway, she stopped to catch her breath before she skipped off the curb toward a small island of pavement with a thought to hail a cab, but with her vision obscured by the heaps of snow, she managed to jump—and this she realized with a gasp as the ground rumbled beneath her—directly in front of a massive truck. If time did not entirely stop for Anna, it slowed, just as she had always expected it would in the final seconds before her death. With no chance to escape forward or back, and still clutching her change of clothes, she raised her face to the sky: her blue eyes turned opalescent in a last glimmer of winter light and she begged her parents to help from the afterlife, to arrange with whatever power was responsible for this senseless calamity to delay it a little longer; even half a day would suffice.

Whether as a result of this prayer or thanks to some deeper instinct, she felt something stir within her, something she had long trained herself to recognize but had never surrendered to with such abandon; possessed by her Isolde, she turned toward the truck and in the fraction of a second remaining unleashed her power: "*Wer wagt mich zu höhnen* [Who dares to mock me]?" she screamed, filling each note with the same vengeance that had marked her recent rehearsals. If no less aggrieved, she felt satisfied: the line had been delivered with a potent mix of force, indignation, and curiosity. Her mind grew quiet, even serene; any doubt about her ability to sing had been laid to rest. As she opened her eyes, the truck seemed to pass slowly through her, as if the sublime quality of her voice had momentarily turned her body to light.

She looked past the surrounding snowcapped peaks at the looming apartment buildings, which seemed to sway in the deepening night, and as much as she longed to join this darkness and its promise of tranquillity, of belonging to nothing and everything all at once, she knew that it was not yet hers to take. She heard a thunderclap, and everything turned white. A moment later she found herself safely on the sidewalk, where she looked at the passing traffic and a few errant pedestrians, hunched over and seemingly concerned with nothing but managing their own treks through this temporary wilderness. Anna was not dead; time, she observed with gratitude and awe, had resumed its unsteady course. She placed a hand on a snowbank to confirm her return to a more familiar world, the same one—she remembered with a jolt—in which she was about to sing for thousands of other souls, each in its own way as desperate as her own.

3

Der Mann ohne Eigenschaften

NEW YORK CITY, 2001. Walking into Demoiselles, the French bistro on Fifty-fourth Street, Martin allowed his eyes to wander over the plush burgundy banquettes that curved into the distance and the folds of drapery that cascaded down from the caliginous heights. Though pleasantly full, the room was not overcrowded or frenetic, like so many newer restaurants, and he savored the quiet but insistent clink of silver and crystal above the hushed conversations. He spotted his friend Jay at the bar, clutching a glass of what he knew would be a Highlands single malt not less than twenty years old, undiluted by water or ice. They had known each other since boarding school, and though a year had passed since their last meeting, a

September birthday dinner was a tradition; Martin's fell on the eleventh and Jay's was the nineteenth: both were turning forty-one. They shook hands—a vestigial gesture of Martin's past—before they embraced and returned to the bar. Martin ordered a drink and made a toast to their respective survival through four decades and a friendship that had endured more than half of this time, after which they spent a few minutes discussing Jay's wife, a former opera singer who now sat on the board of Juilliard. Although Martin had grown up listening mostly to rock, in part thanks to Jay, he had become interested in opera, and he often wished that his job allowed him more time to attend performances.

"So bring me up to speed, Vallence," Jay said as he pushed his wire-rimmed glasses to the bridge of his nose. "Seeing anyone I should know about?"

Martin shook his head. "Nothing serious—work is still too crazy."

Jay responded with a bark that Martin recognized as a laugh. "Didn't you say last year that you wanted to—and I quote—get a life?"

Martin smiled and patted his not insubstantial paunch. "I also wanted to lose some of this." At over six feet tall, with an often goateed, bearded, or at least five-o'clock-shadowed face and barely an inch of skin not covered in fur—and as much as he liked to avoid labels and the illusory "communities" so often associated with them—there was no getting around the fact that he was a "bear," and possibly even a "daddy bear" now that he was safely into his forties. "I'll get there," he promised, "but there's a ton of work at the firm right now—Internet stuff—'start-ups,' " he said, making the quotation marks sign with his fingers.

"Even after the vaunted 'crash'?" said Jay—returning the quotations sign. He could afford to be glib, given that his grandfather had

left him enough to make finances a negligible concern. Martin nodded as Jay continued. "So job aside—what else? How's the rest of
your year been?"

"I can't complain." Martin shrugged.

Jay laughed. "You can to me!"

Martin reconsidered the question. "Okay, how about a few nag-
ging problems on the health front I could live without?"

Jay grimaced. "Hello, life after forty."

"Indeed," Martin acknowledged before outlining a list of symptoms with which he had been bothered in the past year, including episodes of numbness in his hands and feet, maddeningly itchy armpits,
an arthritic knee, and problems sleeping as a result of an unrelenting
need to piss on some nights, particularly—and here he paused to signal the bartender for a second round—after drinking. "Sorry if that's
too much information before dinner."

Jay brushed off the apology. "Christ, Vallence, we're forty-one,
not fourteen! Physical decline should be expected and embraced at
our age, except by those of your jockish ilk, who try to perpetuate
youth with tricks and mirrors."

This was not exactly fair. Though Martin had started all four
years in goal as a hockey player at Cornell—and had long enjoyed
his athleticism and accompanying good health, a few extra pounds
and his HIV-positive status notwithstanding—it was also true that, in
keeping with a tradition of goalies, he had largely avoided the weight
room and most forms of cardiovascular exercise, with the possible
exception of having sex, which—as much as he tried not to think of
it in such clinical terms—was probably the best thing he did for his
heart with any regularity. Because Jay was more or less acquainted
with all of this—except the more salacious details of his romantic
escapades—Martin felt no need to defend himself on such terms.

Jay waited for the bartender to replace his tumbler. "So what does your doctor say?"

Martin shrugged. "No idea about the hands and feet—and as for the other stuff, about the best he could come up with was prostatitis."

"Oh, that's a good one," Jay said, shaking his head. "Completely vague and incurable."

"You have it, too?"

"Try not to sound so cheerful," Jay remarked. "I was born with it—weak bladder, stabbing pains in your balls, insomnia—these things come and go."

They were led to their table, where they considered the menu for a few minutes before Jay picked up the thread of the conversation. "Well, if health is the issue—and even if it's not," he said after they ordered, "my recommendation is to retire, as soon as possible."

"At forty-one!"

"Yeah, why not—you've been raking it in, right? How much do you really need?"

Martin pondered this idea. "Okay—as a man of letters, describe for me a typical day in the life of Jay Wellings."

"Let's see," Jay mused. "Get up between nine thirty and ten, read the *Observer*, the *Times*, and—since I trust you—the *Post*. Drink coffee, do the crossword puzzle—in the newspaper, incidentally, and *not* on the Internet—read some more, maybe even thumb through *The Economist* so I can pretend to be interested in politics or foreign policy, meet someone for lunch—this could be you in the future—go to an exhibit or the theater. Watch Oprah or some other junk food once in a while. At night go to a show or the opera. Or more television. Or maybe one of those dinner parties Linda drags me to where I'm expected to make brash, unpredictable comments to the squeamish delight of the other guests."

Martin smiled slyly. "You don't sound too happy about it."

"What's happiness got to do with it?" Jay again barked. "You have to assume that existential malaise—which is not quite the same as boredom, incidentally—is a constant of modern life, and live accordingly."

WHEN A FEW minutes later Jay left for the men's room, Martin observed his friend's slouching gait and was reminded of the day they met in boarding school, where they had been roommates beginning in tenth grade. He remembered the first time he had seen Jay, slumped on his bed against the wall, effectively two-dimensional as he sat reading a small yellow book, his hair short and parted on the side but still messy, like he hadn't combed it in weeks. After an introduction limited to an exchange of first names and a handshake flimsy enough to make Martin feel relieved that his father—who would definitely have broken Jay's fingers and made a joke about it—had already left, Martin stood stiffly, trying to think of the best way to proceed. He spotted a postcard-size photograph of what appeared to be a rock band taped to the wall. "Who's that?"

"The Velvet Underground," Jay muttered as he stood up and took a step toward his desk, on which sat an impressive stack of stereo components. When Martin didn't immediately respond, he added: "You know—Lou Reed, 'Walk on the Wild Side'?"

Martin nodded. He liked the song but wasn't familiar with the Velvet Underground. "So who else do you like?"

"The Ramones," Jay answered in what to Martin seemed like a needlessly abrasive tone. He knew that Jay was from New York, which made him wonder if everyone there spoke like this, or if he had done something beyond revealing his ignorance of the Velvet Underground to offend his new roommate. Jay picked up a record from a pile scattered on the floor, shook the LP out of the sleeve, and placed it on the turntable, where after dusting it off he set down the needle with a finesse and a sure-handed authority that Martin could not help but admire. Jay turned to Martin. "You're probably into disco."

"Uh, no," Martin said as he brushed a mass of black curls away from his eyes.

"Well, good for you." Jay again seemed to sneer but then, to Martin's pleasant surprise, in the next few seconds managed—after pulling out a small wooden box from his desk drawer—to produce and light a joint, which he offered to Martin with a friendly and almost apologetic shrug. As happy as Martin was to accept this apparent peace offering, as the Ramones kicked in, he was repulsed by the obnoxious simplicity of the music; the drummer could barely hold a beat, the bass and guitar players played the same two or three chords over and over, and worst of all, the singer didn't so much as sing as half-croon and half-yelp his clipped lyrics. After returning the joint to Jay, Martin picked up the cover and stared at the four "freaks"—the term for "burnouts" in Pittsburgh, or at least in Cedar Village, the town where he had grown up—in ripped jeans, black-leather jackets, and bowl haircuts, wearing expressions ranging from completely vacant to somewhat defiant as they stood in front of a graffiti-covered concrete and brick wall. While Jay sat on his bed reading and smoking, Martin listened more carefully to the music as he reexamined the cover, and now—whether because he was a bit high or because he had gotten used to the sound—he noticed that one of the Ramones had his middle finger pushed out of his pants pocket as if giving him—i.e., the viewer—the finger, which made him laugh, and if the songs—e.g, "I Don't Wanna Go Down to the Basement," "Now I Wanna Sniff Some Glue"—were idiotic, they were pretty fucking funny in a way that his parents, for starters, never would have understood.

"So?" Jay asked after side two ended, less than thirty minutes after side one began. "Crap or not crap?"

Martin observed Jay's wiry arms, which like those of any geek looked as if they would have been taxed holding anything heavier than a pair of dice, except there was something ungeekish about Jay that fascinated Martin. It was not only the music he liked and his obvious facility at getting high but also his thick, expensive-looking chinos—even though they were beyond wrinkled and had one ripped knee—and button-down oxford-cloth shirt, which unlike Martin's was frayed around the collar and tucked into his pants in a few random spots. "I can't decide if it's the worst thing I've ever heard," Martin managed with an almost bashful smile, "but right now let's say it's the best."

SOME TWENTY-FIVE YEARS later at Demoiselles, as Martin watched the elongated flecks of chandelier in the curving silver handle of his butter knife, he tried to decide why the memory—as much as he would always love Jay and the Ramones—left him uneasy. He considered his vague if incessant dissatisfaction with work and thought about whether—questions of finances aside—he could ever really "retire," as Jay had recommended. Cutting back on his hours would be one thing, but—as much as he understood the impulse—it seemed like an option better left in the realm of the hypothetical, at least without a more concrete reason. Health problems aside, he could see himself shrugging off the same idea a year from now and, to be fair, wasn't horrified. As he saw Jay walking back to the table, he remembered something else from high school, which left him with none of the melancholy of the earlier memory. Again he heard music, although it was nothing he could place beyond an ethereal dissonance—a wash of distortion—and a slow, hypnotic beat that perfectly matched that of his pulse. He knew he was drunk but didn't care; he felt limber and relaxed as he peered through the smudges on his wineglass and welcomed the forgotten scene. This time, it was a few days later and they were at the window of their third-floor dorm room, flinging Martin's Led Zeppelin LPs against the Dumpster outside, where each of the broken shards reflected a different fragment of the bright September sun.

4

Il n'existe pas deux genres de poésies; il n'en est qu'une

NEW YORK CITY, 1960. It was almost noon when Anna heard a knock at her bedroom door. Her domestic entered carrying a silver platter covered with telegrams from friends and colleagues both old and new, offering congratulations and making requests to consider this or that role or to talk to so-and-so, while at least five claimed to know that critics from the *Times* and—even better—*This Is Our Music* planned to write rave reviews. With her head buzzing, she went to the kitchen and ate two soft-boiled eggs and a roll, along with drinking some very strong coffee—Viennese by birth and temperament, she was not partial to tea—before making a round of phone calls. As exciting as it was to consider what she had done, to rehash the details left her jittery and anxious in the solitude of the afternoon, and as she contemplated the prospect of singing in London, Paris, Milan, perhaps even Vienna, she could not escape a premonition of what the days after these spectacular nights might offer. To this point her out-of-town commitments had been relatively light, nothing like what she expected going forward, and even if she surrounded herself with people—the staff from opera houses and hotels, her fellow cast members, perhaps even a personal assistant—she worried about loneliness; it was such a common lament among top singers, after all, though one she had never liked to consider with too much seriousness for fear of being presumptuous.

Still, she wondered if her Isolde performance was only the first in a line of life-altering dominoes about to topple. She smiled at the memory of swooning over her ex-husband—an industrial tycoon fifteen years older than she was—in the early days of their relationship. While that hadn't worked out—as she acknowledged with a familiar mix of relief and disappointment—she hadn't given up; in the decade since their divorce, she had dated others, including a doctor (boring), a lawyer (argumentative), and even a dentist (fussy), all pleasant enough but none of whom had ultimately left her wanting to rip out her heart and offer it up with his to the endless night.

She returned to her bedroom and flipped through a stack of cards she had collected the previous night at the after-party—per the Met custom, held at Demoiselles—with a thought to find one that had been given to her by the friend of a donor; both men were seated at her table. Over dinner, she could not shake the sense that the friend was watching her with a pleasant (though not invasive) intensity as she greeted a steady stream of well-wishers like a bride in a receiving line. Several times she glanced in his direction, and meeting his gaze made her feel almost giddy, like they were sharing a joke about this performance after the performance, before he returned to the endless plates of escargots and bottles of champagne that appeared in front of them. They managed to exchange a few words across the table, enough for her to learn that he, too, was from Europe and that French was his native language, although he was also fluent in German. When she stood up to leave—after being distracted by still more patrons who wished to convey their admiration—she felt a pang of disappointment to find him already gone; that he was a big man, with a wide chest and broad shoulders, made his absence seem that much keener. She slowly turned toward the entrance of the restaurant and, as though she had conjured him up, spotted him walking toward her. He shook her hand—his grip neither too strong nor too flimsy—offered his congratulations, and gave her his card along with an entreaty to visit his shop—he was, she had learned, an antiques dealer—*n'importe quand*.

Anna considered the card's pleasant weightlessness as she flipped it over to read his name—Lawrence Malcolm—and the address and phone number of his business in Greenwich Village. While she was not so naïve as to think he would be the love of her life, she was not about to abandon the idea, either, especially after the threat of loneliness that had so recently frightened her. She also loved old things as a rule (notably Boulle furniture, French landscape paintings, and first editions of Musset and Bergotte) and collected with the same level of financial impunity reflected in the apartment itself, a sprawling duplex with views of Central Park. She dialed his number and was pleased when he answered on the second ring, as if he had been expecting her. "Mr. Malcolm?" she began. "It's Anna Prus—"

"Yes, yes—what a nice surprise, Mrs. Prus. How are you today?"

The enthusiasm of his response—unfeigned to her ear—seemed to affirm that the attraction she had felt the night before was not imaginary or the result of too much champagne. "Fine, thank you—I wasn't sure if you were going to be in this afternoon, but I thought I might take you up on your offer—"

"Avec plaisir," he said. "I'll be here until at least six o'clock."

"Perfect—I'll see you soon." Anna put down the phone, and as her hand passed through a beam of sunlight, she realized that the emerald stone of her ring was the same color as his lovely eyes.

AN HOUR OR so later, after being dropped in front of a storefront on Vanadium Street, Anna stepped out of the taxi and admired the curving row houses and cobblestones of the block, reminiscent of old Europe but somehow—and she recalled something to this effect that Lawrence had said the night before—less melancholy. After checking the address, she ascended a stoop and pushed open the front door; a silver bell echoed across the dusty shop and the bright winter sun filtered in through the naked trees outside. She spotted Lawrence behind a desk, partially obscured by a filing cabinet.

"Anna Prus," he said with a nod and closed his ledger, into which he had been entering figures—as she noted with appreciation—with a feather quill. "You're by far the most accomplished singer I've had the pleasure to welcome here." He took her fingers in his own and lightly kissed her cheeks, in the European manner, close enough for her to feel the soft scratch of his short beard.

"I'll bet you say that to all of your clients," she replied as she opened her overcoat and took in the contents of the room. There were armchairs, dining chairs, desks, secretaries, and other pieces, which radiated with a glow of iron and dark mahogany. The walls were lined with paintings and etchings, several of which resonated with an azure tone that reminded her of the sky outside. She smiled at him. "Your collection appears to match the graciousness of your words."

"You're very kind." Lawrence made a slight bow and after taking her coat invited her to sit. "Could I offer you a drink? A whiskey or perhaps some cognac?"

Anna opted for the former, and Lawrence soon returned carrying a tray with two glasses, a crystal flask, and a bottle of water. She received the glass with both hands, almost cupping them, which allowed her right palm to caress the back of his left hand, a gesture that seemed neither to surprise nor to displease him as he sat down across from her. "An Irish whiskey for an Irish princess," he toasted before nodding at her. "So—how do you feel after the big debut?"

She savored the ambient heat of the alcohol. "It's a bit unreal," she confessed. "I have to keep pinching myself, especially when I think about doing it again."

He nodded. "I haven't been to the opera in years, but you made me think it was worth the wait."

"I thought I overheard you say that," she remarked, catching his eye as if they were still flirting in a crowd of people, "which surprised me."

"It seems unconscionable, doesn't it?" He laughed and explained: "When I was younger, I was beyond idealistic—not just about opera, as you can probably imagine—but when things in the rest of my life didn't work out exactly as I hoped, I gave it up—I didn't want to be reminded." He looked up at her. "If that makes sense."

"It does," she emphasized and—prompted by his questions—described moving to New York City from Vienna with her parents, followed by high school in Washington Heights and conservatory at the Manhattan School of Music. Minutes vanished as they talked, and not once did his expression develop that maddeningly distant quality she associated with men who were merely indulging her, as if they couldn't quite imagine that singing was as important to her as their art (or more frequently, business affairs) was to them, nor—like certain opera fanatics she had met over the years—did he seem to want to exploit her experience to become more of an insider, to be regaled with backstage stories involving singers more famous than she was. She was struck by the certainty of having already met him at some forgotten point, which—though he had denied this the previous night—heightened the pleasure of talking to him alone for the first time. "So yes, I was idealistic, too—painfully so," she said, circling back to his original point. "I used to kill myself preparing for roles. I read philosophy and psychology, I studied the Eddic myths—I spent hours in the library—I wanted to be an 'intellectual' singer."

He refilled her glass and passed it to her, and perhaps allowed his hand to remain under hers for a fraction of a second longer than the first time. "What changed?"

"A few years ago I went in tears to one of my teachers after an audition, and she said, 'Anna, you have a beautiful voice—just use it!' And it finally dawned on me that I was thinking too much, that I needed to tell my story instead of the history of the world, whether it was the frustration of being a foreigner, the joy of conservatory, the love and disappointment of my marriage, or—perhaps more than anything—losing my parents."

"I know what that's like," Lawrence responded with a sympathetic nod as she observed him over the rim of her glass.

"You never told me," she said in a brighter tone, "what brought you to New York."

"Europe," he said softly and quickly, like he had been expecting the question, and with a kind of remorse she recognized in so many who had moved here from abroad. "What started as a sojourn has lasted—well, let's see—more than two decades." He swirled the whiskey in his glass.

"And do you have any family in Europe?"

"No." He shook his head. "Both of my parents were only children, as was I."

"Were you ever married?" she ventured, knowing the question might have been intrusive had she not already described her own marriage and divorce, a mostly amicable separation—as she was quick to point out—that she attributed to their age difference and widely divergent interests; for one thing, she confessed, he had detested Wagner.

"I don't think I'm the marrying type." Lawrence shook his head.

She raised an eyebrow. "You've never fallen in love?"

"I didn't say that!" he insisted and then seemed to reflect. "But not for a long, long time."

"Don't you miss it?" Anna asked as she remembered herself earlier in the day. Despite her intention to keep the conversation light, she knew from the rasp in her voice and the pressure in her temples that, as much as questioning him, she had exposed herself. "You see what Isolde does to me." She smiled through glistening eyes as she retrieved a tissue from her bag.

He set down his glass and waited a moment. "I don't often admit it—but yes, I miss it every day, and sometimes more, if I'm being honest."

She sighed wistfully, sensing that his response had pulled them together, as sometimes happened on a dance floor when she and a partner shed an initial formality, leaving them to float through the rest of the song. "I always hoped it would get better as I got older," she added quietly, almost speaking to herself.

"I think it does." He nodded. "You reach an age—or perhaps I should say I've reached an age when I'm not sure I could live through it again."

She appreciated his candor but was reluctant to agree with the sentiment, as much on her behalf as on his. "Don't you think that wanting to be loved is part of being alive?"

"I don't know if I want to answer that," he concluded, smiling sadly in a way that nevertheless seemed to acknowledge his agreement.

THEY SAT FOR a little while longer as Anna again contemplated her surroundings. She noticed a golden penumbra surrounding a closed door and felt herself wanting to move, to explore, to understand what had brought her to this room, only one of thousands or even millions in the city, many filled with people trying to unravel the threads of their past or their future, to feel for a few seconds like they were in control of not only themselves but also the ones they loved, or perhaps—like

her—hoped to love. She got up to stretch, and Lawrence, as if detect-
ing the train of her thoughts, also stood; his eyes filled with a mix of
resignation and inspiration, he stepped away from the table and beckoned her to follow. He led her to the back of the store, where after
passing through the door Anna had just observed they were confronted by a blinding sun streaming in through two large windows.
Like a moving silhouette, Lawrence—who maneuvered through
the crowded space with agility—made his way across the room and
closed the slatted blinds, which turned everything to bronze; then,
after returning to an adjacent wall, he invited her to sit next to him on
a bench in front of an upright piano positioned away from the light.

On the music stand was an old score, which he closed and handed
to her. It was not a published edition but a manuscript bound in a
faded orange-velvet binding, tied together with a blue silk ribbon.
She recognized *Tristan und Isolde* written in large cursive letters on
the front, along with the name Richard Wagner and the date April 14,
1860. Taking this into her hands, Anna whispered her astonishment,
questioning what she held, and heard him confirm—in a voice so
soft it sounded like it could have been in her mind—that yes, it was
an original copy, one of only a handful, which had once belonged
to Pauline Viardot, who as Anna knew had sung at the first reading
in Paris. She placed the book on her knees and slowly, reverentially,
flipped through the pages. It seemed impossible that a piece of music
to which she and so many others had devoted their lives had once existed in such a fragile state, a few sheets of paper and lines of ink that
could have easily ended up in the fires of obscurity.

She passed it back to Lawrence, who without being told seemed
to understand her desire to hear this opera as if it were a hundred
years earlier and they were releasing it into the Parisian night like a
flock of white doves. He placed it back on the stand, opened to the
middle of the second act, and began to play. As she shifted her gaze

between the written music and his hands, she suspected that he, too, was—or had been—a performer, a musician and possibly a singer, which made her want to hear his voice; it didn't matter how unpolished or crude. She wondered if she might prompt him and hesitated, recognizing the incongruity of uttering a note in such a venue, never mind that her voice was in strict recovery. A day earlier, she never would have done it, but after her Isolde—or perhaps *because* of her Isolde—she no longer felt constrained. She saw herself after the show in her dressing room and knew that under the piles of roses and the fading roar of the audience, there had been the tiniest doubt, not about the quality of her performance but about the rest of her life, and how it could ever measure up. Now, to feel so exquisitely alive—so full of suspense, this far removed from the theater—made her grateful.

She made her entrance, barely marking the notes, after which— as if she had decreed it—Lawrence responded in turn. Enshrouded in the music, they marched forward as a virtual orchestra seemed to attach to his fingers. No longer concerned about the wear of her previous performance, or the impact on the one scheduled three days later, she sang—*"Lass mich sterben!"*—and he responded with equal force. She lost all sense of time beyond a dim awareness of the twilight slowly giving way to the dark. Their voices so clearly belonged to each other—*"Hehr erhabne Liebesnacht!"*—that it felt equally inevitable, however long after they stopped singing, but before they had exchanged a single word, to find herself in his arms, their actions scripted but uninhibited, like they had rehearsed this scene a thousand times, crossing into the vaunted territory of instinct that every singer craves as they tumbled and groped toward an equally foregone but necessary conclusion. She still heard music, slowly receding as they kissed, violently at first and then with more tenderness, as she gasped under his weight and gave in to the desire to possess him—*höchste Liebeslust!*—in the same way he possessed her.

WHEN ANNA AWOKE, the room was black except for a rutilant glow around the windows, the last remnants of the dying sun. Lawrence gently pushed himself away from her, and they sat for a few seconds on opposite ends of a couch across from the piano. As she caught her breath and listened to him do the same, she tried to imagine how she would have reacted the previous day if someone had described this scene to her, which made her smile. "That was unexpected but wonderful," she said as Lawrence lumbered across the room and switched on a torch lamp next to the piano; the light filled the space with shadows.

He turned toward her as he picked up his pants from the floor. "Magical music can sometimes lead to magical acts, *n'est-ce pas?*"

"*Bien dit,*" she concurred and stood up to retrieve her own clothes. She went into a small bathroom, where she took a quick shower. As she dressed, she savored a sense of exhaustion that had escaped her earlier in the day and knew that the performance had finally ended; her Isolde was gone, or for now at least sated.

When she returned to the front, he offered her a package. "I thought you might like to spend some time with this," he said, and she didn't have to look inside to know it was the *Tristan* manuscript. If it was an extravagant, improbable gesture, she appreciated that it resonated with the same spirit with which they had just sung to each other and made love in the back of his antiques store.

"Thank you." She nodded, then winked at him. "And when should I return it?"

"Whenever you'd like," he said, before alluding to a trip he was about to take to Europe—something he did every year for his business—that he expected to last almost three months.

"Three months!" she cried.

"Three months," he repeated as he kissed her good-bye. If I know anything about the opera, it will go by much quicker than you can imagine."

As Anna rode back uptown, any disappointment she felt was allayed not only by the afternoon she had just spent but also by the prospect of looking forward to something beyond—and outside of—the impending performance run, which as Mr. Bing had confirmed was now hers. She felt happy; it had been a perfect day after a perfect night, and she did not want to be greedy. She considered the manuscript on her lap and absently contemplated the spinning galaxy of light—from the buildings and storefronts, the surrounding cars—splayed out across her in the backseat of the slowly moving cab.

5 . . . .

The Marble Index

PITTSBURGH, 1960. On September 13, two days after her birth in a hospital near Warren, Pennsylvania, an infant girl was brought home to Castle Shannon, a small town built on a former strip mine southwest of the city. The Sheehans lived in a split-level ranch on Hamish Road, which—like so many streets in Pittsburgh—began and ended at no particular point but could be found on the curve of a steep climb before quickly disappearing over the hill or winding into a ravine. John parked the car in the driveway to let Gina out so she could go in the front door instead of through the garage. Like her husband, Gina was on the short side, and despite years of trying to lose weight would never be described as thin. As much as she regretted that, she was thankful for her long lashes and large, expressive eyes, which she had liked to think of as "doleful" ever since her seventh-grade boyfriend had learned the word in a poem. She was also proud of her mane of black hair—inherited from her Italian father—which was tied up in a white silk ribbon she had worn for the occasion because it matched the buttons of her powder blue dress.

She had met John at the same industrial-supply company where they still worked. John, after starting out in the warehouse, had recently been promoted "upstairs" into purchasing, while Gina was in accounts receivable. They had been married for almost three years with no luck getting pregnant—and not, as John was quick to point out, for lack of trying—before consulting doctors and, with all the tests inconclusive, deciding that adoption was the best option. Their priest had put them in touch with an order of Dominicans located about halfway to Erie, and just a week earlier they had finally received the call. Everything inside was already done, from the crib to the border of little yellow ducks John had stenciled over the pale green walls. "John, did you ever cut these back?" Gina called down to her husband as she walked up the sidewalk with the baby cradled in her arms. Though it was a small thing, she had dreamed about this day for a long time, and not once did her fantasy include a straggly yew blocking her entrance to the house.

Her mother, Bérénice—or Bea, since nobody could say anything but Bernice, which she hated—pushed open the screen door with one of her toothpick arms and beckoned with the other. "Quit harping, Gina—*allez-y*—get in here!" Bea was originally from Bruges—where she had grown up speaking French before immigrating to the United States—and in the course of things had ended up in Pittsburgh with her husband, an Italian steelworker who had died a few years earlier. She had moved in with John and Gina to help with the baby (though Gina was also scaling back to three days at the office) and because her old house in Baldwin—where Gina and her brothers were raised—had too many ghosts and memories for one woman to withstand.

Gina and Bea sat down on the couch to admire the new baby. John came in with diapers, extra blankets, and formula, which he put on the coffee table in order to marvel at the baby's tiny fingers, which he held gently with his own. "So . . . Maria?" he asked as he moved his palm over her fuzzy head—she already had more hair than he did, he joked—and looked at his wife with eager eyes. Gina had become infatuated with the name Maria at the dentist's a few months earlier— not long after they started the adoption process—when she'd seen an old *Time* magazine with "Soprano Callas" on the cover, and she had proposed the name the second they received confirmation from the nuns. Even now she could remember reading about the "fat, lonely girl" who returned to Manhattan as "queen of the world's opera." Gina had stared at the cover for the better part of an hour, hypnotized by the glamorous dress, the Spanish-medallion earrings, and the un- forgettable eyes, tawny and Mediterranean like her own and with quite a bit more shadow than she was used to wearing, but which she had subsequently started to mimic on her Saturday nights out with John.

She glanced up at her husband. "You still like it, right?"

"Yeah, sure." John nodded at his wife and—since his mother-in- law had left for the kitchen—allowed his hand to travel up her neck to a sensitive spot behind her ear, which made her laugh. Although he had initially preferred Mary—after his Irish grandmother—he knew it had been smart to give in, because Gina's smile made all the grief and hassle of the past two years seem worth it. He felt a familiar desire— there just the way it was supposed to be, nothing forced or scheduled about it—which also made him happy.

. . .

So CHRISTENED—AND OFFICIALLY baptized the following weekend by Father Gregory—Maria Sheehan began life unremarkably except for the strength of her cries. "This one has four lungs, not two," Bea noted one day with a mix of admiration and fatigue when Gina got home from work.

"She's going to be an opera singer," Gina replied.

"On verra." Bea shrugged as she lighted a cigarette. *"On verra."*

Gina had not been interested in opera growing up—it was too "old-world," like her parents—but lately she could not get enough of it. Not long after seeing the Callas article, she bought an LP of arias and was shocked by how what had once struck her as so old-fashioned now seemed so vibrant and sensual, as if the music were caressing her. She and her mother had listened with tears running down their faces as they remembered Gina's father, who liked to play Caruso while he canned vegetables in the basement of their old house. Hearing her mother sing along—somehow she knew all the words—reminded Gina of being young, when her skin used to tingle and itch because she craved something before actually getting it—on a birthday or Christmas—so that, for a few hours, she experienced a numb bliss that made her feel like the luckiest girl in the world.

Six months later, it was Bea who made another important discovery, on one of Gina's workdays. Maria would not stop wailing, and all of the usual remedies—feeding, burping, changing her diaper, walking her, or setting her in front of the television—were fruitless until Bea plunked the screaming baby into her crib and went back to the living room to drown her out with a Callas record. As soon as the music came on, Maria stopped crying, only to resume with full force twenty minutes later, when the first side of the LP finished. If the baby could hear the record, she remained content, staring up with bright, limpid eyes.

"So is she *française* or is she *italienne*?" asked Bea, referring to the traditional rivalry between the operatic powers, when Gina got home from work.

"I think she likes horrible music," suggested John, who remained immune to the charms of La Callas, especially when the Pirates were on the radio.

"John, be quiet," said Gina—whose authoritative demeanor was well-honed thanks to her accounts-receivable experience—before sending him into the kitchen to check on a chicken cacciatore her mother had put on the stove a few minutes earlier. She picked Maria up from her crib. "You see, she is going to be a singer."

"*Oui, ma fille.*" Bérénice smiled. "*Mia bella* likes the opera very much."

Spurred on by this discovery, Gina soon added to her record collection, and not just arias but thick boxes of LPs with complete versions of *La Bohème, Tosca,* and *Norma.* These were a splurge, but she couldn't resist, not only for Maria's sake but also because they gave her such a voluptuous sense of fulfillment. She loved the way her pulse quickened when she walked into the record store down-town to ask the clerk his advice on what to buy; she felt as young and excited as a teenager but without the crippling insecurity. She and Bea played the records constantly: "*Qui s'en fout?* That we must hear again," Bea liked to say as she dangled a toy in front of Maria with one hand while holding a cigarette and a magazine—and often a gin and Coke—in the other.

Though John was often perplexed to find himself on such a strange island, where his wife—on those days she stayed home—and mother-in-law were as likely to be laughing over some new facial expression of Maria's as crying over the fact that she would never meet either of her grandfathers, he appreciated that his wife liked classical music. While he couldn't resist an occasional quip, he understood that opera was one of those women's things it was better to keep his nose out of, plus he felt it gave him—or them, as a couple—a level of "class" that had been absent in his own family. Then, too—not that he was about to discuss this with anyone, even the guys at work—there was no question that Gina, whether because of the music, because of motherhood, or both, was becoming more adventurous, not just in how she made up her eyes and the fit of her dresses—which were somehow a little tighter in all the right places—but in the bedroom, where she now did things she had never done before, rendering him senseless for the duration, unable to do anything but mutter "Oh, jeez" over and over again.

"How did you learn how to do that?" he asked when it was over.

"Did you like it?"

"Couldn't you tell?"

She pushed a strand of hair back from her round face. "Kiss me," she demanded, and he did.

ONE NIGHT, WHEN Bea and the baby were already in bed, Gina was watching TV with John when she—or actually John, who was turning the dial—stumbled across a broadcast of *Tosca* starring Callas, with Tito Gobbi as the evil Scarpia. It had been a tough day for Gina; Maria couldn't keep anything down, and Bea had likewise been *trop malade et trop fatiguée* to help. Gina recognized the angry, luminous eyes on the screen and yelled at her husband to stop.

"What?" John asked, as he furiously turned the dial.

"That—that singing, that opera—turn it back!" Gina was thrilled to recognize her idol's expression flash with a vengeance far beyond what she had seen on the LP photographs.

John sagged. "Really?"

Gina looked to her husband with an expression that mirrored the one she had just seen on the television. "Do I look like I'm kidding? I'm tired of baseball."

"Okay, have fun." John yawned. "I'm hitting the sack."

Gina raised her cheek for a quick peck but kept her eyes glued to the unfolding drama. Seeing Callas in action was better than watching any movie, so that, within a few minutes, she felt like she was the one stuck in a small town in Italy, negotiating with the chief of police for her lover's release from prison. She stared in disbelief as Scarpia dictated the terms of his bargain, and swallowed hard with resolve and disgust as she understood that Tosca would have no choice but to offer up her body to this horrible man. When Tosca drove a knife through his back and watched him collapse to the ground in a pool of blood, Gina had never imagined that revenge could feel so good. And at the end—when she realized that Mario was dead, shot by the executioner's squad—she felt her own heart break as if it were the first time she had even been in love, so that she understood why Tosca ripped herself away from the guards to jump to her death.

When it was over, Gina saw her reflection in the fading hues of the television screen and knew that she wanted to die, too. The simplicity of this wish was breathtaking and undeniable: she longed to be released from the mundane burdens of Castle Shannon, from working and shopping and cooking and cleaning and everything else that seemed to leave so little time for anything fun or different. She wanted to be young again, but this time confident and talented and pretty, so that like Callas she could travel the world to perform on ornate stages framed by velvet curtains and then go to parties on silver yachts. She wanted to drink champagne, to smoke long cigarettes, and to laugh outrageously with her head back before making love to ten different men, each one more handsome than the last. She wanted a private banker to bring her a thick stack of hundred-dollar bills at the beginning of each month, to spend on white pearls or fur coats or to give to the poor if she were so inclined.

Then she remembered the other Maria—*her* Maria—and

imagined her daughter waking up without her, and knew she was not prepared to leave, not ever, not even in her wildest fantasies. Her cheeks were wet as she walked to the bathroom, where she looked in the mirror and smiled at her folly—Maria would be up in less than five hours—and rapped a knuckle against her head the way her father used to do playfully. She tiptoed into her sleeping daughter's room and kissed her, vowing that she would help Maria not only to vanquish such feelings of remorse and dissatisfaction—however vague—but also to harness them, to take flight and never look back.

6

The Apology of Socrates

PARIS, 1846. Lucien Marchand, nine years old, was already dizzy with excitement when his father covered his eyes and gently led him down the hallway.

"Can I look yet?" he could not resist asking.

"No—and don't squirm," Guillaume said. "Just a few more feet."

Lucien could not imagine what his father was about to unveil, given what he had already seen in the last hour, their first in a new apartment on the Île St.-Louis. Though he had known about the move for months—ever since Guillaume was awarded a life tenancy for providing the beleaguered emperor with a cure for what in polite society was called *la condition infernale* (or in medical terms, *impotentia coeundi*)—he still couldn't quite believe he was going to live on the Île. He didn't doubt his father—who was, after all, a botany professor at the École normale supérieure—but it was the kind of disbelief he associated with certain animals at the zoo (especially zebras and giraffes), the steaming engine of a train, the glass-covered arcade on the Rue Des Esseintes, or really anything else that was amazing to behold but that it would never occur to him to possess. The way the Île floated in the middle of the Seine, with its stately façades quietly peeking out from behind the trees at the rest of the city, made it seem like more of a magical ship than a place where people actually lived, and one that would surely sail away before he could board.

They were not in the main residence of the Hôtel Georges—which like most mansions on the Île was occupied by high nobility, in this case, Prince and Princess Milhelescou of Romania—but in a previously unused apartment next to the servant quarters. This was still a big improvement over their old lodgings, as Lucien had confirmed a few minutes earlier, running wildly through the space as if to capture it and then giddy and breathless as he turned in circles, trying to count all the doorways. The library was already filled with shelves and shelves of his father's books and treatises, and a window in his new bedroom looked out onto the courtyard, where he had just seen the gilded carriage of the princess pull out to the street. Downstairs was a basement filled with brick archways—this was where Guillaume planned to set up his laboratory—and a secret passageway that led to a triangular plot of land at the tip of the Île, with enough room for a greenhouse and a garden, and where Lucien—lying on his stomach—had managed to dip his fingers into the frigid March waters of the Seine.

"Now?" Lucien begged as his father steered him around a corner.

"Now." Guillaume laughed as he removed his fingers.

Opening his eyes, Lucien was knocked a step back by what he saw, so that Guillaume had to prop him up. He was confronted by a massive piano—a true grand, an Érard—which occupied the room with the quiet majesty of a mountain. Stunned, Lucien slowly walked around it once, and then again, tentatively caressing the dark curves of the body and the gigantic wooden legs until he arrived at the front, where he counted more than seven octaves of keys, or two more than on the piano he regularly played.

He reached out and played a low C that rattled the windows as he turned to his father with wide eyes. "Is this ours?"

"It belongs to the princess," Guillaume said, "but she already has one, if not more. When I told her you were a young musician, she agreed to let us keep it here." He helped Lucien pull out the bench. "Go ahead—it's okay, try it. You only live once."

Lucien stared for a few more seconds before he decided to start off with a chromatic scale that, while not particularly difficult or useful, was one of his favorite exercises. His fingers nimbly flitted up the keyboard, from the groaning bass to the chirping high keys, a hundred miles away at the other end, and as he listened to the notes reverberate off the walls, he felt like he had wandered into a house full of butterflies. He next played a few thundering chords that made his father cover his ears before he turned to something more delicate, if not quite as pleasing, a popular French piece—"Dans le ciel" by Albert Delève—he had been working on with his music teacher.

He was about to begin another when he glanced up and was surprised to see his father's eyes red and teary. "Is it Maman?" he asked, referring to his mother, who had died during a cholera epidemic almost seven years earlier. She, too, had been a singer, but because Lucien had been only a toddler at the time, he never remembered her in more than a wisp or a fragment.

"Yes." Guillaume nodded. "But please, don't stop—that's why it's here."

"Do I sound like her?" Lucien asked, knowing that his father often described her voice as a beautiful coloratura, capable of projecting ten shades of love or hate in a single note.

"Very much." Guillaume smiled sadly as Lucien returned his attention to the keyboard and began a new song.

. . .

This was the first of many hours Lucien spent with the piano after they moved in, though as the weather improved and summer beckoned, he also liked to join his father outside. The triangular tip of the Île offered the illusion that the city was flowing by on either side of the river, particularly since the garden possessed an implausible stillness, interrupted only by the birds and the insects, rustling leaves, and lapping water. While it was the best summer Lucien could remember—or imagine—as July gave way to August, he could not ignore a familiar dread as he envisioned the start of school, which led him to dream about stowing away on one of the barges that regularly passed by on the Seine.

He had always hated school, not so much because he was a terrible student but because of an overwhelming tedium he associated with almost every subject. He enjoyed learning things from his father but found his teachers—and the books they relied on—uniformly uninspiring and couldn't imagine why he should care so much about math or grammar or history, when all he wanted to think about was music and the opera. His incorrigible tendency to daydream and to hum—and to play an imaginary piano on his desk or sometimes on his knees—made him an object of scorn among students and teachers alike, the latter of whom were even more mystified given Guillaume's affiliation with the country's most elite university.

Lucien would never forget a horrible day the year before when he had been sitting in the corner of the school yard during morning recess, quietly singing to himself, and a group of his classmates had jumped out from behind a tree with the intent to pin him to the ground and deliver a ferocious series of kicks and punches. Lucien had managed to escape and fight back, and during the ensuing scuffle—because he was lanky and strong—he had succeeded in bloodying the nose of one of the attackers, which led his teacher to accuse him of instigating the altercation.

"How?" Lucien asked, still defiant as he rubbed the dirt from his elbows and knees and glared at the others, who corroborated the teacher's misunderstanding of the event.

"Did you play the game with everyone else as I instructed?"

"No," Lucien admitted.

"What were you doing?"

"If you have to know," Lucien said as he twisted a lock of black hair around one of his fingers, "I was singing."

Guillaume was called in to discuss the matter with the flustered teacher and the headmaster. Because such meetings were practically annual events, he was adept at making the case for why Lucien should be permitted to continue in a small academy populated by similarly situated children of professors and government officials, none of whom shared such a distracting desire for the stage. "I understand that—at least for now—he is very much his mother's son," he offered before explaining their loss—in case anyone present was not familiar with the course of events, and even if they were—which never failed to make Lucien's attachment to her more poignant and forgivable. That Guillaume spoke softly and seriously, with a slight accent—he had been raised in Greece—made his words appear somehow more earnest and reasonable than they would have coming from a native speaker, while his striking eyes, which possessed the diffuse quality of celadon—and which Lucien had inherited—also worked to give his audience the impression that his mind was still in the laboratory, uncovering important secrets of the earth, while his heart remained forever buried with his wife.

GUILLAUME'S DISCUSSIONS AT home with Lucien on the subject were another story. Though he professed no expectation that his son would follow him into the sciences, he made clear that at a minimum Lucien was expected to complete lycée.

"That's eight more years!" Lucien objected as his first summer on the Île waned and he confessed to his father his desire to leave school altogether.

"I went to school for more than twenty years," Guillaume responded. "I'm sure you can manage half of that."

"But you were good at it."

"I know you're as smart as any of them—and I'm sure your life would be that much easier if you applied yourself."

"I apply myself to music."

"You'll have plenty of time for that after you turn seventeen," Guillaume reasoned, "if that's what you still want to do."

"But school is so boring," Lucien complained.

Guillaume laughed and Lucien sighed, knowing he had little choice but to follow his father's directive. He allowed himself to be distracted by the reddish hue of his forearm, which he held up against his father's swarthier skin.

Guillaume, however, was not quite ready to abandon the topic. "You know, Lucien, your mother would have told you the same thing about school," he said and ran his fingers up to his son's neck, making him laugh. "As much as she loved the theater, it wasn't all she was interested in—that's why she married me."

LUCIEN OFTEN DREAMED about his mother, and she was always singing, but he could never remember what she looked or sounded like once he resurfaced from the depths of his sleep. During the day, he sometimes became convinced that she—or her spirit—was nearby.

"Can't you feel her?" he cried to his father one afternoon that summer, when they were again in the garden. He pulled at the edges of his eyes to both sharpen and distort his vision, as if that might help him to see her. "She's here—I know it!"

"I doubt that," Guillaume said before he paused and looked around. "But I'm happy to tell you that you're not completely crazy." He sat down on a bench and pointed at a row of trees across the river. "You see those?"

"I might," Lucien responded, not particularly pleased with the direction this exchange was taking.

"Your mother used to wear a perfume made from an extract of tilia, which as you can see are in bloom, and whose scent is being carried here on the breeze."

Lucien sighed. "Why don't you ever want to believe in ghosts—or souls?"

"Because I'm a scientist," Guillaume offered, "and ghosts and souls are the basis of folktales, superstitions, and religion, which as we've talked about have been the source of too much needless, irrational harm."

"And you don't believe in God either?" Lucien asked glumly, although he already knew the answer.

"God is for those who don't know how to think," Guillaume said with a nod. "Or are too lazy to figure out how something really works. A hundred years ago, if someone got sick and died, people would say things like 'It was God's will.' Too many people are still like this."

"Do you think if Maman were alive now and got sick, you would be able to cure her?"

"Not yet," admitted Guillaume, whose smile seemed to indicate that he was more amused than troubled by his son's question, "but someday, I'm sure there will be a cure for what killed her—and for every other sickness, too."

Since his wife's death, Guillaume had devoted his research to the increasingly validated theory that many diseases could be prevented if molecular compounds—either derived from or resembling the pathogens in question—were delivered to the body in proper doses, allowing it to build a resistance. At the university, he worked with a team on cholera, rabies, childbed fever, and syphilis; in his new quarters, he planned to devote his spare time to an even more radical concept, albeit one that had tantalized his predecessors for centuries, namely that the most debilitating disease of all—the aging process— could also be greatly inhibited by means of a vaccine, if the proper ingredients could be discovered. As he often discussed with his colleagues, there were pockets of humanity around the world—most notably in the Ural Mountains of Russia, the Gobi desert, and the jungles of the Amazon—said to live more than two hundred years, and he believed that understanding the fauna (primarily) and microorganisms (secondarily) of these regions would eventually provide the key to bringing such longevity to the people of France.

"So does that mean we could live forever?" Lucien asked when his father explained his reasons for cultivating such exotic plants in the greenhouse; some had enormous vein-covered leaves and twisting tendrils that Lucien found monstrous, so that—while he wouldn't have admitted such a childish fear—he preferred not to be alone with them.

"No, of course not. But much longer than we do now—assuming you weren't killed by a bullet or run over by a carriage."

As much as Lucien disliked school, it made him proud to consider his father making such an important discovery. "But how—how will you figure it out?"

Guillaume turned so that the reflection of the sun off his hair— once curly and dark like Lucien's, it was now short and flecked with gray—caused Lucien to squint as he looked up. "You may have a scientific future in you yet," he noted as he pulled his stopwatch from his pocket and handed it to Lucien. "You understand how a watch works, with gears and dials?" Lucien nodded as Guillaume split open the stem of a rose, where he displayed the fibrous system that transported water and nutrients from the roots to the leaves and flowers. "Plants and animals—and humans—are not so different in some ways. We're all made out of tiny parts into bigger, more complicated bodies. What I do is figure out how foreign substances interact with these parts. Certain things will make them stronger, while others make them more efficient, the way oil will prevent gears from rusting." He looked down at Lucien and blinked. "My job is to discover what will do both."

7

Taking Drugs to Make Music to Take Drugs To

NEW YORK CITY, 2001. After his dinner with Jay at Demoiselles, Martin woke up fascinated by the way his head and stomach undulated, and estimated he would need at least a year to recover. It almost made him resolve never to eat or drink again, but on further reflection he decided that he felt little contrition for having indulged with barely any restraint (e.g., he had not eaten red meat) in the epicurean phantasmagoria of the four-star French restaurant. He supposed he could have limited himself to a few glasses of wine instead of the five bottles he and Jay had shared, but he remained committed to the idea that each course demanded its own selection, nor could he regret ordering the second glass of port, which the acidulous taste of the cow's-milk fribourgeois had so clearly demanded. Jay could probably be blamed for the cognac that had accompanied the dessert tray—compliments of the establishment—with which they had ended the meal, but Martin's protestations had sounded weak and emasculated even at the time.

He turned his head and slowly focused on the clock: it was already after 7:00, and most sad to consider, he had a 9:15 conference call scheduled at his office. He needed to allow at least an hour for the car service downtown—he was in Washington Heights, just north of the George Washington Bridge in Manhattan—which gave him slightly less time than that to get ready. He forced himself to roll over onto one elbow so that he could reach out with his other arm for the six aspirin he had placed on his bedside table the night before, and after swallowing these with the aid of a glass of water placed there for the same purpose, he collapsed back onto the pillow, granting himself a reprieve.

He gazed into the kaleidoscope of his ceiling and assessed the situation: he was hungover to be sure, but he also detected something else lurking in his condition that was decidedly more psychological, although it did entail a faint numbness—a certain syrupy sensation— that seemed to spread throughout his body, not completely unlike what had recently been afflicting his hands, although less painful, and possibly even pleasurable. He remembered a summer day when he was thirteen years old, and how—for the first time in his life—he had woken up possessed by a similar sense of unease; he did not feel sick, exactly, but he did not feel healthy, either, as though he were a piece of leftover food on an unwashed dish.

This particular morning had arrived after seventh grade, a day or so after he had returned home from two weeks at hockey camp. He was on the screened-in porch off the back of the house, where he liked to sleep when it was warm enough, and was stunned by a sudden lack of motivation to do anything, even blink. As he looked through the mesh screen at the backyard, it seemed like every color had been bleached from the world, which itself was about as exciting as a corrugated box.

Around eleven, his mother, Jane, leaned through the pass-through from the kitchen and asked if he wanted breakfast, a question to which he responded with a blank stare. "Earth to Martin," she said.

"What? No—that's all right; I'm not hungry."

"Is something the matter?"

He finally shifted his eyes in her direction. "I guess I'm tired."

She seemed to consider this for a few seconds as she plucked an errant thread from the front of her bright orange turtleneck top. "I'm sure you are."

Martin understood this to be a mild rebuke for having spent two weeks of summer playing hockey, so he responded in kind. "Do you think hockey is a cause or an effect of my fatigue?"

Jane responded by rolling her eyes in an exaggerated way, which—as crappy as he felt—made him smile for a second as she continued. "Okay, Mr. Cause and Effect, I'm going out for a few minutes to run errands and drop off some papers to your father. I don't suppose you'd like to come?" Martin's father, Hank, was second in command at the same industrial supply house Jane's father—i.e., Martin's grandfather—had started almost thirty years earlier.

"No, I'm too tired," Martin said.

"Well, I suppose this officially marks the start of your adolescence," Jane declared in an airy tone. "Maybe I'll check in later, then? Oh, and by the way, don't forget about those paints I ordered for you." She smiled at him. "That might cheer you up."

"Okay, thanks," Martin said with more enthusiasm, but one that as soon as his mother was gone gave way to a new fog of ambivalence. Most days, he could spend hours painting a goalie mask—he had a collection of almost twenty—pleasantly intoxicated by the epoxies and urethanes, but in his current mood, the thought seemed as enticing as a game of "school" with his little sister, Suzie.

He contemplated the lazy turn of the ceiling fan until the sun moved over the tree line, invading the porch and driving him upstairs to his room. He pulled down the shades, flicked on the power button to his stereo, and moved the arm of the turntable over to *Houses of the Holy*.

He was listening to it for the second time when his sister poked her head around the door. "Martin," Suzie yelled, "Mom's back and said to turn it down."

"What?" Martin barely raised his head from where it had landed on the edge of the bookshelf after rolling off his pillow. "Get out of here."

"She said turn it DOWN!"

Martin reached over and turned off the power, so that the whole system ground to a halt with a vicious scratch, right in the middle of Robert Plant's howl at the end of "D'Yer Mak'er." He eyed his sister. "Happy? Now could you please disintegrate? I'm serious."

He went downstairs to the kitchen and ate three bites of a peanut-butter-and-jelly sandwich his mother made for him before he decided that—definitely not up for mask painting today—he needed a change of scene. He grabbed a hockey stick out of the basement and walked over to the tennis courts at his old elementary school, but the turnout was meager, as this was prime vacation time in Cedar Village; in fact, the Vallences were leaving the following weekend for their annual two weeks at the beach in Loveladies.

On his way home he took a shortcut and ran into some freaks behind the school. "Hey, Vallence," one of them greeted him; it was Dunfree, a tall, skinny kid with white hair.

Martin knew Dunfree from science class, where even though Martin was more of a jock than a freak, they had talked about Led Zeppelin and the Who and speculated about perpetual motion. "What's going on?"

"Science experiment," Dunfree answered as he blew some smoke into the face of a little sixth-grade freak as he tapped at his pocket. "Want one?"

Martin was hardly the rebellious type; he was on the advanced science and math "tracks" at school, where he always received high grades—which pleased Jane—and was considered one of the better hockey goalies for his age group in Pittsburgh, which made his father happy. He had no trouble believing that smoking was a pretty good way to get cancer and suspected his parents would kill him if they found out, yet none of this seemed persuasive when he considered the possibility of a cigarette breaking up what so far had been the most boring day of his life. So he accepted and was not disappointed by the nauseating rush that ensued a few minutes later as he picked up the basics of inhalation.

He had just finished when a second group of freaks—all girls—showed up. Among them was Monica "Kittens" Gittens, who Martin was pretty sure had "liked" him the year before, in seventh grade. After a brief debate, they decided to go en masse to check out the woods up behind the golf course, where Dunfree claimed once to have found fifty dollars in the mud.

"This is so lame," Monica declared to Martin not long after they arrived. "Want to go for a walk?"

Martin thought about how she used to look at him in math class whenever Mr. Pethil did something stupid—he was always transcribing the equations incorrectly from the book—because she and Martin were inevitably the first to notice. Martin had "gone out" with a few girls in seventh grade, but never for more than a week, and had been a little afraid of Monica because she was friends with some of the eighth-grade freaks. But he was taller now and almost an eighth grader himself, which made him more confident. "Okay," he said. "Where?"

"Follow me," she said, but not more than twenty yards into the brush, she pulled him aside, away from the others. "Want to see something?"

"Is it a perpetual motion machine?"

"Don't be a dork." She pulled him up to her and put her face close to his, so he could stare into her irreverent eyes. "You like me, right?"

"Yeah—I mean—do you like me?"

She ignored the question. "How come you never talk to me then?"

"Because I haven't seen you all summer."

This seemed to please her, and when she smiled he did, too.

She brushed her lips against his. "Do you know how to French?"

"Yeah." Martin adjusted the boner in his pants so it wouldn't be so obvious and then kissed her for a while, far longer, in fact, than he had any other girl. Eventually she allowed him to put his hand under her shirt—he knew that guys were supposed to go for this, but no other girl had ever let him before—and rub it against her bra.

"Should I take it off?" she asked. Martin nodded, and she told him to take his shirt off, too, which he did, after which they kissed some more. "Now take off your pants."

"Really?"

"Come on," she said and slid her hand down and unhooked the top button of his jeans. "Unless you don't want to."

"No, I want to." He raised himself to a kneeling position so that he could pull down his pants and underwear. He watched as she positioned herself in front of him and delicately wrapped her fingers around his cock. It took only a few tugs to jerk him off, but as amazed as he was to see it happen, he looked down at the ground and gulped when he realized that he no longer wanted to be anywhere near Monica Gittens.

"That was cool," he managed while he struggled to pull up his pants.

"Was that your first hand job?" asked Monica rather clinically as she wiped her palm on the back of her jeans, down by the ankle.

Martin shrugged, not wanting to admit or deny this. "Are we going out?"

"Yeah, but I have to break up with Todd Mealy first."

"You don't have to."

"Whatever you want," said Monica, annoyed for reasons that eluded Martin, who couldn't understand why she would ever be more interested in him than he was in her.

In his room that night, he couldn't decide what to think. One second he would tell himself that it had actually been pretty awesome to get a hand job from Kittens, but in the next he would admit that he felt a bit disappointed, since sex in any form was supposed to be "a" if not "the" highlight of life. If the thought of a blow job or going all the way—which he bet she would do if he could get a rubber— didn't exactly thrill him, he knew that his ambivalence was another symptom of the ennui that had been infecting him since that morning, which now seemed a hundred years away. It occurred to him that he could no longer envision doing anything—whether playing hockey, painting masks, smoking, or now fooling around with girls— that would give him any great pleasure. Not that he would necessarily object to any of the above, but if he were asked whether he was happy, or nervous, or excited in the middle of doing said activity, the answer, even in the best-case scenario, would be something along the lines of "possibly."

He wondered if all adults felt this way and just lied about it, and if the most he could expect from life was a flicker of whatever was supposed to make it worth living. The question made him feel weak and dissatisfied until in the next second he concluded that to experience this type of ambivalence—and more important, to be conscious of it—was, if you could look at it from another angle, sort of a revelation, because at least you could pinpoint a few things that didn't make you incredibly happy, which in theory should expand the pool of things that might.

Almost thirty years later, Martin grew aware of the bleating alarm clock. It was beyond time to get up, and even though the aspirin had effectively transformed his hangover into a distant and not entirely unpleasant thud, he felt troubled by many things: it was 7:45, and he was running late to a job—and a career—that no longer thrilled him; he was now forty-one, which for all intents and purposes made him a senior citizen in gay years, and which—though he had never had any trouble before—made him worry whether or not he would still be able to attract the kind of man, almost always younger and without exception thinner, he tended to prefer. And while he was rarely inclined to regret being single, this, too, was beginning to feel like a liability as he considered the vague outlines of his future. Or if being single wasn't a liability—because he frankly enjoyed the freedom it offered—the uncertainty he felt, in either case, demonstrated how complicated the variables of time and experience made the calculation of what made life worth living.

Given all of this, he would not have predicted that he was about to launch himself off the bed to face the day—his birthday—with a smile. Yet to his own surprise, this is what he did. On his feet, he wobbled for a few seconds with a hand on the wall and considered that, if nothing else, at least he could state with greater certainty any number of things that did not make him happy, e.g., sex with men who didn't kiss, extreme temperature fluctuations, postwar American political hegemony, and the color beige, to name just a few. He pinched the ends of his fingertips and was relieved to feel them; after staggering to the bathroom, he presented himself to the mirror, where he pulled his face back and forth and rubbed his hands over the silver-tipped hair of his buzzed head.

"I look like shit," he admitted but detected something in the air—if not redemption, at least curiosity and maybe even some desire—which no doubt explained the mischievous glint in his slate-blue eyes.

8

The Diary of One Who Disappeared

PITTSBURGH, 1965. By the time Maria was five years old, she had developed an amazing ability to sing in Italian and French. *"Chants, mon petit oiseau,"* said Bea, who reverted more and more to her native French when she spoke to her granddaughter, as though it were the language of children, and Maria would almost always oblige, offering up any number of things she had memorized from the records that were always playing.

As much as Gina appreciated her daughter's talent and her mother's encouragement—which mirrored her own—she was bothered when Bea told Maria that the best singers gave their voices to God. Gina was starting to hate church; nothing Father Gregory said resonated with her, and she could barely listen as he droned on about the evils of communism and the deteriorating moral fabric of a country where so many young people had clearly fallen into league with the devil. I'm one of them, Gina thought as she visualized her own nonprocreative acts in the bedroom. Even the memory of his voice—nasal and all-knowing—made her skin burn, so that she feigned sickness on many Sundays as the rest of the family got ready to go to mass.

"This is how you thank the good people who brought you this child?" Bérénice whispered to her daughter's unresponsive back on one such morning.

"Ma, drop it," Gina whispered back. "I'll go next week."

Because she didn't want to influence Maria negatively, however, Gina didn't stand in the way when Bea brought Maria to church, sometimes three times a week to make up for Gina's neglect. Nor could Gina deny that Maria seemed to love it; nothing outside of *La Bohème* made her happier than to sit in a pew transfixed by the agonies of the wasting man nailed to the cross, or to allow her eye to wander between the stained glass and the antiquities that glinted in the filtered sunlight as if placed there by the hand of the Almighty Himself.

At home Maria spent hours leafing through Bérénice's saint-and-martyr tomes, dreaming of the day when she, too, might be pierced with iron hooks, mauled to death by beasts, or burned at the stake. Bea taught her prayers in Latin, the holiest language of all, dressed her up as a nun—a venial sin in comparison to the indulgences Bea could expect to receive for indoctrinating her precious Maria into the faith—and together they would recite the litany: "Mother, hear me, immersed in woes! *Ave, Mater dolorosa, martyrumque prima rosa, audi vocem supplicis*," Maria cried, having memorized it.

"*Fac, ut mortis in agone, tua fidens protectione, iusti pacem gaudeam!*" Bérénice responded, as her black eyes beamed out of her wrinkled face with the fervor of salvation, though her command of the English was not so strong: "Only a death and agony we peace for our soul!"

They played this game until they collapsed onto the floor weeping, at which point they would crawl into each other's arms, overjoyed with the promise of divine redemption. Though the five-year-old

Maria did not yet grasp the literal meaning of these incantations, she understood that, by repeating and memorizing whatever Bea placed in front of her, she was acting, which gave her a certain power over her grandmother, who most assuredly was not.

Gina suspected as much. "Ma, she only likes the costumes," she protested to Bea. "Why don't you play house or school with her?"

"What mother ever complained that her daughter prays too much?" Bérénice replied. "Besides, you think I make her to do this?"

"No, but she sees you and—"

"So now we're ashamed?"

"I just want her to be normal," Gina said, exasperated. "I don't think most girls her age are memorizing Latin."

"So she is not *normale.*" Bérénice shrugged. *"J'aurais dire qu'elle soit extraordinaire! Vraiment, je te jure, ma fille,* what is wrong with this?"

It was not a question that Gina felt comfortable answering, given her fear that there was something abnormal deep inside her, hollow and vast except for those few blissful seconds when she could fill it up with music. Gina wanted Maria to experience this bliss, but without the emptiness from which it seemed to arise.

AFTER MARIA STARTED kindergarten at St. Anne's, it quickly became clear that she was anything but normal. Her fellow five-year-olds were less than charmed by her tendency to walk like a penitent and to murmur in Latin, and she could not fade into the background when she was the tallest in her class, with skim-milk blue skin and straight black hair that reminded the other children of spider legs. One of the girls told everyone that Maria's green eyes were the same color as her cat's, which confirmed a collective sense that Maria was not quite of them, particularly after she made the mistake of telling them she was adopted.

In second grade she was dubbed Morticia, and everyone said she was from Transylvania and drank blood. Inspired by the deluge of house cleaners on the market, a group of enterprising girls invented an imaginary "Morticia Spray" to "disinfect" any chair or desk where she happened to sit and made money selling refills for the imaginary cans. Because Maria had so little reason to smile at school, she often wore the dazed expression of someone just hit over the head, which only egged the others on, given that their victim appeared so deliciously addled by their efforts.

As she got older, Maria occasionally devised plans to improve her lot. In third grade she decided to stunt her growth, thinking that if she were the same size as her classmates, they might not hate her as much. Gina was not happy when Maria announced her plan one night at dinner. "Maria, honey, you can't change how tall you are," Gina declared, putting down her fork. "Your size is your size. It's just the way you are."

"Then why do you try to lose weight?" Maria responded.

"That's not the same. That's because—"

"*On mange comme un cochon?*" interrupted Bea. Though pencil-thin, she had spent the past twenty-five years resenting that her daughter had inherited the buxom shape of her own mother-in-law, who though deceased remained an object of hatred because she had moved in with Bea and her husband in the years before her death to torment Bea with the same kind of comment she had just made.

Less affronted by these remarks since her marriage—John liked her figure—Gina stared at Bérénice with a mix of tenderness and foreboding before she addressed her daughter: "Maria, if anyone makes fun of you for being too tall, it's only because they're jealous." She turned to her husband. "John, tell her."

"It's true, honey." John nodded. "Someday you might be able to dunk a basketball."

"I think what your father means," Gina continued, shifting her glare from Bea to John, "is that it's what's inside of you that's important."

Completely unconvinced by her mother and secretly abetted by Bérénice, Maria was soon wrapping her feet like a Chinese princess and cramming them into shoes four sizes too small; she slept on the floor of her closet, her head and feet at opposite walls, hoping to compress the millimeters that were being tacked on at night. To her mother's chagrin, not to mention her teachers', Maria began to slouch, so that the instant she touched a chair anywhere, she slid down the back of it until her chin was only a few inches above the desk or table in front of her, her knees bent as if she had just been stabbed in the back during her nightly prayers. At school she began to walk like a victim of osteoporosis, which only made everyone hate her more.

Since Maria had no friends, Gina and Bea filled in as best they could. Gina took the secular lead with hopscotch, jacks, mumblety-peg, paper dolls, and cat's cradle. They buried jars of cut flowers and months later rediscovered them. When the weather was nice, they sold leaves and grass, sometimes at exorbitant prices, to an assortment of blocks and dolls, or to John or Bérénice. Meanwhile, prayer sessions with Bea evolved into more complicated rites of communion and confession, not to mention the sacraments and gruesome reenactments of martyr deaths in the kitchen, which between the knives and forks and ketchup bottle offered all sorts of possibilities.

This was how Maria's theatrical—and then operatic—skills began to develop; in fourth grade she suggested to her mother that they put on a play in which the characters sang to one another. Using color-coded crayons, Maria was soon writing operettas featuring anywhere from three to ten characters, all of whose vocal lines she invented and committed to memory, along with some written parts, always the easiest, which she reserved for her mother and Bérénice, whom she also directed in the design and construction of sets and costumes. Each week Maria ran a rigorous rehearsal schedule that left her exasperated with the failure of the other actors—again, Gina and Bea—to master even a single note, but then on Saturday afternoons they held performances, with audiences comprising the same blocks and dolls—once again fleeced for tickets, although a few lucky ones were called upon to appear as supernumeraries—and John, who could be counted on to attend as long as curtain times were scheduled between innings of the game. Some of the more memorable productions included "Maria Grows Shorter," "Maria Adopts a Baby," "Suzy Polomski Gets Hit by the Bus," "The Slaughter of the Innocents," "Bérénice in Purgatory," "Felix the Procurator and His Wife, Drusilla," and "Maria Leaves Pittsburgh for a Vacation in St. Louis," a somewhat controversial show because of last-minute changes imposed by censors alarmed by the original concept, "Maria Leaves Pittsburgh Forever."

MARIA'S MUSICAL TALENT never attracted attention at St. Anne's because the subject was taught by a well-intentioned but tone-deaf nun who played the same six records over and over while the children followed along with a book. At home, Maria sang constantly, not just in the musicals but alone to accompany her imaginary wanderings with the saints and martyrs. In her room, the world dropped away and was illuminated by shafts of gossamer light; more rarely, it would all go dark and she would be left shivering and fearful, though of nothing she could identify or explain. Then in seventh grade, hope arrived in the form of a new music teacher named Sister Mary Michael, a relatively young and pleasant-looking recruit. For the first few days of school, Maria admired the new sister from afar and looked forward to impressing her with a song. She had listened to enough children—and worse, adults—to know that most were miles away from the notes, even when singing simple melodies. But on the first day of music class, Maria discovered that Sister Mary Michael, despite her cheerful demeanor, was as tone-deaf as anyone she had ever heard, except even worse because unlike more modest souls, the sister seemed to have no idea how far off she was. She began the class by butchering one of Maria's favorite hymns, "Tell Us Now, O Death," in a monotone so flat and cavernous it almost knocked the wind out of Maria.

It occurred to Maria that she might impress the nun by offering to sing it herself, so that her teacher could perhaps hear the difference. The sister took this suggestion in exactly the wrong way: "Are you saying something's wrong with my singing?"

"No, Sister." Maria shook her head, regretting that she had ventured to raise her hand. "It's just that—" Maria stopped, knowing she was trapped.

"Please . . . continue."

"I—I don't know."

Sister Mary Michael's smile froze on her face and she extracted a ruler from her sleeve with a deft agility that left the other children gasping in fear and delight at the anticipated flogging of Morticia. The nun shushed them before she addressed Maria: "Perhaps you're right—you *should* demonstrate how it's done."

Maria felt tears running down her face, but it was too late to back down.

"Come up to the front of the class, where everyone can see you."

As Maria sang, she was not at St. Anne's in Castle Shannon but in a small village in the mountains of Europe, where she saw Saint Agnes of Bohemia leaving the convent on her way to tend the lepers. In response to this devotion, Maria filled her song with hope and purity; Saint Agnes in turn nodded at Maria before she went into the hospital, a gesture of reassurance that gave Maria the strength to finish the song—"Deadly whisper in my ear, finally my time has come"—with a quiet insistence entirely appropriate for this small but significant performance.

Maria opened her eyes to find Sister Mary Michael scowling at her, obviously less touched than Saint Agnes of Bohemia. "Thank you, Maria," Sister Mary Michael said not even one second after Maria had finished, ruining the tranquillity of the moment. "Now you can please leave for the principal's office."

"Why?" Maria turned to her, crestfallen that the sister was not basking in the proffered glory.

"That you even have to ask shows how much you have to learn." The sister addressed the other students, who, sensing bloodshed, leered at Maria. "While this is indeed a music class, it is, like all of our classes, foremost about respect and working together." She returned to Maria. "Now go."

Maria felt as if she were being lowered into a cauldron of boiling lava, her flesh burning from her body in great scalded chunks, except unlike a saint, she felt no love or forgiveness as she retrieved her books from her desk and glared at every student before she arrived back at Sister Mary Michael, who now stood next to the blackboard. "This is fucking bullshit," Maria declared as she reached the doorway. Though she addressed nobody in particular, there was no mistake, thanks to her excellent diction, about what she had said; it was loud enough that it surprised even her, for she had never said the word *fucking* or *bullshit* to anyone, let alone a nun.

In response, Sister Mary Michael wielded the dreaded ruler high overhead in one hand and took three quick steps with the obvious intent to grab or perhaps slay Maria, who twisted away with enough force to cause the sister to spin into a quick but indelicate pirouette before landing with a thud on her behind, at which point the class erupted into screams and shrieks; for St. Anne's, this was mayhem for the history books. Possessed by nothing but a desire to escape, Maria bounded out of the room and down the hall before she slipped out of the school through a back stairwell. Tears burned her eyes and made her fall many times in her frantic rush to get home, where she arrived a few minutes later with skinned knees and bloody palms.

Gina had never seen her daughter in such a disheveled state and grew even more alarmed when, instead of running to her for comfort, Maria stormed into her room, where she slammed the door. Moments later the phone rang; the principal was on the line, accompanied by Sister Mary Michael. "This is a very serious matter," she said after laying out the details of the felony. "I have every intention of expelling Maria."

"Expelling? She's never given anyone any trouble," Gina protested. "I'm sure there must be some explanation."

"I don't know if I would characterize Maria as trouble-free."

Gina felt flustered, as if she were about to get expelled, but then had a vision of her daughter singing in the living room, at which point all her doubts about Maria seemed to congeal into a hollow vessel she wanted to smash in the heat of accusation. "Nobody understands her, that's all. She's very talented—and whatever she said about the sister's singing, I'm sure she was right."

"I'm sorry, Mrs. Sheehan, but whether Maria was 'right' or not is beside the point. Assuming the decision is made to accept Maria back into the school—which is far from certain—may I suggest perhaps a little less emphasis at home on Maria's wants and a little more on fitting in?"

Gina felt relieved after she hung up, and even proud that Maria—who knew how to sing—had given the sister what she deserved. But the second this thought crossed her mind, it was followed by new doubts: Gina wondered if they had played too much music over the years, or if she had overindulged Maria with her backyard productions; after all, the consequences could be serious. Except as she listened to Maria's muffled cries through the bedroom door, she knew it was too late. A wave of sadness and empathy brought tears to her eyes, and she felt certain that her daughter was afflicted with the same longing as she was. If this, too, was a relief to admit, it gave way to a new fear that if Maria could actually mold her talent into something great and timeless, it would take her places Gina could not begin to imagine.

9

Expériences nouvelles touchant le vide

PARIS, 1851. One afternoon not long after Lucien turned fourteen, he answered a knock on the door and to his astonishment found the Romanian princess peering in as though she had stumbled onto the entrance of a cave. "You're the son?" she less inquired than demanded, as a pair of domestics hovered behind her.

To this point, he had observed her only from a distance, usually as she entered or exited the courtyard—always in her carriage—or when she hosted one of her famous galas, which were said to be more extravagant than royal coronations. For her most recent one—held a few months earlier, in the middle of February—guests were invited to dress in the manner of *"il y a cent ans"* and thus wore prerevolutionary masks and dominoes bedecked with jewels and feathers or, for those many inclined to go beyond this basic requirement, yards of silk and velvet—for the women—while the men wore cravats and powdered wigs, some in eccentric shades of blue and orange. There was a procession that led from the Right Bank over the Pont Constantine and featured a Russian countess who arrived in a dress made entirely of black pearls and white silk, upstaging an elderly marquise in partridge feathers and diamonds, while another—to the delight of Lucien and the servant children watching this parade—managed to trip on her way out of the carriage, causing her wig to bounce off her head and into the Seine.

As for the princess, though she seemed quite old and her dresses tended to accentuate a wide, flat rump and an ungainly, fleshy neck—which in combination with her bulging eyes, bulbous nose, and thin lips gave her the appearance of an emu—she nevertheless waded through her guests with an unhurried and deliberate quality, so that—whether kneeling down to share a confidence with an even older duchess, smiling benignly at a duke's antics, or clasping her large-knuckled hands in front of her chest in a show of delight—her performance possessed a grace and dignity—and even suspense— that had long intrigued Lucien.

Confronted with her at such an unexpected moment, he took several seconds to respond. "Yes, Your Highness," he managed, "my name is Lucien Marchand."

"Lucien, I'm enchanted," she said and frowned. "But please, young man, Codruta will suffice."

"Yes, Codruta."

"That's better. Now, you are a singer, if I'm not mistaken? The one I've heard practicing downstairs?"

Lucien nodded and then hesitated. "Is—is there a problem?"

"That depends, but I would hope the answer is no, since I'm here to invite you to sing at my next *mercredi*." This, as Lucien knew, was her weekly salon, reputed to be one of the most prestigious in the city for the emerging composers and writers honored to attend. Though it was something he had often considered a natural step in his own musical career, which made him wonder exactly how he might go about introducing himself to the princess, it had never occurred to him that such a fortuitous invitation might arrive at this juncture. She held out an envelope between her thumb and her index finger, like the stem of a wineglass, before she turned it over in a slow arc and offered it to him. "I've also invited a young daughter of a friend of mine to perform, and thought it would be appropriate to enhance the program with additional *jeunesse*."

Lucien murmured his thanks as Codruta pivoted, a slow maneuver that reminded him of a battalion on a parade ground, before she retreated down the path to the street, where he could see a man-servant in livery waiting next to a carriage. Back inside, he traced his fingers over the calligraphic letters of the invitation as though memorizing a map to a secret treasure.

WITH JUST THREE days to prepare, on Monday he skipped school, which in light of his father's periodic directives he continued at best to endure. If anything, the past year had only increased Lucien's desire to vacate academia for the stage now that he was fourteen and—because his voice had broken—he could sing with a strength and authority that had obviously been beyond him as a child. His teacher claimed that he would develop into a natural baritone, which disappointed Lucien a little, for he had always wanted to be a tenor, to play the hero and the lover, to break hearts, to kill and be killed, and—it must be admitted—to be paid accordingly for delivering such high, aching notes.

With a thought to find something appropriate to wear, he went to a tailor on Rue St.-Honoré, where he managed to spend all of his spare money, in addition to some his father had given to him, on a new black velvet jacket with silver silk wristbands. On Tuesday he skipped school again and—still wearing the jacket—rehearsed until he developed a slight rasp, which delivered him into a panic until the following morning, when his prayers were answered and his voice was fine. Once again he skipped school, a decision he almost regretted as he watched the minutes crawl by like slugs on one of his father's plants until he finally sallied forth to the entrance of the Georges to be escorted by one of Codruta's footmen through the courtyard. As he walked, he attempted to move with the same deliberate quality he had observed in the princess, and in doing so he felt indescribably mature; when he glanced at his apartment's tiny window, he saw a younger and more childish version of himself peering out.

But once inside, he was dismayed to find that, despite his preparations, he felt cowed by the crystal chandeliers, gilded picture frames, and assemblages of velvet, silk, taffeta, and moiré that greeted him at every turn. Then, in the bright reflection of a ten-foot mirror, he was ashamed to notice a serious defect in the stitching of his jacket, so that it appeared lopsided as it rested upon his shoulders. Although this was in fact the reason he had been able to afford it in the first place, in his excitement he had convinced himself that it would be easy to camouflage, and he now regretted his stupidity. Dejected, he could barely bring himself to smile as Codruta led him into a drawing room and introduced him to the members of her *petit clan*. His mood did not improve when she placed him at a small table with Marie-Laure de Vicionière and her daughter Daisy. "Codruta informs us that you're a very promising young singer," Madame de Vicionière offered as her daughter sipped tea.

"She's most gracious," Lucien responded as he leaned to the side to allow room for his own tea to be poured.

Madame smiled indulgently. "Do you have a teacher?"

"My mother was a singer, but she died when I was three, so some of her friends at her theater—the St.-Germain—have helped me."

"How kind." She glanced at her daughter. "We've not been to the St.-Germain, have we?"

"It's not—" Lucien stopped as he realized that he was about to disparage his mother's theater for no good reason. It was not the Peletier, to be sure, but it was far from the worst opera house in Paris, with a respectable repertoire of bel canto, romantic, and patriotic fare by the likes of Delève, Theron, and a few other Parisian composers.

The St.-Germain was also where he had made his best friends as a child. He fondly remembered scurrying through the backstage tunnels and corridors, where he used to hide in the props, collect fallen flower petals from the soprano's bouquets, dress up in wigs, and spy on the singers as they made costume changes or—just as frequently, it sometimes seemed—made love, often in unconventional arrangements that Lucien had long understood (even before such things were made explicit to him) were not always appreciated beyond the society of the theater.

"It's not far away," he finally concluded with more confidence to atone for his initial hesitation.

"We've been so busy lately," Madame continued in a distracted manner.

Lucien turned his attention to Daisy. "Do you have a teacher?"

Marie-Laure replied on her daughter's behalf: "When Daisy started singing I thought nothing of it, but then a friend of mine— regrettably not here today, or I'd introduce you—pulled me aside and said, 'Your Daisy has the voice of a nightingale,' and insisted that we immediately present her to Monsieur García."

"You're a student of Manuel García?" Lucien again addressed Daisy, amazed that someone so young could have been taken on by the famous teacher, although as soon as he said it he began to worry about how he would sound in comparison.

"Well, no." Marie-Laure shook her head. "Or at least not yet. He assured us that Daisy has enormous reserves of untapped potential but cautioned against singing too much. I suppose you've heard what happened to Jenny Lind?"

"Yes, madame," Lucien said, now disappointed, for despite his nerves he had begun to think that if he impressed them, his performance might open an avenue to the professor. He watched Marie-Laure turn to her own daughter, as if to say "You see?" Daisy in turn smiled with just a trace of disdain as she directed her gaze past her mother's clucks.

Daisy had pretty eyes—they appeared almost turquoise against the pale green satin of her dress—and he wondered if she might like to kiss him, and if he would want to kiss her back; he thought of another game he used to play at the theater in which the loser (or winner) was locked in a closet for a few minutes with another chosen at random. He found that when he was given the chance to be alone with one of the girls, most were more intent on giggling and squirming away from him than actually kissing, but a few times he and another boy had snuck away to do the same, and they had kissed much harder, so that Lucien could still remember the unsettling sensation of their teeth clicking together. As for Daisy, while he decided that any verdict would have to wait until he heard her voice, he smiled back at her with gratitude. Their moment of shared impatience with adult superficiality made the room seem less constrained as he sipped his pomegranate tea and helped himself to a second macaroon.

CODRUTA SOON REAPPEARED to announce the *commencement* of a musical interlude. "We are very fortunate this afternoon to have Daisy de Vicionière, who I have been assured has a talent to match her most youthful beauty—does anyone detect a note of jealousy?— and Lucien Marchand, who in the most neighborly of gestures—and

I mean that quite literally—has agreed to sing for us." Daisy arose from her chair and curtsied before she went to the piano, where she accompanied herself on a pair of popular songs by Gustave Theron. Lucien relaxed the second she opened her mouth, for her notes neither pierced his heart nor hovered like trembling soap bubbles; she did not lack talent, but to hear her gave him nothing beyond a somewhat tedious sense of enjoyment, the way he sometimes felt sitting through a tired production at the St.-Germain.

After Daisy had finished and received a polite round of applause, Lucien's turn came. He went to the piano, where he delivered Gluck's "O del mio dolce ardor" followed by Monteverdi's "Lasciatemi morire." Although Lucien at fourteen was only a fraction of the singer he hoped to become, it was obvious to all present that his voice already possessed an intrinsic beauty and a natural legato that were the hallmarks of real talent. As his last note hung in the air, even before Codruta approached to embrace him as she whispered "Bravo" into his ear and presented him with a dozen white roses, he knew that he had accomplished exactly what he had hoped. Turning back to her friends, the princess dabbed at her eyes with a napkin and thanked the two young singers for raising the spirits of all present on what otherwise could have been a perfectly drab afternoon.

10

Rembrandt Pussyhorse

NEW YORK CITY, 2001. It was eight o'clock by the time Martin had showered, dressed, left his house, and lunged into a waiting car service. On the West Side Highway, he watched the river

glide by under a startlingly clear sky and continued to feel nicely se-
dated by the aspirin he had taken, at least until the car accelerated out
of the Fifty-seventh Street exit heading crosstown and went directly
over a crater-size pothole, which launched Martin several inches off
of his seat, not once but twice, as both axles traversed the gulley.
"Jesus-fucking-christ," he muttered with a laugh and was reminded
of the "brain damage" he had suffered as a child as a result of the
vaunted potholes of Western Pennsylvania.

"That's a Pittsburgh pothole, Marty," his father, Hank, used to
say as he barreled right through on the way to a game or to practice, usually at around eighty miles an hour. "Our tax dollars hard at
work."

"Why didn't you go around it?" the ten-year-old Martin responded, as he did on such occasions.

"Potholes are like problems." Hank gripped the steering wheel
with his muscular hands. "You gotta meet 'em head-on."

Usually Martin would have accepted this advice with an affable
grin, but on this day—as he now remembered—he was planning a
minor insurrection, at least as far as Hank was concerned. "Dad, I
want to play goalie," he declared.

"You mean permanently?" Hank grimaced as the car bucked up
and down. "You're one of the best skaters on the team."

Martin was prepared for this. "I thought you said goalies have to
be good skaters."

Hank frowned, obviously regretting the adage. "That's true," he
admitted and rubbed a finger against one of his sideburns. "You also
have to be kind of crazy, right?"

"Yeah, so—I'm crazy," Martin said, trying to joke.

Hank was not amused. As every hockey player knew, goalies
were strange, aloof loners who displayed all sorts of freakish behavior, e.g., talking to the goalposts or knitting sweaters between periods

in the case of Jacques Plante, probably the best goalie in the history of the National Hockey League during his tenure with the Montreal Canadiens. Hank's theory was that the stress of the position would make anyone a little "wacky," something he did not want happening to his son.

"Is this because of the mask thing?" Hank asked. "Because being in the net is different, you know. You're in the firing line—front and center—and those pucks can really sting."

"So?" Martin responded with a level of disdain he knew—because of the implication that Hank felt otherwise about physical pain—would effectively transform the discussion into a dare. He referred to a practice a few weeks earlier when he had taken a turn in net. "You saw me—I was good."

Hank did not admit or deny this. "Well, let me talk it over with your mother," he said. "I have a feeling she's not going to be too comfortable with you between the pipes."

Martin shrugged, because he had already talked to Jane, and as expected, she expressed no preference about what position he wanted to play. Though he had yet to question the dynamic between his parents in which Hank—who had played at the University of Michigan, where they met—was as obsessed with the sport as Jane was ambivalent, much less how love could bring together such very different people without any consideration of what the union might look like fifteen or twenty years later, he was quite aware that they said things to him that they did not necessarily say to each other. When he took advantage of this discord to achieve his own objectives—or "goals," as he would years later realize in a frisson of Jungian insight—he began for the first time to note within himself a certain disdain for his parents (although it was far too amorphous for him to identify as such, again until much later), as though their failure to communicate was an expression of their stupidity, and not their humanity.

Martin offered his opinion that Jane would not object.

"We'll see," said Hank. "But promise me one thing: no knitting, okay?"

Martin laughed. "Don't worry—I'm not that crazy."

WHATEVER THE UNDERLYING motivation for the switch—and there were probably several—the goal crease proved to be the best place for Martin. The on-and-off nature of the position gave him plenty of opportunity to daydream when the action went to the other end of the rink and even—to Hank's chagrin—sometimes when it was in his own.

"What happened, Marty?" Hank liked to ask after a soft goal. "You were on another planet out there."

"Entropy," Martin stated succinctly, one of his stock answers to avoid explaining that a loss could not be avoided when the Zamboni had not circled the ice ten times. In an early and unconscious attempt to reconcile his conflicting affinities for art and logic, he spent a lot of time developing an intricate set of superstitions, which he liked to believe could dictate the outcome of a game far more than his performance, e.g., each of his pads had to go on and come off in the same order, he never allowed the bottom of his stick to touch anything but the ice—but if it did, he would have to tap it against the ceiling three times to "purify" it—and before the first face-off of each period he always skated back and forth between the goal pipes exactly seven times. He also preferred to be the last one on the ice at the beginning of a game (but the first one off at the end), and he was always careful not to touch any of the opposing players' clammy hands during the traditional postgame handshake. None of this he divulged to his father. "Sometimes it's inevitable," he said.

"It didn't seem too inevitable for the other goalie," Hank noted. "He looked pretty sharp."

"You mean my opposite?" Martin said, using a terminology he had likewise developed, albeit for a different—but equally unconscious—reason, namely to distance himself from his father.

"Yes, your opposite," sighed Hank.

"He did look pretty good," Martin admitted and softened a little before he continued. "Next game you can be sure that my opposite's opposite will prevail."

Any aggravation these tics caused Hank, however, was exceeded by the pleasure he took in his son's talent and skill as Martin—despite the occasional lapse—continued to improve. "You may be adopted, but when it comes to hockey we have the same DNA," he declared.

"That's for sure," Martin responded eagerly. At this age, because he was adopted, he liked to acknowledge the influence of his parents, as if he were no different from any other kid. That he even resembled them in some ways—e.g., his blue eyes were very much like Jane's and he often wore the same serious and intense expression as Hank—also made him happy, and sometimes he liked to surprise people with the truth of his adoption, as if to prove a point about it not making a difference.

As MARTIN GREW older and detected a growing tension between Hank and Jane—albeit one, in keeping with the mores of Cedar Village, they were not inclined to display—he began to hope that he would not end up like them after all. Except, already more similar to them than he realized, he did not directly address the issue but rather exploited it, particularly after he tried out for and made Pittsburgh's most elite "travel team," the Royal Travelers, which took him—and Hank—out of town quite a bit more than Jane would have wanted. On any given weekend beginning in the winter of sixth grade, Martin found himself in Cleveland, Detroit, Toronto, Chicago, Philadelphia, or any other city within a seven- or eight-hour radius from Pitts-burgh. While this traveling entailed many hours in the car, most of which he spent either reading or goofing around with other kids on his team, he liked the sense of escape that came with it—although from exactly whom or what was not a question he was yet asking—so that he inevitably felt let down when he and his father pulled into the driveway on Sunday night.

One Christmas break, when he was fourteen, his team made the finals of a tournament in Buffalo, which meant that he had to skip a Prokofiev ballet—something "cultural," as his mother liked to say—Jane was planning to take him to with his sister. At the hotel, Martin overheard his father on the phone in a relatively heated discussion with his wife: "This is a big tournament, and thanks to Marty, we're doing a lot better than expected. We beat the Junior Sabres, honey! Do you really think it's fair to ask him to leave now?"

Martin was struck by the way circumstances so often contrived to make things as difficult as possible; it was almost as if he had known this would happen the second his mother had ordered the tickets a few months earlier, even though the tournament had not yet been on the calendar. While it pained Martin to picture his mother on the other end of the line, he also didn't want to leave, and he appreciated his father's ability to deal with a thorny situation.

This admiration lasted until they were in the car on their way to the rink a few minutes later, and Hank tried to joke about it. "So, I guess you're disappointed you won't be able to see all those pretty little ladies prancing around onstage?"

Martin found himself incapable of playing along. "What if I told you that they're incredibly limber?" he responded in an ironic tone meant to downplay the lack of irony. "Or that I actually like Pro-kofiev?" The moment the words left his mouth, he regretted it: any loyalty to Jane aside, defending ballet was a tricky proposition for a fourteen-year-old hockey player—even if he was a goalie, of whom some eccentricity was expected and for whom limberness was a necessity—particularly one who was not totally unaware of his ambivalence toward girls and everything that implied. In effect, he had drawn into sharp relief a difference between himself and his father, but one he could view only with discomfort.

Given that Martin—at least at the time—could barely appreciate his need to employ these conversational hedges, they were completely lost on Hank. "Well, let's just say that anything's better than opera," Hank offered. "All those nuts running around screaming their heads off really give me a headache."

"That *is* stupid," Martin agreed, now deciding to take a different tack and outdo his father. "Who ever came up with the idea of people singing to each other anyway?"

"I'll tell you who"—Hank leaned over in his seat and ripped a fart that, remarkably, was louder than a passing truck—"there's a kiss for you—some group of queers who got together in Europe and wanted to torture us American men three hundred years later."

Martin rolled down the window. "Then why do you even go?" he asked, alluding to Jane's subscription to the Pittsburgh Opera and the fact that she required her husband to attend.

"The same reason you're going to go, too," Hank said. "Because your mother likes it, and it's our job to keep her happy. Believe me, kiddo, if they're happy, you're happy. That's lesson number one in relating to the other half of the species, Marty. You gotta keep 'em happy."

ALTHOUGH MARTIN DIDN'T respond to his father's comment at the time, over the course of the following year he would often think back to this advice, particularly since Hank seemed so disinclined to follow it himself. Once again, hockey was—at least superficially—the source of conflict, after Hank proposed sending Martin to boarding school beginning in tenth grade. Despite Hank's best efforts, hockey remained a "second-class" sport in Pittsburgh—unlike in his hometown in Michigan, where hockey was a "religion"—and so he concluded that the solution was not to bring hockey to Pittsburgh, as he once hoped to do, but to send Martin to hockey. It did not occur to Hank that by doing this, he would lose the very thing that had allowed him to remain largely oblivious to his wife's frustrations with their marriage but instead justified the idea with the noble and even sacrificial overtones of acting in his son's best interest.

Jane didn't buy any of it and expressed her displeasure to a degree that Martin had never before witnessed. "I can't believe you want him to leave home to play hockey," she cried more than once. "What about meeting his teachers? What about his first girlfriend? I want to take pictures of him with his date for the prom. I want these things to be part of my experience as a parent, as a mother—does that make sense to you?"

"Of course it does." Hank could afford the luxury of seeming reasonable in these exchanges, knowing that Martin was firmly in his camp.

Jane was aghast. "You've already made up his mind."

"Do you think he'd want to hear you say that?" It was now Hank's turn to act hurt. "He's a smart kid, Jane—he can think for himself."

"Hank, how can you say that when he's spent his entire life playing hockey, just to make you happy?"

A heavy sigh from Hank seemed to conclude the discussion. "I think you should take a look at who's really being selfish here."

Martin was both disturbed and—though he didn't like to admit this—oddly exhilarated to see this unprecedented fissure, particularly when he knew that there was no longer any compromise he could make—short of dividing himself in two—to keep them both happy. He was beginning to detect the existence of some chthonic vein of truth—though whether in himself, the world, or both, he could not have said—that could be mined only away from his parents, so that he sometimes viewed their discord with satisfaction, as though they deserved the misery they inflicted on each other; but then he would feel disgusted with himself, and it would occur to him that he had already been split in two, just not in the way anyone could appreciate.

Worn down, Jane eventually agreed to visit. On a winter day in February 1975, they left a Pittsburgh still euphoric from the Steelers' first Super Bowl win over the Vikings, and five hours later arrived at the school—Cranbrook, about twenty miles north of Detroit. Founded in 1928 by a newspaper baron and designed with an un-limited budget by the Finnish modernist Eliel Saarinen, the campus looked like a piece of Versailles that had been transported to Michi-gan via Fallingwater. While Hank remained oblivious to the artis-tic splendor—except to express admiration for the obvious cost of building and maintaining it—Martin knew from his mother's quiet gasps that it resonated with her in exactly the same way it did for him; except while he observed the passing landscape with a remote and barely elucidated pleasure, she discreetly cried when confronted by the serene juxtaposition of snowy woods and hulking works of abstract sculpture. Even the hockey rink, situated outdoors in a small wooded ravine, exuded a last-century utopian charm, as if you ex-pected to see ladies in petticoats skating arm in arm with gentlemen in tails and top hats, and so it seemed impossible—until you heard the sharp crack of the sticks against the ice and saw incongruously large and fast boys brutally hurling each other into the boards—that it actually housed a hockey team that was one of the best in the state.

By this point, however—after they had toured the Tudor dormitories on the boys' campus, complete with verdigris roofs and slender iron-casement windows, and an art museum that would have been at home on Albert Speer's Unter den Linden—Jane's reservations about hockey were beside the point. Aesthetically, everything— even the sleek, neoclassical fountains where water nymphs reposed and dripped small icicles from their languid mouths and fingertips— "worked" here, and Martin knew that to be confronted with such a magical combination of extremes meant that his mother had lost the battle on her terms. The school was exactly what she would have wanted for herself and, as a result, she had no choice but to join her husband in offering it to him.

BACK IN NEW York City, Martin's car thudded to a stop at the corner of Fifty-second Street and Seventh Avenue. He signed for the fare and stood on the sidewalk for a few seconds to cool off in the dry September air. The car pulled away, and he was distracted by an eight-story video screen across the street, where flocks of dot-com-branded seagulls careened in circles above a white beach before evaporating over the thousands of midtown commuters. As he walked toward his building, his thoughts returned to his parents, and he noted that in his memories they were very close to the age he was now, which made him smile wistfully as he imagined them—Hank and Jane Vallence of Cedar Village, and the suburban sheen of perfection that implied—plagued by the same doubts and longings he associated with his own life (Exhibit A: the malaise with which he had been afflicted after waking up just a few hours earlier). He had long considered his parents so different from himself, if not exactly dissimilar in certain limited ways, but now—as he placed his hand on the cool metal handle of the revolving glass door—it seemed that to be a decidedly nonheterosexual (and single) attorney in Manhattan did not create such a wide gulf after all.

11

Meine Musikdramatische Idee

PITTSBURGH, 1972. Maria transferred to Honus Wagner Junior High—the public school in Castle Shannon—where some former classmates who had already made the move promptly rechristened her Morticia, a name that seemed even more appropriate in light of rumors about her having slit a nun's throat at St. Anne's. She remained as ostracized as ever; even her teachers were reluctant to engage her—and vice versa—for while she never made trouble and received passing—if unremarkable—grades, they were busy with more vocal students or intimidated by the way she towered over them. At home, she closed down her musical productions with Gina and Bea and spent time in her room, where she stared at the ceiling or mutilated her old prayer books, crossing out the contents line by line until the books were filled with brittle pages of lead.

Unnerved by her daughter's bleak intensity, the way she could look right through her and make her feel like she didn't exist, Gina tried to lull the old Maria out of this new one; she cooked her favorite lasagna, played her favorite records, and with Bérénice even pulled out some of their old costumes—made of plastic bags and thousands of paper streamers—and tried to reprise some of the former hits in the backyard. To Maria, these numbers appeared juvenile and wooden, and it embarrassed her to see her mother and grandmother dancing around outside with lipstick smeared all over their faces and mops on their heads, never mind the awful singing.

This frustration sometimes boiled over, such as on the night Gina asked Maria if she wanted an extra helping of her grandmother's meatballs. "Nonna Bea made them just for you," Gina added. "And they're reallllly good—"

"I don't care," Maria interrupted.

Gina's eyes narrowed. "You don't care that she made them, or you don't care if I serve you more than one?"

Maria looked up and knew that a line had very clearly been drawn, but it was one that she was more than ready to cross. "Does it matter?"

Gina took the plate and moved it several inches to the side of the table. In a fluid gesture that recalled the vengeance of Tosca, she thrust it toward the floor, where it landed with less of a shatter than a thud. "That's what I think of that," she declared, before turning on her heel and exiting the scene. Bérénice cast a gleam of approval toward John, who was already trudging back from the kitchen with a towel and a garbage bag.

He glared back at his mother-in-law and shook his head—he hated fights—before he addressed Maria. "I want you to go apologize to your mother."

"Why—what did I do?"

"You mouthed off."

"I mouthed off?"

"Maria, I'm not fighting with you. All I'm saying is that you need to apologize to your mother. And it wouldn't hurt if you cut her some slack."

"Fine." Maria backed down with a grunt before she pushed her chair away from the table and tromped down the hallway to the closed door of her parents' bedroom.

"Ma, I'm sorry," she began, straddling the thinnest line between sincerity and sarcasm, at least until she heard sobs on the other side of the door and felt an unexpected pang of remorse that led her to try to remember why she had been so angry. "Ma, I mean it. Come back to dinner. I don't know what I was saying. If you want, I'll eat twenty of Nonna's meatballs."

Gina opened the door, her expression hopeful, as if Maria's promise to eat meatballs were a vow of unconditional love. She threw her arms around her daughter for several seconds—something that instantly depleted most of the small reserve of goodwill and patience Maria had just put aside for her—and together they went back to the dinner table.

LATER, ON HER way to bed, Gina could not resist a detour past Maria's bedroom, for in her mind the storm clouds of so many months had broken. "Good night, honey," she said.

"Good night," Maria replied automatically. She noticed that her mother had crossed the threshold and now hovered inside her room. "What?"

Gina cleared a spot on Maria's bed and sat down. "I want you to know that I was once your age, too, and I thought the world was a horrible place—kids at school called me fat, and I never could imagine a boy liking me. And I stopped talking to anyone because I figured that things might be easier if nobody ever noticed me."

Maria stared at the floor as the outer edges of her vision began to kaleidoscope. "I'm not you."

"Of course not, honey. That's not why I brought it up."

"Then what?"

"One day after school, Nonna Bea took me aside and we had a little talk, sort of like this, except she said, 'Gina—this moping, she starts to get on my nerves, but if you want to mope, then mope!

But you still have to help me in the kitchen because we are not rich.'"

Maria suppressed a smile at the thought, but she still suspected that Gina was about to allude to some allegedly happy event from their shared past—one of their old backyard theater productions, or how Maria used to sing along with the Callas records—with the implication, as Maria saw it, that she was now somehow inferior to what she had once been. "So you want me to do more dishes?"

"No—it's not that," Gina spoke with deliberation. "I understand why she said it, because in her case it was true—she couldn't afford to have me moping around, with my father and brothers to take care of—even though I really hated her at the time, you know? I don't even know why I'm telling you this, Maria, except I don't want you to give up. You have something in you that—someday, somehow—is going to come out. I don't want you to ever forget that."

"Forget *what?*"

"That you love music, and if that sets you apart from everyone else, that's the way it is."

"So?" Maria responded, though more tentatively because she knew there was something different about her and that it involved music, the way it took her to mountains and lush islands and most of all great, teeming cities. It was not just when she sang, either, but when she listened, so that she still craved the operas her mother played in the living room after school, and she would surreptitiously crack her door to hear, at least until Bea walked by and accused her of doing just that. Or on Saturday afternoons, during the Met broadcasts, when she would sit on the end of the couch and flip through a magazine—or absently blacken in the eyes and teeth of the people in the ads, which she knew her mother hated—as though it were a punishment to be there. She could hear melodies in the flipping pages of a book or the scuffing of her feet against the floor, and could feel music in the midst of her sexual fantasies, in the warm caresses of unknown hands and fingertips that would ultimately deliver her away from her angry restlessness for a few seconds.

Gina paused and took a deep breath. She felt fragile and lifeless and barely intact, like an egg whose insides have been blown out through a pinhole. It did not occur to her that what she said to Maria was truer than she could have imagined, and that, as long as she wanted Maria to escape, there was a part of her that would not resist pushing her daughter away in the most effective way possible. "Maria, you can be so much more than I was."

Though moved enough to wrap her arms gingerly around Gina, Maria felt shocked and even a little affronted. Did this mean that Gina's effusive cheeriness was just an act? Was she really miserable? And even if she was, was it Maria's fault? Why couldn't her mother just leave her alone? Or better, why couldn't her mother just acknowledge the ambivalence Maria now felt toward everything—including, or especially, music—particularly if she felt the same way? Maria was suspicious, as if she had recognized a complacence in her mother that would have to be overcome in herself.

MARIA WAS HALFWAY through tenth grade when the music teacher was replaced by Kathy Warren, a trained soprano who created a sensation thanks to her straight blond hair, bell-bottom blue jeans, and turtleneck sweater. It was unimaginable to the student body that someone so young (in truth twenty-eight, despite a rumor that she was seventeen) could be a teacher, and they watched her every movement in collective astonishment until she was officially introduced at assembly, after which most of them vacantly stared at their shoes or at the cotton-ball-size snow flurries floating around outside.

Later that day, Kathy stationed herself outside the chorus room, where she stopped students to lobby them to sign up for her class.

Maria—late for geometry but in no rush to get there—drifted past, and Kathy did not hesitate to step in front of her to make a pitch. No longer as thin as she had been, Maria at sixteen possessed a body that called to mind the sleeping hills and valleys of Western Pennsylvania; her hair was as black as her skin was pale, while her large eyes had been transformed into pools of jade. If her fellow students still hated her, they left her alone; there was a sense that if sufficiently provoked, she might ignite their own pubescent insecurities into wisps of smoke she would brush away with a flick of her outcast wrist. Maria gritted her teeth and glowered at the petite and slender Kathy, whose cheerful expression repulsed her. "What? Really? No."

"Come on! A bunch of other kids have signed up—including a few cute guys—"

"I don't like music," Maria uttered, being more deceptive than untrue, given that it never left her alone.

"Okay, what about guys?"

Maria scowled. "In chorus class?"

"Yeah. You'll see, it'll be fun—singing is good for the soul!" Kathy leaned in and spoke in a more conspiratorial tone: "Plus I told everyone else if they don't like it after two weeks, they can drop and go back to study hall—no questions asked."

Maria's lips creaked into something closer to a smile. Whether it was Kathy's diction or her posture—or even that "good for the soul" business—Maria suspected that a "real singer" might finally help her to understand what made her so different, and the temptation to find out was more than she could resist.

She went to school the next day accompanied by dreams of triumph, but as the minutes ticked by, she began to wonder if perhaps she wasn't so musical after all, since with the unhappy exception of Sister Mary Michael's seventh-grade class, she had never sung for anyone outside her family. It took every ounce of willpower just to walk, one painful step at a time, to the chorus room, where she could not even bring herself to look at Kathy. The bell rang to signal the start of class, and as Kathy stepped onto a small platform with an upright piano to take attendance, Maria felt the dread of impending execution as she listened to the names being called. When hers arrived, it was all she could do to raise her hand six inches off the desk and respond, "Yeah."

As Maria spoke, one of the junior varsity football players elbowed his friend and muttered, "Morticia has big ones," which caused some snickering among his jockstrap friends, who had signed up thanks to a general consensus that Ms. Warren was the hottest teacher in the history of Castle Shannon High.

Kathy stepped out from behind the piano to address directly the offending parties. "I don't know what you jag-offs are laughing at," she said, employing her native Pittsburgh vernacular to full effect, "but before we go any further, let me be clear: I expect my chorus at all times to maintain an atmosphere of respect; that means no whispering or laughing at anyone, unless you want your balls handed to you on a platter."

Because Kathy—in another bold move to demonstrate her access to the highest echelons of power—had already been seen eating lunch with the varsity football coach, she quickly obtained the necessary murmurs of assent. She returned to the piano and sang a Joni Mitchell song that made every heart in the room skip a beat when she cooed the line "Marcie buys a bag of peaches." Without exception they sensed in Ms. Warren a hip older sibling with great reserves of knowledge about life—and most important, sex—who commanded their respect and provided fodder for their own unceasing fantasies. Even more than the base physicality—fascinating as that could be—Kathy's singing represented a broader awakening for Maria and the other students, who were confronted by the idea that someone in their immediate proximity—as opposed to a movie or a rock concert—could exude such a nonpornographic sensuality, as though they had been dropped into a forest in springtime. Maria found herself staring at one of the jocks, less with anger over his comment than with curiosity as she imagined him with his clothes off and a lock of his long, feathery hair wrapped around her finger.

12

Kritik der reinen Vernunft

PARIS, 1852. Now fifteen and close to a head taller than Codruta, Lucien stooped to kiss each of her cheeks before stepping back to allow the waiting domestics to guide her into a chair. Over the past year, she had invited him to sing several times at her salon and also to afternoon tea, during which they discussed many things, including music—they shared a passion for Beethoven and Donizetti—the swaths of construction in Paris, and Lucien's continuing ambivalence toward school. Once situated, the princess beckoned to a seat opposite her own. "Please," she commanded as a second pair of servants entered the room carrying large silver trays laden with a tea service and an assortment of fruit and pastries. As these were arranged on the table, she tilted her head and scrutinized him. "So tell me—how did your final assignment go?"

Lucien regretted having mentioned it at all, but it had been weighing on him at their last meeting, a few weeks earlier. "Well, it's done," he answered evasively. "I finished the year."

The late-afternoon sun angled down through the west-facing windows and reflected off the gilt rococo, an effect that seemed to turn her eyes to marble. "And did you ask your father for help?"

"Not exactly," Lucien admitted, obdurate for reasons he couldn't quite explain. "I did look through some of his books."

"Imagine," Codruta mused, "the son of one of France's most accomplished scientists refusing to ask his father for help." She focused on Lucien. "What's the problem here?"

"I'm not sure," Lucien began unsteadily. "I wanted to ask him—I really did—but then it was due and I knew he would be angry because I waited until the last second, and then..." He trailed off as Codruta beckoned toward one of her domestics to fill her cup.

"Lucien, please—I'm not your teacher or your father," she said. "I understand you don't want to follow in his footsteps, and I wouldn't recommend it if you did." She paused to dip a slice of pineapple into a warm bath of chocolate sauce. "This kind of adolescent sabotage is not becoming of a young man of your abilities—and I don't just mean for singing."

Lucien felt his cheeks flush as he fixed his gaze on a cluster of jade grapes that served as the centerpiece on the table. "I just wish he understood what it's like for me!"

She nodded. "I don't blame you—as we've discussed, academic studies were never my forte, either—but you have to view the situation from his perspective. His concern is for your long-term welfare, and while countless others share your love of the opera, only the very best can expect anything resembling a civilized existence in return."

"That's a risk I'm willing to take," Lucien insisted. "As I said to him—"

"Please don't upset yourself," Codruta interrupted. "It's your father's passion for music that makes him suspicious. He loves to hear you sing, of course, but as a scientist, he is inclined to want an objective validation, which as we both know doesn't exist."

"Shouldn't your opinion count for something?"

"You flatter me, but no—my opinion here counts for nothing."

"Then what do you suggest?"

She waved at a domestic, who lowered the blinds a fraction of an inch, effectively eliminating the glare while allowing the room to maintain a most pleasant shade of amber. "I am not a miracle worker," she said, "but I have a plan, which—assuming you're amenable—may prove suitable to us all."

EXACTLY ONE WEEK later, Lucien arrived at 3 Place d'Aurifère, the home of Manuel García, who was probably—as Madame de Vicionière had remarked the previous spring at Codruta's *mercredi*—the leading voice teacher in Paris, if not in all of Europe. Codruta had arranged the audition for Lucien on the condition that if the professor felt anything less than certain about his prospects, Lucien would return to lycée in the fall. It was a deal Lucien had accepted with something approaching glee but that he now considered with some terror, given what was at stake. With close to an hour to spare, he peered over the stucco wall into the mansion's courtyard, where boxwood mermaids posed seductively above reefs of flowering azaleas and hawthorns, but this occupied him for less than two minutes and led him to cross the street into the Bois de Boulogne, where he sat on a bench to watch the cherry blossom petals drift down like snow flurries. He watched a couple smile at each other as they strolled past, their hands discreetly locked together, and felt jealous; everything and everyone around him seemed to have given over to the fervor of spring, while he was left with nothing but questions.

A few days earlier, at an outdoor café on the Boulevard St.-Michel, a girl with high cheekbones and curly golden hair had smiled shyly at him from her table, where she was sitting with an older couple, probably her parents, and though he could easily have taken a seat nearby and flirted with her—she had essentially issued an invitation—he had ignored her. It was not until later that it occurred to him that his reluctance was rooted in the same ground as his desire to leave school, as if to return such a predictable gesture would have placed him among the throngs who populated the most generic, mundane sectors of society, the very ones he wanted to escape with a career in the theater. More intriguing had been a man near the Pont Neuf who in the dusky twilight had looked at and through him while touching the brim of his hat with one hand and suggestively shifting his other in the front pocket of his trousers. Though Lucien had again walked past, not acknowledging the gesture, he understood that he had witnessed a type of code, one that he had first become aware of at the theater and that left him wanting to know more.

With the hour almost up, Lucien drove all such thoughts from his mind; the last thing he wanted was to appear confused or lonely to Manuel García. He reminded himself that he was only fifteen—with his life ahead of him—and after gently slapping his cheeks and jumping up and down a few times, he walked with renewed determination to the mansion. After he rang the bell, a footman in scarlet livery appeared and led him through the front entrance into a huge reception foyer, where Lucien asked for and was given a moment to admire the vaulted ceilings some three stories above before he was ushered into a smaller if no less formidable drawing room, and here left with a promise of the professor's imminent arrival.

Minutes came and went. Lucien worried he would wilt like a parched flower in the white light that caromed off the mirrors and crystal, but he dared not remove his jacket, since he had yet to meet Monsieur García and wanted to make the most of his first impression. When he finally heard footsteps, he drew himself to attention but could not restrain himself from smiling rather too broadly—almost gawking—at the professor, who in contrast to the huge dimensions the man had taken on in his mind, was quite short, slender and balding, with the droopy eyes of a hound. Lucien felt more composed during an exchange of pleasantries as the professor led him down a hallway and into the music salon. This room also featured twenty-foot coffered ceilings but was less formal, thanks to a faded oriental rug, an old armchair—threadbare in spots, as though someone actually used it—and endless shelves of musical scores, books, and stationery.

García sat down at the piano, lifted the cover, and tossed off a few chords with an ease that announced the presence of a musician of serious ability. *"On commence?"* he asked as he flattened the sheet music against the stand. Lucien nodded slowly but intently, wanting to convey his appreciation for the jolt of adrenaline that prefaced any performance of meaning. But just before his entrance—and apparently less focused than he thought—he detected a sound, not so much a knock as a light tap, something that distracted him enough so that—*putain de merde!*—he missed his cue and instead offered up something between a gag and a cough.

Wearing the shocked expression of one who has just seen the tip of an arrow emerge through his chest, Lucien contemplated whether to hurl himself out the window, even as the knocking resumed with greater force. García, who had also heard the knock but, presumably less nervous, had chosen to ignore it, stopped playing and yelled that whoever or whatever was there would have to wait. A garbled but impassioned female voice responded, and with a sigh of resigned frustration that Lucien understood conveyed the sad fact that even the best voice teacher in the world could not conduct an audition without being interrupted by annoying trivialities, García got up and, in one quick motion that sent the piano bench stuttering back along the wood floor, took three compact steps to the door, which he opened just wide enough to allow one of his professorial eyes to peer through. "Pauline?"

"Oui—c'est moi." There in the foyer—thanks to his height

Lucien could see over the professor—stood Pauline García Viardot, one of the city's most famous sopranos and—not coincidentally— the younger sister of Manuel. Lucien admired her pale, oval face, framed by a single strand of hair that had come loose from her bun; she had her brother's large, intelligent eyes, but on her they seemed fragile and sensitive. She leaned forward over the bulk of her crino- line to place one of her weightless hands on her brother's forearm and in hushed tones begged him to assist her with something.

Lucien felt a pang of dread as he wondered if she had somehow detected his missed entrance, or if perhaps she was annoyed that the audition had even been scheduled. On the verge of a mea culpa, he stopped as she raised her eyes in his direction and smiled, a ray of serenity that contained no trace of seduction but—just as he would have hoped—only the reassuring condolence an established singer might give to a younger one beginning a climb toward the lofty peak where she now stood.

The professor and his sister disappeared, leaving Lucien alone in the music room. As he waited, he parted the drapes with a thought to open the window, but the casing was stuck and he dared not push too hard for fear of breaking a pane. He pressed his palms against the cool glass as he regulated his breathing and decided that he preferred the heavier, more expectant air inside, suffused with the sweet scent of the burning lamps and the long shadows of the room.

A few minutes passed before Manuel García swung open the doors. "You're still here?"

"Shouldn't I be?" Lucien replied thickly, as if he had swallowed a jar of ink.

"Most of my singers are not in the habit of missing their cues," the professor addressed him curtly. "As I explained to the princess, you are quite a bit younger than I would normally consider, and your lack of concentration seems to validate my suspicion that this audition is premature."

It had not occurred to Lucien that the professor could be so merciless, but as soon as he recognized the trait, he realized that he would have to respond accordingly unless he wanted to return to another year of classroom drudgery. "Professor, I understand your concern," he began, "and whatever dismay you felt a few minutes ago is not only one that I share but one that is compounded for me by having made the mistake." As Lucien spoke, he thought of Pauline Viardot and knew that he would do anything to join her ranks. "With your indulgence, I'll sing without the piano this time."

The professor's expression remained stern, but he relented. "That won't be necessary," he said as he took his seat and began to play. "But this will be your last chance to impress me."

LESS THAN TWO hours later—after an exuberant dash through a dusty field of construction adjacent to the Rue de Rivoli—Lucien was back on the Île, where he found his father in the garden. "I have important news," he began in a rush, before describing the audition with the famous professor and how he had managed to redeem himself. "I think you'd be very impressed," he barreled ahead. "He's extremely scientific—after he listened to me sing, he took measurements of my chest and waist and he looked down my throat and up my nose, all of which he declared to be in the proper proportions for a singer."

Guillaume barely lifted his eyes from the table, where he was comparing two leaves and entering figures into a notebook. "So you're going to be his student?"

"Yes, exactly!" Lucien cried, as if to make up for his father's lack of enthusiasm, "and if all goes well I can expect to enter the conservatory in two years." He stood facing Guillaume for several more seconds and realized that he had yet to deliver the most important—or at least controversial—element of the news. "Which means I don't have to return to lycée this fall."

"Is that so?" Guillaume responded quietly as he folded his hands in front of him and looked directly at Lucien. "And what if I said you did?"

"Do you understand who Manuel García is?" Lucien challenged. "I would be one of his youngest students ever—it's practically a guarantee."

"Surely he doesn't expect you to train with the same rigor as a more mature singer, much less drop out of school," Guillaume pointed out, with a degree of insight Lucien found maddening because it was exactly what the professor had said; that he was not to sing too much—beyond basic exercises and the occasional recital—and instead should focus his attention on learning as much theory as he could, to provide a sufficient foundation for the conservatory.

Lucien tried to explain all of this, but Guillaume interrupted him. "Lucien, my objection has nothing to do with your desire to sing or to learn everything you possibly can about music. I love your voice, not only because it's yours but also because it reminds me of your mother. But she was married to me, most obviously, and so could afford to fail—singing was a passion, not a necessity."

"It's a necessity for me," Lucien insisted.

"I mean an economic necessity." Guillaume shook his head and waved at the mansions that loomed up behind them. "As we've discussed many times, despite our surroundings, I'm not a rich man, and—"

"Codruta has already promised to be my patron," Lucien responded. "She'll provide whatever I need."

"Yes, she mentioned something to that effect."

This information rendered Lucien speechless for several seconds. "She did? When?"

"A few weeks ago, before she arranged the audition."

"So you knew about it?" Lucien felt betrayed by both of them.

"Don't be angry. It was the right thing for her to do—"

"And what did you tell her?"

"I encouraged her to set up the audition, because I didn't want to deny you the opportunity to meet and possibly work with the famous professor, but I also told her that you're too young to accept her patronage," Guillaume replied more gently. "I know it's difficult, but try to think of yourself at the age of forty, and what you would do if singing wasn't enough. Think of the thousands of young men and women who come to Paris each year with the same dream—you've seen how they line up outside the theaters for even the smallest roles—and most are starving! Half the drunks and beggars in Paris are failed singers."

"Most of them don't know anything, and none of them has Manuel García—or Codruta!"

"I understand the man's reputation," Guillaume said, "but what if you lose your voice? Or what if something happens to Codruta?"

Lucien steeled himself. "Do you really think that three years of lycée will make a difference?"

"Yes, I do," Guillaume insisted. "It's a natural breaking point; it establishes that you attained a certain level of scholarship—"

"Only because of you!"

"That's what parents do." Guillaume sighed. "We work to give advantages to our children." He focused more intently on his son. "You need to be able to support yourself without relying on your voice—at least until you're older."

Lucien stared at the ground as it swirled in front of him. As much as he wanted to leave school, he knew Codruta would never help him if he made a rash threat to disobey his father. He wasn't sure if he was angrier at Guillaume for being so stubborn, at Codruta for conferring with Guillaume, or at his mother for not being alive to help; but as this last thought crossed his mind, he stumbled upon a third option, as though she had whispered it into his ear. "What if—what if I get a job at the theater?" he ventured, tentatively at first but then with more enthusiasm as the idea materialized. "With props or costumes, maybe even with the stagehands! I could begin as an apprentice— it wouldn't cost anything—and then I would earn enough. And just like you said, I wouldn't rely on my voice."

Guillaume pondered this for a few seconds. "Well—it's a thought."

"I could become a carpenter!" Lucien begged his father as tears of relief and certainty escaped his eyes. "Please—I'll go tonight and speak to some of the men. I'm sure I could do something."

After considering him for a few more seconds, Guillaume nodded. "Okay, go see what's available," he said. "If you can get an offer at the theater—in carpentry or some other area; it hardly matters what, as long it's a skill or a trade—I'll consent."

13

Spiderland

NEW YORK CITY, 2001. Martin entered his office building with enough time to buy and then drink a double espresso from the coffee shop in the lobby, and then—because the first went down so well—a second, along with a chocolate-chip muffin that unfortunately looked much better than it tasted and—because he was trying to eat less junk—a banana and an apple. While this breakfast vanquished all remnants of his hangover, he considered the hordes of the nine o'clock rush with less enthusiasm as he tried to remember what had prompted him to agree to a conference call at this ridiculous hour, especially on his birthday. After easing himself back into the lobby—and perhaps there was a god—he spied not one but two empty elevators, the closer of which he ran to catch in the hope of avoiding a clump of office workers chattering away not far behind him. He reached it at the same time as a tall, excessively thin woman in a business suit whom Martin recognized from another firm. She pressed the Close Door button so that the doors clunked shut only millimeters beyond the zebra-striped fingernails of a secretary attempting to trigger the sensor. "Oops," she said to Martin as she extracted her cell phone from her bag and flipped it open. "Wrong button." He smiled benignly at her but felt queasy as he observed her dark hose, closed-toe leather heels, thin pinstripes, and network-anchor hair; while they rode up in silence, he could not shake the feeling that she might turn on him with some sort of perfectly constructed opening statement that would expose him as woefully unprepared for the day ahead.

He was reminded of his ex-wife, Amanda, whose appeal had been similarly imperious and unreal. Before they met, during Martin's junior year in high school, Cranbrook had offered Martin everything he—and his parents—could have wanted (except for his actual presence, in Jane's case): as a sophomore, he had made the dean's list and the varsity hockey team, and as a junior, he was well positioned to be the starting goalie. Living away from home had also made him more forgiving toward Hank and Jane; as his roommate, Jay Wellings, pointed out, there wasn't much point in rebellion when your parents lived three hundred miles away. But for all that was good, he could not escape a longing for something more than schoolwork and hockey, or even getting high, listening to cool bands with Jay, or messing around with girls, all of which he had done with varying degrees of success and satisfaction. After considering the problem, he concluded that it might have something to do with having a more "serious" girlfriend; while the thought of becoming a drooling, love-struck dimwit held no appeal, he began to scan the crowd more earnestly, with the hope of finding the perfect girl staring back.

He first noticed Amanda in his second-semester pottery elective, where he was intrigued by her thin shoulders, boyish hips, and long, slender neck, and over the course of a few weeks, he grew more entranced as it became clear that she was a goddess of the ceramic studio, able to transform mountains of clay into spinning beehives and then one perfectly formed cylinder after the next, which in turn were followed by massive pitchers, urns, and vases. While he often allowed his eyes to linger on her, she seemed oblivious; there were no accidental glances or nods hello, just an inscrutable gaze with her sleep-deprived eyes that sent twin shivers of adrenaline through him, one at the thought that she wanted nothing to do with him or anyone else, the other at the prospect of doing something—anything—to ingratiate himself with her.

He turned for advice to Jay, who assessed the situation: "For you and many others in this warped environment, her appeal lies in her aura of decadence," his roommate said. "You understand that, right? That for someone like you—varsity hockey, dean's list—she represents the underlying fatigue you feel for your superficial displays of perfection."

"Who says I'm fatigued?"

"My point exactly," Jay rejoined. "Nevertheless, your plight has moved me to pity, and so I can do some reconnaissance. Very discreet to spare you the agony of a public rejection, though I must go on record to say that you will not be the first or the last to lose your bearings navigating the shoals off the rocky coastline that is Amanda Perry."

That Friday, Jay caught up with Martin on the quad. "Good news, Vallence: Ms. Perry is amenable to a brief excursion. You are to meet her at the pottery studio tomorrow at four, after which I would suggest something informal, perhaps a stroll through the woods—bring some entertainment, of course"—he tapped his backpack, where he kept his one-hitter—"to determine if there is the necessary rapport."

The next day Martin met Amanda at the studio, where they talked about music—she liked Roxy Music and David Bowie—which seemed to confirm that they were two lost souls who against incalculable odds had found each other. Still, because there was a part of him—even deeper and less acknowledged—that was afraid of exactly what Amanda might help him find, he remained somewhat aloof and was careful to mask the depth of his feelings for her as he mentioned older or more obscure bands—the Stooges, the Modern Lovers, Big Star—that he professed to love more than any others.

They eventually left the studio and walked around the lake to the Greek amphitheater in the woods behind the girls' campus. In a shaded alcove next to the stage, Martin extracted a joint from his pocket. As the sun disappeared below the tree line and the forest around them became somber, the smoke they exhaled mixed with a wet mist that covered the entire theater in a shroud. Martin was struck by how attuned she seemed to his desires; like him, she was not incapable of enthusiasm but never appeared too earnest or overbearing. When they kissed, her mouth fit over his in a perfect mix of cool passion and—somehow, again—detachment that left him simmering, if not quite ignited.

This "date"—a word they never used—was followed by others, until at some point, back at the amphitheater, she mysteriously extracted a foil-covered package—a rubber—and pressed it into his palm. When he admitted to her that it was his first time, she tore it open and unrolled it into place before she pushed him onto his back.

"Don't worry—it's a lot easier than calculus," she teased before she kneeled down and officially began the exercise.

At first, as she rocked back and forth and he tried with mixed success to match her rhythm, he feared that this, too, would join the decidedly muted delights offered by—among others—Monica Gittens and his first hand job; Julie Hayes, who had kissed him for an hour; and Barb Peters, who had somewhat presciently put a finger up his butt. Then he detected something dispassionate in Amanda—never once did she lose that faraway look, even when she came a few minutes later and instructed him to do the same—which seemed to be the perfect complement to his own ambivalence and—miraculously— left him wanting more.

SHE BROKE UP with him just before graduation. They had been accepted into different colleges, and when Amanda declared that a long-distance relationship would be untenable, Martin listened to the words as if they were being whispered at him from across a desert. Though he felt sorry, he was not close to tears, for it had already occurred to him over the last few months that his feelings for Amanda had not crossed—and would not cross—into the realm of serious love or infatuation.

A decade later, when one day on the subway platform he heard a low female voice, eerily familiar, which did not so much call out his name as state it—"Martin. Martin Vallence. Hey, Martin, over here"—he was no longer so presumptuous, and his longing for Amanda was not so obtuse, but rooted in a more tangible hope to alleviate the far more acute desires that had taken hold during the intervening period. So when he confirmed that it was Amanda, still vaguely but unapologetically masculine in the manner of certain runway models, and she examined him with the same passive but not displeased expression he remembered from high school, he felt more than grateful; he felt redeemed. He had staked a lot more on meeting the girl of his dreams—or his past dreams, which in Amanda's case meant the same thing—and his hands trembled, so certain was he at this moment that her arrival was predestined to save him from the parade of men who increasingly inhabited his thoughts and fantasies.

He restrained the urge to touch her. "Amanda?" he asked, although he already knew the answer. "What the fuck?"

"Nice to see you, too, Martin." She pushed a strand of hair—still the color of wet sand—behind her ear and spoke in the same faintly mocking yet seductive tone he remembered.

He looked into her shadowed eyes, which made her face seem even more appealingly gaunt than he remembered. He quickly explained that he lived in the city now and worked as a rock critic, the New York correspondent for the British weekly *Music Machine*, a job he had inherited from Jay Wellings. "So do you live here?" he asked, trying to seem nonchalant but praying that she would say yes.

She nodded and explained that she was an assistant to Louise Bourgeois and also had her own sculpture studio on East Broadway in Chinatown, under the Manhattan Bridge. "Give me your hand," she instructed as she fished a pen out of her pocket and quickly scrawled a number across his palm. "Call me," she said before jumping through the closing subway doors with the offhanded grace of a gazelle.

THE WEDDING WAS held a year later in an abandoned synagogue on Ludlow Street, where Amanda and her friends installed close to a hundred piñatas featuring a range of fantastical creatures that created the illusion of a Miró sky. They were married by Amanda's cousin—a mail-order minister—and during the ceremony, as Martin looked out at the guests and noted an assortment of bored, smiling, and tear-streaked faces, it occurred to him that underneath the ironic trappings of the event he and Amanda had so carefully choreographed, their wedding was not very different from the millions that had come before and would no doubt come after. While such a realization would have tainted his enjoyment of almost anything else—to wit: was there anything worse than seeing a favorite band appropriated by the shallow mainstream of popular culture?—deluded by his desire to escape himself, he felt only happiness as he kissed the champagne away from Amanda's lips amid the calculated mayhem of the moment.

It took not even six months for this phantasm to be obliterated by the prospect of an entire life together. At first he pretended as they went to art openings and rock shows, and made the rounds of their usual East Village haunts. He strained to imagine her as aloof and imperious, and devised a million new ways to please her; he took her to Sammy's Roumanian, he surprised her with dozens of black tulips, her gave her advance copies of new albums by the Cure, Kate Bush, and Echo and the Bunnymen. At home in bed, he assiduously licked every pore of her body as she lay impassively under him, while in public, he always marked her with a touch of his finger on her arm, a kiss on the shoulder, even as he unconsciously shied away when she tried to reciprocate, so that in his mind she retained the magnetic yet feline quality he had always admired. None of it worked for long, and unlike in the past, he saw himself in her hands no longer as a spinning mound of unformed clay but rather as a horribly deformed pot—slimy and off center—with no destiny beyond the slop bucket.

Martin's decision to go to law school the following year proved even more problematic when Amanda showed no enthusiasm for discussing the basic tenets of the law he was obliged to acquire. Her power over him waned to new lows, and as he thought about her during the day, or passed her sleeping body on his way in or out of the apartment, he felt disgusted with himself. He started having sex with men—secretly, of course, but so detached from any sense of Amanda's reality that carelessness was more a given than a question—which both exacerbated the situation and perversely made it more exciting, as if he really were getting away with something.

One afternoon toward the end of his first year, she came home and tossed her bag with some violence onto the bed before she sat down across from him and drummed her fingers on the kitchen table. They had been bickering about something the night before, and she was annoyed that a gallery owner had blown off a studio visit with her.

"Is there a problem?" he asked, petulant. "I'm trying to work."

"I don't know why you ever went to law school," she answered, less aggravated than fatigued. "You actually used to be kind of fun."

He responded as if she were responsible for his hidden and unceasing desires. "Fuck off, Amanda."

"Martin, what the fuck is wrong with you?" she yelled back, provoked. "You look at me like I'm a piece of shit. Do I make you sick? You make me sick! We never talk, we never fuck—are you gay, Martin? Is that why I make you sick?"

"You wish," he responded, trying to control himself but shocked that she had seen through what was apparently little more than a thin veneer. He felt an urge to make angry love to her, which he knew was idiotic, rooted in nothing more than a desire to prove her wrong, but which in turn made him even more irate. "Is there anything else you want to blame me for?"

At this point her anger seemed to break as she beat her hands against the table in frustration. He was horrified to see real tears emerge from her eyes and spill down her cheeks. Until this moment, it had not occurred to Martin that she had also been losing patience with him, that he was actually the one who had taken on the exact characteristics—cool and aloof, vaguely angry—he had once found so beguiling in her.

He felt a newfound resolve and addressed her calmly: "Aman—I'm sorry—I think we made a mistake—"

"Fuck you, Martin," she said, in exactly the same tone he had used a few minutes earlier. "You think an apology for wasting three years of my life is enough?" She now continued without emotion, flat and distant as a mirage. "You have these expectations, Martin, and I'm not sure where you get them, but I always get the sense that neither one of us is living up to them, so how can you ever be happy?"

"That's a good question," Martin admitted, passing his hand in and out of a beam of sunlight on the kitchen table.

She winked at him. "So you really want a divorce?"

"Don't you?"

"You bet, but it's going to cost you."

"Are you threatening me?"

"No, I'm telling you. I want this apartment, Martin, and you're going to give it to me."

"Why should I do that?"

"Because I already know, Martin."

"Know what?"

"I know you haven't exactly been at the library studying all these nights—"

Martin felt the hard metal of the gun she had placed at his temple. "What are you talking about?"

"What part of not being at the library didn't you understand?"

There was a part of him that wanted just to admit it, to confess, but at the last second he panicked and offered a dose of feigned sarcasm: "I love it when you condescend to me, Amanda."

She shrugged. "Fine. Let me spell it out for you—you've been having sex with guys you meet—"

Martin interrupted her. "You're making this up—"

"Am I?" She flipped open a nearby copy of the *Voice*. Her tone was shaky but rehearsed, and he realized that she had planned this. "Hmmm—this one sounds good, doesn't it? Bi-curious MWM—married white male—seeks same . . ."

He felt a strange sense of dislocation, the way he imagined it might feel to have his head cut off but to retain consciousness for those several seconds as it rolled across the floor or stared up at the sky from the wicker basket. Except the numb quality did not fade to black but continued for what felt like years and years, as though he were living every second of his life in reverse. Unable to talk, he staggered to the bathroom, where the deception he saw in these images of his past seemed to accumulate into something visceral, so that he could no longer contain it. To be sick was actually a relief, because it was a distraction from the reverberating echo that each of his many professions of love for her now seemed to hold; it was really the cruelest kind of lie, something you wouldn't wish on an enemy, let alone someone you had shared a bed with for three years. He realized that if someone were to ever do the same to him, he, too, would be filled with rage, except even as this occurred to him he knew he had done this to himself, which was exactly why he was kneeling here on the bathroom floor with his head in the toilet like a strung-out junkie.

Yet after a few minutes, when he was in every way purged of his desire for her, he was struck by the idea that however torturous and ugly the route had been, she had in fact guided him to a certain truth; granted, it was ugly and rough, but it was his to own, and his relief at finally admitting this—of finally grasping this most basic idea, i.e., that he was incapable of loving Amanda—made his tears feel almost hopeful as he allowed himself to be comforted by the cool porcelain against his cheek. His head stopped spinning, and for at least a little while the future seemed ordered and attainable, even when he returned to the kitchen and found Amanda gone, having left only a note with instructions to call her lawyer.

MARTIN'S ELEVATOR STOPPED and his legal colleague exited, leaving him alone with his memories. He had not seen Amanda since the divorce settlement—a dreary session in which they signed documents in her lawyer's conference room and did not once make eye contact—but from periodic reviews of her art had gleaned that she subsequently married a prominent dealer and otherwise appeared to lead the life she had always seemed—if not quite professed—to want. Although the settlement had been financially punishing for a few years, as he thought of her now, he could only admire the manner in which she had eviscerated him, exactly in the way—he could now admit—he had always hoped she would. If she had not appeared, he would have needed to invent her; otherwise, he might have languished even longer in the purgatory he had fashioned for himself. In the silver reflection of the metal doors, he saw an image of the two of them at an outdoor café on Bleecker Street, where they used to go for espresso after shopping for used records. She was sitting across from him, her legs crossed and one elbow resting on the table, a cigarette dangling from her fingers as she looked past him at nothing. He was pleased to detect a continuing resonance in her angular beauty and indifference, the way her placid expression betrayed just a trace of exasperation at the poor service delivered by the world around her.

14 . . . .

The Experience of Our Generation: That Capitalism Will Not Die a Natural Death

PITTSBURGH, 1976. If Maria, once she joined Kathy Warren's chorus, did not consider her voice to be particularly beautiful—or at least not as beautiful as Kathy's—its sheer size and agility in comparison to the wobbling, scooping efforts of other students was obvious, and so she was not surprised when Kathy began to ask her to demonstrate certain passages for the rest of the class. In contrast to how she felt about speaking, Maria never felt any anxiety about singing; she opened her mouth and her voice appeared. But as much as she tried, she inevitably failed to summon this fearlessness on those rare occasions when she was called on in her other classes, or when talking to a boy, or doing anything else that made her nervous, all of which left her feeling at odds with herself as she tried to understand why she could be so able in one respect and so limited in others. Because singing was so easy—and because those who heard her regularly expressed their appreciation of her talent—it often seemed that in the rest of her life, she was just acting and—judging from the audience—not doing a particularly good job of it, either.

At the end of the semester, Kathy rewarded her with a solo at the school's graduation. For the student body at large, this was the first chance to hear Maria, and when they realized it was Morticia on the stage, singing with an impassive confidence that made the leaves around the stadium seem to rustle—especially for those many who were tripping through the ceremony—on what was otherwise a stifling day, there was a collective whisper of astonishment. Though it quickly gave way to boredom and impatience, Maria savored this wave of attention even as she saw an infinitely flat sea behind it.

After the ceremony, Kathy unveiled her plan to have Maria enter the following year's Heinz Recitals, a statewide high school competition whose winners received scholarship money for college or conservatory. When Maria heard this, her mind began to simmer with implications that went far beyond the competition; she saw herself leaving behind so many things—her home, Castle Shannon, her family—traveling the world, stepping off airplanes and being taken to important theaters, where her voice would create riotous storms among countless admirers.

Meanwhile Kathy was describing the details of what they would need to accomplish over the course of the summer to prepare. "So what do you think?" Kathy asked. "Are you up for it?"

Maria was still floating miles above the ground and so did not so much respond as issue a proclamation: "I would be honored and delighted," she said in a serious tone that—as she registered the effect on Kathy, who only squinted up at her—snapped her out of it and made her laugh. "If you really think I can win," she added more hesitantly.

Kathy returned the smile. "Even if you don't win, it'll be good for you," she promised and led them out of the stadium and back to the empty hallways of the school.

As THRILLED AS Gina was by the news, she felt torn that night when, after dinner, a premonition of Maria's empty bedroom in a few years made the house feel as sad and lonely as that cavernous place in her soul, except one that not even the promise of music could fill up. As if on puppet strings, she veered into her daughter's room, where Maria was on the bed reading a book about opera that Kathy had loaned her. "I was just wondering," she mused to her daughter. "Do we have to pay Miss Warren for these lessons you're taking this summer?"

Maria immediately detected—and resented—the distant tone

in her mother's voice, and the happiness she had felt that morning vanished as she considered new doubts and fears—namely about the competition—that Gina's question brought into relief. She looked at her mother with the kind of disdain she felt certain she would feel for herself if she didn't win, as if such a result would doom her to staying in Castle Shannon forever. "You can call her Kathy," Maria said curtly, "and no, you don't have to pay for anything. I just need you to drive me to her house after work."

Gina took a step back. "I suppose I should check with your fath—"

"Since when do you care what he thinks? Why can't you just say yes?"

"Honey, what's wrong?" asked Gina, who could not understand why Maria had to make things so hard. "I'll get you there, don't worry. Just remember who told you not to give up singing in the first place," she remarked as she walked out the door.

"Good—then maybe I'll stop!" Maria yelled at her mother's back.

Maria stared at the door and fantasized about hanging herself from the light fixture or diving off the roof, just so that from the great beyond she could see the shocked look on her mother's face as her body tumbled past. She couldn't understand why Gina had to say such stupid things—like Kathy would make her pay for lessons!—instead of just helping her. Still, even this much reflection was enough for Maria to decide that she really didn't have the energy to get out of bed, much less commit suicide—besides, the roof was not really high enough, and she could imagine just breaking her leg in the bushes—so she absently returned to her dreams and made a vow that, no matter where she went, she would leave Gina and everyone else she knew behind.

THE FOLLOWING WEDNESDAY, as promised, Gina drove Maria to her first session at Kathy's in Cedar Village, where she was living with her parents until her wedding—she was engaged to a reporter for the *Post-Gazette*—which was scheduled for the fall. The Warrens had a neoclassical mansion complete with three Doric columns that made it look—as Maria would later realize—more like a bank than a house, but at this point in her life Maria was nothing but awed as she walked up a flagstone sidewalk lined with rosebushes and marigolds in matching beds carved out of a freshly watered lawn, which glistened in the dappled sunlight under a pair of towering pin oaks. A weather-beaten gardener waved hello, and she felt embarrassed, as if to acknowledge someone from her own social stratum might expose her as a fraud.

Mrs. Warren greeted Maria at the door. "Is that your mother?" she asked caustically as she looked at the car lurking at the base of her driveway.

Maria felt intimidated by this woman's patrician nose and conch of ivory-colored hair. "Yes." She smiled weakly.

Mrs. Warren eyed her. "Don't you think I should meet her?"

Maria's heart sank at the thought of Gina entering this domain of riches she alone had procured but, with no choice in the matter, she waved to her mother to stop and ran down to relay the invitation, which—of course, Maria bitterly noted—Gina accepted.

Gina made her own ascent up the Palatine Hill before stepping into the two-story entrance foyer with a direct view of a curving, marble staircase to the second floor. She took this in with eyes wide but hardly gawking, which did not prevent Maria in the next two minutes from dying of embarrassment as each innocuous syllable left Gina's lips in the course of exchanging pleasantries with the formidable Mrs. Warren.

Fortunately for the skittish Maria, Kathy soon descended like Freia from Valhalla to escort her to some distant wing of the mansion, while Mrs. Warren presented Gina with a cup of coffee and a plate of cookies. As they chatted about their daughters, Mrs. Warren gleaned that the Sheehans did not have a piano. "I'd be frankly overjoyed to give you our spare—it's an upright—if you would arrange to have it moved."

"You have *two* pianos?"

"Well . . . yes." Mrs. Warren did not bother to hide a befuddled expression that seemed to be caused by Gina's failure to grasp the meaning of the word *two*. "That's why I'm offering you one. If your daughter is as talented as Kathy says, then she should have a piano."

"I'll talk to my husband tonight." Gina beamed. "Now that Maria's getting serious, I'm sure he'll understand."

Back in Castle Shannon, where the bald spots in the lawn and the shag carpet stood out in sharp contrast to the manicured landscaping and serene berber of Cedar Village, John—who wished to see nothing but a new color television being hauled into the house—was less certain that this was such a good idea. "You know, it's not exactly cheap to move one of those things."

"John, she's giving it to us. They cost hundreds of dollars in the store!"

"If she's a singer, why does she need a piano?"

Gina tried to remember how Kathy had phrased it. "There's a lot of theory—music theory—that she should learn on the piano."

John scowled. "You don't know what you're talking about."

"No, John, you don't know what you're talking about! Singing is the one thing she's ever done where someone besides anyone living here said, 'Maria, you're really good at that,' and you may not care that much about music, but it's important for her—it really is—even if she doesn't have a professional voice. And if we can't get a new television until next year, that's just tough. I know if she was a boy who was good at football or baseball, you'd be the first one lining up to get him all the right equipment."

"Except the great thing about football and baseball," John pointed out, "is that they don't cost anything."

Gina frowned. "If I have to ask your mother for the money, I will." This was a serious threat, because Mrs. Sheehan was a barely functional alcoholic who spent her days playing bingo and her nights calling her children to deliver sherry-induced vitriolic diatribes about what worthless failures they were, something they all endured because of her habit, the following morning, of calling them back, not remembering a word but suffering from a huge hangover and a vague feeling of remorse, to announce her intention to purchase the victims of her assaults expensive gifts. Gina had discovered that this cycle tended to correspond with losing streaks by the Pirates of more than six games—which was why she read the sports pages almost as fanatically as her husband—and that she could influence her mother-in-law by dropping hints about how nice it would be to have a new hi-fi or electric mixer, or even a $150 chaise.

"Fine, get the movers." John gave in, and the following week, the Warrens' old piano was installed in the living room upstairs while, in a carefully negotiated compromise, the big television and couch were moved downstairs into the room next to the garage, so John could invite his buddies over to watch the game without having to worry about spilling pretzel crumbs on the carpet.

15

A Kind of History of My Life

PARIS, 1860. Lucien stepped in front of a mirror in his bedroom but after a moment of consideration shook his head and began to unbutton the white shirt he had chosen, with a thought to replace it with one that was black. The evening ahead promised to be exciting in many respects: Codruta had invited him to a reading she was hosting for Richard Wagner, after which he planned to go directly to the Pérégrine, a new music hall in Montmartre to meet his friend Gérard Beyle, a fellow stagehand at the St.-Germain. Now twenty-three, Lucien had finished his studies at the conservatory and—still on track for the operatic stage—was appearing in recitals around the city, including the recent Soirée d'Avril, where in addition to his impressing *tout le monde* with his voice, a young Russian countess was overheard to remark that he resembled less a typical Gaul than a young Greek champion of the javelin. His impressive physique—he was as tall as his father but wider in the chest—could in part be attributed to his job at the theater, where he had worked as a carpenter and stagehand since negotiating the compromise with Guillaume.

Though he was now used to the work, during his first season he sometimes feared he had made a mistake. He had started in August, and spending twelve or more hours each day in the sweltering heat, hauling around heavy pieces of wood, iron, and whatever else—not to mention breathing sawdust and paint fumes—left him exhausted. But with no desire to return to school, he persevered, and in October, the demands of the job diminished considerably and he was frequently needed for only a few hours, most often during the actual performance. Each subsequent year had followed a similar pattern, which had given him plenty of time to focus on his musical training, even after he started at the conservatory.

There had been other benefits to the job as well, particularly in the early years, when he was so much less experienced in the ways of the world. Hardly a night passed that a crew of his coworkers— often joined by some of the singers—didn't go out to a nearby bistro to *faire la fête,* and it didn't take him long to learn to drink too much and vomit ferociously in the alley behind the bar, an experience he had found oddly joyful—at least until the next morning—as he stumbled home between the arms of two other men, with the lamp-lights of the new boulevards spinning through his vision.

Nor would he ever forget one evening that first April when—a few minutes after he had arrived at the theater for his shift—a sou-brette named Cathérine Deville appeared in the hall and beckoned with a small curl of her index finger. *"Bonsoir, "* she said with a wink. "Do you think you could assist me with *une petite quelque chose?"*

"Bien sûr, madame. " Because Lucien had heard rumors about her, he was not completely surprised by the invitation, and in fact had already admired her small-waisted figure and ample breasts, which featured prominently in her stage costumes, and most of all her voice, which at its fluttery best managed to land squarely on every note with deceptive grace. At this point—in terms of love—he continued to be intrigued by all permutations offered by theatrical society, and he liked to imagine that he would need to try many before deciding which suited him best.

But his bedroom fantasies in no way prepared him for the real-ity of Cathérine Deville, so that when they arrived at her dressing room—not much bigger than a closet—and she turned to face him after shutting the door, close enough that he could feel every breath, he felt weak and thought he might faint as she traced one of her small fingers down the front of his shirt.

"Do I make you nervous?"

"I'm sorry, but I'm worried that you are, well . . . more knowledgeable than I."

"That's probably true," she admitted. "Are you a virgin?"

He blushed. "I'm only sixteen."

Her eyes narrowed. "You—sixteen?"

Lucien leaned back on the door and nodded; with a full beard and arms hardened from the better part of a year in the theater, he knew he looked older. He detected her skepticism and regretted that his curiosity had delivered him into such a tenuous predicament, in which he had to assume, like any performer taking the stage without adequate rehearsal, his humiliation could be the only outcome. "I'm sorry," he muttered. "I should leave."

"No, *mon chère*, stop—*viens*." She reached out for his belt and pulled him a few steps forward, enveloping him in the fragrance of her hair, the top of which reached only to his chin. *"Dis-moi,"* she continued sotto voce, "do you find me attractive?"

"I think so." Lucien immediately regretted the sound of this and quickly added: "Your voice is . . . superb."

"Do you really think so?" She flounced her hair in a gesture that conveyed a mix of sarcasm and perhaps—he hoped—appreciation. "Of course, you know I didn't invite you here to listen to me sing—"

"I didn't mean just your voice."

"You're very sweet, but I wouldn't want you to be disappointed with your first time."

He tentatively placed his hands over hers as she steered him onto a small stool next to her dressing table. She ordered him to unbutton his trousers, which he did, and led her to note with approval that his nerves had not prevented him from functioning in the expected manner. She then took his hand and placed it under her loose-fitting chemise, resting it on the velvet folds of her stomach for a few moments and then moving up to a breast, which she told him to caress gently. This, too, he did, before she escorted this same hand on a trip below her waistline, where his fingers undertook a brief exploration that, to his regret, raised as many questions as it answered before she extracted him with a smile that again made him nervous, at least until she bit the top of his ear and whispered that he was doing fine.

She removed her own undergarments and, in one fluid motion that caused him to gasp, stepped forward to straddle him on his lap. "Don't worry," she said and squirmed a bit as she leaned down into him, burying his face in her chest and clasping her thin arms around his neck. *"Ça va bien?"*

"Ça va bien," he answered, though wedged between Cathérine and the wall, he felt a bit constrained and hoped that she didn't expect a lot more from him.

She laughed and began to pant and thrust. *"Mon enfant,* stop thinking so much!"

Only then did he understand what the poets meant by the boundless rapture of being everywhere and nowhere at once, as waters rushed and fires raged; he exalted at being initiated into this magical rite and wondered how he could ever have had any doubt; he swore his everlasting gratitude and devotion to Cathérine Deville, whose every pleasure would henceforth be his only occupation. Except as he returned to consciousness in the same uncomfortable position and watched as she, too, opened her eyes—which only seconds before had trembled slightly under closed eyelids—to reveal a frank expression that contained no hint of love or everlasting gratitude but simply the perfunctory appreciation of one who had just received a kind assistance from a stranger, he wondered if the waters had been more a trickle and the fire but a tiny spark.

"What is your name again?" she asked, as she dismounted in an efficient motion that made him feel like an actual horse and dispensed a quick peck to his forehead.

He felt a new and dispiriting ambivalence. "Lucien," he answered petulantly and did not take pains to disguise the shattered pieces of his heart.

"Lucien, are you upset, *mon chère?*"

Her tone, he noted, held not a trace of earnestness, but that she had recognized and mocked his hurt made it seem ridiculous. He laughed at the child who had entered this room however long ago, who could not understand that what would occur could barely be considered more than the shake of a hand, and that to attach love or hate to such a little thing was preposterous. But then he felt deflated, as though he had opened a gift wrapped in gilded paper, only to find a book written in a language he did not understand. He looked at Cathérine, who in turn glanced at her makeup table—a show was scheduled, after all, and she needed to get dressed—and he understood that there was no need to explain any of this to her. "Why would I be upset?" he replied brightly.

She placed one hand on her chest and the other to the side as she performed a short arpeggio. "Good-bye, Lucien," she sang and then remarked, "Thanks to you, I shall be in very good voice tonight."

Lucien had barely a second to consider this as he backed into the hallway and there literally bumped into one of his fellow carpenters, a short, compact man with mischievous eyes and a mustache that looked like a push broom. He was new, but Lucien liked him, if for no other reason than that he had seen him laughing at the antics of some of the other members of the crew Lucien also found amusing. Lucien froze as he wondered if and how he should acknowledge the moment, and he was greatly relieved when Gérard—that was his name, Lucien remembered—simply stepped to the side and looked back at the blushing Lucien, tipped an imaginary hat, and said, *"Bonsoir, monsieur"* in a low voice accompanied by a sly smile that told Lucien—well, of course, what else would he be doing in the soprano's dressing room an hour before curtain?—he knew.

Over the next few days, when he saw Gérard, they continued to nod at each other, as if they shared a secret understanding, though about exactly what remained unclear. As luck would have it, the next week they were assigned to work together on a new production. They barely had time to talk while the show was going up but after the opening spent an hour each night in proximity waiting for the end of the first act, when they were responsible for rotating a giant turntable, the gears for which were located on a secluded platform directly beneath center stage. It wasn't long before Gérard alluded to having seen Lucien leave Cathérine Deville's room, and Lucien saw no point in denying it; he even expressed some of the doubts the experience had raised for him, thinking it might be helpful to get the insight of a married man.

"You're not in love with her," Gérard responded, confirming Lucien's suspicions. "Which is not surprising, even if most men here would line up for the chance to serve Madame Deville. So what's different about you?"

Lucien did not appreciate the aggressive tone. "Is it wrong to want to combine the emotion of love with the act?"

"No, but is it wrong not to want the emotion? Just to take a few moments of pleasure and leave it at that? To forget about life and all its problems for a minute?"

Lucien felt disarmed. "No—of course it's not wrong, but—"

"Then what's the problem with Madame Deville?"

Under siege, Lucien responded with a question of his own. "Would you line up to service her?"

Gérard shook his head and placed one of his hands just above

Lucien's knee, where it rested heavily. "No, because she offers me neither the possibility of love nor pleasure, so I would respectfully decline."

Lucien considered this as a stampede of feet pounded overhead. "Have you ever been in love?"

"I have."

"And did you know it from the start?"

"It's not something that can be easily hidden. It starts with a glance, but where pleasure is easily satisfied, love devours. You feel sick, you want to cry and shit and puke, you feel like you're going to die if you're not attached to the other person, if you can't touch them and feel their breath on your cheek."

"Your wife?"

"*Merde.*" Gérard scowled but managed to shift his hand up onto Lucien's thigh. "We're happy on most days if we don't kill each other."

Lucien felt his throat become parched as he understood that Gérard was making a proposition very much along the lines of the one made to him by Cathérine Deville, except somewhat less explicit, which was only to be expected given that he was married—*un vrai mec*—with thick fingers and a crooked nose that made him look like he had spent a few years as a prizefighter. Not that Lucien was completely shocked, given how often he had wondered what drove men together, and whether he might possess the same impulse. Aware that the time for prevarication was over, he grabbed Gérard's hand and pulled it up to his crotch. "Is this what you want?"

Gérard leaned close to him, so that Lucien could smell a mix of sweat and grease. His voice was like gravel. "That, my friend, is for you to tell me."

Lucien could only nod, but he did not flinch as Gérard leaned over and deftly went to work. Though Lucien could barely breathe, his mind raced with questions: why did the rough nankeen of Gérard's shirt, which he gripped with one hand, and the stubble of his cheek, which he caressed with the other, please him so much more than Cathérine's softer cottons and silks? Did this mean that he preferred men in general, or was there another woman with whom he might be better matched? Would he ever get married or have children? Fortunately, before he could dwell for very long on any of this, he remembered Cathérine's direction and gave himself to the rushing waters and raging fires, which for a few seconds sent him spinning disembodied across the night.

Then it was done, and with no time to spare they both rushed to their spots behind the gears. Lucien glanced at Gérard, who did not meet his eye as he concentrated on the task at hand, and this disappointed him. Perhaps, Lucien reconsidered, Gérard had not been so much better than Cathérine, and he had only been tricked by his desire into thinking so at the time. He wondered if it might be best going forward to push aside his desire if the second he satisfied it, he would be left with an even worse condition of disillusionment.

At the intermission they sat down to bread and cheese. "Cat got your tongue?" Gérard asked as they sat in an uncomfortable silence.

"No," Lucien lied, for he was in fact at a loss for words. "I just don't understand—"

Gérard laughed. "You just had your first time with a man." He shrugged as he broke off a piece of baguette.

"It just seems strange to go from such extreme desire to"— he paused for a second—"well, what are we?"

"You mean us? We're not Romeo and Juliet, if that's what you mean, but we can be friends . . . "

Lucien failed to appreciate the humor in this. "Would you do it again? With me?"

"Yeah, sure." Gérard shrugged. "Not this second, though."

Lucien felt a twinge of disappointment, for despite his earlier admonitions, he felt something more for Gérard, which had already been reignited during this short conversation. He continued in a more cavalier tone. "So do you still sleep with women?"

"I am married," Gérard said, a little harshly, but his expression became more reflective as he turned toward Lucien. "But not really, no."

"You sound melancholy," Lucien observed.

"That's the way life is—it excites you for a little while and then it pulls the rug out from under your feet."

"But—" Lucien began to ask, then stopped, as it occurred to him that the answers he wanted from Gérard were ones that neither this man nor anyone else could ever provide. He felt more alone than he could remember and, as he considered this, could not prevent a few tears from escaping his eyes.

Gérard put an arm around his shoulder. "You'll be okay—you just need to live a little. I'll show you around. Paris is full of hidden surprises."

"What about love?" Lucien responded, for although he appreciated the gesture, he still wanted to pout.

"Don't worry—you'll have your heart broken like the rest of us, and then you'll wonder why you spent so many years craving it."

"But how do you find it?"

"It'll find you. Trust me."

The agitation he sensed in Gérard pleased Lucien, who felt reassured that, whatever the nature of their relationship, it was at least not marked by ambivalence or boredom. "But not with you?"

"I can love you," Gérard sighed, "but just a little bit, and only once in a while."

While Lucien at twenty-three was still friends with Gérard—and had enjoyed similar encounters with a number of others—he had yet to fall in love, or at least in the way Gérard had described. Though he tended to justify this defect by reminding himself how busy he remained between work and singing, he sometimes feared his continuing isolation, not only on those nights when his bed seemed vast and lonely but also when he considered his development as an artist. Every music teacher he had trained with inevitably and repeatedly made the point that the greatest opera singers were not necessarily the ones with the strongest, most talented voices but those who could convince an audience that they had been subsumed by the characters they portrayed, a process that required great reserves of both empathy and experience. Like a painter with only two colors at his disposal, Lucien worried that he would never be able to express himself fully if he had not experienced the complete gamut of emotion.

But with nothing to be done at the moment, he buttoned up his shirt and turned his attention to the evening ahead. He had been interested in Wagner since the composer first arrived in Paris with the hope to mount a production of *Tannhäuser* at the Paris Opéra, and had become something closer to obsessed after attending the symphonic concerts at the Théâtre des Italiens; unlike so much French fare these days, this music had nothing quaint, charming, or airy about it, which made him feel young, reckless, and invulnerable, immune to the conventions of polite society, as if he should be scaling mountains, hacking through dense forests, or perhaps writing tomes of scandalous epic poetry.

Along with his black shirt, Lucien opted for black pants, a black cravat, a black overcoat, black shoes, and—to complete the effect— black kohl, which he rubbed around his eyes. "My dear, you look like an opium addict," Codruta observed a few minutes later when he presented himself in the music salon of the Georges, where she was arranging chairs, or rather dictating the arrangement to a pair of her domestics.

"You don't approve?" Lucien responded. "I thought we agreed that Wagner's music was romantic and funereal."

"At my age, I don't like to be quite so literal," she remarked, although as Lucien knew, her interest in Wagner was also relatively unrestrained. She had seen his operas in Vienna and was said to have been instrumental in convincing the emperor to offer the *Tannhäuser* commission. More recently, she had taken the unusual step of publicly allying herself to his cause—by way of a petition of support signed by more than fifty of her noble peers—to counteract the more conservative elements in Paris, who were scandalized by everything from Wagner's nationalistic tendencies to his penchant for expensive clothes—he reportedly ordered thirty tailored suits from Charles Worth in a single visit—to his refusal to insert a ballet into the second act of his opera, as per the French tradition.

Without waiting for a response, Codruta officiously guided Lucien to a settee positioned at an angle to the back wall and an adjacent bay window, thus offering him a clear sight line to the piano and the view outside. "Do you think your romantic heart can withstand the burden of being extremely quiet for the next few hours?"

Lucien nodded, knowing that only four others—all important musicians—were slated to attend. In recognition of Codruta's patronage and support, Wagner on this night planned to unveil Act II of his newest opera, *Tristan und Isolde*, a five-hour piece of music rumored to be "unperformable" because of its extreme dissonance and the extraordinary strength and stamina required of any singer undertaking one of the leads. All of this added to the charged atmosphere when a few minutes later the guests began to arrive; from his spot at the window, Lucien recognized Pauline Viardot—still one of the city's top sopranos—as she emerged from her carriage and tottered through the gates looking rather pale and tense, which Lucien more than understood given that she would be sight-reading in front of not one but two notoriously temperamental composers, as Hector Berlioz was also on the guest list.

Lucien had met Pauline several times over the years—he continued to train with her brother—and she greeted him warmly. To his delight, she even went so far as to offer to lend him the *Tristan* manuscript after the reading if it proved to his liking.

"What do you think of it?" he asked.

"It's innovative but difficult," she said and glanced around, as if to make sure the composer was not within earshot. "To be honest, it makes my head swim a little"—she laughed—"but I don't want to prejudice you."

"I can't wait to hear it," he said truthfully, and she winked at him as Codruta swept back into the room accompanied by the pianist Karl Klindworth, a protégé of Franz Liszt. Next was Berlioz, who with a furrowed brow and an immense, swirling head of hair appeared to be thinking only serious thoughts, and finally Wagner, surprisingly diminutive with eyes like tiny buttons and a stern expression framed by large muttonchops. He marched in wearing a golden velvet cape with red trim and pants to match; under his arm he carried a leather briefcase containing another copy of the score. Codruta briefly introduced the men to Lucien, whose presence as a young singer of high pedigree seemed to cause no consternation; all in turn offered a perfunctory hand for Lucien to shake before returning to their seats, arranged in a semicircle next to the piano. A few minutes passed in conversation before Klindworth began to play, and he was soon joined by Wagner and Viardot singing the parts of Tristan and Isolde.

Lucien leaned forward to listen. The music was slow and dense, yet jarring to the extent that at times it sounded like two works being played at once, with each taking turns pushing to the surface while the other lurked beneath, giving the piece a constant, shivering sense of anticipation that was almost maddening for its lack of resolution. There was a sense of grandeur but unlike in Wagner's earlier work, one that evoked not mountaintops or dark forests so much as urban landscapes; or that's how it seemed to Lucien as he stared past his reflection in the window at the flickering lights of Haussmann's new boulevards, which stretched out into the blackening horizon, with the music reminding him of a certain delirium and fatigue he sometimes felt wandering the city streets, of looking for something but not quite knowing what, as each creaking door, rolling carriage, and waft of savory heat from the patisseries and bistros washed over him, filling him with longing and possibility.

He thought of the night ahead, and could see himself walking past the syphilitic beggars of Montmartre to meet Gérard at the Pérégrine, where—just as they had done a few weeks earlier—they would be confronted by hundred-foot spires and turrets painted in gold leaf, illuminated by overlapping shafts of limelight. Inside, they would meander through a labyrinth of candlelit tables and gas chandeliers, gawking less at the entertainers who danced or juggled or tumbled through rings of fire than at the merchants—dressed in silk suits with fur-lined collars and gold monocles—discussing stock prices on the bourse, accompanied by slender nymphs who sat silently by under tiaras ringed by variegated gems casting kaleidoscopic halos around their bored, waxen faces. They would watch suave, white-gloved aristocrats who kept live falcons perched on their wrists as they kissed each other for an entire minute, full on the lips.

The more he listened, the more convinced Lucien became that this opera—as if it were a transcription of not only his unfolding fate but that of a new generation—was leading him through the backstage of an expanding, mutating city, where a nocturnal chaos reigned under the orderly rules of the day. He saw that if he wanted to fall in love—the one thing he missed in his life more than any other—he would have to embrace a similar disorder, to inhabit two or more very different and possibly conflicting roles. There was no point making distinctions between art and love; as with air and water, he needed both.

16

Je n'ai pas oublié, voisine de la ville

NEW YORK CITY, 2001. Martin got off the elevator and—already thinking about his conference call—sauntered through the glass doors at the entrance to his firm. He turned left into reception, where he was confronted by the unprecedented sight of at least a dozen secretaries and one or two attorneys—like him, most of the attorneys rarely arrived before ten unless they had some business reason for doing so—running into and out of the conference room on the southwest corner of the building.

"What is this?" he asked no one in particular as he stood in the hallway outside.

"We're being attacked!" cried Darla Rodriguez, a nineteen-year-old from Riverdale who worked for one of the senior partners.

"Attacked?" Martin stuttered.

She nodded and brushed away tears from her cheeks. As best as he could gather from her halting explanation, someone had flown a plane into the World Trade Center.

"Holy shit—are you serious?" Martin replied as a few others rushed by and confirmed that something along these lines was indeed happening. A new series of shouts erupted; apparently there had been another hit.

"Oh my god!" Darla cried, looking up at him with eyes watery and trembling.

"It's all right, Darla," he offered, despite feeling that it was anything but. "Feel free to—uh, leave, okay? Go home." He could not, he realized, bring himself to say "evacuate." "Don't worry about Karen," he added, referring to her boss. "I'll—I'll talk to her tomorrow or something."

She nodded and rushed away, at which point he descended a flight of stairs to his office, where a quick glance out his window confirmed that both towers had been hit by something. Stunned, he sat down at his desk, where he spent a few seconds staring at the walls. A few years earlier, he had painted them—or technically, had them painted—in thin, tremulous strips of green, ranging from a very flat, grayish hue to a bright lime, on which he had stenciled in a barely detectable cursive font the words *Pseudoreality prevails*. At the time, his intent was to pay sly tribute to Musil and the goings-on in his office at any given time, but as he now considered the prognostic impact of these words, he felt slightly nauseated, as if he were the one who had caused the disaster outside.

"Pseudoreality prevails," he said heavily as he turned to again confront the scene, which the hard and artificial blue of the sky made seem less real, as if he really were just watching a movie.

HE SAT PARALYZED for a minute or so, until the logical part of his mind began to function. "I bet it's a terrorist attack," he muttered and could not resist a premonition about the political ramifications of some idiots flying planes into the Twin Towers, a thought followed by a thin hope that whoever had engineered this fiasco was an American. Then again, he reconsidered, did it really matter who had done it? He remembered the many times he had attempted to temper Jay's pervasive pessimism in their political discussions with Hegelian dialectic, but how could he ever again argue that progress and evolution—in any kind of moral or political sense—was anything but a phantasm of propaganda meant to deceive stupid people everywhere?

Like me for forty-one years, he thought, with less bitterness than wonder, which for the first time led him to consider—given his location in a Manhattan skyscraper—his own safety. He jumped up, closed his briefcase, and was about to run back to reception when he paused, deterred by the thought of all those crowded elevators; no, more than deterred—the idea of being crammed into a small space like a member of a herd of petrified cows made him feel sick.

Short of breath, he collapsed back into his chair, where he picked up the phone and listened for the dial tone. Reassured by this—a fact that both amazed and annoyed him—he decided to call one of the other attorneys scheduled for his 9:15 conference call.

"Oh yeah, it's off," his fellow doctor of jurisprudence confirmed after Martin reached him on his third attempt.

"So what's going on? Have you heard anything?"

"As far as I know, someone hijacked a fleet of commercial jets and flew at least two of them into the towers."

Martin digested this information before he spoke.

"So there are more?"

"I don't know—there could be," said the esquire, who worked on the forty-fourth floor of a building on Fifth Avenue where Martin had been any number of times. "I'm getting out of here, though."

After he hung up, Martin pictured what was going on just outside his door—and, he reckoned, in every other building in Manhattan—as his coworkers fled for their lives. It was not difficult to imagine them rushing through the halls, carrying picture frames, documents, laptop computers, bananas, bottled water, and bagels as they flooded toward the hated elevator banks. He wondered if the elevators were even working, or if they had been shut off due to planes flying into the World Trade Center.

He stared at his phone, and it rang. "Marty—thank god I got through—have you seen this?" It was his sister, Suzie, calling from Massachusetts.

To hear her voice made his chest collapse, as for the first time he pictured real people on the planes and in the burning towers. "Yeah, Suze," he said hoarsely. He cleared his throat and tried to sound more cavalier, which at that moment seemed to be the only option short of breaking down. "Front-row seat."

"What are you doing there?"

"I don't know," Martin admitted. "Everyone's leaving, but I can't face the elevator right now."

"What?" She barely paused before responding. "Martin, you're in shock. Listen to me: leave now, okay?" Her tone softened. "Seriously, big brother—do you want to get hurt on your birthday?"

Martin shook his head "No, I don't—I'm leaving—don't worry, I'll be fine."

"Okay, good," she said. "Call me when you get home."

"I will," he promised and gently hung up the phone.

MARTIN KNEW THAT his sister was at least partially right, and it now seemed unreasonable just to sit in his office during an apocalypse. "I should go," he resolved and again picked up his briefcase and took a step toward the door. But the word *evacuation* reeled through his mind, and he resented the idea of being forced to go anywhere on someone else's schedule, particularly that of some dumb terrorists, wherever they were from. He mentally apologized to his sister and vowed not to succumb.

He went back to his desk, where from a lower drawer he extracted a bottle of whiskey, the depleted contents of which he noted with remorse before he realized that a second one behind it was completely full. As he poured himself a shot, a chill went through him that was not exactly unfamiliar but that he had not felt in many years, namely since those horrible months before he tested positive for HIV. He had not been particularly sick at the time, much less bedridden—to the contrary, he was working more than ever—but had nevertheless been unable to shake a vague but unsettling cold and frailty, as though his bones were already deteriorating in his body. Yet he could barely acknowledge the symptoms, much less the idea that his life might be ending, even after the doctor informed him of the verdict.

It was not until much later—when the death sentence had been effectively commuted by his "cocktail" of meds—that he felt more capable of describing the chill in terms of something he had gone through as a child, i.e., the "temperature inversions" he used to experience on summer vacation, those odd days at the beach when a ghostly fog would drift in from the sea and leave your skin damp and raw no matter what you were wearing. He realized that the terror he experienced as an adult was a sense not only that something was seriously wrong—which, of course, it was—but also that it was simply a matter of time before the tide came in and swept him out forever. As Martin considered the scene in front of him, there was something similarly indescribable and terrifying about it, but by the same token, his earlier confrontation with mortality—and his continuing familiarity with it, in the form of the pills he took every day, each one a rock in the temporary jetty—explained his reluctance to cave in to his fear. What he saw outside hovered so much more distantly than what he had already endured, and still did, even if the virus was suppressed. Rather than flee death, he felt obliged to confront it, to stare it down, to meditate on it and even to mock it, all in the attempt to gain some kind of power or control.

He poured himself a new drink and proposed a toast, as much to his reflection as to what lay beyond it: "To the shittiest birthday ever," he saluted, glass raised, "and even worse, one I will never forget."

THE WHISKEY NULLIFIED Martin's thoughts for a few seconds as a slight tingling spread from his stomach to his fingertips. Though he was not about to leave—despite the chills that continued periodically to pass through him—it occurred to him that he might find some solace in one of his LPs. It was only when listening to music that he had ever been able to grieve, to cry real tears of anger and remorse as he pictured his life ending at such an absurd and unanticipated juncture, and how hard it was to tell the younger version of himself— with whom he inevitably associated such songs—the sad news.

He weighed his options carefully; far from wanting to denigrate or belittle the moment, he wanted to reflect its gravity in a mournful and perhaps even resigned way that acknowledged a sense of aching fear, of melancholy and impotence. Almost of its own accord, his hand reached over to his shelves and extracted *A Gift from a Flower to a Garden,* a double LP by Donovan, a work Martin had always associated with the kind of pathos displayed by a precocious child on the verge of madness. On the cover, Donovan could be seen in a lavender-filtered photograph dressed in an Indian caftan and appearing to offer the listener a tufted poppy. It might have come across as a caricature of hippie idealism—the musical ghetto where Donovan was so often pigeonholed—were it not for what appeared to be dark rings around his eyes, an effect of the saturated exposure of the shot and his barely tinted sunglasses, as if he were already haunted by the manic dreams he offered.

As Martin listened to the crack and hiss of the needle against the vinyl, followed by Donovan's whispered lyrics, he looked out the window and was newly astonished by the amount of smoke that continued to pour forth from the towers. More unbelievably, the north tower began to vibrate like a corrugated sheet of metal before it buckled and collapsed, as if a bomb had been detonated underneath it. As a mushroom cloud erupted from the site, Martin remembered a passage in which Thoreau described the deafening groan of the last of a stand of majestic white pines being felled by two woodmen with a crosscut saw. Though he could hear nothing except Donovan's soft voice and an acoustic guitar, the destruction at hand seemed no less egregious, although the remorse he felt was as much for the building and those he imagined inside it as for himself, as if just by being alive he was in some way responsible for this monstrous act.

MARTIN'S HEAD POUNDED slowly and even dogmatically to such an extent that he was reminded of a tolling church bell. Determined to finish what he had started, he poured himself another shot and flipped over the record; as he swiveled back to face the window, beads of sweat rolled down the sides of his face before falling onto his shirt, where they were absorbed into his body like long-forgotten aspirations. Though his eyes remained fixed in front of him, he realized that he was no longer watching the smoke and fire of a random act of destruction but viewing a memory that exerted a far more personal form of terror.

His thoughts turned to his graduation from high school, which seemed as bucolic and naïve—and lost—as a Donovan song. If his experience at boarding school had generally allowed him to appreciate his parents from afar, on this morning, with them present, Jane's pronouncements on art and aesthetics had frustrated him almost as much as Hank's crude pragmatism. Also bothersome were Jane's false sighs of commiseration about his breakup with

Amanda—whose appeal she had never grasped—while for his part, Hank could not stop bleating a stream of trivia and advice about Martin's upcoming year. College hockey, Hank recalled more than once, had been the best experience of his life, not to mention the route by which he met—nudge, nudge—the best woman in his life.

When the ceremony was over, good-byes issued, and everything packed, Martin was relieved to be driving home in his own car, where he and Suzie surfed for radio stations and made fun of their parents. They even laughed at Jane when the family stopped at a rest area in Ohio and—because she had always hated thunderstorms—she suggested they get a hotel.

Hank brushed her off. "It's just a few little clouds," he scoffed. "We're only a couple hours away."

Martin, still impatient with his parents, had basically ignored this conversation and instead amused himself by reaching around his sister's back to tap her on the shoulder, the way he had done years earlier, until Jane looked at her children. "You two all right?"

"Uh—yeah, sure—quite all right." Martin saw himself answer coolly and robotically, the way he used to talk to his mother to disguise his true feelings, which back then he would have characterized as annoyance or irritation but which he now understood to be something closer to fear, not of the storm but of Jane's ability to glean information about him that he was just beginning to understand himself.

None of this was mentioned at the time; instead Suzie entered the scene, just as he expected her to, because as often as Martin tried to forget all of this, it was engrained in his memory like the lyrics of an odious pop song from an otherwise forgotten era of his youth. "No offense, Dad, but I'm sticking with Martin," she informed them.

Nor could Martin forget how, in response, Hank stuck out his tongue and trotted back to his car.

Nor how a few seconds later, Martin was in his old car, the make, model, and year of which he noted with aching precision, along with the garish cranberry hue of the upholstery and even the chrome buttons of the tape deck and radio, which like any stereo worth hearing at the time was "customized."

They were back on the highway, and as usual—because Hank had a heavy foot—Martin was following. He saw the blur of the first heavy, thick drops of rain hitting the windshield and could feel Suzie beside him as she watched the side of a truck roar past about six inches from her window. "Check it out, big brother," she said, putting her palm against the glass. "The water's coming right through— it's a miracle."

"It's called condensation, Sherlock," Martin corrected her, "but I'm glad it makes you happy."

Martin whispered the word *happy* at the same moment he heard it now. In his memory it was like a gunshot instantly followed by his sister's scream, which reverberated across these many years, joined not only by the vulture screech of the brakes but by Martin's own involuntary cry, as if he were reacting for the first time. It happened fast—two seconds at most, maybe three—and he pounded the arms of his chair, an involuntary echo of his chest slamming against the steering wheel, constrained only by the seat belt as he skidded to a stop and—hands shaking—threw open the door.

Numb with panic, he stumbled forward a few steps but then caught his balance and sprinted toward a blurry heap, which as he approached became increasingly focused but also mangled and—with a truck behind it, on its side like a fallen horse—incongruous; somehow the car had been flipped, but there was also something—a piece of steel, an I beam—sticking through it, so that it lay on its back at a strange angle, like a spinning top that was no longer spinning.

Frantically Martin ran around it; one side of the car was crushed, while the other—the passenger side—was slightly more elevated, and here he dropped to his knees; through the cracked window, he could see his mother—she was still in her seat but upside down—and his father beyond her, but it was raining so hard that he could not tell if they were hurt or could speak or even move. The smell of gasoline was thick, and he knew he would have to get them out before anything caught fire. He had already checked the doors, and none would open, but he noticed that a back window was cracked a few inches, and after brushing the water away from his face, he crawled over and called in to his mother and father, to let them know that he was there and that they shouldn't worry because they were going to be fine and help was already here—and as he said this, he could hear the wail of sirens and see the flashing lights reflecting off the wet pavement, so he knew it was true—and he twisted his ear down to the gap and tried to listen, and he seemed to detect a low moan, which gave him hope. He sat up and put his hands on the window and pulled, so that the whole thing just fell out and crumbled like a sheet of ice.

All of this took only a few seconds, and Martin heard a familiar voice in his head—his goalie voice—telling him to be calm, be calm, be calm. His hands and knees were cut—badly—but now he was able to crawl at least partway in through the window to the back. Inside, he still couldn't see much of Hank, who was on the other side of the beam, but Jane was pinned to her seat—somehow he knew that she was broken; there was nothing in here that wasn't—but still alive; she seemed to be breathing, and he ignored the blood running down her twisted arm. He asked if she could hear him, and there was a response—low and garbled, but it was there—which drew him farther in, so that by turning over he could see the side of her face. And even though one of her cheeks had a gash across it and her forehead was already swollen and misshapen, at least her eyes were open and he knew she recognized him because her lips were moving and her eyes were searching and her fingers reached for him. He wanted to reassure her, to tell her that all of this mangled steel and broken glass and blood was just a bad dream, that it wasn't as bad as it looked, that it was going to be all right as soon as he got them out, but when he tried to speak, he realized that he was already talking, that he hadn't stopped—"Mom, it's going to be all right," he kept saying over and over—and he believed it, and for a second he even paused to think about what he should do next, because he knew he had to get out but he couldn't leave, either.

He felt something pulling at his legs, and it was hard and rough so that he grabbed at the edge of the seat to hang on but his hands were filled with shards of glass so he couldn't really hold on to anything, and just a blink later he was back out in the rain being pulled across the pavement and he screamed at the men holding him that she was alive, that his mother was alive, and he strained against them to get back, he clawed at the asphalt looking for something to hang on to so that he could shake them off, and even after the blast, they had to sit on him as he pounded the unforgiving ground with his blood-soaked hands and feet.

IT WAS NOT something he ever wanted to remember—or so he had told himself for years—although that had never stopped him from getting to this point, where as he did now he braced himself for the inevitable, breathtaking pain of knowing, and the desire to detach himself, to skirt away and imagine his parents already flying. Except this time, as much he wanted to, he did not—could not—wander off but rather felt his mind slow to survey the scene, not all at once but in bits and pieces, interrupted by short gaps of breathless, almost instinctual determination. Soon he was awash in forgotten details: the oddly muted sound of the explosion—really more of a pop than a bang—that ignited a small inferno; the heat of the asphalt under his palms, the evil hiss of a burning wreck in the downpour, his sister's wet shirt and the convulsing sobs that shook her as she sat beside him hugging her knees while the EMTs and bystanders raced around yelling and screaming, the bloodred tint of his vision; and most horrible of all, the motionless silhouettes in the burning wreckage in front of him.

Yet even as all of this seemed to compound the shock and grief, his mind kept turning over the image of the rain, the way all the drops seemed to bounce off the pavement in an infinite number of perfect little explosions. It tugged at him, so that he could feel the drawers of his mind slamming open and shut as he desperately looked through them for an explanation; then, miraculously, he found what he was looking for: again he was at the beach with his family, this time literally in the ocean, in a churning surf that crashed over him with furious insistence as the rain smacked down hard around him, each drop bouncing off the roiling sheen of the salt water, almost as reflective as an asphalt highway. In this memory, Martin was not sobbing but yelling with a hoarse, adolescent glee; it was a hurricane day at the beach—not to the point of evacuation but one of those days when you weren't supposed to go in the water—but he and Hank didn't care; they went in anyway, and Martin loved every second because, even if it was macho and stupid, it was wild and uninhibited and violent, and he knew how to handle the rough surf.

He knew why this memory had come back to him, and why it allowed him to confront the scenes of the accident as never before; it was as if, he realized, rather than escape—detach himself—he had dived under the turbulence, where for a few seconds he could surrender to the larger currents—i.e., of life and death—before resurfacing to confront the aftermath; and though he was flailing as he was pulled and thrown by forces so much larger and more powerful than himself, to swim through like this, however feebly, gave him a flicker of hope and strength, so that when he looked down at his fingers, he was almost surprised to find they had not been stained with the color of these new tears.

HE REACHED AROUND to turn up the volume on his stereo, where Donovan sang as seductively as he had on the radio more than twenty years earlier; the song was the last thing Martin heard before leaving the car, moments after Suzie had found it on the radio and declared it worth listening to. He knew that, just as it had done outside, a tower had given way in his soul; it had been there for him to behold but then shuddered and collapsed and now was gone, leaving an empty space marked by an intense but purposeful sorrow and a vague long- ing for something that he still couldn't quite see but that nevertheless resonated with a beauty he could only describe as defiant. Far from disturbing him, the diagnosis of this condition—this gap, this void, this chasm, this HIV of the psyche that without exception afflicted everyone—made him strangely optimistic. He felt a rush of under- standing as he stared simultaneously at his reflection and at the dusty cloud in the distance beyond it.

"Wear your love like heaven," he whispered to the unfamiliar man in front of him, who stared back with silent but knowing eyes.

Second Act

Irony

17

Dial M for Motherfucker

PITTSBURGH, 1977. From the backseat of her airport taxi, Anna admired the pale green fringe of the ancient hills of Western Pennsylvania, which rippled past her in the April sun. She was here to serve as a judge for a state high school singing competition and, despite some minor qualms about the hotel she had booked, was looking forward to it. Having retired from professional singing four years earlier, she now taught at Juilliard, which, as she liked to tell her friends, offered a "balance" that had been lacking in her career, allowing her to remain immersed in the opera but without the associated indignities. By this she did not mean the actual singing, which she would always miss. Even after she had appeared in most if not all of the major houses in the world (and often repeatedly), there was something astonishing to her not only about stepping out to perform in front of thousands but also the entire process leading up to these incredible nights, the theatrical alchemy by which it all came together—though inevitably at the last minute, and just when she would find herself on the verge of despair about some facet of a production—the backstage crew, who created the lighting and costumes and sets; the stage managers and directors, who dictated everything from the position of her hands to erupting walls of fire with the precision of army generals; the conductors and musicians—many of them musical prodigies in their own right—who immersed themselves in the scores of the (mostly) dead composers whose spirits seemed to hover in the theaters in which their works were performed.

It was rather other facets of the life, even beyond the expected pangs of loneliness—which had not failed to materialize but for which she learned to brace herself—that had increasingly tried her patience; the way management—and always after opening night, when she was most exhausted—required her to share a ten-course meal with the biggest patrons, who invariably liked to interrogate her about the most intimate details of her life; or how she couldn't go out-side—particularly in Europe—without sunglasses and a scarf over her head, unless she wanted to be accosted by an autograph hound or relentlessly subjected to the details of one of her past performances, as though she had not been there herself. These were not things that had bothered her in the beginning—to the contrary, she had been charmed the first hundred or so times she had been approached by a stranger—and she understood that such nuisances were insepara-ble from the kind of career she had always sought. Over time she began to understand why so many famous singers were notoriously "crazy," and rather than succumb to the same impulse—and with her voice by this point showing some wear, as more than a few crit-ics were eager to point out—she decided to walk away completely, knowing that, after more than a decade in the spotlight, she no longer had the same drive as she had ten or twenty or thirty years earlier. She was proud of her career; she still received her share of notes and letters, along with the occasional entreaty from an autograph seeker, but all in moderation, allowing her to respond with the patience and grace she felt the great majority of her fans deserved. Her students also inspired her; she worked hard to prepare them, both vocally and emotionally, for the future they so desperately wanted, even if they could barely explain why, which of course was just the way she had been at their age.

She was dropped downtown at the Soldiers & Sailors Memorial—a monolithic Beaux Arts auditorium designed to recall the tomb of Mausolus at Halicarnassus—where inside she was introduced to her fellow judges. As she took her seat, she contemplated the dusty, unused quality of the theater—as if it had spent the past seventy years in someone's attic—and wished there could be a middle ground between the stifling and history-laden intransigence of Europe and the reactionary disregard for the same that seemed to be the rule in her adopted country. But one of life's pleasures at fifty-seven was to have relinquished such epic battles: helping one of her students master a difficult passage, taking a twilight walk along Central Park, or (because she now collected them) finding a rare manuscript or painting—these were the smaller, more obtainable victories that satisfied her most.

THE COMPETITION BEGAN, with each singer taking a moment to shine—though some more brilliantly than others—before giving way to the next. Perhaps an hour had passed when they reached the final entrant in the soprano division, a striking but ungainly creature named Maria Sheehan, who—poor thing—tripped while making her entrance and had to windmill her arms a few times to catch her balance. It would have shattered anyone's nerves but in Maria's case created a perverse magnetism, so that, for the first time in the day, Anna detected a palpable suspense. She could hear paper rustling and the crossing and uncrossing of arms and legs; a few rows behind her, someone coughed, and she resisted the urge to send a nasty glance.

Maria regained her composure and took her position with an improbable if no less alluring stillness; she did not look nervously at her shoes or at the piano, or concentrate with furrowed brow on some point in the middle distance. Her expression was both less aware and more self-absorbed than those of the other girls, almost as if she

were granting each member of the audience the honor of entering
her cocoon. Anna wondered if this girl would be the first of the day
to possess a voice to match her intriguing aura, and—though barely
conscious of this—also began to formulate a question about who
Maria might really be; at this point, it was mostly in the spirit of curiosity, such as sometimes happened when she saw an attractive young
man or woman on the street, perhaps walking out of a store, hailing a
cab, or even standing beside her on an elevator.

She remembered her tryst with Lawrence Malcolm, which occupied the same realm as the Isolde debut with which it would always
be linked, existing somewhere between a memory and a dream. For a
second she was there, in the back of his store, overflowing with confidence about her burgeoning career and a belief that she could bring
this kind of serendipitous, passionate love affair along with her, so
that her future had seemed like a precious metal untarnished by any
difficulty or regret. In the weeks after Lawrence left for Europe, she
wrote to him several times and he responded with cheerful postcards
from abroad, the stamps of which she caressed as though touching
his lips. Which is not to say her interest in him was obsessive; as he
had predicted she had too much else to think about between singing
and the endless complications of her new life, which—intoxicating
as it had been to consider in the abstract—was nerve-racking in the
actual flood of offers, counteroffers, and agreements, not to mention
unceasing demands for interviews and information said to be required
by the insatiable public in light of her new status as a "sensation." But
to know it was just a matter of time until he returned had been—just
as she had hoped—a kind of palliative or life raft in these first few
months, as she—like any singer who had ever gone through this phase
of initial scrutiny—struggled to keep her bearings amid the turbulence of so much attention.

When complications—if one could use such a term to describe an unexpected pregnancy with twins—had arisen, their lives together, albeit largely imaginary at this point, became fraught with difficulty, and Anna could no longer envision them together on a sort of oasis. She debated whether even to tell him—this was part of a larger and more painful debate about how to proceed, if at all, with the birth—and ultimately decided to write to him, less with the intent of gaining his approval than out of her consideration of what it would be like to be in his position; she would, she reasoned, want to know. So she informed him of her intention to give the children up for adoption—though not opposed to abortion in theory, she hated the illegality of it—while offering the hope that he, as someone who seemed to appreciate the demands of her art, would understand; as she wrote these words, she began to feel a new hope that the event might even bring them together in unexpected ways.

On the day she mailed this letter, fate again intervened and delivered to her a notice from his law firm informing her that Lawrence had died in a car accident on his way back from Capri. She had dropped the sheet of paper and—filled with a bitter premonition—thrown the crumpled envelope across the room. For a second she detested her voice, which—like one of those beautiful but destructive flowers in a garden—seemed to have blossomed only at the expense of her capacity to love; it didn't matter that the mere existence of Lawrence would appear to disprove this idea, or that their love was anything but certain given that they had spent only a few hours together; what mattered was that he was gone, and nothing could bring him back.

This angry bitterness had not lasted but—as Anna reflected upon it now—was quickly transformed into a more wistful sadness (albeit one that had never completely faded). She could now appreciate what had happened; not his death, certainly, but the way it had brought into sharper relief the choices she had made and ultimately—despite the momentary doubts—reinforced her understanding of where she still needed to go. It had been an emotional turning point, a recognition of the strength and self-reliance she needed to march forward with an almost fanatical conviction about her relationship to the opera, one she now understood—in addition to the most practical kinds of focus and discipline—was necessary to sing at the most competitive levels. It was not that she had sworn off men—if anything, her rise made her more attractive—but after Lawrence, she always viewed them with impatience, as if they were a baser part of life, a necessary diversion before she took her true nourishment from the stage.

There was one concrete element to Lawrence's death, namely the *Tristan* manuscript he had lent to her. After she recovered from the shock of the news, she called the firm to ask what she should do with it; the attorney in question suggested she keep it, given that Lawrence's actions could just as easily be construed as making a gift as they could a loan, and Lawrence had no heirs making claims on his estate. So she kept the manuscript but not the twins—fraternal, a boy and a girl—a decision that, as difficult as it had been to make, was not one she had ever been inclined to regret; to raise them herself would have been as unfair to them—she knew she never could have provided the kind of home she felt they deserved—as it would have been to her, making her career an impossibility.

Still, at this second, to note Maria Sheehan's black hair and the blue tone of her skin—so similar to her own—along with her unusual height, made Anna's heart pause, if not quite skip. She probably would have disregarded the idea completely had she not been in Pittsburgh, the closest city to where she had given birth. She reminded herself to concentrate, and the logical part of her mind reasoned that there were probably hundreds of girls in Pennsylvania alone who fit the same description. But as soon as she heard the voice, her questions went from a trickle to a flood, one made all the more powerful and intoxicating—if alarming—by the thrill of discovery, the certainty that this girl had something to offer. A quick glance at her fellow judges confirmed the obvious talent on display, and Anna leaned forward, swept away by a wave of remorse as she considered that this could be her daughter, the same one whom she had given up seventeen years earlier but whom she had never touched or exchanged a word or a smile with, much less changed a diaper for or punished. It threw her entire life into doubt, and she could not stop the tears from spilling down. She did not so much fight this emotion as let it pull her into the deeper waters, where just floating and breathing, she became aware of other currents—hope, desire, resolve—that slowly brought her back to more solid footing; perhaps if she had been given two lives, she might have also been a mother, but with only one at her disposal, she would never regret the choice to be a singer. If anything, to see Maria only reinforced the certainty that if she had to do it again—even at this second, confronted by this voice and the staggering possibility that it was related to her own—she would make the same decision.

As Maria finished her song, Anna knew she would do everything in her power to bring this girl to New York and, with any luck, transform her into a singer for the history books. It hardly needed to be said that she would never whisper a word to anyone about a biological relationship; this was not a second chance to be a mother but a first to be a teacher. Anna dried her eyes, ran her fingers through her hair—these days she kept it short—and repositioned her scarf around her shoulders. She felt something familiar pass through her, a queasy sense of anticipation, and realized that she was quietly singing to herself, just as she had always done in her career during those excruciating, delirious minutes before taking the stage.

18

The Psychology of the Transference

PITTSBURGH, 1977. After winning the Heinz Recitals, Maria—with Kathy Warren's help—prepared her application for Juilliard. She recorded a selection of songs and arias, and in early September sent them in with the necessary forms and essays. Less than a week later, Anna called to let her know that everything was in order. "We're inviting you to audition. The committee was very impressed . . ."

Maria had not enjoyed the recording process, particularly the playback, which to her ear made her voice sound shrill and forced. "Really? I thought the tapes were"—she caught herself before she said "crappy" and substituted—"less than outstanding." When she spoke to Anna, she liked to think she had swallowed a pill that had already transformed her into the famous singer she wanted to become.

A few days later, Anna called again to inform Maria about a few administrative details pertaining to the audition before she asked about Gina. "Will your mother be coming to New York?"

To Maria's consternation, the two women had developed a surprising rapport at the awards ceremony and had talked several times since about tuition and other practical arrangements. "She might," Maria answered, "although she hasn't mentioned it."

"Please let her know that I'd be happy to answer any questions," Anna offered.

"Okay," Maria responded, "but—just so you know—my mother doesn't really like New York, and Kathy's been there, so—" Maria realized as she said this that she didn't want her mother to go, and she wanted to see how Anna would react to this possibility.

"Whatever you and your mother decide is fine with me," Anna said in an efficient tone that left Maria with the impression she wouldn't interfere.

After hanging up, Maria went into the kitchen, where Gina was making dinner. "That was Anna," she said, as she sat down and absently began to shred a napkin. "She wants to know if you're coming to New York."

"I will if you want me to."

"Well, sure, but I didn't think you really wanted to go, and well— since Kathy's driving, I already asked her."

Gina frowned. "I'm sure Kathy would be happy to drive both of us." She sighed as she set down her spoon and walked toward the door. "But if you don't want me to go, just say so."

"I didn't say that," insisted Maria, annoyed that Gina was taking this in exactly the wrong way.

"Then what are you saying?"

"I don't know—just that it might be easier if—"

"Does that sound like an invitation to you?"

Maria shook her head but, having gone this far, found herself unable to stop. "I think it might be better if we all went up together after the audition, if I get in."

"Honey, you're getting in," Gina muttered as she tossed a dish towel on the counter and left for the living room. "But if you don't want me there, that's fine. Just let me know if you need any help from your *mother* before you leave."

Maria had second thoughts and chased after Gina. "Are you really upset? Because if you are, I could call Anna and make sure—"

"I'm not upset, Maria. Please—just do what you have to." Gina paused. "I mean it."

This thin display of stoicism provided the justification Maria had been looking for all along, so with equally exaggerated pretense, she stormed off to her bedroom.

An hour or so later, Maria crept past the living room, where Gina and Bea were watching television, and she was only mildly surprised to find them both crying, since the news often had this effect on them. She stopped for a second to watch with one foot in the hall in the event her earlier perfidy had caused these tears, but when her mother looked up at her, Maria's heart stopped: something was really wrong. "What's going on?"

"*Mia bella.*" Bérénice raised her wrinkled face to Maria. *"La Callas! Elle est morte,"* she whispered.

"But she's not that old, she's only—" Maria paused. "How did she die?"

"Fifty-three," Gina said. "They think it was a heart attack."

To see her mother and Bea in tears, and to digest the news about Callas—whom she had secretly been hoping to meet now that she was Pennsylvania's top high school soprano—also caused something in Maria to snap, so that seconds later she was sandwiched between them on the couch, sobbing along through the aspirin commercial that preceded a short retrospective on Callas. She had apparently died alone—a recluse—in her Paris apartment, which made no sense to Maria and for the first time made her question whether the fruits of her own artistic dreams would make her happier than she was now. She saw herself at fifty-three and wondered if her own mother would be alive, and considered that most certainly Bea would not, and felt bereft at their prospective departure in a way that made her regret what she had done that afternoon.

"Ma," she sobbed to Gina. "I didn't mean it—I want you to come to New York. Anna said to call—she wants you to come, too!"

"It's okay," Gina stroked Maria's head, which now lay on her shoulder. "We can talk about it later."

THOUGH GINA'S OFFICIAL position toward her daughter was for-giveness, she, too, had been frightened by the specter of Callas's lonely death, and felt that it was only right that Maria get a true taste of the life she so desperately sought. "I thought about it and decided that I'm not going to New York," she declared to her daughter a few days later. "I don't want to distract you."

"You won't, Ma—"

"You and Kathy can go, and then we'll all plan a trip up there in the spring, when it's nicer weather—your father and grandmother can come, too."

"But Ma, I want you to come. I was just in a bad mood. I didn't mean it."

"I know, and I appreciate it, but really—I think it's best if you go alone this time."

That fall, an unprecedented formality descended upon the Sheehan household. Dinners devolved into conversations between Bérénice and John about the Steelers, who were in pursuit of Super Bowl number three, and after a terse exchange of presents at Christ-mas and a subdued New Year's Eve, the week of the audition finally arrived. Gina softened the night before the scheduled departure and offered to help Maria pack, a process that required the delicate maneuvering of an arms-reduction treaty when Gina insisted on placing into the valise a navy blue gown that Maria had never liked and that they both knew would later be replaced with a black one she did.

Before any of this erupted into open warfare, John came in to say good-bye, as the next day he had his weekly inventory meeting at the company and the idea of disturbing Maria at six o'clock in the morning held no appeal. "I'm hitting the sack," he said with a yawn. "Remember, if anybody gives you a hard time for being from Pittsburgh, just mention Franco Harris and Jack Lambert."

Maria looked at Gina, and they both laughed. "Dad, I'm sure the admissions committee isn't too concerned about the Steelers."

"Then maybe this will help you," he said and flipped her an Indian-head nickel that he explained had been his good-luck charm when he was a kid. "The day after I found it I hit my only home run."

Maria thanked him and even shared a smile with her mother before she popped it into one of the penny loafers Gina had bought her for the trip, and John kissed her on the cheek and went to bed.

The next day, Gina drove Maria to Cedar Village, where the snow-dusted trees glistened in the morning sun. She remarked how beautiful it would be on the turnpike, a comment not acknowledged by Maria, whose morning stupor prevented her from thinking about anything except whether the stupid snow might stop her from getting to New York City. Gina sighed, remembering her daughter before they had grown so distant. Her baby was about to leave for New York, and it seemed like only yesterday that they were dancing together in front of the hi-fi, Maria perched on top of her shoes with her thin arms wrapped around the backs of her legs, Bea hollering out from the kitchen to turn it up, *prego!* Gina reminded herself that Maria was a teenager, and at least she wasn't running around with some long-haired boy doing who-knew-what like those kids she saw hanging around the shops on Castle Shannon Boulevard. Nor did she forget that this was exactly what she had always wanted for her daughter, from the second she saw the picture of Callas—God rest—almost two decades earlier, and though she could feel the old, familiar emptiness, she tried to console herself with the thought—in fact, she had just read an article about this while waiting in line at the grocery store—that this angry insolence was a cultural phenomenon, that mothers everywhere were letting go of their teenage daughters with the expectation that one day soon they would all come home.

MARIA AND KATHY drove east under a looming sky that extended into the curving climbs through the Appalachians of central Pennsylvania. Maria began to feel better as they descended from the mountains and passed Harrisburg, and by the time she caught her first glimpse of the World Trade Center from Route 80 and then the entire skyline, glimmering in the last speck of sunlight like a long diamond necklace, her spirits were flying. After they crossed the George Washington Bridge and made their way down the West Side Highway, she expressed surprise that New York City was so close to such a big river, something she had never really considered, though it was perfectly obvious from a map. "It's like New York has everything Pittsburgh has," she exclaimed, "except ten times bigger!"

"Just remember," Kathy noted, "that goes for singers, too."

After checking in at the hotel—the Callaghan, across from Lincoln Center—Maria happily agreed to Kathy's suggestion to opt out of the hotel's dining room in favor of an exploration of the neighborhood. On Broadway, Maria was enthralled by the parade of business suits, dresses, tracksuits, platform shoes—even in winter—and shearling coats. Everyone, it seemed, had a "look"—some combination of fear, aggression, and street couture—unlike anything she had known in Pittsburgh, which made her worry about her lack of the same, and how she would have to go about changing that unfortunate condition. She was struck by how the many different shops on Seventy-second

Street—shoes, a butcher, a diner, buttons, beds, televisions—had no intrinsic order but still seemed to fit together like the ingredients of one of Bea's leftover stews. She enviously watched a woman perhaps a few years older than she was hurry into a dry cleaner's, pick up some garments, and rush back out onto the street, which was filled with the honking of countless yellow cabs swerving through traffic. She inhaled the smell of pizza from a nearby parlor and laughed at a fat, old man waving his hands in the face of a teenager with a large Afro who appeared somehow to have offended him. Kathy pointed out different buildings, some with flat, modern façades, others dripping with the carved monsters and deformed gargoyles that seemed at first to leer at Maria but then with a wink to tell her, no, she was one of them.

THE NEXT MORNING they went to Juilliard, where at the appointed time, Maria took an elevator upstairs and followed signs through several long hallways to another waiting area filled with her fellow young prospects, who sat in a collective cloud of body odor and perfume. At some point her name was called and she stepped into the room, where she felt like a speck looking up at the faces of Mt. Rushmore until she recognized Anna Prus beaming down at her. As she sang, she imagined taking Anna's proffered hand and together arriving in the center of a circle of twelve marble statues, all of which Maria faced one by one as she made a slow 360-degree rotation. And as her eyes met with each frozen woman, the woman's mouth would open and add her voice to Maria's, pianissimo and then forte, so that by the end of her piece she heard a chorus that awed and terrified her, for while their mouths moved, their eyes remained lifeless and cold.

Back downstairs, she found Kathy and burst into tears: she cried inconsolably, so that all who walked by the young teacher holding the hand of this girl and gently reassuring her must have thought the kid had really blown it. They walked all the way across Fifty-seventh

Street to Madison Avenue, where Maria—now more composed—gasped at the prices of silk scarves and a gold pen, which she knew would amuse her father. She called home twice, but the line was busy both times, and then—because she still felt uncertain about her audition—decided it would be better anyway to wait until the next day so she could tell Gina about *A Chorus Line,* which she and Kathy planned to see later that night.

At dinner, they rehashed the audition and decided that it had probably gone better than Maria initially thought. Kathy ordered her red wine, and Maria loved the way it sat placidly in its enormous glass, which became cloudy and opaque as she ate. Slightly drunk, she floated through the cold night air to the theater, where she watched the crowd of people milling around in front of the box office with a sense of disbelief that anyone could be lucky enough to experience this more than once. But the intensity of the show made her nervous, and she had to resist the temptation to chew on the ends of her hair; watching professional performers, she could not help but envision herself among their ranks—given that this was now her aspiration—yet they were so polished and unguarded, as if they had not the least trepidation about revealing the darkest corners of their souls for everyone to see.

MARIA WAS STILL in bed when the harsh ring of the hotel phone abruptly awakened her, and she opened her eyes to the opalescent light of dawn. She felt a pang of guilt—she should have called home again—even before she saw Kathy reach from the adjacent bed to answer. Already hoping it was a dream and knowing from the brittle texture of the bedspread it was not, she heard a hushed gasp and two footsteps, followed by Kathy's fingers, first touching the top of her head and then her shoulder.

Maria sat straight up, her stomach in knots even before she saw Kathy's face, quivering as she wiped tears from her eyes and tried to mouth the words. "What?" she asked, her voice a round whisper absorbed by the upholstered headboard and the crumpled sheets and blankets.

Still unable to talk, Kathy looked away, shaking her head back and forth.

"Kathy?" Maria cried.

Sinking to her knees, Kathy leaned on the edge of Maria's bed and looked up. Her lips moved, and even before a sound reached her ears, as if her nightmares had preordained it, Maria knew the word was *fire*.

19

Concluding Unscientific Postscript to the Philosophical

PARIS, 1860. As Codruta did every December on St. Ignatius Day at the Georges, she hosted a *fête des rêves*, at which, per the custom in her native Romania, she served roasted pig and plied her guests with plum brandy and mulled wine. Lucien halfheartedly performed a selection of Christmas songs before helping himself to two glasses of each, which left him pleasantly drunk but still estranged from the festivities. He stood at the edge of the ballroom among the potted palms and banana trees as a couple drifted past on the dance floor—heads back and laughing, they were in perfect step—and he felt a twinge of sadness as he pictured himself the previous spring, enthralled by Wagner's new opera and certain that falling in love was as imminent as the end of the piece.

He wasn't sure exactly what the problem was; unlike many others, he was not ashamed of his romantic interest in men and had never hidden his inclinations from those nearest to him, whether his friends from the conservatory, his colleagues at the St.-Germain, Codruta—who in any case had surmised years before—or even his father, who as a man of science did not believe that such a well-documented aspect of human behavior could be ascribed to a "perversion" and moreover was obviously not unfamiliar with the mores of the theater in which Lucien had always felt most at home. Nor did he lack for opportunity; at her *mercredi*, Codruta regularly introduced him to painters, poets, and rich young aristocrats, an endeavor undertaken with the understanding—and in this she was like most members of her artistically oriented milieu—that he would always be a "bachelor," an oblique but convenient term that would allow him to move through both theatrical and civilized society (where it was not uncommon for two such bachelors to share an apartment) without undue controversy of the sort that would arise in more restrictive quarters. Which is not to say he—or she—was naïve, or had any misconception that such arrangements were not to be shielded from large swaths of the population. Every situation, he knew, called for a different level of discretion: as Gérard had taught him, Paris was filled with bistros, parks, quais, and tunnels where he could go without fear of being harassed, while other places were to be avoided at all costs unless he wanted to be beaten or arrested (which he did not).

Whatever the broader implications, the fact remained that while he had met any number of men who he felt sure would be considered by most to be handsome, intelligent, and artistic, none had ever set his heart on fire. Even worse—for there was no logic to support this—he still could not shake the feeling that his fate was tied to that of Wagner, who over the same period had managed to get banished from the city. This had occurred following a disastrous *Tannhäuser* run at the Paris Opéra, where a claque of conservative apes from the

Jockey Club had ruined the performances with shouts and whistles, leaving management—via the dictate of the emperor—no choice but to cancel. While this fiasco was bad enough, what was still more demoralizing to Lucien was that everyone—even Codruta—seemed to agree that *Tristan* would never get produced, in Paris or anywhere else; the composer was too old and too controversial to be headed anywhere but obscurity and ruin.

The only good to come of it, at least from Lucien's perspective, was a *Tristan* score, which Pauline Viardot—going beyond her promise at the reading—had ended up giving to him after he confessed to her the extent of his infatuation for the piece. No matter what anyone said, he still planned to study it closely. To console himself, he sometimes leafed through it, fantasizing about the day when he would be famous enough to demand a production of this forgotten opera, thus resuscitating Wagner's reputation, where it would shine next to his own.

JUST AS LUCIEN was on the verge of slipping away, Codruta appeared to announce her intention to lead him on a short tour of the room. "I want to perform a little experiment," she proposed. "Stand up as tall as you can—as if you were about to sing—and turn yourself in a circle." Lucien gamely followed her instructions as she gently pushed his right arm. "Not too fast," she continued as he turned. "Now tell me—and don't think about it—who catches your eye?"

Having finished one revolution, Lucien indulged her by completing a second; and while most of the room passed in a blur, he found his attention—just for a second—focused on a short, compact man who stood on the periphery of a group perhaps thirty feet away. Oddly enough, he seemed to observe Lucien at the same moment, although with perhaps a trace of ridicule, if not disdain, which sent a shiver of embarrassment through Lucien as he considered that he was literally being turned in circles by the princess.

Lucien returned his attention to Codruta. "Okay, him," he said as he bent down to speak into her ear, where from behind the mass of her hair he could more surreptitiously observe the man, whose evening wear displayed a hand-tailored quality typically acquired on the Rue St.-Honoré.

"You don't know who that is?" she asked, smiling benignly as if she could have predicted this all along.

"Obviously not," Lucien muttered, for once impatient with her.

"How charming—I seem to have struck a nerve." She looked through him toward a group of dancers exiting the floor before she continued. "His name is Eduard van der Null. He's Austrian, he comes from a noble family, and like you he has inspired heartbreak among some of my more desperate peers. He's also involved in the opera, but unlike you, he's no longer aspiring." She fixed her inscrutable eyes on Lucien. "If only he lived in Paris, he would be perfect."

Lucien could not restrain himself from looking back at the man, though his gaze was no longer returned. "Is—is he a singer?"

"Fortunately no. As we've discussed, that's rarely a good idea." She paused and shook her head, as if the question required some consideration. "He's an architect," she murmured. "Probably the most important outside of Paris—at least on the continent. He's been commissioned, if memory serves, to build the new opera house in Vienna."

"You mean he's like Garnier?" Lucien asked, incredulous.

"Effectively, yes—that is my meaning."

Lucien brushed away a pang of something that felt like stage fright: "Is he attached?"

Codruta nodded. "I expect this will be your biggest challenge, with Herr van der Null."

Lucien was unabashed. "Who's his lover?"

"Not who, but what," she answered while casting a stern eye at Lucien. "Like someone else I know, his first love is his art." Hearing this, Lucien could not resist another glance toward Eduard van der Null, who in light of this information—and also because he was probably a decade older—seemed to possess a dignified reserve that inspired Lucien with a sense of understanding, as if they belonged on two sides of the same coin.

After a slow procession across the floor, during which Codruta paused not so much to greet as to acknowledge several guests— with whom she shared opinions about anything from the unseasonably frigid weather to the quality of the *mousse au chocolat*—she and Lucien reached their destination, a perfectly timed arrival that led her to envelop Eduard as he stepped away from a conversation. "Herr van der Null, what a delightful honor to see you this evening," she greeted him, in a tone that managed to convey both intimacy and hauteur, as if they were cousins who as children had shared summers in some distant castle. "I'd like you to meet Lucien Marchand, who in case you missed him earlier is one of our most promising young singers." Lucien extended his hand for Eduard to shake as she continued. "Which is to say that I expect he'll be singing in your new opera house."

"I would look forward to that," Eduard replied as he released Lucien's hand and seemed to wink—or perhaps it was just a raised eyebrow—which pleased Lucien, who understood the gesture to represent the formation of an unspoken alliance in this repartee with a grande dame, notwithstanding the fact that she had clearly intended this. "And I would hope even more," he added, "that you would be there to witness it."

"That's very kind of you." Codruta frowned. "But I regret to say, at my age, I don't travel as well as I used to. Tell me," she said, "do you still have that lovely café on Kärntnerstrasse, perhaps a block below St. Stephen's?"

"You mean Joséphine?" Eduard suggested.

"Yes, that's the one." She beckoned for them to lean in. "I have an amusing story for you. I went to Vienna as a girl before I had ever been to Paris, and so when I arrived here, I was rather shocked to see the same thing everywhere. 'Isn't it odd,' I said to myself, 'how all of these cafés are just like the one in Vienna?' Of course, that was before I realized that all great ideas originate in Paris and go on to enlighten the rest of the world!"

The two men laughed, at which point Codruta turned away—with a slight tilt of her head as if someone had just called her name—and extricated herself from the conversation. As they watched her part the sea of guests, Lucien realized that he liked Eduard's voice—not only for the deep tone but also for the faint Austrian accent of his French—and that he was pleased by his lips, which were not as thin as he had initially thought, and the grayish hue of his blue eyes, which except when lit by amusement were wolfish and melancholic.

Lucien wanted to impress Eduard—somehow to address him as more of an equal than as an awestruck child—but felt momentarily at a loss with no script to follow or notes to sing. It helped that he was taller than Eduard and aware that—thanks to his beard—he looked older than his years. "Have you known Codruta for very long?" he began and felt good about the question, which seemed appropriate under the circumstances.

"Oh, about three minutes," Eduard admitted, and again they laughed in appreciation of her performance.

"She knows a lot about everyone," Lucien noted.

"It might be offensive if she didn't use such tact," Eduard responded, an observation that impressed Lucien not only for its accuracy but for the succinct manner in which it was delivered, a quality he knew was often lacking in himself. "Have you known her for long?"

"I suppose I have." Lucien explained how and why she had come to assume a role of such importance to him.

"I can attest to the importance of good patrons," Eduard nodded. "You can never have enough of them—or at least in my work."

"Have you designed many buildings?" Lucien asked, trying to sound more confident than he felt, given that he had not studied architecture with any seriousness. He and Gérard sometimes argued about the merits of different buildings they encountered in their wanderings around Paris, with Gérard predictably favoring more utilitarian structures, such as warehouses and factories, while Lucien tended to prefer the ornamental and baroque.

"A handful—or five to be exact." Edward paused and seemed to consider Lucien before he continued. "It seems hard to believe as I stand here now, hundreds of miles away from any of them, if that makes any sense, but each one was really an odyssey, if not an ordeal. Though in retrospect it becomes more inconsequential, just another thing that people pass on the street."

"That's how I sometimes feel about singing," Lucien said, trying not to be awed, less by the extent of Eduard's experience and how much it eclipsed his own than by the older man's ability to reflect on what he had done—and with such lack of conceit—in a way that impressed Lucien as an ideal measure of both an artist and a person.

With better sense than to elaborate on this idea, he asked Eduard about the opera house in Vienna, and they spent several minutes discussing the project, which had not progressed beyond drawings and models. Lucien had always been curious about the acoustic properties of different theaters—specifically, why some were so much better than others—a topic about which Eduard not surprisingly displayed a lot of expertise, while Lucien was not shy about voicing his opinions concerning what did and did not work with regard to ideas Eduard mentioned. This led to a wider discussion of opera—they heatedly debated the merits of Wagner, with Eduard displaying somewhat less enthusiasm than Lucien, although he understood Lucien's disappointment about the Parisian fiasco—and then a more specific discussion of Lucien's own training and aspirations as a singer.

Before Lucien knew what had happened—for it felt like just a few seconds earlier that Codruta had introduced them—he heard applause on the dance floor and realized that more than an hour had passed; the party was ending. While they had talked with some intensity, Lucien was unsure if Eduard had any desire to continue the conversation beyond the party; in fact, the pensive coolness that had initially attracted him now made him nervous as he tried to ascertain Eduard's intentions.

"Well, it seems to be winding down here," Eduard remarked with a shrug that seemed to confirm Lucien's fears. "But I've very much enjoyed meeting you."

"Likewise," Lucien offered tepidly, dismayed by the ambivalence he detected. "Are you going back to Vienna soon?"

Eduard nodded. "Tomorrow afternoon."

"Tomorrow afternoon!" Lucien cried, unable to restrain himself. "Will you be coming back soon? I'd like to see you again—I don't know when I've enjoyed talking to someone so much."

Eduard pursed his lips and considered Lucien for a second before he laughed. "I find myself oddly defenseless." He looked at his watch. "I really must get back to my hotel to supervise the packing," he explained, "but if you care to come along, I could be persuaded to share another drink."

Lucien nodded—of course he would go, and might have killed himself had Eduard not invited him—but if in one second he felt as if he were made of light and air, and was tempted to mock the moody, downcast version of himself who had been moping around under Codruta's wing just a short time earlier, in the next he felt his throat constrict, less in anticipation of the night ahead than with sadness as he envisioned the next morning, when he would have to say good-bye. It pained him to think of living so far away from Eduard, but he decided it was a good, universal kind of pain—a pain of real love, perhaps—and one that needed to be experienced to be understood.

20

A Section That May Be Skipped by Anyone Not Particularly Impressed by Thinking as an Occupation

NEW YORK CITY, 2001. The towers were gone. Martin turned away, no longer able to watch. He spent a few minutes on the Internet, where he read that the attacks appeared to be over—a fourth plane had gone down in a field in Pennsylvania—but the city was effectively paralyzed. He gathered some documents from his desk, inserted them into his briefcase, and paused: did he really need any of this paperwork, filled with the hieroglyphics of law and business? He remembered Jay's suggestion that he quit his job, and far from fanciful, it now seemed necessary, as if having witnessed such a radical event demanded from him an equally radical response. He considered his office, and already it resonated with the sepia tones of a faded photograph.

He walked empty-handed toward reception, observing desks

covered with half-eaten muffins, uncradled phones, open spreadsheet applications, and other evidence of evacuation. He rode down the elevator and walked through the lobby and he tried not to think about anything—especially what he suspected would be a seven-mile walk home—as he inched forward in the compressed isolation of the glass chamber of the revolving door. The sidewalk was both better and worse than anticipated, for while the day remained pristine, and de-manded to be acknowledged as such, the sun was too bright, which made the acrid smell of burning chemicals and broken gas lines—not to mention the unprecedented sight of the thousands trudging past, diverging around him as if he were a rock in a stream—all the more surreal. He stood paralyzed by the procession: although a few people here and there seemed to be heading east or west, hardly any-one went south, with the great majority marching up Seventh Av-enue toward Central Park. Again Martin condemned the terrorists for destroying the ordered chaos of the city, the hypnotic ebb and flow that bore no relation to this muted, downtrodden parade of refu-gees, but with no choice in the matter, he immersed himself in their ranks.

He had taken only a few steps when his attention was diverted by a pickup truck, the bed of which held an assortment of ghostlike fig-ures whose dust-covered clothes led him to assume that they had been much closer to the site of the falling towers. While this scene aroused his sympathy, he found himself distracted by a second group—civilians, as far as he could tell, and apparently uninjured in any way—running alongside of and in front of the truck, furiously wav-ing and shouting at those before them to move out of the way. The ardor expended on this task hardly seemed necessary given how will-ingly and without exception everyone stepped to the side, but every member of this fanatical troupe of directors wore an identical expres-sion of importance—each a self-anointed model of altruism—as they cleared a way for the victims, who had already taken on the aura of martyrs surrounded by acolytes.

As Martin watched a second truck drive by, he heard a woman next to him quietly remark to her colleague: "Do you think we could hitch a ride if we poured vacuum cleaner bags over our heads?"

Martin could not help smiling to himself, comforted by the thought that whatever else the terrorists had accomplished, they had failed to destroy the New York City hallmarks of sarcasm and irony, whether employed in the spirit of irreverence or to mask the more painful and traumatic implications of what had happened. Nor was he sorry to be subsequently absorbed in a tangential and equally facetious discussion taking place among an attached group of cynics and misanthropes; they spoke about famous death marches—Bataan, the Trail of Tears, the Holocaust—and concluded with great certainty that this present walk out of Manhattan would surely be listed among them before they next engaged in a series of quips about how lucky so-and-so was to get out of a presentation for which he was not completely prepared, which led someone else to complain about all of the truly shitty buildings in New York City that could have been destroyed in lieu of the towers.

How true, Martin thought, grateful for the distraction and unable to restrain himself from mentally adding Madison Square Garden to the hypothetical list. As for the World Trade Center, the consensus was that while the view from the top could be impressive, nobody was going to miss the trashy mall in the basement.

"Oh my god—do you think anything happened to Century 21?" another woman interjected with the true pain of calamity.

Martin remembered shopping there, as much for the clothes as for the cruising, when a shared glance seemed to offer the potential fulfillment of a lifetime's worth of pent-up fantasies. This period had lasted through his marriage until some years after, a predictably adolescent phase of his life—and surely his "sluttiest"—during which (particularly after his divorce) he had maintained a large divide between his ideals and his actions. Most naïvely, he had assumed that after coming out, as a matter of course he would find the male equivalent of Amanda (or at least the Amanda of his dreams), who would guide him through the haze that seemed to surround the question of exactly who he was. As this person failed to materialize, he alternated between periods of despondence and periods of manic anger—these latter episodes marked by increasingly reckless behavior—but without (and this was most problematic of all) acknowledging either.

HE REMEMBERED THE first time "it" happened—for he used to think about these encounters with the passive quality of an innocent bystander—not long after his engagement, when in an impressive feat of wayward logic, he had reasoned that, with things going so well, it would be a good time to have sex with another man—just once, he reminded himself—to confirm that his fantasies were merely the products of an immature version of himself about to be permanently outgrown. The decision made, he took the necessary steps with surprising ease: one afternoon after Amanda left for work, he turned to the personal pages of the *Voice,* scanned through the "bicurious" offerings, and selected one that quickened his pulse—28yo WM 6'0"/165 br/br. He jotted down a short response with his own statistics—27yo WM 6'3"/215 blk/bl—before he sealed it up and took it to the nearest mailbox, where he inserted it with shaky but determined hands. This small but symbolic deed accomplished, he returned home in a state of breathless arousal, which after handling in the usual manner led to an intense guilt as he reflected on his incipient betrayal of Amanda—his fiancée!—only weeks before their wedding.

He officially wavered and for a few minutes swore that he was done with this business once and for all, and that under no circumstance would he show up at the coffee shop on Third between First and A he had suggested as a meeting spot. That night, in the effort to atone for his misdeeds—hypothetical as they remained—during sex with Amanda he kissed her with such intensity that she asked him if something was wrong, which annoyed him just enough so that the following day he began to reconsider his earlier decision, as if she now deserved to be cheated on; not like a major affair or anything, he again reasoned, but a dalliance, something that would be a little secret with himself.

He pretended to debate the issue, going back and forth like this for the rest of the week, until to his alleged shock he found himself at the appointed time outside the appointed coffee shop, where he spotted in a booth a man who more or less fit the description of the ad. He decided to leave, but as he walked past the doorway, his legs made a right turn and carried him through, and the guy nodded at him in a casual but conspiratorial way to confirm that he was indeed the object of Martin's epistolary desire. Though momentarily disconcerted, Martin managed to reach out and shake the man's hand as he slid into the other side of the booth, as if they were old friends.

Between his signal to the waitress for a cup of coffee and a comment on the weather, he examined "Boris" and decided that he was not bad-looking, Russian or Polish maybe, with the stained fingers of a working-class man and a wiry build that appealed to Martin. "I'm a little nervous," he confessed. "I've never really done this before."

"Girlfriend?"

"Engaged—you?"

Boris raised his left hand to display a wedding ring. "Married."

"Does she know?" Martin whispered.

"Are you fucking crazy?"

"Just paranoid. So where is she right now?" Martin thought of Amanda at work at Louise Bourgeois's studio in Brooklyn.

"Out of town." Boris frowned. "So you really haven't ever done this?"

"No," Martin responded a little aggressively, as if the idea were insulting. "You?"

Boris stirred his coffee. "So you want to come over?"

Martin started to say sorry, he didn't but once again was vetoed by something else that directed him to pause for a few seconds while he looked at the last rays of daylight reflecting off the back of a spoon on his saucer. "Okay, sure," he said, as if accepting an invitation to go play a game of checkers.

They soon arrived in the apartment, a fifth-floor walk-up on Tenth Street. Breathless from both anticipation and the ascent, Martin followed Boris through a rusty kitchen and a cluttered bedroom to a living room, this last space illuminated by a dusty twilight that filtered through a pair of large windows, which judging from the coagulated paint around the frames, were sealed shut. Boris wordlessly began to unbutton his shirt, prompting Martin to do the same, which led to a rather somber removal of pants and underwear, this last item providing a stark reminder of what exactly they were doing here and led them to approach each other, tentatively at first and then with the overwrought ferocity of bad actors as they fell groping onto a brown corduroy couch.

Even as it happened, Martin felt perplexed by what had driven him here and wished that he could fly back to his apartment, purged of all desire except for Amanda. He remembered getting wasted in college, those magical nights when, two-thirds of the way through a party, at say 2:00 A.M., he would arrive at a perfectly lambent moment of intoxication and desire, when the world became plastic and surreal as he fell into the arms of his teammates, sliding down their sturdy, muscular frames to his knees as they caressed his thirsty lips with the end of the beer tap. At the time, there was nothing he wanted more than to cross that unspoken line, yet now that it was happening, exactly as he had fantasized, he could barely stop from laughing at the disappointment he felt, and was consoled only by the growing certainty that he would never do this again. But determined to go through with it, he felt a saliva-moistened thumb twist his nipple, a tongue in his ear, his cock being gripped by a hand that looked like it could break it; he saw himself as if from afar, in a series of freeze-frame poses that both alluded to and mocked the pornographic overtones of the encounter, until at last he gave up and for the briefest of seconds knew what it meant to be tied to the tracks as a train roared overhead, giving him a taste of what his dreams had long promised and for once did not fail to deliver.

As soon as it was over—and though it felt like an eternity, only six minutes had elapsed—he returned to his senses. To see their naked, cum-streaked bodies made his spirits plummet, and as he glanced around the room, he was convinced that, as at any crime scene, the arrival of the authorities was imminent. Feeling polluted and ruined, he made his escape as quickly as possible with no objection from Boris, who watched him leave with a knowing—and to Martin, annoying—smirk. He hated Boris at that second almost as much as he hated himself.

Walking home, he began to feel better; after all, he had gotten away with it, and Amanda would never have to know. There had been no fucking, and he felt confident that there never would be, so for once AIDS was not a concern—to the extent that the disease was always lurking, even in his fantasies, as the inevitable outcome of such twisted desires—or more to the point, he would not be dying from sex with Boris. Thus his disgust quickly mutated into a more familiar detachment. He decided that gay sex was not unlike a drug; he was happy to have tried it but did not see himself becoming addicted. He replayed the previous hour in his mind with the sort of satisfaction of a job well done, and, for the first time since he could remember, felt certain he was completely and permanently free from desire for another man.

AS MARTIN RETURNED to the present on a very different walk home, he found himself in a less compacted crowd, and one that on the whole seemed more sullen and reflective than the one he had encountered earlier, as if the reality of what they had collectively witnessed was finally starting to sink in. As Martin continued to dwell on the episode with Boris—along with the many more that followed, most with men he could no longer begin to recall beyond the vaguest details—he felt relief and a form of gratitude (to the extent that such things were even possible in the larger context of this moment) in light of the murky, delusional waters from which he had arisen. For many years, sex had presented itself as an ordeal through which he could never pass without "collateral damage"—in his case a combination of guilt and denial—which over time had impeded his ability or desire to distinguish between what was "safe" and "unsafe," at least in the heat of the moment, and it was only after testing positive that he learned to act with more patience and consideration, for himself and for others.

Similarly, in a way that had been far beyond him twenty years earlier, he could now appreciate the advantages being gay offered him, not only in terms of access to the infinite reserves of seriously attractive men in New York City—some percentage of whom could be counted on to return his interest—but also for allowing him to see the world through different eyes—his own—to find beauty that in the past he would have overlooked or ignored in the effort to appear different than he really was. As Martin considered this, he felt a spark of desire—though more abstract than physical, a form of optimism, really—that he knew would be difficult if not impossible to reconcile with everything he had just witnessed (both in the present and in his memories), not to mention the accompanying waves of shock and sadness that continued periodically to wash through him and make him weak in the knees as he headed north. However small or illogical, he knew it was there, and he did not want to question or—worst of all—malign it; instead he resolved to keep it burning in a remote corner of his mind, unexamined for the moment but somehow reassuring as he returned his attention to the more pressing problem of getting home.

He was distracted by the sight of a young suit, maybe in his late twenties, in a double-breasted coat and a candy-striped tie, with shaggy hair and aviator shades; he wasn't walking with anyone, and his vaguely distracted, antagonistic aura seemed both appropriate and frankly seductive to Martin. But now that he was forty-one and not, say, twenty-nine—when the fate of the universe had so often seemed to hang in the balance of possessing a stranger—Martin easily restrained himself from making any kind of overture. There would be other days, perhaps, but what could he possibly say today—a disaster day—that wouldn't sound ridiculously trite and mundane, so that he would be left wanting to slit his wrists the second the words left his mouth? He again considered the multitudes around him and realized that each person had a story, yet—at this juncture—he could not bear the thought of hearing a single one.

21

The Past Unfolds in the Wax Museum like Distance in the Domestic Interior

NEW YORK CITY, 1978. In the fleeting image of a dream, Maria could see her parents at home asleep, in their bedroom underneath the attic. On the roof, a little silver light landed like a snowflake and burrowed down to ignite an exposed electrical wire next to a shopping bag full of old Popsicle-stick stage sets. While the first flames seemed innocent enough, small and curious as they explored their new surroundings, licking here and there, in just a few seconds they grew into a crackling fire and then a rabid inferno that ate through the ceiling to ravage John and Gina, whose souls had departed long before their bodies dissolved into the molten memories of their daughter's childhood. Delivered to her in the hazy fog of awakening, this image was as ephemeral as a black-winged moth in the night, and so it fluttered away before Maria was fully conscious of it, although she knew it was true because Kathy was holding her and they both were weeping inconsolably. Maria already felt the shock and grief and worst of all the guilt, which made her long to follow her parents in death—but not her grandmother Bea, who was safe visiting Maria's uncle for the weekend—and not painlessly, either, but like Saint Hippolytus to be drawn and quartered by wild horses.

Though she did not die in the hours and days that followed, a period that took her back to Pittsburgh to witness the charred remains of her home before she was shuttled around by an assortment of relatives, Maria felt increasingly numb, so that there were many times when she was sure her heart was beating slower and slower, and she was led to wish that it would stop completely. She was installed in her aunt and uncle's house, where she shared a bedroom with Bea, and where the two of them were prone to view each other with a mix of shock and a kind of wariness or survivor's guilt as they were to find themselves clutched in each other's arms with tears of disbelief running down their cheeks, just as they had done when Maria was a child but now without any acting. When she thought of her old life, the one she had inhabited just a week earlier, Maria saw two versions of herself—a singing one and a nonsinging one—and she could remember thinking that the singing one had taken her to beautiful, peaceful sanctuaries, whereas the nonsinging one existed in the boring and functional world she had otherwise tolerated; but in her new life, both of these seemed to be disappearing islands from which she had been cast adrift.

She managed to sing one last time, at the funeral, and even those most disinclined to the emotional tides of music marveled at the power of Maria's voice in the coruscating light coming through the stained glass above the altar, a sign that the deceased had not, after all, lived in vain. For a moment Maria forgot where she was, seduced by the familiar scent of flowers and the iridescent pinwheel spinning before her eyes; except as she sang, the smell made her nauseated and the colors made her dizzy, so that she had to put out her hand to steady herself, and though she wouldn't have thought it possible, she was left more bereft knowing that this magical landscape was no longer one in which she felt at home.

WHEN MARIA RETURNED to school the following week, she went to her classes and ignored the stares of the students who often regarded her with less sympathy than awe, wanting to involve themselves in the fanfare surrounding such a tragedy. In the past, there had been much she hated about her life—school, her classmates, her summer job—and things she loved: mostly singing, but also her parents, the thought of whom now filled her with guilt and regret as she remembered what she had done to exclude her mother from the trip to New York. It made her feel reluctant to do anything but float through the day somewhat aimlessly, like a fallen leaf in the wind. There were those, she knew, who detected this change in her and tried to console and reassure her. Her aunt and uncle and grandmother spoke to her about God; Kathy Warren, who drove her to the mall and helped her pick out new clothes, encouraged her to sing; Anna Prus, who called from New York, prodded Maria to describe the most mundane details of her day. Maria did not resist these conversations but found herself saying things to please her audience and then doing quite the opposite, such as when she told Kathy and Anna that she was starting to practice when in reality she would sit in her room and absently stare at the Indian-head nickel her father had given to her. It was not a malevolent form of lying—she said these things with a vague intention to follow through—but a resistance to returning to her old self that she ultimately had no desire to overcome.

There were implications to this change at school, where her former, monolithic disdain for her classmates was also something she no longer had the energy to uphold, particularly when she was the center of so much perverse attention. A pudgy girl named Rhonda, who sat next to Maria in the back of her math class, one day invited her out to the smoking area, and Maria shrugged and went along, and didn't really mind when Rhonda taught her how to inhale and hold the smoke in, so that it made her throat and lungs burn and her stomach queasy. Nor did she refuse when Rhonda—who wore black eyeliner and sometimes smoked her cigarettes through a long filter like rich people in old movies—asked Maria to go to a party that weekend. It wasn't that Maria particularly liked Rhonda, but she didn't hate her, either, so it was just easier to tag along and listen to her pronouncements about how most people were stupid, selfish losers. They went to the house of some kid whose parents were away or upstairs, and although Maria didn't say more than a word to anyone—except a few to Rhonda, who periodically appeared with things to smoke or drink—she liked that nobody hassled her about singing or anything else from her past or (former) future life. She sat on a windowsill, all but invisible in the dark, waiting for the next thing to carry her away.

There was a boy—Joey Finn—who like Rhonda was a freak and sometimes smoked with them after math class. He lived down the street from Maria's new house and was famous for having convinced his parents to let him install in their basement "den" four couches— one on each wall—a television, a two-hundred-gallon fish tank with a pair of oscars that made short work of goldfish, and a stereo with two speakers, each the size of a small car. Maria started going to Joey's after school and learned to get high; once she even dropped acid and watched the massive subwoofers morph into faceless lips mouthing the words to *The Dark Side of the Moon*. Usually there were other kids around, but one day Maria was the only one, and when Finn sat next to her on the couch and started to rub his hand up and down her leg, she didn't stop him, and soon enough he was kissing her, and even though there was a part of her that didn't want to kiss him back, his more obvious desire easily outweighed her reluctance, so that she didn't really mind when he pulled his pants down and told her to suck it, because this was where her life was taking her, and it didn't seem any better or worse than anything else.

It was also how a few days later she ended up back at Finn's—she walked past his house twice a day—and he said he wanted to go all the way and she didn't really care about that, either; even the pain when he awkwardly rammed into her, or the vague disgust she felt as her hands traveled from his long, greasy hair over his acne-covered back and bony ass, seemed far away, really no more than distorted images to accompany the dull and muted strains of music she could barely hear, as if her life were being played in a movie theater three doors over from the one in which she sat.

MEANWHILE IN NEW York City, Maria's name had already acquired an almost supernatural aura, thanks to her mind-warping audition—which was saying something at Juilliard—and news of the fiery death of her parents. There were those who denied her existence, an urban myth that gained traction after her failure to respond to the acceptance letter was leaked from the admissions office. There were times—given what Anna suspected about her own relationship to Maria—when Anna was inclined to believe this as well, which always led her to pick up the phone and call Maria, because to hear even a few syllables in that voice reminded her of what she had witnessed in Pittsburgh—and then later at the audition—and increased her resolve to bring the girl to New York. With a thought to counter the inevitable chorus of doubters—all of whom had their own agendas to promote—Anna staged conversations with her friends in the Juilliard lobby in which she referred—in full voice, almost singing—to "this little robin's remarkable determination" and her "unrelenting desire to make a new start at Juilliard," and informed admissions that Maria would in fact be attending in the fall but needed an extension to supply replacement copies of papers lost in the fire.

Though she didn't want to alienate Maria—whom she did not begrudge this period of mourning—Anna worried that Maria's grief would lead to other, more active forms of self-destruction. Such fears were confirmed when she called Kathy Warren and learned that Maria had skipped chorus a few times and had also been seen smoking outside the high school, which though not alone a cause for panic was enough to make Anna think the time had come to intervene. She considered a visit to Castle Shannon but ultimately opted for the phone, reasoning that it was best to engage Maria *voce a voce*.

Bea answered and made the sign of the cross. "Thank you and please—you must save her," she pleaded. "Every day I am more— *comment dire, j'ai peur*—" Once again Bea was reverting to the language of her childhood, as if speaking in French would erase the memories of what had come after. *"C'est trop dur."*

"Je comprends, je comprends." Anna tried to reassure her, though she was also nervous. *"Ne vous inquietez pas—est-elle chez vous?"*

"Momento." Bérénice went to retrieve Maria, while Anna listened through the line. "Maria, *bella,* is the nice German lady singer."

"Tell her I'll be right there." Even through the phone, Maria sounded far away to Anna, particularly when she remembered how excited she had been at the Heinz Recitals and before the audition.

"Merde! You tell her yourself," Bérénice said, after which there was a long pause before Anna heard footsteps approaching and the clank of the receiver knocking against a wall, or perhaps some cabinets.

"Hello."

Anna took a deep breath. "Maria, it's Anna. How are you today?"

"Fine, thank you."

"How's school going?"

"Not bad."

"And your singing?"

"It's okay," Maria said.

"Well, there's certainly no need to push yourself right now," Anna replied, "but I was a little concerned that we didn't receive your acceptance letter. Did you mail it?"

There was a long pause before Maria answered. "No, I guess I didn't."

Anna let some time pass before she spoke. "Maria, my heart breaks every time I think about what happened to your lovely parents, but there's no reason to compound this tragedy. I can't imagine they would have wanted anything except for you to sing, don't you think?"

"That's true."

Anna knew she was not reaching Maria and tried a different tack. "When I think of your voice, it's a little painful for me, and not just because of what happened, or because I think you're beautiful and talented, but because it reminds me of when I was your age—or perhaps a bit older—and trying to come to terms with what it means to have this; except for me, it wasn't so much a talent or a skill as a secret language, a way to describe the world that made it seem wonderful and the rest of my life dull and drab by comparison. But after I lost my parents, life became painful for me, and I really struggled for a few years. I could barely sing—my voice felt lost to me. Do you understand this?"

"I'm not sure," Maria said, but there was a trembling, hesitant quality to her response that Anna found encouraging, since it seemed to reflect the churning of real thoughts.

"We're born with a gift," Anna continued, "and for a while it seems magical and gives us great pleasure, but there comes a time when it no longer satisfies us, except unlike a toy or a dress it's not something we can just outgrow, because it's part of us, and when you first begin to understand this, it can feel like a curse, so that you regret having been given the gift in the first place. If your voice feels different because of what happened to your parents, that's natural— it's part of growing up. And though you can never go back, you have the option of really learning how to use it in a way that will still bring you—and countless others—a lot of joy. Because—trust me—most people *don't* have it, but it's through us that they find at least a little piece of it in themselves."

For a long time there was no sound, until Anna heard the raspy choke of tears. "I wanted it so much," Maria sobbed, "but I just don't know if I can anymore."

"It's okay," Anna reassured her and listened until Maria had stopped. "I'm here."

"How?" Maria asked miserably, and Anna resisted an impulse to cry, as much with empathy as with relief at having broken through.

"First I want you to send in the letter," Anna said with hope and encouragement, knowing that Maria only needed to grasp the life preserver in front of her. She outlined a plan to bring Maria to New York after graduation; she would get her a part-time job and an apartment—with a roommate, another incoming singer—before classes began in the fall. "I'll be here whenever you need to talk," she added quietly, almost wistfully, as though speaking to a younger version of herself.

MARIA HUNG UP and felt stunned, but in a very different way than she had a few months earlier. She looked down expecting to see fragments of whatever it was she had been encased in exploding around her on the floor and then went into the bedroom, where her grandmother was lying on her bed, rosary beads in hand, her wrinkled cheeks wet from tears. "You spoke to the frau?" she asked. "She is *vraiment* not so bad for a German, *mia bella*. I hope—"

"I'm going," Maria said as she retrieved the Juilliard letter from under a stack of books, the exact place she had put it a month earlier, when it arrived. She sat down next to Bea and showed it to her. "This summer—she's helping me. I start school in the fall."

"*Dieu merci,*" Bea responded and kissed both of Maria's cheeks before she insisted upon kneeling next to the bed and saying a prayer of thanks.

As Maria watched her grandmother, she felt a familiar exasperation but was thankful that it was not marked by the same ambivalence that had so recently clouded her thoughts. As she listened to her grandmother's incantations, and remembered how much as a child she had loved praying with Bea, like two performers before an audience of God, she realized that what she felt was something entirely new, a combination of exasperation, ambivalence, nostalgia, and even a certain detachment, as if these were all different hues of paint on a single canvas, which she had the sense to step back from so that she might appreciate it.

She considered the letter, which continued to feel heavy in her hand, but less with obligation than with portent. She thought about what Anna had said about her "gift" and how she could have been describing the musical landscapes that Maria had inhabited for as long as she could remember but that had seemed so foreboding and unattainable at her parents' funeral. She knew she was still adrift but was more determined, even if the thought of finding something she might not recognize frightened her almost as much as not getting there at all.

22

Original Stories from Real Life

VIENNA, 1864. Though it was February and the temperature outside well below freezing, Lucien was not deterred as he trotted down the spiral stairs of his apartment building, two steps behind Eduard. He knew that, despite the cold, stepping out into the open air—where the winter sun refracted through the mist to create an almost perpetual twilight of orange and pink pastels—would be like stepping into a dream. It was one of his favorite things about Vienna, and something he often thought about when he was inclined to miss Paris.

Still, there was a limit to how fast he liked to move in the morning, and Eduard was testing it. "Please, slow down just a little—you're making me dizzy!" he begged as they circled closer to the foyer.

"I know—I'm sorry," Eduard said and stopped in front of the door to wait. He quickly placed a finger on Lucien's lower lip in lieu of a kiss. "I told you—I don't want to be late."

Lucien lightly bit the finger, shook his head like a dog, and then just as quickly let it go. "Okay—that's better—*on y va.*"

Outside, they continued at a brisk pace past the university—where Eduard was an adjunct professor—toward the center of the city, making a detour around a vast field adjacent to the Ringstrasse, where the new parliament buildings, all in different stages of construction, could have been mistaken for ruins. After crossing into the old city, they walked past the Spanish Riding School, where Lucien insisted they spend a few seconds admiring the horses—steaming after their morning exercises—before continuing on to Graben-strasse, where a strip of yellow tents extended in either direction in the center of the wide thoroughfare.

"Is there anything else I need to get?" asked Lucien as he withdrew from his pocket a list that they—along with Heinrich, Eduard's longtime domestic and cook—had made in anticipation of dinner that night, to celebrate Lucien's third anniversary in Vienna.

"I don't think so"—Eduard shook his head—"but if you see anything that looks good—"

"Pomegranates, perhaps?" Lucien joked, knowing that these were Eduard's favorites, but were no longer in season.

"If you love me you'll find them," Eduard replied with a wink, before he doffed his hat and turned toward Kärntnerstrasse—which led directly south to the site of the new opera house—leaving Lucien in the growing throngs at the base of St. Stephen's.

Now on his own, he meandered through the tents, which in this corner of the marketplace were filled with barrels of strange gourds, dried lemons, coriander seeds, cinnamon sticks, and other spices. After buying a few things—bartering down the prices like a true Viennese—he went back to the street and paused in front of a plague monument to consider the tower of writhing bodies and skulls; in Vienna, death was honored the way Paris paid tribute to military victories, a distinction Lucien realized he had come to appreciate as he turned to orient himself by way of the cathedral rooftop. Looking up, he ignored the shouts and cries of the surrounding merchants and allowed himself to be momentarily hypnotized by the vibrating mosaic of orange and green against the pale white sky.

As he walked back to the apartment, he was struck by how three years in a foreign city could feel at once so fleeting and so epic. Like a tourist, he was always discovering unmapped streets, dusty bookshops with rare prints and old editions—sometimes in strange Eastern languages he didn't even recognize—and courtyard cafés that served tortes whose recipes were said to be kept in vaults under the imperial palace. At the same time, it often felt as though he had never lived anywhere else. Like many Viennese, Lucien had learned to move with a methodical deliberateness that announced an awareness of life's difficulties and a corresponding desire to avoid them whenever possible; his German was close to flawless, and he had made new friends to replace the ones he had left behind.

That he was still singing—albeit again, more in German than in French—added to the sense of having lived nowhere but here, as if his art trumped—or transcended—any geographical consideration; it also helped that, since arriving in Vienna, he had achieved a consistency in his upper range that allowed him to entertain the idea of tackling certain roles that would have been quite beyond him at the conservatory. In addition to performing periodically at recitals and salons hosted by a number of Eduard's friends, Lucien was working with a new teacher, who agreed it would not be unreasonable for him to start auditioning in the very near future, possibly as soon as the fall.

When he considered differences between his old life and his new, the most important was not the atmospheric light, or the Turks and Arabs who ran the markets—or even the Viennese themselves—but Eduard. To say they had fallen in love undoubtedly captured the intensity of their first months together, when even the briefest separations—during a phase when they had traveled back and forth between the two cities—had been enough to send Lucien into despair and for the first time he had understood what Gérard had meant on that night at the St.-Germain; and now that he and Eduard lived together, Lucien felt he could have predicted the more mundane if pleasurable aspects of love, the obvious and expected benefits of sharing a bed and meals and evenings at the theater, along with the trivial annoyances and spats that occasionally accompanied the same.

What he could not have predicted, and what he thought about as he walked up the stairs laden with spices, flowers, and pastries, was how to live with someone was in effect to become that person; it was not just that he sometimes threw his shoulders back or held his teacup in a way that mimicked Eduard, or even the uncountable number of small jokes and shared gestures that seemed to carry one day into the next, but most of all how Lucien found that he could—when alone, walking through the city or sitting in a café—observe a scene with Eduard's brand of intellectual objectivity. Just as Eduard professed to admire the fire Lucien brought to his singing—which he assured Lucien would be reflected in the final plans for the opera house—Lucien knew that Eduard calmed him down; he was less likely to find himself in tears, and his dreams were no longer filled with endless hallways through which he ran panicked, unable ever to find the door.

He remembered the first time he had seen one of Eduard's buildings, a church a few kilometers west of their apartment, just off the newly widened Lerchenfelderstrasse. The structure was not particularly remarkable—as Eduard had warned him, his original design had been scaled back by church officials for both aesthetic and financial reasons—but inside he was confronted by a staggering display of stenciled patterns spiraling up each of many walls and braided columns, painted in soft hues of gold, teal, and burgundy, and interlaced with repeating motifs of flowers, leaves, and fleurs-de-lis; above it all hovered an enormous dome that resonated with the mottled blue tone of a robin's egg, as if to beckon those below with the luminescent promise of emancipation.

"I feel like I'm flying," Lucien remarked as he made a wide circle before taking a seat on a pew next to Eduard.

"That's the idea." Eduard grinned bashfully, clearly pleased to have made a favorable impression.

"I can't believe it was controversial," Lucien noted more seriously, for Eduard had described to him in some detail the factions who had objected to the design.

"I couldn't believe it, either," said Eduard, in a harsh whisper that Lucien had never heard, while staring through him with a dejected anger that seemed improbably close to the surface, given that the building had been completed several years earlier. Eduard briefly shook his head as if to drive the vision away before he smiled at Lucien and continued in a more placid, resigned tone. "Honestly, there's no accounting for taste—or bad taste, as the case may be. They wanted angels and cherubs, and I—or we—insisted that color and pattern were more than enough."

"Sometimes I really do envy my father," Lucien noted as he again looked up. "At least his work is measured in numbers and results. Even if it takes a long time—and I know from him that it usually does—eventually either you cure a disease or you don't." Since moving to Vienna, Lucien regularly received updates from Guillaume, who in his son's absence continued to work as feverishly as ever, both in his own lab and at the university, on the same projects that had occupied him for as long as Lucien could remember. Although Guillaume frequently emphasized that a cure for any of his diseases—this was how he often referred to them, as if they were his charges—remained on the distant horizon, he seemed satisfied with his progress. Or maybe, Lucien sometimes considered, his father didn't really care about finding a cure for cholera—much less aging—so long as he was engaged in the work, which because it was driven by a love for his dead wife, brought him closer to her. But it was a solitary endeavor, and Guillaume—and in this respect he was very much a scientist, at least as Lucien understood him—showed no sign of suffering from the kind of artistic angst to which Eduard had just alluded.

Eduard nodded. "What's also good about science is that it's constantly expanding—adding new knowledge on top of the old, or replacing it—which is something a lot of art critics—the same ones constantly bemoaning the slightest change because it offends a nostalgia they hold for some lost period of their youth—would be well served to understand." He smiled wryly at Lucien. "Look at what happened to Wagner."

"Don't remind me." Lucien rolled his eyes. "But how do you know if it's good—if it's really original and not just contrived—when you're doing it? Nobody sets out to make something limp and derivative, right?"

"In my experience, you never really do," Eduard mused, and

Lucien could not help but note a certain melancholy that seemed to hover over him as he spoke, as if the obvious success of the result had been tainted by the ordeal of getting there. "You just have to trust a gut feeling—an intuition—and hope."

THAT NIGHT AT dinner with Eduard, as they reflected on the previous three years, Lucien playfully tested the hypothesis that he had changed—and for the better—since coming to Vienna.

"You think?" Eduard replied. "How so?"

"I'm more mature," Lucien ventured. "Don't you remember how, when we met, you were always saying how young I was?"

Eduard laughed. "That's because you were always in tears."

"Yes, I suppose I was." Lucien sighed, and smiled as he thought of himself breaking down at the door of Eduard's Paris hotel, then again when Eduard took him to Beethoven's apartment for the first time, and then when he first saw the green copper dome of the Karls-kirche, built to honor the victims of a devastating plague in 1713, which had annihilated half the city's population.

"It's nothing to be ashamed of—it was endearing," Eduard said more reflectively. "You know, I also cried when you left for Paris the first time—"

"No you didn't!"

"Of course I did," Eduard said. "It may not have been an epic tantrum, but I can still feel the back of my hand as I held it up to wave to you, and how it felt as the tears evaporated in the wind."

"I was on the train," Lucien replied. "You never told me—you were always so stoic."

"Well, one of us had to be." Eduard grinned as he picked up his fork.

As Heinrich cleared their plates from the table, it occurred to

Lucien that—as with the city itself—it was impossible to know every facet of another person; it was a chaotic undercurrent of love that he wouldn't have been able to predict but that he now felt able to embrace, given his faith in the venture as a whole.

Rather than expound on this thought, he turned the question around. "So—do you think you've changed?"

"Yes, I hope so," Eduard said after a few moments. "Before, I was miserable, and now I'm—"

"Slightly less miserable?"

"Exactly." Eduard leaned back in his chair. "Today after my meeting, I was talking to August," he said, referring to an associate in his office, "and telling him about our dinner, and how three years had passed since you moved here. And he said he was quite aware of the fact, given that I've not really yelled at anyone during the same period, or at least not the way I used to."

"You used to yell?"

"Not every day, but I was a lot more likely to snap." He smiled at Lucien. "You might say it was the wrong kind of emotion—or at least not the sort of thing you want to put on display."

"That's hard to imagine," Lucien admitted, although he felt pleased by the idea that he had affected Eduard in this way.

"What's strange to consider now—or perhaps not—is that I really had no idea what I was like, or how miserable I was. I thought it was normal to scream at someone about stupid things beyond anyone's control—a delay in a delivery or a shortage of materials, inevitable problems that crop up in any project. Or even worse—if you can imagine—were the days when I'd find myself completely incapacitated by pressure, whether real or not—or probably some combination—so that August would have to come over and get Heinrich to drag me out of bed to finish our plans on time or whatever else to make some deadline." For a second he stared through

Lucien, lost in the memory. "It's like I was possessed by demons, but didn't know it."

THE NEXT MORNING, Lucien woke up groggy; they had enjoyed more than a few glasses of absinthe before going to bed, which in combination with so many kisses and caresses never failed to leave him with the sense of having spent hours in a moonlit field of wildflowers, pressed hard against the wet earth and staring up through the blossoms at the slowly spinning stars. He turned his head toward the clock; it was past nine, and Eduard—with his usual discipline— had already left for work; if a part of Lucien regretted his absence, he was also relieved that Eduard's demons remained so far at bay.

At the breakfast table, Heinrich offered him a cup of coffee and a croissant with *confiture et beurre,* along with the morning newspaper. When a few minutes later he opened this last item, Lucien noticed a small headline that made him drop his butter knife on the table, where it landed with a clang. "Wagner Rescued by Ludwig," he whispered, and then repeated it with more excitement to Heinrich, who was passing through the dining room on his way to water the orchids. Not believing it at first, Lucien three times read a short account of how Ludwig II, the recently ascended King of Bavaria, had in one of his first official acts summoned Richard Wagner to Munich to relieve him of his financial debts and to grant the composer an official position at the Munich Hoftheater, where his new operas would be produced. *Tristan und Isolde* was to be the first, with a world premiere scheduled to occur in March of the following year, assuming—and this, too, he read aloud, as if to confirm that he was not dreaming— suitable leads could be found.

23

Loveless

NEW YORK CITY, 2001. Martin stood up from a park bench at 110th and Riverside Drive, where he had been resting under the Medusa-like branches of an allée of American elms. The unusual silence of the surrounding neighborhood—the empty playgrounds, the lack of stereos and traffic—made him think of the suburbs, and as he resumed his walk north, he wondered if the attacks would result in large numbers of people moving out of the city. It was an impulse he could understand, given that he had left the more manic environment of the East Village—where he had lived for close to a decade—for his current house in Washington Heights, this during a period of his life when he, too, had felt under siege—although he would not have used such an expression, he realized, until today—forcing him to take steps that might have seemed drastic, if not reactionary, to a younger version of himself. The most important of these steps, not coincidentally taken just a few months after he was diagnosed with HIV, had been the decision to switch law firms, effectively jettisoning his former career as an entertainment lawyer—i.e., representing bands—for a new (and ultimately, just as he had hoped, far more lucrative) practice negotiating technology ventures.

Of less practical importance, but equally emblematic of a larger need to "reshape" himself, was his growing appreciation for opera at a time when he had felt saturated with rock. Given this, it hardly seemed coincidental—at least in retrospect—that the opportunity to buy his house had arisen after he saw his first *Tristan und Isolde*, just a few weeks before starting his new job. He could still remember the performance; though he had suffered through much of the first act—the music felt lugubrious, and the vaunted dissonance failed to impress him—he managed to return for the second, and as the piece moved deeper into the love duet, he felt his resistance erode, so that, as the doomed pair sang about their longing for love and death, the music seemed not only to locate the anger and grief that had been weighing on him like a swallowed rock but also to dissolve it into something benign, even potable.

Too stimulated to go home after the show, he left the Met and meandered down Broadway to Joséphine, the Viennese café on Fiftieth Street. Inside he admired the tall, beveled mirrors, marble-topped tables, and dark wood paneling, all of which seemed to recall old Europe perfectly without denigrating it, while the mix of decadent society types, artists, whores, and junkies added an intoxicating fin de siècle verisimilitude to the scene. He ordered an Irish whiskey and casually watched a table of attractive young men, whose animated conversation and games of flirtation further entranced and soothed him with the thought that there were some good things about the world that would never change.

The room was filling up when Martin was approached by an older woman—perhaps in her sixties—who caressed a long strand of black pearls in one hand as she addressed him. *"Excusez-moi,"* she began and then switched to English, "would you mind if my entourage joined you? As you can see, tables are now scarce, and I see no reason for a handsome young man to sit alone."

Martin did not mind. *"S'il vous plaît,"* he responded in his rather tortured French.

"Je m'appelle Ghislaine," she continued and nodded to a man who appeared to be around the same age, "and this is my husband, Arthur."

Martin also nodded to the gentleman, whose intense eyes and lean body did not fail to catch his attention. Perhaps it was for this reason that he was less than surprised by Ghislaine's next words:

"I am also accompanied by Jean," she said and patted the hand of a younger man next to her, "who—because I believe in candor at my age—I will disclose is my *amant du jour*." Martin nodded at this man, whose long chin and messy blond hair pleased him somewhat less, as Ghislaine turned to the fourth member of their party, a man who—thanks to his robust build, length of the nose, curve of the ear, and swarthy skin tone—bore more than a passing resemblance to Martin, as if they both had ancestral roots in the same village in southern Europe.

Ghislaine acknowledged as much in her introduction. "And here I present you with your doppelgänger, Leo," she continued with a small bow as everyone laughed, "who in the interest of fair play I will also disclose is Arthur's lover. He shall sit next to you, for his English is by far the best among us."

As soon as Leo sat down, it dawned on Martin why he looked so familiar. His stomach flipped at the thought, even though he felt faintly ridiculous to acknowledge it, after all of the rock stars—and in some cases, musical heroes—he had met.

"Are you a singer?" he asked tentatively.

"Yes—opera," Leo confirmed.

"*Tristan?*"

Leo raised an eyebrow. "You know it?"

"I was there tonight," Martin admitted. "I was very moved—it was my first time."

Leo seemed to waver before he responded. "So I've made you an expert."

"I've been called worse." Martin shrugged and then sipped his drink. He might have been more disappointed by the chill he detected in Leo's voice if he had not long before trained himself to expect the worst from artists whose music he professed to admire. It was always a delicate procedure, given his assumption that someone on the level of Leo Metropolis had no particular need for his approval, but Martin still felt it better to acknowledge his admiration than to pretend—as some of his former music industry colleagues always did—that he felt no particular attachment to an artist's work.

To change the subject, Martin asked Leo where he was originally from and learned that he had grown up in Paris, although his father was from Greece.

"And you?" Leo asked in a tone that fell somewhere between dismissive and playful.

"Well, I'm American—I grew up in Pennsylvania," Martin replied. "But I was adopted."

"I see," Leo mused. "Well, my mother was from the South of France, so if our passing resemblance is any indication, I think it's probably safe to say you have some Mediterranean blood in you." Another round of drinks arrived; while Ghislaine and the others resumed their own conversation across the table, chattering in French, Leo again turned to address Martin. "So you don't know who your birth parents were?"

"No. The records were sealed, and my interest has always been more superficial—more of a conversation piece than a real desire to know."

"And your adoptive parents know nothing?"

"No," answered Martin and then briefly explained what had happened to Hank and Jane.

"I'm sorry," Leo murmured and then seemed to look through Martin for a few seconds before he returned his gaze to him. "Although if it's any comfort—and please don't take this the wrong way, because I speak from my own perspective, which I understand often places me far outside of the norm—I sometimes like to think that death, at least in the case of those we truly love, allows us to appreciate what they have done for us in ways that are not possible when we're all here, constantly changing and fixated on how to get from one day to the next. Death offers us the chance to reflect on who they were, which of course is a way to understand ourselves. As painful as it can be to see them go—and I don't mean to diminish the sense of loss or grief we all feel—there is also no greater gift."

Martin, who in the surrounding mirrors could see an infinite number of Leos repeating into the distance, was struck by the man's eyes—the way they glinted like jade in the shadowy light—as well as the beguiling tone of his voice, both of which made Martin remember he was talking to a man whose performance had shattered him only hours earlier. "I see you take your *Tristan* to heart," he remarked, not unappreciatively, for Leo had accomplished the difficult trick of acknowledging death with neither cold detachment nor the uncomfortably overwrought displays Martin had come to expect from a certain percentage of others with whom he shared this information.

Leo's expression barely changed as he nodded. "Let me guess—you're thirty-three?"

"Very good." Martin laughed, less unnerved than slightly astonished in a way that sometimes happened during such barroom conjecture, and also relieved to move away from the maudlin overtones of their earlier conversation. "How'd you guess?"

"Woman's intuition?" Leo also laughed, then shrugged in a charmingly self-deprecating way that gave Martin the impression that it really had been nothing more than a lucky guess.

"And you're . . . fifty-two?" Martin replied, taking care to shave a few years off his real guess.

"That's not something we singers are ever inclined to disclose," Leo said, pursing his lips in what struck Martin as less a flamboyant gesture than an allusion to one.

Martin extinguished his cigarette; he didn't really care how old Leo was but remained curious. "And—and do you still live in Paris?"

"Yes." Leo smiled. "Although I still keep something here."

"'Here' meaning?"

"I have a house in Washington Heights."

"Washington Heights," Martin repeated, as if trying to place it. "Uptown?"

"You're familiar with it?"

Martin shook his head. "I don't think I've ever been north of Columbia."

"That's too bad," Leo said. "I'm about ready to sell." He smiled at Martin. "And since fate—or Ghislaine, if there's any difference—has brought us together, I thought I'd give you first dibs."

Martin resisted the temptation to roll his eyes, having over the years endured his share of sleazy come-ons and farcical invitations that made sense only in the inebriated aura of night; in Leo's case, however, there was a pleasing ambivalence to the offer—a complete lack of desperation—that intrigued him. It was the sort of conversation that pulsed through uncountable bars and cafés and restaurants of Manhattan every single night and—whether anything materialized or not—served as a barometer for any potential relationship, even one that could be expected to last no more than a few minutes. "Okay, I'm game," he answered. "What kind of house?"

"A small-but-charming kind," Leo playfully replied. "It's perched on the cliffs of Washington Heights, and has the loveliest views of the Hudson. It's also secluded in a way that in my experience is most difficult to find in Manhattan."

"Why would you want to be secluded in Manhattan?" Martin asked, although even as the words left his mouth, it occurred to him that—though he had never thought about it in these terms—he could very much understand the desire. He saw a new version of himself, devoted to his new job during the day and returning home each night to somewhere peaceful and distant, not so far away from the heart of the city that he would obsess about leaving or missing it, but far enough so that he would not be distracted by those parts of his life he was ready to leave behind.

"Isn't that for you to tell me?" Leo smiled and to Martin's disappointment got up from the table; apparently Ghislaine was ready to leave. Before he stepped away, he presented Martin with a calling card. "Here's the address," he said. "If you have any interest, I'll be there tomorrow afternoon—come up and I'll show you around." He then shrugged. "And if not, *à la prochaine.*"

"Until the next time," replied Martin, who already suspected—or was beginning to hope—it would not be very far away.

THE NEXT DAY, after referring to a map of Manhattan, he walked to 14th Street and Eighth Avenue, where he took an A train all the way up to 190th; having no idea what to expect as he emerged from the station, he was surprised to find a hilly neighborhood, filled with five- and six-story prewar apartment buildings, that on the whole resembled a European city more than an American one. The streets were quiet and clean, and this part of Washington Heights, at least, seemed to have little in common with the "drug-infested" quarters to the south and east about which he had read; Martin knew that, as with Harlem, large swaths of the neighborhood had given way to a form of blight and disrepair that mirrored what he had seen in the East Village during his first years in the city.

He walked west to Letchworth Terrace, a street just one block long that jutted out from Cabrini Boulevard, and here paused in front of a stone wall to admire the view. To the south was the George Washington Bridge, while the sheer cliffs of the New Jersey Palisades extended impressively to the north. The bridge seemed to bring the same order to his thoughts as it did to the cars streaming over it, and as he considered the river, he was struck by a stillness and a grandeur that had nothing to do with the more frenzied atmosphere in which he had lived for the previous twelve years. It was difficult to believe he was still in Manhattan, but the certainty that he was added to the allure; as he looked farther south, at the outline of midtown, he felt as if a fever had just broken. The city had always seemed alive to him—and in ways that were increasingly difficult to romanticize—but from this vantage point it appeared less monstrous than benevolent, and in his admiration he felt an encouraging spark of love and possibly forgiveness.

He went to the end of the street, where Leo's property was situated behind a brick wall. He admired the deco motif in the wrought-iron gate and then peered through at the top stories of the house, which were just visible above the forested hillside. To see even this much filled him with longing and purpose, for already the house seemed to resonate with an aesthetic reminiscent of his prep school; it was, he noted, something his mother would have loved. He wanted his life to be marked by the same grace that allowed this house to erupt out of the cliff and to hover magically—presumably there was some sort of cantilever onto which it was built—above the river. As he walked down the steps, he looked up at the mottled brick exterior, which reflected the pink and orange tones of the western sun, and then kneeled down to touch the moss growing between the cobblestone pavers leading to the front entrance. He observed a lush wisteria growing up and over the southern façade, its woody vines wrapped around several of the drainpipes, before cascading over a railing that appeared to give way to an outdoor terrace.

He questioned moving so far uptown when he could afford to live almost anywhere on the island. He thought about how many hours he would be working at his firm, and how he could expect on many nights to arrive home at one or two in the morning, and then head back to the office after four or five hours of sleep, and whether he would regret not buying an apartment on, say, Columbus Circle, only a ten-minute walk to his office. No sooner were any of these arguments made than he dismissed them; just as he now intended to give increasing amounts of time to the lawyerly side of himself, he wanted to offer what remained something serene and contemplative, completely removed from the clubs and bars and bathhouses that had marked his life during the previous years.

He stood on a small stoop and rang the bell, reminding himself that he was no longer drunk and there was a good possibility that Leo had changed his mind. When the door opened a few seconds later, Martin looked into a shadowed hallway beyond which he could see the sky, azure and shimmering. He tried to speak and could not, and for a moment regretted appearing so weak in front of a man he barely knew and from whom he might be buying a house; it was not a good way to start a negotiation. Flooded with intuition, he didn't care if a few coughs and tears weakened his position; he knew he would gladly pay whatever it cost. "I can't pretend," he managed, as he looked up at Leo. "I'm ready to buy."

Nor did he protest as Leo invited him through the door, where he kissed each of his cheeks and in a whisper acknowledged his failure ever to be surprised.

24

The Motion of Light in Water

NEW YORK CITY, 1978. After a long bus trip, a harrowing walk through Port Authority, and a taxi ride across the neon extravagance of Times Square, Maria arrived on the Upper West Side of Manhattan, where she rang the buzzer for what she hoped was her new apartment. She had spoken briefly on the phone with her new roommate, Linda Pasby—another incoming singer, a mezzo—and was worried about meeting her. As much as she wanted to like Linda, if only for Anna's sake, Linda's cheerful demeanor—combined with the knowledge that she was from Beverly Hills—made Maria think they might not make the best match. She felt greasy and exhausted by the trip but forced herself to smile as the door opened and she was confronted by Linda, who just as Maria had pictured her was petite, with short blond hair and very white teeth. She wore a T-shirt with an iron-on decal of a horse, the widest bell-bottoms Maria had ever seen, and a silver necklace with *Linda* spelled out in large, cursive letters.

"Wow—you really *are* tall!" Linda exclaimed and then added, "Hey, sista, can ya spare an inch?" in a Bronx accent as she assumed the swagger of a panhandler.

Maria took a deep breath and hoped that her smile looked more genuine than it felt as she stepped into a small living room and peered down a narrow hallway toward a tiny kitchen with a half-size stove and refrigerator. "I can't believe I'm here," she said. "It's actually bigger than I expected."

Linda gave Maria a complete tour of what was a ground-floor garden apartment. "Don't you love Anna?" she mused at one point before she flapped her arms and tilted her head slightly. " 'My lee-tle robin,' " she cooed. " 'New York is such a von-da-fool city.' "

If it was jarring for Maria to hear someone poke fun at Anna, who had played such a serious role during the least funny part of her life, she resolved not to show it as they arrived at her new bedroom, which was about eight feet wide by twelve across, with a dingy window that faced a neighboring apartment building. She put her suitcase on the bed and pushed aside the curtain to peer out the window, where she was confronted by a view of the basement of the building next door.

"The view's incredible," Linda noted, "so don't pass out or anything."

Maria decided that she liked the dusty, unswept quality of the alley, which was what she had imagined for an apartment in New York City. She even liked the gray block façade, which as she watched became momentarily illuminated by the sun's reflection in the air shaft. She pulled on the metal bars.

"Don't worry," Linda reassured her. "My father triple-checked all of them."

Maria nodded. "That's all my grandmother has been saying to me for the past month." It felt strange—and sad—to think of Bea so far away, but rather than express this, Maria decided it might be a good chance to let Linda know she was not the only one capable of improvising on the fly. "'Maria, *faites attention,*'" she said, assuming the accent, "'this city, *elle est assez dangereuse.*'"

Linda seemed at least interested, if not totally impressed. "She's French? *Très chouette.*"

"Actually Belgian." Maria nodded and felt a spark of pride at having initiated this exchange. "Where are your grandparents from?"

"Palm Springs." Linda frowned and continued more hesitantly. "Anna told me about your parents, and I wanted to say I'm very sorry, and even though I don't really know anyone who's ever died, if you want to talk about it or anything, I'm actually a pretty good listener—"

"That's okay—thanks." Maria kind of hated Linda for bringing it up, but she also kind of admired her for the same reason. In any case, Linda no longer seemed to be made of plastic, and Maria detected an expressive quality in her brown eyes that made her curious about her new roommate's voice; presumably, she would be very good, and Maria wanted to know exactly how good.

While Maria unpacked, they spent a few minutes aimlessly talking about Los Angeles, where Maria had never been but which Linda assured her was not as exciting as New York. Maria showed Linda a picture of Bea she had brought with her in a small frame.

"Oh, she looks so tiny and cute!" Linda said. "Is she going to visit?"

"Maybe, but not anytime soon." Maria shrugged. "She's pretty old and way too afraid."

"Well, we can take care of her—just looking at her makes me want to move to Europe!"

Maria took the frame back and placed it on her dresser. The photograph seemed so small and distant, and looking at it made her feel utterly alone; it was like one half of her brain kept asking what she was doing here, while the other half knew it was perfectly obvious. As Linda's last comment continued to reverberate, it also didn't seem fair to Maria that she should be rich and pretty, with two living parents—and four grandparents—and even though she understood why Anna had put them together, it seemed like a stupid, obvious choice that didn't give Maria enough credit for what she had been through. But when she took her eyes off the frame and looked up, she was pleasantly surprised to find Linda already gone—as though sensing Maria's need to be alone—and it again occurred to her that, like a Russian doll, there was more to Linda than she had initially thought.

THAT NIGHT, ANNA took them out for Japanese—another first for Maria; but determined to shed her provinciality, she let Linda coach her through the basics and tried everything. As they ate, Anna explained that both girls would be starting summer jobs the following week as administrative assistants in the fund-raising department at the Metropolitan Opera. To hear that she would be going to the Met, even in the context of a summer job, awed and intimidated Maria, which then made her feel embarrassed, given that this was only the smallest step toward where she wanted to go. It made her wish that she could be more like Linda, who seemed to take the news in stride, or perhaps even with a trace of derision, as if it were no better than any other summer job, which was probably true given that it was going to be a lot of photocopying and filing.

"Really—photocopying?" Linda asked with a raised eyebrow. "I thought I was going to be giving a master class with Leo Metropolis!" Linda had already discussed her admiration for the heldentenor, whom she had seen perform the previous spring in Milan but whom Maria—again to her chagrin—had never even heard of.

Anna smiled at Linda and responded in kind. "My understanding was that Mr. Metropolis was all set, but your agent skewered it by asking for too much money."

As Maria observed this and other such exchanges throughout the meal, she began to understand that the conversation often worked on two levels, and perhaps even three, as Linda managed to acknowledge her subservience to Anna, to mock it—but lightly—and yet to draw Anna in, which made them seem more like equals, if only for a few seconds. Though Maria chimed in a few times, she felt that everything she said was a beat too late, and when Anna and Linda smiled at her, their smiles were rooted more in indulgence than in appreciation. It made her feel weighed down, and try as she might, she could not help brooding as she wondered if her past would inhibit her in ways she could not even predict. Several times she tried to laugh—to at least convey her understanding of a joke—and it got stuck in her throat, and she was always relieved when the waiter arrived to fill their water glasses. As much as she wanted to join in, she found she could do little more than wrap her hand around the icy glass, as if to prevent her new life from slipping through her fingers.

As the summer progressed, she began to feel more comfortable—in her apartment, at her job, at dinners with Anna, and with Linda—or at least more able, so that after only a month in the city she looked back at the nervous girl who had frozen up at dinner with pity and disdain. Because New York was so different from Pittsburgh, her past began to feel more like a harmless callus than a malignant growth; she often felt as if she had died in the fire, and could now discuss her former self with a certain objectivity, a distance that sometimes made her wonder if she had ever lived there at all or was just now waking up from a bad dream. When the subject of John and Gina came up—as it invariably did, since she was introduced to many new people—she learned to explain that they had died some time ago in an accident, and for the uncouth who couldn't resist pressing her, she made it clear that she didn't feel comfortable discussing the details. She found that with practice—and she did practice, alone in the bathroom, in front of the mirror—she could convey the information without seeming too vacant or needy, like it really had happened to someone else.

She struggled more when classes started in September, particularly during the first few weeks, when she walked past the practice rooms and heard the muffled strains of a Paganini violin caprice, a Rachmaninoff piano concerto, a Rossini aria, and other offhanded feats of musical genius. Several times she found herself alone in her room, absently examining her father's Indian-head nickel, thinking about nothing, just the way she had done during those months after the fire. She remembered what Anna had said to her about the musical language of her childhood, and how it required more work to understand as an adult, and she would feel motivated by the diagnosis. She would set down the coin and stand up with greater awareness of her spine, the position of her head and neck, the way the air moved in and out of her lungs—or any number of other things about posture and technique that she had learned—and walk out of the room as if taking the stage, already transformed into who she wanted to become.

Of the new singers, Linda was the quickest to establish herself among the faculty, and moreover—in addition to having a gorgeous voice that sounded like it belonged to someone twice her age—she knew about all the big singers and had managed to see quite a few of them, not only in the United States but also in London, Paris, and Milan. If this occasionally made Maria jealous, it inevitably gave way to a fascination with and even admiration of her roommate. Maria was particularly interested in Linda's ability to convey a hypnotic melancholy that seemed to have no relation to her sunnier personality, which led Maria to hope that, once she figured out exactly how to go about it, she could make the veritable wealth of sadness at her disposal that much more powerful.

She mentioned this idea to Anna at one of her lessons but in the next breath confessed a new fear. "I'm worried that I'll never be able to do the same thing," she confessed, "because—well—"

"Because you lost so much?" Anna suggested.

"Yes." Maria nodded.

Anna took a few seconds before she responded. "First of all, I want you to remember that there's never been a singer who has not spent decades learning how to breathe—with consistency—and you are just getting started. And right now, that's all you should worry about; questions of interpretation can come later. Eventually your singing will need to be personal, but for now, it's not a problem that you are so detached."

Given that Maria had never told Anna about her episodes of

slipping away—when she would lie in bed absently rubbing her coin—it frightened her to think that her teacher could detect this in her singing.

Anna placed a reassuring hand on Maria's elbow and spoke in a more consoling tone. "Try not to compare yourself to Linda. It's a process, and eventually you'll understand not only what it's like to build up walls but how to knock them down, though not completely, because you always have to hold something back, too."

Maria felt tears about to spill and knew she was on the cusp of something, though as much as it felt like a revelation, she feared it could just as easily be a breakdown. "Will it have to be my parents?"

"That will be for you to decide," Anna replied, even softer. "It might be a boy you used to like, a lost love. It might be someone who was mean to you in elementary school, or even someone you were mean to." She smiled. "It took me forty years before I learned how to tell my story."

Maria nodded. It was such a simple concept to understand, and it even gave her a certain appreciation not only for what she had endured but also for what she would continue to face going forward. But the idea that she would regularly have to embrace her life like this made her uneasy; if experience was a bridge to her island, it felt increasingly rickety as it crossed over deep chasms she was just beginning to detect.

25

The World as Will and Representation

MUNICH, 1864. Lucien paced back and forth in front of the Hoftheater and tried not to be too nervous about his audition. It helped to think of Eduard, who while unable to join him on the trip but having been to Munich many times before, had gently derided the design of the opera house for its stilted resemblance to the Greek Parthenon. Lucien spent a few minutes absently watching Bavarians—including some very attractive young men in lederhosen—stream across the plaza before he checked the time and made his way to the Maximilianstrasse, the grand boulevard that ran adjacent to the theater. As he walked along the sidewalk, he dragged his fingertips against the rough stone foundation for good luck and tried to imagine doing this every day on the way to rehearsal, if only he could get the part.

At the stage door, he was greeted by Hans von Bülow, the Kapellmeister of the Munich Opera, with whom he had arranged the audition. As Bülow led him backstage, they talked about Lucien's train ride, the beautiful weather—it was now June, and much of the English Garden was in bloom—and other innocuous subjects, all of which helped distract Lucien from the task at hand. After being escorted into a rehearsal room, he recognized Wagner, who jumped up from his seat and vigorously shook his hand. "Well!" he exclaimed. "If your voice matches your build, then we should be in luck."

Although the composer displayed a leering, adolescent grin that might have bothered Lucien under different circumstances, at present it felt closer to a relief than an affront. It gave Wagner a pedestrian quality that seemed absent in his music, and made Lucien think he could actually impress the man.

"You look familiar to me," Wagner continued, examining him more closely. "Have we met?"

"Yes, maestro." Lucien nodded. "I was at your reading in Paris— the one hosted by Princess Mil—"

"Yes, I knew it! How is La Codruta? Have you seen her?"

"Good, yes, I—"

Wagner interrupted him with a wink. "You wouldn't know it to see her now, but in her youth she was—well—not to be ignored, if you catch my meaning."

"I'm sure I do," Lucien offered benignly. "I saw her last month in Paris, and she said to send her warmest regards."

"I'll make a note to write to her as soon as I have a minute to spare," Wagner promised, but in an absent tone that made it seem as if the thought had already slipped his mind. "She was always a bright spot for me in that miserable city."

Lucien resisted the temptation to agree with the composer and an even stronger one to disagree—it occurred to him that he was already being tested—and instead summoned the spirit of Codruta as he responded. "Maestro, I'm sure the princess would be most pleased to hear from you, just as she was overjoyed to learn about your recent success."

"Very good," Wagner replied. "But Herr von Bülow tells me you're not living there anymore?"

"That's right—I moved to Vienna a few years ago."

"So that explains your German."

"As with my voice, it's been a subject of much study," confirmed Lucien, pleased by the compliment.

There was a conspicuous throat clearing from Bülow—now at

the piano—and Wagner's expression grew stern as he stepped back to direct the proceedings. After Lucien had warmed up with a few short songs and exercises, they turned to the third act. They worked for close to an hour, a process that to Lucien felt more like a rehearsal than an audition, particularly when Wagner barked at him to repeat something. A few times Lucien lost his bearings and was unsure of exactly what the composer wanted, but any confusion did not seem to hold them back for more than a few seconds. When they finished, they stood speechless for a few seconds, until Bülow and Wagner nodded at each other and Lucien discreetly wiped his forehead with a handkerchief. Oddly, he felt more nervous now that it was done, and had to subdue his shaking knees and chattering teeth as he shook Wagner's hand and allowed Bülow to escort him back to the stage door. As much as he longed for some affirmation, he refrained from asking, knowing that doing so would make him appear weak; instead, after Bülow pleasantly thanked him for coming and allowed that Lucien should expect to hear from them soon, whatever that meant, Lucien nodded back and firmly—but not too firmly—shook his hand and said in an equally pleasant tone that he hoped he would.

BACK IN VIENNA, Lucien ignored Eduard's advice not to think about it and gave himself fully to the torpor of the wait. He spent hours lying on the couch, where occasionally a cat walked across his chest or Heinrich delivered lemonade and ice. Even his father's most recent letters from Paris were filled with an uncharacteristic degree of frustration—apparently Guillaume's latest round of experiments had resulted in little more than new questions—that seemed to validate Lucien's ennui.

As June gave way to July, the increasing heat left him wanting to do little more than watch the sweat form on his arms and evaporate in the twilight. He found it impossible to concentrate on anything but the audition, and any earlier convictions about his performance gave way to new doubts and forgotten details, along with an inability to determine whether they were real or imagined. He could almost hear his voice wavering where it most certainly had not, and it seemed that Wagner had been less impressed than chagrined that Lucien—a detestable Frenchman—would dare to sing his work.

"Why haven't they written?" he asked Eduard in a panic after most of July had passed—almost twice the length of time Bülow had initially indicated Lucien should expect to wait—and he had yet to hear a thing.

"Because they've completely forgotten you," responded Eduard. "Didn't you see the newspaper today? They cast someone else—another Parisian, I think?"

Lucien ignored him. "Do you think I should write?"

"Of course not," Eduard said more earnestly as he shook his head. "I think they're both very busy and perhaps have one or two other things to finish before they confirm that you're the singer they want—"

"I'm tired of waiting!"

Eduard laughed—they had discussed this many times—and he pushed the rest of his strudel toward Lucien. "Here—eat this and you'll feel better. I promise."

"That would be nice." Lucien sighed, but accepted the proffered remedy.

When he finally received word from Bülow in mid-August offering him the role, with rehearsals slated to begin in October, it didn't quite meet Lucien's expectations. It wasn't that he didn't feel a certain ecstasy or validation, or that he didn't enjoy the party Eduard threw on his behalf, but he found himself worrying about leaving Eduard for so many months and about whether the Bavarian cuisine would make him sick; he perversely wondered if his audition had perhaps been too good, so that Wagner and Bülow would be disappointed when they discovered his German was not as flawless as he had led them to believe, or his upper range not as uniformly consistent as the piece required.

WHEN HE RETURNED to Munich, the theater was already a beehive of construction. Ships, castles, and costumes needed to be built or sewn, and then rebuilt or resewn when they inevitably fell short of the maestro's expectations, and with increasingly extravagant materials, including African mahogany, Mesopotamian lapis, Chinese silk, and the finest wigs from Italy. Although such expenditures were known to raise eyebrows among the king's advisers, Lucien was pleased that his own fee was on par with those of leading singers in Paris and Vienna. Besides, his attention was fully occupied by the music and the staging, either of which could be maddening given that Wagner's ideas for every word, gesture, and glance seemed to change on a daily basis. Lucien was regularly put under the microscope and was often left weeping—or seething—with frustration after having failed to deliver exactly what the maestro wanted.

"Do you want to know what your problem is?" asked his Isolde— a Berliner named Pelagie Gluck (who, despite sharing a surname, claimed no relation to the famous composer)—one day after a particularly grueling rehearsal.

"No, but I'm sure you're going to tell me," Lucien said as he removed a towel from his head. In contrast to him, she managed to make perfectly clear when she had been through a scene enough times, informing the maestro that he would have to wait until the next rehearsal if he didn't want her to go insane.

"You believe in it too much," she said, as she retied her black hair in a ribbon behind her head.

"And you don't?"

"I'm here to sing, no more and no less," she stated and then cupped her hands over his ears as she continued in a whisper. "If it were me, I'd cut the whole thing in half—that would satisfy a lot of longing, right?"

Lucien could not help but laugh at the thought. If at first he had found her irreverence distasteful, and had even worried that it would somehow tarnish the production, by this point—in large part thanks to the strength of her voice—he was finding the opposite to be true; if anything, she made him understand that different avenues could be taken to the same place, with one not necessarily better than another. But like everyone in the company at different times, even Pelagie was not infallible, and there were days when he ended up consoling—or assuaging—her with the idea that they were doing something important and universal, even timeless and sublime, and for this reason owed it to the music—even more than to Wagner, as if he were a messenger and not the creator—to push ahead.

Except as often as Wagner preached that they were collectively engaged in the "music of the future," and no matter how much Lucien was inclined to believe this, there were moments when he, too, felt crushed by a despondency that went deeper than his problems in rehearsal; it was the difference, he knew, between understanding the power of waves and actually being battered in the ocean. Gradually he came to attribute this lassitude to an almost constant exposure to the opera; it was not just the scale and its technical difficulty that were daunting—and different parts of the piece remained elusive for each musician—but an almost tangible weight that he had never before encountered, even during his many years at the St.-Germain. Like an airborne sickness, the music seemed to infect everyone—the singers, the crew, even the administrative staff—with a form of despair that drained them of any energy even before the day's work began, as though they were hacking through a malaria-infested jungle. The sad wistfulness that came from constant exposure to a story of love and death was a component but in no way explained the overwhelming sense of futility under which they labored, as if they were required each day to explain the ultimate purpose of life while knowing that the previous day's answer was no longer viable.

26

What Fun Life Was

NEW YORK CITY, 2001. It was close to three o'clock when Martin made it home. Already anticipating the cool air inside—which he kept at a constant sixty-seven degrees from April through October—he paused at the front door to take the keys out of his pocket when he felt something brush against his shin. "Whoa, Nellie," he muttered as he looked down to find a very skinny gray cat peering up at him. Over the years, Martin had seen many strays cross through his front yard; at least a few of them, he knew, ended up in the basement of a nearby apartment building, where the super employed them to keep the mice and rats at bay. Because he had never been predisposed to pets, Martin pushed the cat away with his leg and was about to apologize for not being able to help when he examined it a bit more closely; it didn't seem nearly as mangy as some of the others, and it occurred to him that maybe it had recently escaped from someone's apartment, perhaps even in connection with the attacks downtown. The cat—clearly not afraid—looked back with a certain expectation and intensity that made Martin feel like he was being tested.

"Okay, wait here," he said and went to retrieve from his kitchen a small plate, on which he poured some milk. While the cat drank,

Martin walked down the block to the apartment building, where he found the super's wife watching television in the basement. She seemed a little dazed—like everyone, he supposed—as he briefly explained the situation and learned that she not only knew about the cat—and knew it was a "him"—but had been taking care of him for the better part of a week.

"So do you want me to bring him back?" Martin asked.

"No, not particularly." She dragged on her cigarette and spoke as she exhaled. "Why don't you keep him?"

"Do you think he belongs to someone?" Martin responded.

"Yeah—you."

Martin made a low whistle. "I don't know. I'm not really a cat guy—"

"Oh, Christ, have a heart." She grinned luridly at him. "What is it, the goddam shittiest day in a hundred years or something? The least you can do is take care of a cat." She disappeared into her apartment and returned carrying a few cans of food, a cardboard box, and some litter. "Look, try him for a few days, and if he doesn't work out, bring him back—no questions asked."

Martin felt powerless to say no as he reached through the door to receive the goods. "Okay, yeah—fine—a day or two," he said when he recovered his voice. "Does he have a name?"

"You know, I think he does." She put a hand on her hip. "What was my daughter calling him the other day—wait, I got it!—Dante."

"Dante," Martin repeated. "Why Dante?"

"Because he's a poet?" she quipped and then shrugged. "I have no idea what goes through my daughter's head half the time."

Martin went back to his stoop, where he found Dante waiting for him in front of the door. "Well, go ahead then," he said as he ushered the cat through. "I hope you like sixty-seven degrees," he added, thinking this might encourage the cat to find another arrangement more to his liking.

When Dante did not object, Martin invited him to look around. The cat—who seemed to understand the transaction—began to explore while Martin arranged the litter box in the downstairs bathroom and put away the food. He then spent a few minutes following the cat around as he tentatively poked his head into all of the rooms before going up to the living room, where he sat in front of the window. Given that this was exactly what Martin had been looking forward to—albeit with a drink in his hand, which he now prepared—he decided that, against all expectation, Dante actually had much to recommend him as a representative member of his species. He was attractive, with a bone structure more angular than round, and short fur, so that on the whole he resembled one of those ancient Egyptian hieroglyphs more than anything out of one of those idiotic Sunday comic strips. Furthermore, Dante's large green eyes made him seem quite intelligent, or at least intelligent enough so Martin had to imagine that the cat—as though he were in fact the Italian poet after whom he may or may not have been named—would be able to speak a few words.

Martin finished his drink, pointed at his mouth, and patted his stomach. "Are you hungry?" he asked. "Hun-gree?" he repeated, thinking that Dante might master the basics. "Shall we go see what we have to eat?" he added, and the cat amenably followed him downstairs into the kitchen, which at least partially confirmed Martin's sense that he had acquired a seriously intelligent cat.

To Martin's everlasting gratitude, he had replenished the refrigerator only two days earlier—and not two centuries, as it seemed—thanks to a trip to Zabar's. He offered Dante a slice of turkey breast, which was readily accepted. "Please don't take this the wrong way, but you could stand to put on a little weight," declared Martin, who then felt compelled to add: "You probably won't be shocked to hear that I'm trying to lose a few pounds myself."

Having addressed the needs of his new charge, Martin sliced himself two pieces of French sourdough; on one he spread his favorite Pierre Robert Camembert and on the other placed several slices of prosciutto di Parma and a sweet sopressata. These he took back to his study, along with a bottle of Shiraz he cradled in the nook of his elbow, a large wineglass, and an opener he carried in the fingers of his left hand, which in the course of the past hour or so had again started to ache. Dante, apparently full—although he did not say so, to Martin's slight disappointment—sat quietly on the corner of the rug. "Good job," he paternally addressed the cat, who looked through him with an utter lack of acknowledgment that Martin did not fail to appreciate, for it seemed to reinforce his expectation that Dante was not the sort who planned to run around breaking things, or even needed to be told otherwise.

After finishing his meal, Martin drifted into a state of semi-consciousness in front of the television and found himself confronted with alternating shots of the day's video footage, first the improbable melding of an airplane with a skyscraper and then the tidal wave of rubble at street level. As disturbing as it was, he could not tear himself away from this waking dream; to hover over this unprecedented destruction was to appreciate its power, and even in his less than fully conscious state, he recognized the tug of addiction. This footage—more than nicotine, heroin, anonymous sex, alcohol, ibuprofen, processed sugar, Godard films such as *Contempt* and *Masculin-Féminin*, and the shrouded woman in *Infinite Jest*, but more beautiful and terrifying—had more damning allure than anything he had ever encountered. Were he to copy and edit it into a taped loop lasting an hour or more, he knew he would be doomed.

The ringing phone interrupted this chimera; he checked the

caller identification and saw that it was his sister. "Oh, shit, Suze—I'm sorry," he apologized, explaining that he had walked the entire way home with no cell phone service and had just finished eating. "I also may or may not be adopting a cat," he added before briefly describing how this had come about. "Which means I could need your advice."

"Any time, big brother," she offered reflexively, and in the next second mentioned that their uncle and aunt—i.e., Jane's brother and his wife, with whom Suzie had lived during her high school years—had also been trying to reach him.

"Okay, thanks—I'll call them," Martin said.

Neither of them spoke for a few seconds, as though they didn't want to acknowledge the real reason they were talking on a Tuesday afternoon, and Martin could imagine her running her hand through her short blond hair, the way she had always done when she was nervous. Unlike him, she was thin and waifish, with a button nose and impish brown eyes. Nobody ever believed they were related until it was explained—as if it weren't obvious—that they were both adopted, and from different biological parents.

"So . . . ," she finally said, "are you feeling okay?"

"Honestly? I'm a bit scattered," he admitted, and resisted the urge—for both of their sakes—to tell her about watching the towers, and how he had been delivered into an omniscient state in which he could almost feel the hissing pavement of the Ohio Turnpike under his knees and palms. "I'm having a hard time reconciling what happened with sort of—well, I guess—functioning," he explained. "Like one second I'm slicing bread and the next I'm thinking about . . . not good things."

"I know what you mean," she said, and he did not have to ask to know that she was also thinking about their parents, and the grief-stricken period after their deaths—in some ways, it had never really ended—when life went on in the most mundane ways until for no apparent reason you found yourself thinking about what had been lost.

"What about you—what's it like up there?" he managed and felt more focused as he listened to her describe the details of her day (she was home working on her dissertation), and how her girlfriend, Caroline—a junior high school math teacher—had been confronted with a small legion of parents coming to rescue their children, which—as Martin wryly pointed out—sounded at least ten thousand times more stressful than anything he had endured.

As his sister quietly laughed—although it was closer to an exhalation of relief—he was reminded of another life that seemed very far away, when he was in college and would visit her at their aunt and uncle's house in Connecticut, and how they used to stay up late listening to records. He knew this was a sanitized and nostalgic version of the past, but he also knew that at this point he would gladly take whatever solace he could find.

AFTER HANGING UP with his sister and checking in as promised with his aunt and uncle, Martin retrieved a pint of ice cream (vanilla truffle) from the freezer. He returned to the couch and resumed watching the television but with a thought to avoid more disaster footage, switched the feed to the VCR, where he found himself perhaps an hour or so into *Ludwig*, Visconti's bio-epic about the last king of Bavaria. Martin had watched it countless times, not just for his longstanding attraction to the Austrian lead, Helmut Berger—whose high cheekbones and serious eyes, at once sadistic and vulnerable, never failed to entrance—but for the story of King Ludwig, a monarch tortured by homosexual urges (and in this regard, Martin understood the movie to be an accurate representation of history) who cast aside his political power in favor of financing Richard Wagner and building increasingly extravagant castles. (Ultimately declared insane by the state legislature, the king was deposed only days before his dead body mysteriously turned up in a lake.)

Though Martin understood why the movie was not exactly acclaimed—even among Visconti admirers—for its long detours into melodramatic camp, he had always been hypnotized by the decadent beauty of the king's crumbling empire, at least as it was rendered by the Italian director. Watching now, he was eerily reminded of the Twin Towers footage, except the film was less disturbing to the extent that it struck him as more a reflection of a universal condition than a window through which to observe its horrors. As the credits rolled over the final shot of the dead king sinking into the lake, his face illuminated by watery sunlight, Martin's mind began to churn, as if he were just beginning to acknowledge the implications of everything that had happened on this seemingly endless, unforgettable day.

He thought about Ludwig's mad willingness to do anything, even die, for his art, and recalled the famous photograph of Candy Darling—who along with Edie Sedgwick was his favorite Warhol "superstar"—the one taken in the hospital only weeks before her death from a form of leukemia caused by gender-reassignment hormones. In this photo, she was more beautiful and tragically glamorous than ever, the pallor of her skin luminescent against the cruel and sterile white of the sheets and the drooping roses. Martin had often considered her gaze along with the words she had written at the time: "Even with all my friends and my career on the upswing I feel too empty to go on in this unreal existence. I am just so bored by everything." He had initially found these words tragic and callow, like those of an insolent teenager, until upon further reflection he remembered a scene in the film *Dishonored,* when Marlene Dietrich, distant and defiant, lifted her veil just prior to execution, and it occurred to him that this was the role Candy Darling had adopted for her entire life, and that her eyes were haunted by the same cerebral and pessimistic desire on display in Visconti's film, to inhabit another time better than the one in which she was so sadly imprisoned. That Dietrich, like Garbo, died a recluse—and that these two women had most influenced Candy Darling could hardly be a coincidence. As Martin considered this now, immersed in the aftermath of both *Ludwig* and the New York City disaster footage, he understood better than ever the desire to escape and for a second, he, too, wanted to meet death head-on but in the least violent of ways; he wanted to withdraw, to upraise his existence, to remove himself as much as possible from the mindless cruelty of the present. He wondered if he would have any choice going forward but to resign himself to the past, which made even the prospect of love—which just a few hours earlier had felt relatively, albeit vaguely, enticing—seem hopeless.

Distracted by the rattle of the empty carton against the floor, Martin looked down to find Dante with his head buried in it, lapping up the last drips of the ice cream. "It's pretty fucking good, isn't it?" Martin said, unable to resist a wry smile, and as the words bounced back at him off the blank screen of the television, it occurred to him that maybe—just maybe—he was talking about his life, or at least its potential.

27

The City as a Landscape and as a Room

NEW YORK CITY, 1979. If Maria, as she entered her second year at Juilliard, rarely had the sense that her move to New York was a dream from which at any moment she might be shaken awake, she continued to have doubts. Linda, for one, seemed so much happier than she was, and the same could be said of many of the other students, who while clearly devoted to their practice regimens, managed to find time for friendship and dating in a way that still felt largely beyond her. As often as she craved having more friends or—a much keener desire—a boyfriend, the singer in her would belittle such wants or needs as childish or irrelevant, or at best subordinate to the more important ones dictated by her art.

Linda encouraged her to take chances, to talk to guys instead of just watching from a distance, as they liked to do in the school cafeteria over lunch or tea. While Maria's stock response was that she was too busy or too "stressed" from work, the truth—which she admitted only to herself, at least at first, and only late at night, as if it were a secret even to her—was that she was very much attracted to certain guys and—again, in secret—was not above paging through . the student face book to figure out exactly who they were. Coincidentally or not, almost every one of them was a brass player; these were guys who tended to swagger through the cafeteria looking hungover but unrepentant, like they had just rolled out of bed after sleeping in their clothes, which may have been true, given rumors of whiskey-fueled jam sessions in smoky jazz clubs, but which Maria also liked to consider because it seemed to make the strict adherence to her own training somehow more tolerable. And while she would have had no problem walking up to one of them and singing an aria, the thought of having a conversation—of being "normal" for just a few minutes—petrified her, so for a long time she did nothing at all, and resigned herself to playing out these meetings in her fantasies.

ONE NIGHT AT school, as she walked by a rehearsal room, she noticed the muffled strains of a trumpet and, peering through the window, spotted one of the brass players just as he was emptying his spit valve onto the wooden floor. This particular guy had already caught her attention, and was at or near the top of her list: an unabashedly beer-bellied trumpet player, he was at least seven inches shorter than she was and had a full, bushy beard that in a certain light looked almost red. His name was Richie Barrett, and—as much as she would have preferred not to spend the time thinking about him—she liked his sleepy and somewhat disdainful eyes; that he was black added to the sense of curiosity and transgression as she thought about what it would be like to meet him, and possibly more. On the verge of walking away, she found the courage to push open the unlocked door and walk through as though—or so she told herself—she were taking the stage.

He didn't even look up. "Sorry—I still have seventeen minutes."

"I just wanted to tell you," Maria declared with an expression halfway between a grimace and a smirk, "that other people, who might not like the idea of wading through your drool, use these floors."

"What? A little spit never hurt anyone," he said and dipped his finger in the puddle, then raised the finger into the air with a grin, as if to offer it to her. "Want some?"

In response, Maria cleared her own throat and disgorged a fairly sizable ball of phlegm, which landed at her feet. "You first."

Laughing, Richie left the room and returned a few seconds later with a stack of paper towels, half of which he handed to Maria, and together they kneeled to mop up. "I don't know if we've officially met." He held out his free hand for her to shake. "Richie Barrett."

She felt dazed from the apparent success of her entrance and resisted the temptation to take a bow and leave. "Maria Sheehan," she replied, and liked the weight of his hand in hers. "Second-year soprano."

"I know."

"What's that supposed to mean?"

"Well, let's see, that you're a hot-shit soprano who almost got kicked out for punching Judy Caswell."

"So not true," Maria objected, employing one of Linda's expressions. "I tapped her on the shoulder when she tried to step in front of me during a scene rehearsal. She tripped and hurt her toe, and the whole thing got blown way out of proportion. And I didn't almost get kicked out for it, either. Anna saw the whole thing." Everyone in the school referred to "Anna," so there was no need to explain the reference.

Richie nodded. "Well, between you and me, I think Judy Caswell's kind of a bitch."

"Between you and me," Maria said, lowering her voice to what she liked to think was its most sultry tone, something she had also practiced in front of the bathroom mirror, "the top of her range isn't bad, but her middle sounds like a dying cow."

"Can I quote you on that?" Richie responded as he stepped around Maria and blocked the door so that—when she did not move out of the way—only inches remained between them.

Maria felt seasick with physical longing. "Unless you want to die," she said, "you better move."

"Maybe I want to die."

Moving closer, she tilted her head down. "Maybe you want to kiss me?"

"I think a cup of coffee would be more appropriate," he said and pulled back just slightly. "I hate to play the stereotype."

Maria stepped back. "What's that supposed to mean?"

"I mean, we only met five seconds ago and you're already hot and heavy? You don't think that has anything to do with the fact that I'm black?"

"I never thought of it exactly like that," Maria admitted, as she tried to decide if he was insulted or not, or if she was insulted or not. "I see your point, but I can tell you that of all the black guys at this school, you're the first one I've ever wanted to kiss."

Richie's smile contained a mix of wry skepticism and intelligence. "So what do you have against black guys?"

"Oh, fuck you," she said and laughed a bit uneasily.

"If you say so," he said and inched closer to her, so that she now was in a position to kiss him again.

"You're sending very mixed signals," she whispered.

He looked at his watch and then reached behind her, locked the door, and then pulled a cord to close the blind on the small door window facing the hallway. "We only have fourteen minutes."

They kissed for a few seconds as Maria, gripped by something magnetic and propulsive, leaned into him. She loved how sturdy he felt on his feet and the sight of her own blue hand against the russet folds of his neck added to the excitement, as did his beard—softer than she expected—when it brushed against her face. She knew what she wanted and decided there was no point pretending; he was obviously thinking the same thing. After a furious removal of shirts and unbuttoning of pants, Maria was on the floor, and for once remembered her experience with Joey Finn with appreciation as—with Richie's hairy gut spread out over her—she wrapped her hand around his dick to help guide him into her, where after a few seconds she found it very much to her liking. As he began slowly to move, she dug her hands into his back and in an urgent whisper reminded him that time was at a premium; he responded in kind, pushing to *allegro* for a few minutes before a *molto vivace* finale that left her pleasantly numb and transparent, after which she reluctantly watched her body reappear from somewhere else.

He rolled off, and she tried to speak. "That was—"

"Intense?" Richie looked at his watch. "Shit—we have to clean this place up."

Maria looked at the clock. "Relax—we have four minutes," she joked with the cavalier grace of a veteran before they threw on their clothes, wiped up the floor (again), and—in Richie's case—packed up his music and instrument, which left ten seconds as they walked out past a violinist who appeared at the end of the hall.

Exhilarating as the night had been, by the time Maria got back to her apartment, she felt uncertain. As she considered what had happened, she knew it had been a performance of sorts—and one she had enjoyed—but this also made it feel untenable. She wanted to show Richie a fuller picture of herself, except she worried that it would conflict with the earlier one she had offered of someone strong and brash, with the gumption to push through the door and have sex on the floor of a practice room. For the first time in a long time, she found her coin and let thoughts of nothing carry her away as she fell asleep with it gripped in her hand.

THEY MET FOR coffee the next day. "You know," Richie remarked, "this is what normal people do when they first meet—have coffee, maybe go to a movie."

"Their loss," said Maria, who—despite her doubts—felt incapable of abandoning the more brazen personality she had cultivated the night before. "I don't know about you, but I barely have time to breathe with all the shit they have me doing around here."

"Too true." Richie looked at his watch. "But since by my calculations we have at least twelve minutes together, you could at least fill me in on some of the basics."

"Such as?"

"Okay, I'll start. I'm from Hartford. My father pushes paper for an insurance company, and my mother takes care of my three younger brothers—I'm the oldest. Musically, I'm all about jazz—Miles Davis, Chet Baker, Mingus, Monk—but I like some orchestral stuff, too. Alexander Arutiunian is a hero." He leaned back and sipped his coffee. "Okay, your turn."

Maria felt her stomach flip, and she spoke slowly. "I'm a soprano. I'm not a fan of Judy Caswell. What else do you need to know?"

"Seriously."

"Okay, my favorite singer is Inge Borkh, and Anna likes to think that if I can torture myself for the next twenty years, I might one day have a place in the dramatic repertory—"

"That's an undertaking," Richie said, with a mix of admiration and familiarity that pleased Maria.

"Everyone says you have to be at least forty to attempt it."

"And what do you think?"

Maria sighed. "I'll let you know when I'm forty."

"Okay—what else besides singing?"

Maria swallowed nervously. She hated feeling so naked and vulnerable, despite the fact that this was exactly what she wanted to show him. "I was adopted—I grew up in a small town called Castle Shannon outside of Pittsburgh—I was an only child, but now I'm an orphan because both of my parents died a few years ago in a fire."

"Wow—I didn't know all of that. I'm sorry."

The second he said this, Maria felt the nervous, stricken version of herself deliquesce, to the point where she couldn't even imagine what she had to fear. "It's okay," she said and allowed him to hold her hand. "It was really hard at first, but Anna pretty much saved me. If there's another place where—you know—'life goes on' more than it does here, I'd like to see it."

"You're even tougher than I thought," he mused. "You'll make a good diva."

"Who's stereotyping now?" She smiled.

"I am." He stood up and blew her a kiss from his palm as he ran out, since he was already late for class.

To Maria's relief, as she spent more time with Richie, she found that unveiling parts of herself—and her past—made her not only happier but also hopeful, and not just about their future but about her ability to find a sense of equilibrium, so that she no longer felt so consumed by her singing. It helped that he was equally dedicated to his trumpet—and to her ear, equally talented—so that she never felt guilty spending so many hours on her work, knowing he was doing the same.

One day she declared to Linda that she was in love, and to feel the words roll off her tongue made it seem true. That summer, after Linda went to London with a young artist program, Maria and Richie for the most part lived together; they spent nights huddled in her room—which thanks to Anna had an air conditioner—where their whispers and sighs mixed with the quiet hum of the fan. When they were alone, everything was perfect, and even with her dumb filing and photocopying job at the Met, she had more time with Richie than she could ever have imagined, particularly on evenings and weekends; it was—as they both noted repeatedly—like they were a married couple. They went on walks, and the city—hot and deserted, especially at night—was theirs, so that the streets were a stage and the buildings an audience. When they got home, they confessed their love with no embarrassment or reticence over and over until they fell asleep, dissolved into each other's arms, and when they woke up, Maria reluctantly untangled herself, for she did not want to breathe air that did not smell of him, or taste anything but the salt of his skin.

She showed up to a few of her singing lessons woozy and under-prepared. "I'm living underwater," she admitted to Anna.

Anna did not seem displeased. "All the clichés about love are true, but that's no reason not to give in," she commented and suggested having a cup of tea instead of launching into their usual routine. "Even if it doesn't last—and I make no judgment or prediction in that regard."

Maria was annoyed by a fatalism she detected and an unstated assumption that the real purpose of the experience—like everything else—was to expand the emotional range of her voice. "Why does everything in my life have to be about singing?"

Anna placed a hand on Maria's elbow. "My robin, of course I understand, and I suppose, at my age, one cannot help but feel a trace of jealousy, or at least nostalgia, to see the fresh bloom of love—"

"But what does age have to do with it? You could fall in love, too! What about the men you date? Aren't any of them—"

"Yes, they sometimes serve a need." Anna laughed but then grew contemplative. "Sometimes I think it would be nice to give in to a new love, but—and please don't take this as an insult or an expectation that you should ever feel the same—love is transformative; it takes you to new places. But if you're settled like I am, it's not anywhere you want to go."

"What if you don't have a choice?"

"You train yourself, Maria, and with experience, you know what to expect. Life is not always a brand-new adventure. You meet a man and you recognize something familiar, even desirable, but you don't give in to it. Love is exhausting—it gives you puffy eyes, which is less charming at my age than at yours. Of course there's nothing of interest in life that is not also painful to some degree, and I would rather have less interest and less pain, if that makes sense."

"It doesn't feel painful to me," Maria insisted.

"I know it doesn't." Anna moved toward the piano and played a few chords to indicate that the discussion was over.

ONE AFTERNOON A week before classes started, Maria and Richie were walking hand in hand down Central Park West when Maria noticed a man—nondescript, middle-aged, white, in a cheap polyester suit—looking askance at them.

"Is there a problem?" she demanded.

He turned around, hackles raised. "You tell me. Is there?"

"Not that I can see."

"Stupid bitch," the man muttered before walking away.

"You want to go fuck yourself?" Maria yelled as he stalked off in the opposite direction.

Richie pulled her along. "Maria, why do you let a stupid asshole like that bother you?"

"Because! Why does anyone have to make such a big fucking deal out of the fact that we're holding hands? I thought this was New York City."

"He was crazy! Making a scene doesn't help anything."

"So what if I was making a scene? Am I supposed to just take this shit lying down?"

"I appreciate where you're coming from, but you're not exactly the one with the problem complexion here," Richie remarked.

Maria stopped walking. "What—do I embarrass you or something?"

"Now *you're* being crazy," Richie answered, exasperated. "Why are we fighting about this?"

"Maybe I should just 'chill out'?" Maria added sarcastically.

"Maybe you should. I'm just saying that you might have a lot of things to be angry about, but being black isn't one of them."

Maria heard this and felt something crack inside her. She staggered to a nearby bench and collapsed. She could not believe that she had been yelling at him, as if anything were his fault. "I'm sorry," she sobbed, but even while she hugged him and begged his forgiveness, and he hugged her back and forgave what was barely a transgression, she felt something cold inside her and at that moment realized that the reason she could be icy and intimidating in the halls of Juilliard was that, more than fearing anyone or anything else, she was still afraid of herself.

28

The Fighting *Téméraire* Tugged to Her Last Berth to Be Broken

MUNICH, 1865. Three days before the *Tristan* premiere, Lucien went to meet Eduard at the train station, where he was scheduled to arrive from Vienna. They had not seen each other in several months, a period during which Lucien's rehearsals had reached their highest peaks of despair and intensity, when his hours away from the theater had left him rarely inclined to do much but sleep. It had taken all of his energy just to write the most perfunctory letters, and though he knew Eduard had problems of his own—something about a new oversight committee for the opera house—he had felt too overwhelmed and incapacitated to bring himself to digest the details fully.

It was only when Eduard got off the train and scanned the platform that Lucien recognized in his haggard expression—the sleepless eyes and wan cheeks—a degree of suffering that mirrored or possibly exceeded his own and that he had not been able to appreciate before now; even more alarming, it occurred to him that the rift he had attributed to his own ennui was actually the result of two sides pulling apart. For a moment he struggled to breathe, but when Eduard began to walk toward him with his efficient gait, Lucien felt a renewed tenderness and dedication; his affection, he realized, had only been hidden behind a thin veneer. Giddy with love and resolve, he shouted and waved—not caring if he made a scene—as he pushed through the crowd and caught Eduard's attention.

"You're finally here," he said with genuine relief, as a porter loaded Eduard's luggage onto a wagon, taking care to avoid the puddles that had not quite dried up after an earlier rainstorm. "I missed you."

"Me, too," Eduard replied as he discreetly brought Lucien's finger to his lips and then noted his appreciation of the blue skies, slices of which could be seen through the arched canopy of the station. "It's been raining for a week in Vienna."

"Is everything all right—with the theater?" Lucien asked somewhat guiltily as they made their way through toward the carriage he had hired to take them back to the hotel.

"We're making progress—or at least that's what August keeps telling me," Eduard responded, and if his tone was wry, he did not in any way seem to have detected—much less resented—Lucien's failure to grasp the details.

"Well, I hope you're not yelling at him," Lucien chided. "Or at least not too much."

"No—no, nothing like that." Eduard laughed. "Anyway, I don't want to talk about Vienna. We'll have plenty of time for that later." They were now in the carriage, which pulled ahead with a jerk. Eduard reached out to brace himself but then let his hand fall on Lucien's thigh, where it rested with an enticing weight and familiarity. "So tell me"—he smiled—"are you ready to make history?"

THE NEXT DAY Lucien was back at the train station, this time to meet his father, arriving from Paris. As he waited on the platform, he

thought about Eduard. Their night together had been perfect, a succession of desultory, dreamlike touches before a fathomless sleep. He
had awoken sore and depleted but infinitely calmer as he focused on
his impending performance, as if by giving every part of himself to
an audience of one, he had expunged any lingering doubt about his
ability to perform for thousands. Then at breakfast in the restaurant
downstairs, while drinking his coffee, Eduard had most uncharacter-
istically dropped his cup, so that it shattered on the table. While the
shards were quickly swept up by the staff and a new service put in
place, Eduard had not eaten anything the rest of the meal, which he
attributed to a lack of hunger but which Lucien suspected was a result
of continued trembling in his hands.

"Do you want to bring something upstairs?" Lucien asked.

"No—why?"

"You're really not hungry? You didn't eat very much last night
at dinner, and then, well . . . " He paused, not wanting to draw
undue attention to the coffee spill, which he was sure had embarrassed Eduard. "I don't want you to starve in Munich," he said more
tenderly.

"Don't worry—I'm just exhausted," Eduard said as he caught
his breath on the landing. "If I sleep for a few more hours—while
you pick up your father—I'll feel much better."

"Is anything else bothering you?" Lucien asked.

Eduard's face flushed red. "No—I told you," he emphasized,
causing Lucien to step back, unsure how to react. Before Lucien
could respond, Eduard caught the sleeve of his coat. "I'm sorry," he
said, as he pulled him closer. "My mind is still in Vienna," he continued softly, "but it's nothing to worry about. I promise, if I can just
rest for a bit, I'll be much better this afternoon."

Lucien did not press, and as soon as they arrived in their room,
Eduard went directly to bed. "This is just what the doctor ordered,"

he declared and smiled weakly at Lucien, who felt reassured when he placed his hand on his lover's forehead and felt no trace of fever.

GUILLAUME'S TRAIN WAS on time, and Lucien found him with no difficulty. After returning to the hotel—they were staying at the Kempinski, just behind the opera house—they were joined for lunch by Eduard, who to Lucien's relief seemed perfectly at ease through the entire meal, showing no trace of the stricken character from the morning. As in the past, Eduard and Guillaume seemed to enjoy each other's company, trading insights and opinions about their respective fields, with Guillaume displaying particular interest in the technological advances in architectural materials—new amalgamations of steel and glass and so forth—that allowed for the building of structures that would have been unthinkable a generation earlier, while Eduard was equally fascinated by Guillaume's theories about vaccines and diseases.

After lunch, Eduard returned upstairs to work, while Lucien and his father decided to stroll the Maximilianstrasse. As per orders from King Ludwig, the grand boulevard was adorned for the *Tristan* premiere with high banners in black and gold checkerboard that rippled in the bright June sun.

"It looks like a royal wedding," Guillaume noted appreciatively. "Does it make you nervous?"

"Well—yes—a little." Lucien laughed. He understood that Guillaume—far from doubting him—was only trying to establish the kind of rapport that they enjoyed in Paris but that seemed more tenuous in an unfamiliar city. "And you?"

"On your behalf? Not at all," Guillaume replied. "But I'm curious: is the music really as difficult as they say? I've been reading these articles in Paris—"

"Yes, it's difficult," Lucien admitted, "but far from impossible, or at least not in the way they make it out to be. We had our final dress rehearsal two days ago. It wasn't flawless, but we made it through—"

"Well, of course the doubters will come out in flocks until you do something to prove them wrong," Guillaume said rhetorically before he addressed Lucien. "But you're pleased with it—you're happy?"

"Yes—very much—though I'm not sure *happy* is the right word. There are times when it's difficult to leave the music at the theater, if that makes sense."

Guillaume nodded. "Your mother used to be like that, too—if she was singing a sad part, she would mope around in a cloud of despair, but if it was comedic, she couldn't stop telling jokes, and we'd laugh and laugh . . . " He smiled wistfully as he stood up. "That's why I always liked it when she played happier roles."

Lucien tried to remember the last time they had talked about his mother. "But which did she like better?"

"I'm sure she enjoyed both—that's what she did—but I think she was like you. It's not that she was melancholy by nature, but her favorite music conveyed what she used to call the sadness of life. In this respect, we were very different—we used to argue about it."

"Really? In what way?"

"In the way that I don't think there's anything inherently sad about life."

"You think that even now?"

"Yes, even now," Guillaume said with a shrug. "It's not that I haven't cried and grieved, but I don't see such experience as inevitable. Your mother didn't have to die when she did—it was mostly bad luck, and had things been just a little different . . . " He did not finish the sentence as he looked at Lucien. "No matter how hard life gets, we only get one chance, which is why we owe it to ourselves to make the best of it, for as long as we have."

Lucien nodded, although—as much as he admired his father's conviction—it occurred to him that a difference between an artist and a scientist was that one worked to transform the pain of life into something beautiful, while the other worked to transform it into something negligible.

THEY MADE THEIR way off the boulevard, turning north at the river and in at the English Garden, where they admired the late-afternoon mist rising off the lawn beyond the outstretched boughs of the black pines. They followed a path through a stand of larch trees, which proved to be an unexpected pleasure for Guillaume; as he caressed the feathery, lime green needles of the deciduous conifer, he explained to Lucien that it was one of the oldest species on earth, and one he was hoping to study in greater detail in the future.

"How is your research going?" Lucien asked as they found a bench on which to sit and rest. "The last time I was Paris, you mentioned problems—"

"Yes, I did," Guillaume said, "but as it turned out—and this is so often the case—the moment when nothing seemed to be working, when I was on the verge of giving up, is when I had the breakthrough I've been wanting."

"You mean with the longevity vaccine?"

Guillaume nodded. "Yes, exactly."

Because Lucien had been so young when he first learned about his father's project, and because so many years had passed with so little progress, he had assumed that the experiments would never really end, or at least not successfully. He didn't doubt his father's skill or intelligence, but a palliative for aging seemed much more of a grand ideal than a possibility. As Lucien considered Guillaume's expression, it seemed to convey more than fantasy, and for the first time he began to envision the vaccine in concrete terms; in a flash of understanding and foreboding, he saw how valuable it would be, how kings and queens would spend fortunes to acquire it, while criminals could be expected to resort to their own brand of extremes, a thought that made him fear for his father.

"You haven't taken it, have you?" he asked.

His father shook his head and laughed. "No—no, it's not any- where near being fit for humans. At this point it's only mice."

Lucien felt relieved by this. "Have you told anyone else?"

"No—of course not—you're the only one." Guillaume shook his head and spoke in a low tone. "I likewise trust you to keep it quiet— not even Herr van der Null should know, and above all not Codruta. I'm sure you can imagine what could happen if—if word got out."

"I'm not sure I could," Lucien admitted. Though he had men- tioned this element of his father's work to Eduard, it had always been with the same mix of astonishment and incredulity with which he viewed it himself, and not as something in any way imminent; furthermore, he had never seen Guillaume discuss the longevity vac- cine with anyone else except in the most theoretical terms, as he had done at lunch with Eduard. It occurred to Lucien that the vaccine was like *Tristan*; because most people couldn't begin to conceive of such a thing, there was little reason for debate until proof was in hand, after which all the old assumptions would be buried under an avalanche of newfound certainty.

"The last thing I need," Guillaume continued, "is for some idiot to think he could just swallow some concoction and live for two hun- dred years."

"But isn't that the idea?"

"Eventually," Guillaume admitted. "But for now, it's still much too dangerous—only about five percent of the mice survive more than a few seconds."

"And those that survive . . . ?"

"Well, that's another question." Guillaume smiled. "But if my suspicion is correct, there will be some very old mice running around the Île St.-Louis for the next few decades."

As Lucien pondered his father's news, he alternated between states of awe at the implications of such a vaccine for society at large and something closer to anxious hilarity as he imagined how much more intense Tristan's longing for death might be if he were 150 or 200 years old. He understood this latter reaction to be mostly a function of his nerves, but rather than fixate on it—to the detriment of his performance—he reminded himself that the most likely outcome of his father's work would be the indefinite continuation of the experiments; as Guillaume had said, mice and people were far from the same, and what worked on one could rarely be trusted for the other.

The day of the premiere, Lucien slept late and ate lunch with Guillaume and Eduard. He went to the theater and by five o'clock was in costume. Thirty minutes later the houselights were dimmed; Bülow entered the pit and after a polite round of applause signaled the orchestra, which began the prelude. Lucien moved into position to wait for his cue, and as he listened to the first breath of the cellos, he could almost hear his father and dead mother talking, while in the cascade of strings that followed, he felt his heart beating in time with that of Eduard and imagined them still together in the night.

By almost any measure, it was a good and possibly a great performance, which was not to say there were no mishaps. Several times Lucien or Pelagie came in early, which resulted in cross looks from Bülow as he tried to adjust the tempo of the orchestra; then the ropes on the curtain snagged at the beginning of the second act, which led the third-chair violinist to drop his bow and cause a rather loud screech; and finally, during Brangäne's warning, a lock of hair fell out of Pelagie's wig into Lucien's mouth and made him cough. When he could, he watched the audience from the wings and observed a few people inserting fingers into their ears, though very discreetly, as the rapture of their king was apparent to all. For some, it was destined to be a long night indeed, and Lucien pitied those he saw checking their watches just fifteen minutes into the piece, with more than four hours to go. There were many others for whom the music seemed to take hold: their twitches and squirms abated, replaced by a more transfixed state of contemplation, as if to be exposed to such dissonance and volume left no choice but to place a magnifying glass on their heavy souls. For those being exposed to this process for the first time, it was a trial by fire, while for those like Eduard who were better versed in the art of introspection, the piece was less disturbing than evocative of the inherent ambiguity of life.

When it finally finished, the crowd remained silent until one of the king's men had the foresight to clear his throat, at which point the audience erupted in a display of fervor as unprecedented as the more introverted states from which they had just returned. As Lucien took his bows, he felt like his dreams and memories and aspirations— along with all the petty obligations and responsibilities, all the hopes—had been decimated; the notes he had sung just a few minutes earlier were beyond his grasp, and there would be no way—even under duress—to summon them again until some point in the future he could not begin to think about. As the applause continued, he was reminded of certain mornings in Vienna—especially after he'd just arrived—when he would wake up next to Eduard and for a little while feel sated and content, and for the first time he understood the consummating power of performance and how—as with romantic love—he had grasped this only after years of searching, of craving something he could not have described until after it was found.

29

Blue Monday

NEW YORK CITY, 2001. When Martin woke up on the Wednesday after the attacks, he turned on the radio news and confirmed that the previous day had not, after all, been a nightmare. He called his office switchboard and learned that the building was closed, and after hanging up was startled by a cat walking across his bed, yet another detail in a surreal stream that now returned to him. But if Martin was at all inclined to regret his decision to take in the cat, he found himself entranced by the way Dante—he now recalled his name—methodically cleaned his paws, slowly and deliberately, without apparent concern that Martin might disown him at any moment.

They went to the kitchen, where Martin boiled water for his morning tea and gave Dante breakfast. Eating, Martin noted, was one of the few activities in which the cat appeared most like an animal—really, almost rodentlike—his head bent down to the plate, gulping up and chomping the pieces of turkey breast Martin set out for him. "Don't worry—there's plenty of food," Martin said, and felt pleased when a few seconds later Dante stepped back from the plate—which was not empty—and stretched before sauntering out of the kitchen.

His tea ready, Martin carried it into his study on a tray along with half of a Zabar's cheesecake. He turned on the computer and once again considered quitting his job—or "retiring," as Jay had put it—which had felt so imperative the day before, when he was leaving his office. He pulled up his finances, and it did not take him long to conclude that, while not exactly a moot point, the concern was not particularly vexing. Hardly a year had passed at his firm when he did not receive a hefty bonus, which in turn had allowed him to make a second killing in the stock market after he invested in all sorts of Internet highfliers on their way up and—in a show of pessimistic bravado for his colleagues at the firm—shorted a good portion of them on the way down. All of these gains were now converted into a well-balanced selection of munis and slow-growth funds effectively impervious—to the degree possible—to market fluctuation. He concluded that barring some catastrophe—e.g., the one that had happened the day before—his portfolio could be expected to provide a reasonable per annum in the six-figure range.

He wondered if he could really be happy leading the life of a dilettante and recalled something his father had said to him after eighth grade in the context of giving him his first job. "I think last summer may have been a little too unstructured," Hank had explained. "It's not good for someone your age to sit around too much."

Martin, who at that age had shared Jane's views about the potentially stultifying aspects of the bourgeois workplace, responded with a prepared statement: "Do you think it would be better next year, when I'm a year older?"

Hank laughed but was unmoved. "Sorry, Marty; everybody has to work. It makes you a man. The job is three hours a day. You can work out in the morning, come into the warehouse after lunch, and spend the rest of the night doing whatever you want."

Though Martin was annoyed—if not quite angry—at his father for framing the issue in such logical but repugnant terms, the job—as he now admitted—was actually one of the better ones he had ever held. Although the assembly-line work (screwing a seemingly infinite number of eyeglass temples to frames with an electric screwdriver) introduced him to an almost visceral and at times exhilarating form of tedium he would later understand to be a foundation of modern life, it was genuinely fascinating to watch the piles of tiny screws gradually disappear from the tray in which they awaited their fate like cattle at an abattoir. Sometimes they would briefly fall into perfect formation, twenty-five lined up in each of the ten slits designed to hold them, while at other times, such as when Martin poured in a fresh batch, they would be panicked and chaotic, rolling all over—as if succumbing to entropy—and would have to be corralled by an angry god before they were removed one by one to fulfill a destiny with the nonprescription safety eyeglasses of the world.

This was also when Martin first learned to appreciate the aural tedium of album-oriented rock radio, which at this point in his life was his primary source of music (not counting the classical works Jane periodically introduced him to). To hear the same five or six bands—the Who, the Stones, Sabbath, Zep, Deep Purple, Hendrix; i.e., all the music he would disavow in prep school—over and over was the aesthetic corollary to the assembly line; had he not experienced this firsthand, he never would have understood the appeal of such an extreme, much less the desire to destroy it.

MARTIN'S FIRST "REAL" job after college, as a paralegal at the downtown office of his uncle's white-shoe law firm, had been marked by a similar—if somewhat more complicated—anomie. At first he enjoyed his immersion in the "high-stakes" atmosphere, where millions of dollars were tied up in lawsuits and corporate transactions; as a government major with a concentration in international relations, he felt it was important to understand whether corporations could be said to act more or less rationally than the countries they had displaced. But over a relatively short period of time—perhaps an hour, he joked to Dante—he grew to dislike the work, not so much because it was boring and draining—which it was—or because he had been required to wear a coat and tie—bothersome as that could be—but because everyone at the firm viewed him as a recent Cornell grad and Division I hockey player, which were two facets of Martin Vallence that had begun to resonate with him less and less as he spent more time in the East Village.

He was living with Jay Wellings in an apartment on Second Avenue and St. Marks, surrounded by random flea markets—full of doll heads, bent silverware, and porno mags—junkies and punks, boarded-up storefronts, and anarchist graffiti. Almost every weekend they went to hard-core shows at the Shoe, an abandoned tenement on Tenth and A. The ground floor was essentially a plywood cave with a small riser in the back covered by doormats stolen from restaurants in SoHo, lit by a single naked lightbulb hanging from the ceiling, and adorned with a couple of very tortured-looking microphone stands that seemed to be held together with duct tape and admonition. The smell was sour and rank—they smoked cigarettes as "air freshener"—while the bands were loud and fast and violent. Martin loved it; he threw himself into the mosh pit and emerged bruised but scrubbed, ready for revolution.

This process was not without unexpected repercussions, not only in terms of his increasing displeasure with his law firm work but in a seriously lamentable disinterest in girls and a corresponding desire for the opposite. Given this tension, it could hardly be considered a surprise—although it had felt like it at the time—when one night he found himself smitten by a friend of Jay's named Keith Loris, who helped run the shows. With sunken eyes, a boxer's nose, and a full black beard, Keith had the idealistic and slightly sadistic aura of a young Fidel; he seemed to be everywhere at once, helping the bands set up, checking the PA, and even selling beer. Martin was officially introduced when Jay ordered a few cans of whatever, and during this transaction—they had shaken hands—Keith seemed to regard Martin for perhaps a whole second, a gesture Martin barely acknowledged as he turned away, taking care not to move too fast or too slow, with a calculated air of indifference that he hoped in the deepest corner of his heart might make an impression, though to what end he could not even begin to think about.

THE NEXT DAY at work, with his ears still ringing and his thoughts infected by visions of Keith, Martin found himself unable to bear the more immediate and conceptual proximity of certain associates, partners, and—worst of all—senior partners, all of whom at one point or another in the previous months had corralled him into their offices for teeth-grinding sessions in which they had reminisced about their own glory days overlooking the Cayuga (or the Charles or wherever else), on the ice, or both. Which perhaps wasn't so horrible—i.e., the talking or the listening part—except for what Martin had noticed was an assumption held without exception by every single lawyer that his paralegal position was simply a year or two's hiatus between college and law school, after which he would follow in their footsteps and—as if there could be no higher calling—become a practicing attorney.

To make matters worse on this particular afternoon, Martin was informed by the supervising associate that he, along with a team of his fellow corporate slaves, could expect to remain on the premises for at least the next twelve to fifteen hours, and probably most of the weekend as well, in order to execute some "important" redactions on a mountain of evidence scheduled to be turned over the following Monday to opposing counsel as part of a complex trade-secret litigation between the two largest lipstick manufacturers in North America. In practical terms, this meant cutting out blocks of white paper and pasting them over portions of documents deemed irrelevant— i.e., unresponsive to the opposing party's discovery requests—by the team of associate attorneys and supervising partners, and then photocopying said documents, skills that Martin, along with 99 percent of the population, had mastered in kindergarten.

It was after midnight when an associate named Joe Klint—a tall, preppy guy with an aggressive chin and Clark Kent glasses—stormed into the conference room and threw several sheets of paper down onto the table where they were all working. "Someone's not doing their job," he yelled as he pointed to a highlighted portion of the text that had not been covered. "Wake up!"

"Jesus," Martin muttered.

Klint exploded. "Do you think this is some kind of joke?"

"No, I kind of think it's pathetic."

"Well, if you think it's so pathetic, maybe you shouldn't be working here."

"I didn't say *you* were pathetic," Martin replied, drawing smirks from the rest of the paralegals.

"It's fun to be a wiseass, isn't it? But in the real world, which you obviously haven't quite joined, our client pays my salary—and yours—which doesn't include making stupid mistakes like the one you just made. So don't do it again."

Martin had visions of smashing one of the office chairs through the plate-glass window. It would be so satisfying to see everyone's expressions as they witnessed an act of violence that served the bottom-line interests of nobody except for maybe the chair company and whoever repaired the glass, but it was really the riffing distortion of the previous night that inspired Martin as he addressed Klint: "This is fucking bullshit. I quit."

"Ouch—I'm so hurt." Klint stepped back to address the remaining paralegals. "Does anyone else want to join Martin? If so, please— the door's open."

In fact, nobody did want to join Martin, which barely tempered his joy as he was escorted off the premises; he couldn't wait to tell

Jay—and Keith—about it. But as he was pulled uptown by the somber streetlights of the nighttime city, he began to worry about the implications of what he had done; not in terms of work—quitting had never been more satisfying, and he was already writing music reviews—but in terms of what he realized with a shudder might be love, at least as he understood it; or at least some form of it, because how else could he explain the queasy anticipation he felt even now as an image of Keith drifted past him, and the sense that this entire day had been a performance for Keith's benefit?

As much as he recognized this, Martin was terrified as he envisioned the walking skeletons, many no older than he was, staggering through the city. He saw a future in which, no matter what he did, he would be branded: the homosexual doctor, the homosexual athlete, the homosexual music critic. Martin Vallence, homosexual. To get AIDS, which seemed like an inevitable consequence of his feelings for Keith, was not just to join the ranks of the walking dead in New York City, with their skin sallow and drawn, their eyes intense and hollow, their limbs wasted and starved, but to be a dead homosexual, as though, no matter what else he did with his life, illicit sex—i.e., abnormal, perverted, immoral, unnatural sex—would always be the essence of his lost existence.

RETURNING TO THE present, Martin—while remaining cognizant of the attacks, and everything they represented—could not help but consider the many ways in which his life—or just life in general—had changed since that night, and mostly for the better. For one thing, AIDS—though hardly a laughing matter—was not the specter it had been; in his case, the medicine had worked, and—except for those first few weeks, when he suffered from fever and aches—he had remained free from symptoms since his diagnosis, almost ten years earlier. Above all, he did not feel "branded," or at least not in a bad way.

This shift in perspective had taken many years, of course, and—as he reflected on it now—went a long way toward explaining why he had embraced a career that had seemed anathema to him after college. His decision to go to law school had occurred roughly when he began having sex with men, and while at the time he had framed the issue in financial terms, it now seemed that the former had been done as a way to compensate for the latter. By pursuing a more conventional career, he could prove to himself—and those around him, or at least as he imagined them—that even a "homosexual" was capable of acting in a "productive" manner, doing his part to oil the gears of innovation that pushed society forward. For many years, he had in fact relished the broader approval and prestige that came with a high-paying position in a Manhattan law firm but with the passage of time and the accompanying acclimation to his desires, this motivation had waned; he no longer relied on his career as a crutch for his identity, to justify his existence, gay or otherwise. Although he could understand why others might view a decision to abandon his job at the height of his earning power—to quit, to give up—with a certain disdain, as if even to consider it at such a point in his life (not to mention what was going on in the rest of the country) was somehow inappropriate or even offensive, he now appreciated that by "coming out," he had largely removed himself from such expectations (putting aside the question of whether they were real or imagined to begin with); in effect, for the first time in his life, he felt liberated, free to do what he liked.

He didn't hate the firm—to the contrary, on many days, he enjoyed it—but there were so many other things he wanted to do in the time that remained to him (and here, HIV was a consideration, given that there was no telling how long the drugs would work); he wanted to plant alpine troughs, to cultivate orchids, to learn to speak Russian and maybe Chinese, and perhaps even to quilt; these were only a few items on a long list. And it was not just a desire to culti-vate new hobbies that quickened his pulse with anticipation; as much as he liked and admired some of his legal colleagues, the demands of his practice had relegated even the possibility of almost any new relationship to the margins for many years. Besides Jay Wellings and his sister, he rarely talked to anyone outside work with any regular-ity, while his dating record had been even more sporadic. Although he—like some significant percentage of nonheterosexual men, in his experience—generally enjoyed sex whenever it suited him (this, too, was a perquisite of gay life he had not initially appreciated), simply by going to a gay bar or (more recently) a website, he wanted to learn more about someone else and (by extension) himself, to—why not just say it?—fall in love for more than a single night or—more typi-cally—a single hour. It was a thought that both excited him and—if he wanted to be perfectly honest—made him nervous, as though he were just seeing the infinite horizons of the seas he hoped to sail.

He considered the many things in his life he had quit—marriage, music writing, the East Village, cigarettes, and more—and concluded that no matter how painful at the time, in retrospect it was always the better course of action. "Quitting is seriously underrated," he noted to Dante, who slowly blinked and yawned, stretching his mouth to its widest point before delicately snapping it shut.

30

Ce Livre pourrait s'appeler Les enfants de
Marx et de Coca-Cola

NEW YORK CITY, 1981. As Maria approached the end
of her third year at Juilliard, she thought of her old life in Pittsburgh
with a sense of accomplishment at having put it so far behind her.
When she went back to visit—usually for a few days at Christmas and
at the beginning of each summer—she could not believe she had spent
so many years in a place to which she now felt so little connection. In
contrast to New York City, Castle Shannon seemed depopulated and
uninviting; it made her think that, even if she didn't become a singer,
she would never leave New York, any more than she might cut off one
of her arms or legs. Just as she was now part of the city, it was now
part of her; this was apparent even to her grandmother and Kathy
Warren—the two people she cared about most in Pittsburgh—who
noted that she was a different person now, more confident, mature, and
well-spoken. She still missed her parents on these trips, but even here
their absence seemed less an open wound than a dull ache. At night,
before she fell asleep, if she occasionally felt a tremor of uncertainty
about the future, she was consoled by the idea that she no longer felt so
detached, and was able to think concretely about the steps she would
need to take to become a professional singer. This, too, was an improvement over her first two years at Juilliard, when the nuances of
technique had threatened to drown her, so that she would wake up in
the middle of the night, panic-stricken and gasping for air. If her past
had once weakened her, she now believed the opposite to be true; in
comparison to her peers, she felt she could get by with less, in both
material and emotional terms. She loved Linda like a sister but did not
go out of her way to find other friends; if she relied on Richie, she felt

that she gave as much as she took, and that they provided each other with an equilibrium that would be important as they approached life after graduation and the looming prospect of launching their careers.

This sense of direction and well-being lasted precisely until one day at the end of her third year when Richie came over to the apartment with startling news: he had been offered a job with a jazz band in Paris. Maria wasn't exactly sure why she was so shocked, given that Richie was finishing up his fourth year and—as she knew but had not really acknowledged, at least to herself—had been auditioning with many bands outside the city. But it made her angry, so that when he sat down and began to discuss how they would visit each other as much as possible, and that his plan was to be back in the city within two years at most, she snapped: "Don't even start—because you don't know. You could end up in Turkey or Sweden or Japan."

"So we'll deal." He tapped his fingers against her arm. "We'll be long-distance for a while, that's all."

"Long-distance," Maria scoffed. "My only regret is that I didn't see from the beginning that we were doomed, not for some stupid reason like the fact that you're black and I'm white, or that I'm taller than you, but because you're a trumpet player, and I'm a fucking soprano, which—"

"Why are you so upset?" Richie laughed, and seemed truly perplexed as he squinted at her. "Isn't this exactly what we said we wanted for each other? Would you really want me to pass this up?"

Maria felt a line of dominoes topple over in her stomach. "No, I'm just worried about how I'm going to handle next year without you," she admitted. "Is that selfish enough?"

"Next year will be fine," he said and placed a hand on her thigh. "Just because we're musicians doesn't mean we don't love each other or that we can't make it work."

As much as Maria wanted to believe this—and even went through the motions of believing it, to the extent that they made love during the weeks before he left and made all the necessary plans to write and talk and see each other as much as possible given the practical constraints—she still felt jarred and unsettled, so that when she sat in bed and looked through the various lenses at her life, it appeared blurry and flawed. She really hated Richie then, and told herself that what they shared was not worth anything, or certainly not the return of that dreadful feeling that made her throat hurt, as though it were coated with her regurgitated past.

THE DAY HE left, Maria turned off the air-conditioning in her room and buried herself under the covers. She slept, and in her dreams she watched him walk to the gate over and over, and each time she felt something different—relief, hatred, sadness, doubt, and finally ambivalence—so that when she woke up, she felt more confused and exhausted than ever. She went into the kitchen, where she found Linda brewing coffee and opening a bottle of red wine. "There's only one cure for what you have," her roommate remarked as she took out two glasses and two mugs. "The coffee-and-red-wine diet."

"I'll be okay," Maria sighed, but she had her doubts. "You know," she mused, "what he said is true—I can't deny it anymore. I mean, here I am lying in bed with a shattered heart, and the truth is I'm freaking out because I haven't practiced in two days. That's not exactly normal, is it?"

Linda brushed a strand of greasy hair away from Maria's sweaty face. "When were you ever normal?"

"I know, never," Maria replied with a fraction of a smile. "Except with Richie—what we had was normal, and it still would be if he hadn't left."

"Maria, you scheduled sex around practice," Linda pointed out. "Not normal. But not wrong, either."

In the ensuing weeks, Maria often returned to this idea as she struggled to maintain her attachment to Richie. When she thought of him, she couldn't decide if she missed him or only wanted to miss him, because she hated the pressure of talking on the phone when it was so expensive, and writing letters was not something she had ever enjoyed. She felt an undeniable tedium as she did these things, which led her to question how much she had loved him in the first place. When she began to suspect that she had not, it sickened her to think that—just as Anna had insinuated—she had exploited Richie in order to taste love, rather than given herself over to it entirely, until it occurred to her that he was doing the same thing to her, which made her angry. Then she would remember waking up next to him and— far removed from any music at all except for the vague symphonies that never really left her head—how much she had loved those moments, and she wanted to run away to Paris, no matter what the consequences, until she remembered that Richie had rented a room in a tiny apartment in the 20th Arrondissement, which was supposedly like the South Bronx of Paris, and she knew she didn't really want to trade in her current life for that.

WHEN RICHIE CAME back to visit for a week in August, Maria took the bus to Queens to meet him at the airport, where he already looked very much *le jazz man* in his chinos, dark green fedora, and goatee. While she wanted to be a little cold, when he smiled sheepishly in the way she had always adored, she rushed into his arms and felt awash in love, so that all her fretting and doubting the past few months seemed inconsequential, and she was glad not to have mentioned any of it to him.

It was a perfect moment, this reunion, which led to a series of even more perfect ones as the days unfolded. Everywhere they went, it seemed, was marked by a memory of a kiss or a laugh or even an argument, so that Maria felt as if they were continually looking through a scrapbook. Even when they went to a jazz club on St. Nicholas in Harlem with a few of his new Parisian friends, it felt to her like the creation of a perfect memory as she drank wine and spoke French in the smoky haze of the room. They even reprised some of their old walks through the dead heat of the summer nights, and Maria felt as if the buildings now watched them with a sad if appreciative sense of nostalgia until she promised them that, no, this was the beginning of something new.

It was not until the last full day of his trip that this tapestry began to unravel. Though Maria had been determined not to let any of her fears or uncertainties spoil anything, she woke up feeling feverish and lonely. "Why can't you stay for another week or two?" she cried, pinning him to the bed.

Richie smiled as he rolled her off and pried her fingers from his arm one by one. "I'll be back—*je te promis*—and right now, we have to get going or we'll be late."

"Okay," she sighed, somewhat regretting the plans they had made to meet Richie's friends for lunch at a café in SoHo. Though she had fully endorsed the idea earlier in the week, now she didn't want to share Richie, particularly with people who would presumably be seeing him all the time when they were back in Paris.

Her mood did not improve at the café, where she felt isolated by her lack of real proficiency in the language—Richie's friends had invited two other French friends—and the discussion veered into a Marxist analysis of modern socialism. After lunch she felt better strolling along the West Side piers with Richie, at least until the leg of her jeans got caught on a cleat and ripped the seam almost all the way up to her butt, which even though they both laughed made her sulk on the train ride back uptown.

Back at the apartment, Richie tried to reassure her. "Maria, come on, don't be upset."

She tried to smile. "Who said I'm upset?"

"You did. This morning." He spoke a little shortly, so that she could tell he was also agitated, but then he sighed. "Look, you've been moody all day."

"Well, you'd be moody, too, if you'd had to sit through that pretentious lunch and then had ripped your jeans."

Richie smiled and caressed her arm. "I'm sorry about lunch—and your jeans. I thought it was just going to be the four of us, like last night."

"I know. I don't care about lunch—or the jeans." Maria looked at him and for a second hated herself for acting imperious and ungrateful. But as she considered the greater uncertainty of their relationship, she felt tentative and precarious, as if she had just crashed through one floor and another was about to give way. This vision was quickly replaced by one of her the following year, rehearsing for what she—and to be fair, everyone else at the school—expected would be a leading role in her first production, and she felt a familiar if somewhat crushing sense of resolve as she spoke. "Richie, we need to break up."

"What? Why? Everything has been so perfect, until today—"

"I know. That's just it."

"What are you talking about?"

"I mean it was too perfect. It's unreal; it's dangerous. It makes me want to throw my life away and never sing another note."

"Christ, it's a vacation, Maria. Why can't you give yourself a break?"

"No, it's more than a vacation." She bit her lip. "Nothing feels real to me anymore, like I'm dreaming or maybe even dead. I fantasize about moving to Paris with you, and it scares me. It's like there's this temptation to forget everything I need to start doing as of next week, because it's going to be a lot, but I have to do it and I can't afford to be lovesick anymore."

"I understand, but you don't have to do this." Richie pulled her into his arms. "You're being extreme. You don't have to destroy yourself to sing."

"How do you know?" she demanded as she wrestled free to face him. "How can you say that when you just don't know?"

"Okay, I don't." He shrugged. "But for both of our sakes, I hope you're wrong."

WHEN MORNING ARRIVED, it would have been hard to believe that this day was any different from so many others except they now looked at each other shyly, more like new lovers than like old, and the conversation was generic and forced, related to the weather and the mundane details of how Richie should pack and get to the airport. Though determined not to go back on her decision, Maria felt sadder and weaker than she had the previous night. She interrupted Richie and filled every pause with her own voice, which sounded shrill and artificial.

At JFK they spent a few more awkward minutes at the gate until they heard Richie's boarding call.

"That's you, isn't it," she managed with a gulp.

"Maria, whatever happens—"

"Don't," she begged. "Last night, I didn't—"

"No, you did," he said. "You were right."

She took a deep, trembling breath and began to respond.

"Don't. It's okay," he said, but his eyes didn't quite meet hers.

She understood that to survive these next few seconds she would have to be bigger and stronger—even inhuman—and for once did not have to summon any courage to make this part of herself appear but simply allowed it to happen, even though there wasn't the remotest chance she was going to sing. As if she had put on a costume or a coat of armor, it was someone new—or at least in disguise—who gingerly wrapped her arms around him, though they barely touched as she bent down and kissed both of his cheeks for what she knew would be the last time. With a distant and bemused smile on her face, she straightened up and addressed the air over Richie's head. "Goodbye, darling," she said and kept her eyes from meeting his as he walked around the barrier to hand his boarding pass to the attendant.

She waved one last time and was halfway back to the terminal exit before she leaned against a dingy pay phone and laughed: when had she ever called him *darling*? The answer, of course, was never; yet it had come out so effortlessly, like she had rehearsed it a thousand times. She turned around with the faint expectation that the footsteps she heard behind her belonged to Richie. Seconds passed; he didn't appear, and—as she had to admit—she didn't want him to. She pushed through the glass doors and from the buzz in her ears knew she might have been crying except for the lack of tears.

On the sidewalk, she listened to the empty honks of taxis and the intermittent roar of a passing bus as she waited for her own. It was over ninety degrees outside, and though she could not completely escape the sense of having succumbed to something, it was also a transformation that left her impervious to the hot, muggy air, which seemed like a blanket that could easily be thrown off the bed. Her heart raced as she considered what had just happened, along with the thrilling certainty that whatever grief or loss or failure she felt was momentary, nothing but clouds that could be burned away in the blazing sun of a gigantic career.

31 ....

The Intermittences of the Heart

VIENNA, 1865. When Lucien returned to Vienna at the end of July, he learned that Eduard's difficulties at the opera house were more severe than he had let on. The foundation and exterior walls of the structure were complete—and the addition of the roof imminent—but a committee of retired military men and architects, all of whom Eduard knew and detested but who had managed to get the ear of the emperor, were attempting to mandate design alterations—ranging from the addition of a huge pediment on the façade to a large outer staircase leading up to the entrance—to enhance the "imperial aura of the monument." While their jurisdiction to issue such an edict was being scrutinized by Eduard's allies both in and out of the government—with newspapers running editorials both for and against—the tension throughout the city was palpable; when they went out in the evening, Lucien could feel the stares of Eduard's enemies boring into their backs, and rooms were divided into clusters of those who could or could not be trusted.

One morning—not long into September—Lucien woke up and found Eduard still in bed beside him. "Are you sick?" he asked.

"I'm sick of fighting," Eduard mumbled.

"I know you are," Lucien sighed. "But you can't give up now."

"I can't?"

Lucien laughed uneasily. "I'm not even going to answer that—"

"Why? Just because everything has worked out in the past?" Eduard rolled away. "There's a first for everything."

Lucien ignored him. "Don't you have a meeting?"

"I do," Eduard confirmed. He sat up for a few seconds and then collapsed. "But I need more sleep."

Lucien put his hand on Eduard's shoulder. "Are you sure you're all right?"

Eduard pulled away. "Lucien—please—you're not helping."

"Okay, then—I'll leave you alone." Lucien went to the dining room, where he sullenly ate breakfast, trying to decide if he was more angry about Eduard's dismissive tone or fearful about his despondency. When Eduard emerged some time later, Lucien was relieved to see him dressed, but with his feelings still raw from the earlier exchange, he made a point of ignoring his lover as Eduard rushed out the door.

As it turned out, Eduard managed to make his appointment, and when he returned home that afternoon was contrite. "I'm sorry about this morning," he said. "Don't worry—I'm not giving up."

"Your demons?" responded Lucien, also regretting his earlier anger.

"You might say that." Eduard nodded and smiled slyly as he accepted Lucien's outstretched hand and brought it to his lips.

OVER THE NEXT few months, though the battle continued on many fronts, Lucien made a point to console Eduard whenever he could: he massaged his neck, he brought pomegranate juice to his office, he filled the apartment with black roses and violets. He helped Heinrich plan menus for several dinner parties they hosted for members of the government and nobility whose friendship was deemed critical by Eduard. Though it didn't come naturally, Lucien enjoyed playing a supporting role; he especially liked going to the market with Heinrich, who would suggest a dish with Greek olives, at which point Lucien would say, "No—let's use the Italian ones, which Eduard likes better." And though he was conscious of the fact that Heinrich in certain ways knew both of them better than anyone—and had probably even proposed the Greek olives because he knew that Lucien would enjoy correcting him—it still pleased him to think that, in sum, if one considered not only Eduard's tastes in food or clothing—in which Heinrich probably did have the upper hand—but also the curve of his back, the texture of his hair, the quiet whimpers he sometimes made under Lucien's weight, or even the way he tended to sleep on his stomach with one leg bent and the other straight, nobody—not even Heinrich—knew Eduard as well as he did, which if it was not the only meaning of love struck him as a most plausible one.

TOWARD THE END of the winter, Eduard and his allies achieved several tactical victories to ensure that his original design was to be implemented with only minor alterations. Construction resumed at full speed, and his mood improved greatly, at least until April arrived and brought with it a new and unforeseen problem—if not exactly unprecedented in Vienna—in the form of rain. It started around the middle of the month, which caused little concern until a second week passed without any real interruption, and then a third; when it wasn't drizzling, it was a downpour, and at all times a cold, dank mist seemed to seep through even the thickest walls. Lucien slept under three blankets, and even the usually imperturbable Heinrich walked through the apartment muttering about the green mold that crept into undershirts, bedsheets, buttonholes, and shoe eyelets. At the end of the third week, the Danube overran its banks, and the army was dispatched to build barriers of sandbags.

Lucien felt sick with anxiety each time he looked out the window to assess the infinite layers of gray sky, but when he accompanied Eduard through the fog to check the opera house, he did not have to feign optimism. Though it was unnerving to see the waters rising on the other side of the sandbags, which in turn were stacked higher by the soldiers, there was a majestic quality to the structure that went beyond its sheer heft. Except for a few leaks here and there—mostly backstage—the roof kept the inside dry, and in the somber lamplight, it was easy to imagine the theater filled with operagoers. Several times Lucien and Eduard emerged from these inspections into a deluge, but with the water streaming off the curving dome of the roof in thick, opaque sheets, the building felt as impenetrable as a massive ocean liner. While waiting under the arcade, Lucien always made a point to grip Eduard's hand, and he felt reassured when the gesture was returned.

ONE MORNING—it WAS now May—the rain stopped. Lucien opened his eyes and detected a strange and forgotten illumination coming through the drapes. "Eduard, look!" he cried but reached out to find only rumpled sheets. He quickly dressed and ran downstairs, where Heinrich confirmed that Eduard had already left for the site.

Outside, the sidewalks steamed and glistened in the hazy white light, and as Lucien walked past the construction on the Ringstrasse—on the western side of the site, with all the new government buildings—he barely noticed that it was effectively underwater, with only columns and pilings poking through the surface like a graveyard of masts, or that, to the north, many of the streets were now canals, with water lapping at the windows and doors. He took his usual detour to Grabenstrasse, which though wet was not flooded. Many of the shopkeepers were bringing their goods out to dry in the sun, while farther ahead on the Stephansplatz, only a few puddles dotted the field of cobblestones. Here he paused to admire the cathedral's shining spire, which seemed to offer a benevolent grace and power, and even inspired him to whisper a contingent prayer to a god he had never really believed in.

Running down Kärntnerstrasse, he saw the opera house, and his spirits lifted at the sight of the copper wings of the rooftop, which hovered majestically above the last remnants of silver fog. As he got closer, however, his exuberance was tempered by the realization that the sandbags had given way, so that the entire structure was circled by a moat, perhaps fifteen feet deep. He stood on the edge and peered through the tops of the entranceways—the doors had been pushed open by the flood—into the vast interior. He called out to Eduard but heard only his own voice echoing back across the water. He yelled again and this time heard his name return as soft as a whisper.

"Eduard?" he repeated and was met by the same whispered response.

He found a plank of wood about the size of a small door, on which he was able to kneel precariously and paddle forward. He ducked under the entrance and went through to the lobby, where the water was still and flat except for the debris that seemed to hover ominously in the shadows beneath the surface. He continued forward into the auditorium, where, after catching his breath, he again called out.

"Lucien," Eduard responded, but in a soft, hesitant tone that Lucien almost didn't recognize.

He looked up and saw Eduard perched on a scaffold near the very top of the dome, at least a hundred feet up. He could not suppress a cry of surprise and then fear as he strained to see. "Eduard," he yelled. "What—what are you doing up there?"

"It's over," Eduard replied after a few seconds. Though he spoke softly, there was something about the watery acoustics of the theater that made it seem as if he were only inches away. "They're tearing it down."

"What do you mean?" Lucien replied automatically, as it began to occur to him that Eduard was not just inspecting something.

"It's done," his lover said. "Destroyed. Enjoy it while you can."

There was a flat, hollow quality to Eduard's voice that alarmed Lucien, even as he struggled to understand. "But—but I'm sure it's not as bad as it looks," he responded, trying to sound confident. "Once it drains, it'll be fine. Maybe it'll push things back a few months, but the outside looks—well, it looks beautiful. Did you see some of the other buildings? They're much worse—there's hardly anything left at all—"

"It's just an excuse," Eduard vaguely replied.

"What are you talking about?" Lucien cried.

"'I hope you won't be too offended, Herr van der Null,'" Eduard began in an affected, imperious voice before continuing in a harder, sarcastic tone. "Oh no, thank you, Excellency, why would I be offended? I've only given fifteen years of my life to this, so of course I understand why political expediency demands that you do whatever you must to please the general's cousin. Why let a little flooding go to waste? These things happen! Such is life! Good day, sire!"

Lucien stared up, perplexed. "Who is this?"

Eduard sighed. "I saw the emperor this morning. They're going to demolish it and use the committee plans."

Eduard's words—now that Lucien understood what was happening—seemed to hang in the air for a second before they froze and like a piece of ice fell down to break into shards. The water dripped around him as he responded. "Eduard, they can't," he said and realized that his hands were shaking where they gripped the board on which he sat. "They'll have to kill me—both of us. We'll fight. You know that just because the emperor says one thing it doesn't mean he can't say something else the next day."

"I—I don't know, Lucien," Eduard sighed. "It's too much. I never thought I would say this, but I can't see this destroyed."

Lucien could not contain his dismay. "Eduard, this isn't you talking—it's—it's your demons."

Eduard responded in a resigned tone that—because of its flat, conversational quality—frightened Lucien even more. "You've said it a thousand times, Lucien—it's irreplaceable. You don't build something like this more than once in your life. Losing this makes me less than nothing."

The implications of this statement—not only for the present situation but for their past—took Lucien's breath away. He felt a new tremor of panic as he considered how he could possibly reach Eduard, whose despair surpassed anything Lucien had ever experienced, even during his darkest moments in Munich. It seemed to unveil a wider gulf between them than he had ever imagined, and he saw nothing in his own life—or at least his artistic life—he could use to convey his empathy without sounding condescending and false. Yet even as these doubts occurred, he brushed them away with a desperate certainty that what he and Eduard shared transcended any artistic crisis. He stopped himself from shaking and focused on the still, yellow light surrounding him.

"You can't be nothing," he said, "because to love you would make me nothing, too—and that's not what we are. We're not nothing— I know you don't think that."

Eduard seemed to waver for several seconds before he spoke. "Lucien . . . you know . . . I love you," he said, and there was a tender quality to his voice that led Lucien to think he was getting through.

"I'm coming up there," Lucien cried and started to paddle toward the scaffold upon which Eduard was perched. "We'll go home—Heinrich is making lunch—we'll go back to bed and sleep." He paused to look up, and Eduard took a step toward the ladder from which he could descend. Now drifting, Lucien felt the light on his face and, sick with relief, thanked whatever power had led Eduard to back away. "Eduard—be careful—"

But Eduard did not pivot around as Lucien expected and instead launched himself off the platform. He fell through the gloom, his arms extended like wings, his eyes no longer silver but soft and unfocused as he spoke his final words. "I'll miss you," he whispered before he hit the water, where the heavy splash echoed beneath the harrowing dismay of Lucien's untrained screams.

32

Do You Want Chillwave or Do You Want the Truth?

NEW YORK CITY, 2001. On Thursday morning after the attacks, Martin went to work and arranged an appointment with the managing partner. His intention was to give notice as quickly as possible, but when he walked into the corner office, he was shocked to find his dead father, Hank, sitting behind the desk. Although Hank was now a lean sixty-something man, his hawkish eyes and jutting chin left no doubt in Martin's mind as to his identity. "How's it hanging, Marty?" he asked as he removed his sunglasses from where they had been perched on the top of his head.

Martin did not respond for a few seconds as he debated how to react; he knew he didn't really have time to consider the logic or illogic of what he saw but simply needed to accept it, to adjust to the unexpected terms of this confrontation and proceed accordingly. If he had learned anything in his career, it was that nothing ever went according to plan, and his ability to maintain his cool under the tensest of negotiations was part of the reason he could even entertain the idea of quitting.

"I want to give notice," Martin announced, but in an unconcerned tone generally reserved to describe last week's weather. "I've been thinking about it for a while," he said before alluding to a deal he had recently wrapped up. "I want to leave before I get too deep into anything else."

"Come on, Marty." His father shook his head. "You're one of our top earners. I know this terrorist shit has thrown everyone for a loop, but why don't you take a few days to think it over? Take a vacation if you want—come in next week and we'll talk about it . . ."

Martin hated how reasonable this sounded. "Thanks—I appreciate that," he began slowly, "but like I said, it's been on my mind for a while—Tuesday just kind of sealed it for me."

"Early retirement, eh?" Hank scoffed. "So what are you going to do? Make cookies?"

"I'm not sure yet, to be honest," Martin admitted with some candor.

"Sure you can handle it?" Hank asked. "Have you ever not worked?"

Martin understood that Hank was only trying to get under his skin, that he was embarrassed by the prospect of his son's early retirement, as if to lead a life of leisure had a certain effete quality that did not belong in the masculine world of the corner office in which they now sat.

"I guess I'm not as motivated as I used to be," Martin agreed somewhat evasively, feeling that this would be the best strategy, though as he said the words, he felt them resonate; it wasn't hard to remember when he had enjoyed the prestige of working for a top firm in a city where such associations meant access to certain clubs and restaurants that had once interested him.

"Yeah, some people lose the drive," Hank continued in a predictably dismissive tone.

This provoked Martin. "Don't you ever get sick of this place?"

"No, not really," answered Hank in a grave manner that offered Martin no satisfaction. "It's actually worse when I'm not here for too long, you know, when your mother's dragging me to all those crazy fund-raisers, or the fucking opera. I want to shoot myself."

Martin—again resolved to move ahead with his plan—could only shrug. "I've never had that problem."

"I've always said you cocksuckers get off easy," Hank noted wryly as he stood up and looked through his son.

Martin recognized this to be the end of the meeting and the mark of his new beginning as someone off his father's radar, so it didn't seem worth arguing the point. "In that respect I guess we do."

Surprisingly, Hank's expression softened, and Martin considered confessing some of his real reasons for wanting to retire—which ironically enough were connected to being gay—but before he could say anything, his father spoke, softly, as though confessing a secret. "The truth is, Marty"—he smiled—"I'd give just about anything not to be so addicted to cunt."

Martin laughed uneasily but gratefully, knowing that this was exactly the kind of comment—along with everything it represented—that he wanted to leave behind with the job. With a smile, he stood up and shook hands with the man for what he expected to be the last time, knowing that he would most likely be able to avoid him during the next two weeks, given that they were separated by two floors.

Back downstairs in his office, Martin stared at his bookshelves with relief and—to be fair—some sadness that he would never again consult *Corbin on Contracts*. He decided that he felt a new appreciation for Hank's brand of pragmatism, which however crude contained an element of honesty that had long eluded Martin, at least until now. Beyond any nostalgia, he acknowledged a new desire to forgive Hank, and as the logical part of his brain asked exactly what for, it finally occurred to Martin that he was thinking not of his dead father but of himself.

THAT AFTERNOON, MARTIN arrived home in time to take Dante to the vet, where he was promptly diagnosed with ringworm and taken to the back for treatment. By now, Martin not only had acclimated to the idea of permanently adopting Dante but also was even made so disturbingly bereft by this small separation that he wondered if he might be approaching some line of sanity.

"Do I look insane to you?" he asked the receptionist.

"Yeah, kind of," she answered. "Do I?"

Reassured by this exchange, he sat down to wait and was distracted by a small "adoption center"—a few cages, actually, stacked on top of one another—that sat near the front desk and in which he noticed a cat that looked strikingly like Dante, i.e., small and gray, with the same bottle green eyes. Martin tried to ignore a nauseating certainty that like any obsession, his new one with Dante could be sated only by adding more to the mix, so he pretended to inquire casually with the receptionist about the cat, which he soon learned was a female; like Dante she was a Russian Blue, a year old, or slightly younger.

"And nobody's adopted her?" Martin asked incredulously, as if the streets were not teeming with stray cats.

"Not yet," she answered and added that the cat in question had been brought in from a Dumpster in Park Slope a few months earlier along with a litter of kittens.

"Where are the kittens?"

"They're gone." She shrugged. "Nobody wants a mother—she's 'used'—and she's a little stunted from having kittens so early."

Martin expressed renewed horror at the callousness of the world.

The receptionist laughed at him. "If you're so upset, why don't you take her?"

"I might," said Martin, trying to sound like he needed to be convinced. But in a gesture to his more pragmatic side, he resolved to take a few minutes to ponder the idea.

He leaned back in his seat and observed an older woman sitting across from him who had four carriers in front of her, each with a different pair of eyes peering out. That's me in ten years, Martin thought morosely as he noted her disheveled trench coat and the frayed navy blue scarf tied around her head, although on second glance he decided she was not inelegant and was even pleasantly reclusive behind a large pair of sunglasses. There was something familiar about her, and as he tried to figure out where he might have seen her, she pushed up her sunglasses and addressed him.

"You really should have more than one," she stated, having obviously overheard Martin's conversation.

After his earlier experience with Hank, Martin was not unprepared to recognize his dead mother, Jane, or an older version of her who had somehow moved to New York City to live with cats. It was not just her voice he recognized but her frank blue eyes, which had not aged at all. As he had done with Hank, he resisted the urge to shout or perhaps weep—or otherwise to demand an explanation for why this was happening—and instead considered how best to address her. Nor could he completely ignore a slight annoyance at the intrusive nature of the advice, which as much as he wanted to hear he had not exactly asked for.

"How many—how many do you have?" he managed in what he feared might come off as a needlessly restrained, if not paranoid tone, after deciding that—at least to start—it would be best to keep the conversation on point.

"Seven." Jane spoke softly but also slightly rolled her eyes as if slightly mocking herself—or possibly him—just as she used to do. "They're my children now."

"I can appreciate that," Martin responded more affectionately, and then he told her how he had come to adopt Dante. He considered how much easier it was to talk to his mother as an adult and felt gratified as they spent a few minutes discussing cat food and—of all things—flushable litter. Then he remembered all that they had never said to each other, and unlike when he was a teenager, he saw no reason now to hide anything from her. "I'm never having real children," he said. "For obvious reasons."

If his intent was to surprise her, her placid smile contained no trace of anything but acknowledgment; she clearly knew what he meant. "I think you're being a little too literal," she replied. "Parenting is as much about responsibility—and not just for someone else—as it is about conception."

Martin resisted the impulse to argue with her, to tell her that, except for a few admittedly serious mistakes, he had been responsible, or at least as responsible as most people he knew. The achingly familiar quality of her voice reminded him of when they used to discuss books, and he admired a degree of conversational finesse he now realized was very similar to what had brought him so much success in his work as a deal maker.

"You absolutely should adopt her," she continued. "She'll bring you a lot of joy."

Martin nodded. Something had changed between them; she seemed so much less wounded and unhappy than in his memories, and he was encouraged by the idea that the same could no doubt be said of him. "What do you think I should name her?" he asked with a laugh, pointing at the cardboard sign attached to the outside of the cage. "She's obviously not a Mango."

"Given that you already have Dante, wouldn't Beatrice be appropriate?" she proposed, using the Italian pronunciation.

"Beatrice," Martin repeated as if hypnotized. He remembered how he and Jane had always shared an intuition, and if he felt some regret at how needlessly frightened of it he had been as a teenager, he was now consoled by the thought that they were more like reflections of each other, each able to follow where the other chose to walk.

He went to the cage where Beatrice cowered and trembled in the corner and looked up at him with wet eyes, much more fearful than Dante. Her face was also heart-shaped, but smaller and more angular, except for some very long and prominent nose whiskers that in the reflection of the light gave her the appearance of a walrus. She was really quite tiny, Martin realized, and a bit bedraggled, with some of her fur matted down on the sides of her face and along her belly. Her tail, he further noticed, appeared to be only five or six inches long— perhaps half the length of Dante's—with a little knob on the end, which though not raw or infected made him wonder if it had been cut off in what he imagined had not been an easy life. She covered her face with a paw, and he noticed that this, too, was misshapen; it looked like a mitten. He counted at least seven toes, including one that had an impressive nail in the shape of a lobster claw.

"Did you see her foot?" he asked as he turned back to his mother, who had pushed the sunglasses down over her eyes again.

"She's polydactyl," she replied, her tone still recognizable to him.

"You get that in cats, but it's good luck, I promise—take her home, and you'll see."

THAT AFTERNOON, THE three of them—Martin, Dante, and Beatrice—arrived at Martin's house, where he was disappointed to find that Beatrice was extremely skittish and refused to budge from a spot under the bed, even after he made clear his intention to rescue her from the cruel life she had thus far endured. Days passed, and he was at times disconcerted by his failure even to touch her. Dante by contrast was completely fixated; he spent hours roaming the perimeter of the bed and whining until she emerged to eat or use the litter box, at which point he stayed two inches behind her unless Beatrice—clearly ambivalent about the attention—lost patience and gave him a quick swat in the nose with one of her big paws.

As Martin remembered how much calmer things had been with just Dante, he questioned his attachment to the cats, not to mention his mother's advice. Although Beatrice gradually emerged and began to explore the house, she still seemed petrified of Martin, and would dash out of any room where he happened to find her. After two weeks she still refused to eat if he remained in the kitchen, except when he offered her a piece of cocktail shrimp or a slice of turkey breast—but only from Zabar's, and no more than one day old—which she would deign to receive after emitting a demure, plaintive meow, no louder than the creak of a closing door.

As more weeks passed, he knew that there was no possibility of giving her back; Dante would never have forgiven him, and his mother's words about responsibility continued to resonate. He tried to be patient and remind himself—now that he was giving himself to the pursuit of art and maybe even love—that there was really no deadline. It wasn't like she was ripping up the furniture or breaking things, and he was charmed on those occasions when she did allow him to remain in her presence, for she did not seem ungrateful, just shy. If Martin was surprised to note the existence of such rarefied tastes in one whose life had to this point allowed so little opportunity to indulge—such as when he presented her with a plate of shrimp, cut into tiny bites—he in no way discouraged her, for he did not want to deny his own awakening in this regard.

33

This Screaming Girl Has Suddenly Realized That the Body Lying Under the Blanket Is That of Her Mother

NEW YORK CITY, 1981. Just as Maria had hoped, the resolve she felt after breaking up with Richie catapulted her into her final year at Juilliard with unprecedented confidence. She sang with more poise and clarity, had better timing, and mastered difficult coloratura that just a year earlier would have been beyond her, all of which more than compensated for the occasional pang of missing Richie. A few weeks into the semester, when she auditioned for *The Magic Flute*, she felt only a trace of suspense as she waited for the results: who, she asked, could be better suited for the Queen of the Night, the unhinged, vengeful matriarch attempting to incite her daughter to murder? The answer, at least this year at Juilliard, was nobody, and Maria promptly began work on her first fully staged production, complete with costumes, makeup, and sets; a famous conductor in residence who ran music rehearsals; and a famous director in residence who staged the singers.

The weeks rushed by in a frenzy of preparation; in addition to her music and stage rehearsals, Maria studied biographies of Mozart, read theses on Egyptian initiation rituals and Masonic imagery, and scoured the Juilliard archives for audio and visual recordings, the highlight of which was a 1967 Lucia Popp "Wrath of Hell" aria. Except this aria was so excruciatingly wondrous that—as Maria absorbed it for a third time—she was literally knocked unconscious by the vengeance and fury on display. She slumped to the floor, where she remained until the next morning, when she was revived by an alarmed librarian who discovered her in the A/V room adjacent to the stacks. Apparently uninjured but groggy, Maria staggered back to her apartment, where in a state approaching the catatonic she realized that all of her brilliant plans over the past weeks were nothing but a flimsy façade. Her mind was a void; her ideas about how to bathe each note of her Queen of the Night in the mystical and Masonic waters from which the opera arose had vanished, and worse, the music now seemed inane and nonsensical, just as the idea of singing what was a very challenging part now fatigued her with its pointlessness.

Mystified about the reasons for this condition and increasingly demoralized, she slept for a few hours. When she woke up, she found Linda in the kitchen making toast. "I know what's wrong," her roommate declared after Maria had given her a sullen overview of the situation. "But you're not going to want to hear it."

"What? Tell me."

"Don't get mad."

"I'm not—just tell me."

Linda shrugged. "You're blocked."

"Blocked?"

"Yeah—it's been what, like two months since Richie, and before that you were used to it all the time."

Maria rubbed her eyes. "What are you saying?"

"I'm saying you need sex."

"Right," Maria scoffed as she remembered why Linda's refusal to take problems seriously sometimes got on her nerves.

"Sorry to break it to you," Linda replied. "But you can only work so much."

"So, what?" Maria replied, now irritated. "Am I supposed to just pick up some guy off the street?"

"Mope all you want," Linda said as she rinsed her plate off in the sink, "but you're the one who passed out in the library and spent the day walking around like a zombie only three weeks before your Queen of the Night."

ALTHOUGH MARIA DID not concede the point to Linda, the conversation motivated her to cast off the yoke of sedentary ambivalence in favor of a walk to campus, where she spent a few minutes idly staring at the bulletin board. She spotted an announcement for a master class being offered by Ronald Spelton and knew she should go—she had been planning to—given that Spelton was a Juilliard alum currently playing Rodrigo in *Don Carlos* at the Met. As she stood wavering, someone—and for some reason, she could tell it was a man even before she turned her head—walked up and addressed her. "If you're weighing your options," he said, nodding at the flyer and speaking with a slight accent she couldn't quite place, "Ronald's excellent."

Maria tried to decide if she was annoyed that a stranger had offered unsolicited advice but figured that, under the circumstances, any distraction was a good idea. Also—whoever he was—he seemed important; he was maybe fifty or so, his wide shoulders and slight paunch giving him the look of a knighted actor of the British stage, while a bronze hue to his skin and an impressive nose made her suspect he was Italian or Greek. She guessed that he was a singer and—based on his first-name relationship with Ronald Spelton and a certain ease with which he stood, hands in pockets, as if above the fray—a successful one. "Yeah, I might go," she said and immediately regret-ted the impetuousness of her reply. "I'm sorry," she quickly added. "I'm having one of the worst days ever."

"I know what that's like." He nodded. "Bad lesson?"

She shook her head. "I have a Queen of the Night in three weeks, and I'm feeling overwhelmed and unmotivated."

"*Quelle horreur!*" he said, but then added, "I'm sure you'll be fine."

"How can you be so sure?"

"I can't." He grinned. "But I thought you might like to hear it."

Maria smiled wryly. "I guess I'll take what I can get," she offered before she looked at him more closely. "Please don't take this the wrong way," she continued, "but you look kind of familiar."

"Maybe you've heard me sing?" he suggested, and for a second Maria could see him as a young man, eager to impress, as he affably held out his hand. "Leo Metropolis."

"Leo Metropolis!" she cried, forgetting her anomie.

He laughed. "Is that a problem?"

"No, no—of course not." Maria now felt embarrassed and wished that she had met him a day earlier, before her collapse, which had left her feeling so weak and tentative. "It's just that my roommate saw you in *Walküre* like five years ago," she managed, "and still talks about how great it was, and—well—she'll die when she hears I met you."

"I'm happy to be of service," he said, but in a distant, inscrutable tone that reminded her he was an enigmatic figure in the opera world, a leading heldentenor who performed rarely and only with certain companies, almost always in Europe except for the rare appearance at the Met. Moreover, he refused to give interviews or appear in pub-licity photographs, which helped to explain why Maria didn't recog-nize him. Many who had been fortunate enough to hear him—and his performances were often unannounced—claimed he was the great-est Wagnerian of the century, while others tended to dismiss him as a spectacle, hardly deserving of accolades. Nobody knew where he lived, although she had heard rumors that he was exceedingly wealthy and when not singing could most often be found in castles, seaside villas, and luxury apartment buildings like Anna's.

Maria felt childish for having complained about anything, like he was really going to care. She wanted to emulate him instead of falling back on the brash arrogance and disdain that had possessed her since she'd marched out of the terminal after breaking up with Richie. She saw herself as shrill and forced, displaying a lack of dimension that had literally made her susceptible to being knocked out. "Can I ask you something?" she ventured in a halting but earnest tone as it occurred to her that he was in a position to help. "About singing? Do you ever have doubts? I mean, would you still be a singer if you could do anything else?"

"It's not an easy question," he said before reflecting. "Right now I'd say yes—there's nothing I would rather do—but if you had asked me at another point in my life, I would have said something very different."

"Why—what happened?" asked Maria, at once incredulous and despondent, because she had been expecting a more reaffirming answer from someone in his position.

"When I was your age—maybe a little older—I thought everything was perfect with my career and my life, and maybe it was—I don't know, it's always hard to judge, except for those few minutes right after a performance, when every doubt seems far away—but then I had some real problems, not so much with my singing but with the relationships in my life, and I wasn't old enough to understand that turmoil is inevitable—especially for those of us in the theater—and I ended up in a crisis. I was so sure that my voice was hurting me—or more important, those I cared for—that I gave up singing. I vowed never to enter an opera house again."

Stunned by this information, Maria took a moment to respond. "But how—how was it hurting you?"

He lowered his voice almost to a whisper. "I didn't think I could do both—sing and live. I thought that to sing with any passion was making me too vulnerable, so that I felt wounded both on *and* off the stage, and also too self-centered, oblivious to the suffering of those around me or—even if I was aware—incapable of helping. When you perform, everything seems so alive, and—as much as I tried—I couldn't make myself acknowledge *real life* because by comparison it was so tedious and messy and unrehearsed." He laughed quietly and sighed. "It took me a long time to learn how to separate the two, which also isn't easy, because you can't be two completely different people—you have to give yourself to the stage, obviously, but you have to maintain some kind of distance, too."

"How did you come back?" she asked and already felt a little bereft as she considered the answer, and what it might entail for her or, for that matter, already had. For years she had told herself that there was nothing she wouldn't do to be the best singer she could be, yet the resolution now sounded hollow and frightening.

"One night I went to the opera, and I realized as I was watching it—I was sitting there with tears streaming down my face the entire time, just shy of sobbing, much to the horror of those around me, I'm sure!—I realized it was killing me *not* to sing. I knew I had ostracized myself from what I loved most, and for those few hours I saw my life the way you sometimes do—like you're viewing it as another person—and I knew that I was barely going through the motions, not really enjoying anything or anyone, like I was already dead. There was no love in my life! I knew that I *had* to sing, that it was the only way I could offer myself any kind of beauty or forgiveness, which is ultimately what mattered most. I thought singing was the problem—and maybe it was—but from then on,

I knew it was also the solution." As he finished this thought, he focused his attention on her. "Was that more than you expected?"

"I'm not sure," Maria said, "but thank you—it's helpful." As she spoke, she felt a shift in her perspective, something indefinable but present, so that the previous hours seemed no more consequential than a few errant clouds crossing the vista of her life. As she and Leo spent a few more minutes idly chatting—about some of his favorite roles and her upcoming *Magic Flute*—she could imagine herself like him, a working singer with a battle-weary sense of pride and resignation, which was an end that—at least for now—seemed better to justify the means.

A FEW MINUTES later she arrived at Ronald Spelton's master class. She found a seat near the back of the amphitheater—not surprisingly, it was crowded—and tried to enjoy the mild buzz of affirmation that continued to spread through her in the wake of her conversation with Leo Metropolis. She felt like she had taken a big fall but with his help had landed safely in a pool of water. The only problem was that not more than two seconds after Ronald stood up and began to speak, her resolve was shattered by a dry-throat, finger-biting, twirling-the-ends-of-her-hair kind of attraction for him that had her fanning herself in a room not much warmer than a refrigerator. Despite her earlier talk with Linda—which she now remembered with renewed annoyance—this desire was as completely unexpected as it was undeniable, and she could not take her eyes off him as he paced back and forth in front of the room, lecturing and singing in what might as well have been Martian. Beyond her long-standing attraction for solidly framed men, she wasn't exactly sure why he did it for her; he was probably thirty years older than she was—even older than Leo—and more than a bit trollish, with thick eyebrows, lumpy shoulders, and the perpetually surly leer of someone about to tell a dirty joke; but she could not deny the intensity of his bleak, serious eyes, or how his clothes were tight in all the right places, and she mentally undressed him a thousand times in an equal number of seconds.

When the class ended, she lingered in her seat for several minutes before she went to the front and carved out a position on the outskirts of a ring of students. She stared down at least two others—did they have the same idea?—who tried to insist they were in back of her, but she exerted her seniority to push them ahead. Finally it was her turn, and she plied him with a series of questions related to interpretation, agents, and possible career trajectory—the answers to all of which she already knew—as they walked out of the building.

They paused in the somber glow of the November sunset. "I don't know why," Maria remarked, "but this time of day makes me feel seasick."

"Transitions are tough." Ronald nodded. "Let me guess: you're a night person?"

"I am," Maria confirmed. "I'm always in a daze until three or four in the afternoon."

"That's not a bad thing for a singer, although it can be hell when you have a matinee."

"Or a final dress," Maria pointed out.

"Or a final dress," Ronald agreed.

The conversation seemed to have reached a dead end, and as they stood on the corner of Broadway, Maria decided to move beyond this charade of pleasantries. "So where are you headed?"

"Back to my hotel for a few minutes, then I'm meeting some friends for dinner—"

"You don't have an apartment?" Maria interrupted, determined to keep the conversation on point.

Ronald appeared to hesitate for a second, and Maria wondered if he was on to her, for his tone was perhaps a trace more seductive as he explained, "I always stay at the Callaghan."

Maria suppressed a shudder. "What's that like?"

"It's not bad. I have a little suite with a kitchenette, and there's a nice view of Central Park from the balcony."

"I bet I've seen better," Maria declared in a display of truth and confrontation as she thought of Anna's apartment.

Ronald grimaced and scratched at his tooth, which gleamed through a slightly oily five-o'clock shadow surrounding his mouth. "It's only two blocks away if you want to see for yourself."

Maria looked at her watch. She was supposed to meet Anna in just over an hour. "Okay," she said. "Lead the way."

A few breathless minutes later they were at the hotel, and after what seemed like seconds after that they were on the elevator up to his suite. Then they were inside, and Maria heard the click of the door over the internal din of her racing heart. As she looked past the foyer toward the bed, where the floral print on the bedspread started to kaleidoscope, she wondered what she was doing here, and whether she should politely excuse herself and leave like a fellow guest of the hotel who happened to have stepped into the wrong room.

Ronald tossed his coat on a chair and invited her to do the same. "Um, I don't—," she began to say, hesitating.

"Don't worry, I won't bite." He winked at her. "Unless you ask me to."

"Cut the crap." Maria looked back at him and frowned as she wondered how she could be so attracted to such a lecherous character, yet at this same moment she could not resist finding out what he really looked like under those ill-fitting clothes, and whether he was as good in bed as he was on the stage.

"I sincerely apologize," Ronald said, his tone dripping with insincerity as she dropped her coat and then allowed him to take her hand in his own and bring it to his lips. He looked up at her, and it was only at this moment that he, too, seemed to waver. "Just so we're on the same page," he went on as he lightly kissed each one of her fingers in turn, "this *is* why you're here?"

"I thought," Maria responded in a low, breathy tone that almost made her laugh at the idea of playing such a sexpot, "you were going to give me the name of your agent."

She pulled him up to her and leaned into him, close enough that his taut belly jutted up against her own, close enough that she could see the wrinkles around his eyes and his thinning hair, and so that she could even smell the slightly foreign and mildewed aroma of a man so much older than any she had ever experienced, and like a cheap wine all of this left her both nauseated and intoxicated. She was filled with suspense as she again wondered whether she was actually going ahead with this, but as she lowered her lips to meet his she knew the answer was yes, apparently, she was.

Ronald returned the kiss with some violence before he pushed her away. "Let's not rush," he said as he unhitched the top button of her jeans and caressed the small patch of exposed skin above the line of her underwear. He fell back onto the bed and pulled Maria on top of him, where she straddled him for a few seconds before he rolled her off and then somewhat more forcefully unfastened the remaining buttons on her jeans, which he removed one leg at a time and then dropped, inside out, onto the floor. He dispensed with his own clothes with the calculated speed and acuity of one who had been through thousands of costume changes, first his shirt—to expose a fat, hairless chest of fish-belly white—then his pants, and finally his socks and underwear. For a second he glowered over Maria, who was now flat on her back, before he collapsed onto her in what was practically a body slam—not that she minded, since she was a lot taller than he was, although he definitely weighed more—and attacked her with his tongue. He quickly traversed her body, a strategy that soon delivered her to delirious heights she had never suspected could exist until she realized that he was fucking her with the slow, heavy force of twenty elephants.

The frame of the bed was knocking furiously against the wall, which made her hope that the neighbors were out to dinner. She gasped and writhed under his weight, smothered by a mix of pain—his dick was not long but, like the rest of his body, squat and almost grotesquely hard—and bliss unlike anything she had ever experienced. When, however many minutes later, she regained her senses, she felt more calm than frightened, although both emotions were present. She turned to Ronald and noted how his eyes—shiny, black, and limpid, like those of a seal—stared up at the ceiling as he softly hummed to himself. She observed his bloated body with renewed admiration and disgust. "I can't tell you how much I needed that."

"Uh, anytime?"

Maria laughed and ran her pinkie over the hill of his stomach. "You're married, right?"

He turned toward her abruptly. "Why?"

"No reason."

"That's not exactly an innocuous question."

"Does your wife know that you—?"

"No—and I'd like to keep it that way." He sat up on the bed, his back to her. "It's not like I do this all the time."

"I wouldn't care if you did," Maria said with genuine nonchalance as she got up and went into the bathroom.

After a quick shower, she peered at herself in the mirror and was surprised—but pleased—by who stared back: not only was she older than Maria had imagined but there was a graceful quality to the way she brushed the hair away from her face and turned the spigot on the sink, a physical maturity she would not have believed possible had she not just seen it herself. If there was something flawed about what she had done—to the extent that it was not very romantic—it struck her as a necessary flaw, rooted in a spirit of pragmatism that she would need to balance the rather many uncompromising facets of her future. She thought of Ronald in the next room, old as he was and at the height of his career, and how she had seduced him, and it made her realize that she was no longer a child, or even a student. She felt confident, as if she had mined an intuition on which she would have to rely to motivate and guide her—particularly after she left Juilliard—to practice, to choose her roles, or to make any number of other important decisions related to her prospective career. That she had discovered this in the course of having sex with Ronald, she knew, was not an accident; she saw her father's coin, except she was not holding it in her palm thinking about nothing, as she usually did, but it was slowly flipping through the air—as when he had tossed it to her on that last night in Pittsburgh—and she could see her embossed silhouette as much on one side as on the other.

34

Into the Millennium (The Criminals)

PARIS, 1870. After his arrival at the Gare du Nord, Lucien took a carriage to the Île, where he found his father about to sit down for lunch. As much as Lucien might have wished otherwise, his gaunt expression could not disguise a continuing struggle with grief, even now, four years after Eduard's death.

"I wish you could find a way out of this," Guillaume said as he pulled the cork out of a bottle of red table wine. "I'm sure when you were a teenager you never would have predicted the day I would say this, but you should be singing."

"I've tried," Lucien replied, "but it's not there—I still can't seem to breathe."

Lucien's grief had not been constant; in the first days, his friends had to prevent him from jumping out the window like a trapped animal, and then he had been gripped by an irrational belief that Eduard was not actually gone, so that he ran through the apartment opening and shutting doors. During the funeral cortege, which had snaked all the way from the opera house to St. Stephen's—an honor decreed by the emperor himself—Lucien had bit the insides of his mouth to resist the temptation to wave and laugh at the Viennese who lined the route, absently nodding with their vacant, dull expressions. This initial phase eventually gave way to a more reflective but guilt-driven state, in which he sat for hours, obsessively replaying not just the day in question but their entire past, looking for clues to exactly what had gone wrong—besides the rains and the flood—as if there were still a chance of doing things differently. He could not imagine, for example, why he had not woken up on the morning in question but managed to sleep while Eduard walked out to be shattered by a chance conversation with the emperor; and if their exchange in the flooded opera house had been a final performance, it didn't prevent him from revisiting his lines over and over, like a mad composer writing for the dead.

Guillaume considered him for a few seconds. "When your mother died," he said, "it was devastating in ways you now appreciate, but there's a limit to how many times a young child can see his father in tears."

"How did you manage it?"

"Do you think you're the only actor in the family?" Guillaume gently chided him. "I'm not saying I was very good, but children can be—or at least, you were—a forgiving audience. They're naturally happy; they cry for a little while and get over it—they become distracted by their curiosity about the world and their place in it. You might even say they're little scientists."

Lucien nodded; it made sense, not only in terms of scientific inquiry but also with the kind of larger meaning he had always ascribed to music.

"I'm not saying it's easy," Guillaume continued, "or that you should act like a child—or for that matter, have one—but you have to find something. As I've said to you before, we only get one chance at life, so there's a limit to how much we can squander. I'm not saying you have to sing, but if you stop trying to understand—well, then—"

"You're dead," Lucien concluded, and he did not protest when his father left him to sit alone in the sunlight.

THE NEXT MORNING, Lucien had breakfast with Codruta in the main residence of the Georges, where a retinue of servants was busy preparing for her imminent departure to the Loire Valley for the summer.

"I apologize for the lack of tranquillity," she noted with a wave of her hand at the hallway behind them, "but I appreciate you arranging your schedule so that I could indulge my continuing interest in your affairs."

"It was far from an imposition," Lucien offered truthfully, since he always made a point to visit Guillaume for a few weeks at the beginning of each summer. "My father was also anxious for me to see you."

She nodded. "I won't pretend he didn't ask me to talk to you," she said, "but I don't think it's necessary to repeat his advice."

"No, I don't think so, either," Lucien glumly agreed.

"Not that I'm questioning his motives," she added pensively. "He's worried about you."

"I know—I understand." Lucien nodded. "And I wish I could be more like him—I wish I could work through my grief in a more productive manner—"

"That can be admirable," she offered, "but I don't think that kind of sublimation—while suitable for a scientist—necessarily conforms to an artistic temperament, do you?"

Lucien considered this. "No, or at least not for me," he admitted. "I want to sing—I've tried—but I can't. I think back to Munich, and how at the time it felt like something crystallized in me—as a singer and a person—and though I thought it made me stronger, since Eduard, I feel like it turned me into someone I don't want to be."

She waited several seconds before responding. "It was a beautiful performance," she acknowledged, "and I think it would be naïve to suppose that there would be no costs."

"But death?"

"If you mean Eduard—absolutely not," she emphasized. "As we've discussed before, you can't hold yourself responsible for that tragedy, although I understand the impulse." She slowly arched one of her painted eyebrows. "But I don't think death is necessarily the wrong word to apply here, if we might remove ourselves from its more literal meaning."

Lucien saw himself as an adolescent, nervously sipping his tea and hanging on her every word, and as he watched this vision dissipate, any sadness he felt at what had been lost was—perhaps for the first time—tempered by a relief that he was no longer filled with such improbable hopes and ideals. "My youth?" he suggested.

She tilted her head in a way that seemed to acknowledge his response along with her intention not to reply in a direct manner, which—in keeping with his revelation—he understood was not her place. "As much as we like to think we grieve for others," she said, "it bears keeping in mind that we are also grieving for ourselves and, above all, what has inevitably passed us by."

LATER THAT AFTERNOON, Guillaume—who had spent the day at the university—returned and joined Lucien in the garden. "There's something I need to tell you," he said, "about the vaccine."

They had not discussed Guillaume's work in great detail for some time, and Lucien was operating under the assumption that his father had done little more over the past several years than test the formula on mice, most of which still died. "What's wrong?" he asked and then corrected himself. "Or is it good news?"

"That depends," his father offered cryptically before explaining how a month or so earlier—desperate to get some insight—he had made the mistake of confiding in a colleague at the university about the exact nature of the experiments; had even gone so far as to show him the surviving mice. While the professor in question had been suitably impressed, he had betrayed Guillaume's confidence, and word had since leaked out to the faculty and beyond.

"How far beyond?" Lucien asked.

"As far beyond as you can go," Guillaume sighed. "All the way up to the emperor."

"To the emperor?" Lucien repeated. "Are you sure?"

"Yes—I was summoned to see him."

"You were? When?"

"This morning."

As Lucien digested this news, the surrounding leaves seemed to turn to glass ornaments, clinking against one another in the breeze. "What—what did he want?"

"Well, it wasn't to present me with another award," Guillaume said quietly. "He wanted to confirm rumors about the vaccine, and whether it will work on a human being."

"And you told him . . ."

Guillaume's expression darkened. "I told him the truth, which is that I have made progress with mice—some of which seem quite happy and virile—but as for humans, there remain many questions."

"And what did he say?"

"He wants answers—and sooner rather than later."

"He can't expect—"

"He's the emperor, so he can," Guillaume interrupted. "He was surprisingly frank with me. He didn't pretend that things have been going perfectly from where he sits—between the food riots and the Prussians, he's obviously preoccupied—and even offered that under different circumstances he would be happy to give me more time. But—you know how it is—given the political ramifications of such a discovery, he wants to know if a vaccine is viable." Guillaume shook his head. "In a way I felt bad for him. He seemed very distraught— I could understand his position."

"Meaning what?" Lucien quietly ventured, trying not to jump to conclusions.

"He wants me to test it on someone."

"Couldn't that be murder? Did you tell him it kills more than half the mice you give it to?"

"He wasn't interested in statistics."

"Then why don't you test it on him?"

Guillaume frowned. "That occurred to me, but I thought better than to mention it."

"Then who?"

Guillaume took a deep breath. "Me. I'm going to take it, Lucien. I know you already understand this—I could never force it on anyone."

"He can't do this to you!" Lucien cried.

"No? What would you suggest?"

Lucien's mind raced as he searched his father's face for some kind of clue. "You could drink some harmless concoction—or we could escape; we could leave this afternoon for Vienna—"

"I don't want to leave," Guillaume responded, in a steely voice that conveyed to Lucien he had already dismissed such options. "My guess is that the emperor would have been more than willing to let me administer the vaccine to someone else—after all, he doesn't want me to die, since I know more about it than anyone—but I didn't even explore the option, and had he suggested it, I would have insisted on my own plan." He put his hand on Lucien's knee before he continued. "I'm going to take it first, before anyone else. I had to sooner or later, and it's time—before I'm old and frail. Look at me—I have no intention of dying—I'm much stronger than your average mouse." His smile broadened as he gripped his bicep. "And think of what happens if it works—the possibilities! It would change everything."

"What if it doesn't—what if . . ." Lucien could not complete the sentence.

"What if I die?" Guillaume responded tersely. "Nothing meaningful is ever unveiled without great risk—isn't that what you learned singing your opera?"

Lucien stared at his father and for a second despised him for making the comparison; he wanted to ask his father if he thought killing himself would bring his mother back to life. Then he remembered his earlier conversation with Codruta and knew that he was no longer capable—or even desirous—of following through on such an angry impulse. He was struck by the idea that while his father's research may have been rooted in science and logic, his obsession was a means of coping with the pain of losing his wife, his greatest loss. Like a page being lifted from the score of his own life, the insight gave Lucien new empathy, and he knew his father was right, at least to a degree; there was always an irrational, emotional component to the opera, or at least any worth hearing or performing, and one of the reasons Lucien couldn't—or wouldn't—sing was his continuing fear since Eduard's death of being overcome by the dissonant chaos he had once sought to embrace. For perhaps the first time in his life, he felt more experienced—albeit more destroyed—than his father and knew that his own reservations would mean nothing to Guillaume and—given that he had no power over him—that it would only be hurtful to argue.

"So when?" he quietly asked.

Guillaume exhaled. "I want to remake the vaccine with several alterations," he said more calmly, "to make it more palatable to the human body. Three weeks should be enough."

"Three weeks," Lucien repeated as he began to consider his own options. He could take the train back to Vienna, but such a choice would damn him even more than Eduard's death to a penance of guilt. He could remain as a bystander, offering his help, but this option felt equally weak and reprehensible, particularly as he thought of his earlier conversation with his father, and what his father had done for him when he was a child. He next considered taking the vaccine and knew that doing so was the only honorable choice; the thought of his own death barely made him pause, and the even smaller likelihood that the vaccine might work—if he survived—felt too remote to be a serious consideration. He would lend his hand to his flailing father, even at the risk of being pulled into the churning waters in which he struggled to stay afloat.

The air felt cool on his face—wet from tears—and he could detect a distant, echoing crescendo, a mounting tension that for the first time in years almost made him want to sing. "I'm here, Papa," he whispered and then turned and kneeled, gripping his father's shoulders as if to prop them both up. "I will take the vaccine with you."

Guillaume slowly stood and kissed each of his cheeks, and in his eyes Lucien could see his own. "Great truth requires great sacrifice"—he nodded—"and today you've proven your capacity for both."

Over the next two weeks, Guillaume assembled several new furnaces, which along with test tubes, pans, and bains-marie all had to be tested and calibrated. Lucien was charged with water distillation, a time-consuming procedure in which barrels of water had to be boiled and strained through charcoal and slow-sand filters. He helped organize and measure vials of cinnabar and sulfur, silver and lead, and any number of vegetative extracts, including one from a Mongolian orchid that Guillaume insisted was the most poisonous substance on the earth. Once the procedures began, with a flame burning under every piece of equipment—and a wave of summer heat outside, as though a higher power had placed a magnifying glass over the proceedings—the lab became unbearable; it was a noxious jungle, dank and steaming, and Lucien could not enter without retching. Yet even in this most wretched condition, he was astonished by the speed and agility with which his father—who seemed impervious to the heat and the smell—moved from one task to the next, all the while making precise measurements and notations and recording them in his notebooks. As a spectator, Lucien understood what decades of training had brought to the fore, and while he watched, there were moments when he could not help but be infected by his father's optimism. Death seemed far away, as if it would be impossible for such an ordered, efficient rehearsal process to lead to anything but a successful performance. It was easy to imagine countless others around the world—whether scientists or architects or engineers or artists—undertaking the "unperformable," making people stronger, transforming cities into taller, more formidable places, so that those who had walked the same streets even a generation earlier would not recognize the marvels they now beheld.

ONE MORNING IN early September, Guillaume extracted the new vaccine from a congealed mass of what to Lucien looked like a handful of dripping seaweed. He placed the liquid in a small covered flask, where it was scheduled to remain until sunset, which he had determined to be the best time for a living organism to ingest it. While his father spent the rest of the day cleaning and organizing the laboratory, Lucien stayed in the garden, trying to contain a mix of nerves and adrenaline not unlike what he used to feel before performing. What was perhaps most remarkable to him—except for the vaccine itself—was the extent to which his grief had melted away over the past three weeks; as his thoughts turned to Eduard, a part of him still longed to tell him about everything that had happened, but it was with more enthusiasm and appreciation than loss. He felt Eduard beside him, listening, observing—possibly laughing—and several times Lucien found himself caressing nearby rose petals as if they were Eduard's lips, which made the prospect of his own death more comforting.

As the afternoon began to wane, Guillaume and Lucien went upstairs to the music salon and situated themselves in the slanting rays of amber light.

Guillaume nodded at the piano. "Do you remember the first time you saw it?"

"Yes," Lucien answered. "I never imagined that anything could be so beautiful."

"And do you remember what you played?"

"Of course," said Lucien, trying to sound confident as he thought of the old French song. "I'll never forget—and I'll always be grateful."

They sat across from each other and placed their cups on a low table in front of them. They had agreed that Guillaume would go first, so that Lucien could gauge the reaction and if necessary assist in the event of a problem—for example, Guillaume had discovered that applying gentle pressure on the chest of a mouse could resuscitate it—after which Lucien would take his dose.

"Don't cry, Lucien," Guillaume reprimanded Lucien as he took hold of his son's hand, his expression both triumphant and doleful. "This is good."

"I can't help it." Lucien tried to smile through his tears.

"I know," Guillaume said and released his hand. As the sun passed through the line of the horizon and heaved a final sigh, emitting a few last rays of light, Guillaume raised the cup to his lips. "To life," he offered. "To truth."

"*Deo concedente,*" Lucien managed to whisper back as Guillaume, his eyes shining, eagerly swallowed the murky liquid.

It shocked Lucien how fast it happened, how quickly Guillaume—even before setting down his cup—fell onto the chair and rolled to the floor, where he began to convulse. Without a thought, Lucien held him down and ripped open his shirt to massage his chest as Guillaume continued to thrash for perhaps a minute or more—Lucien could not watch; it was too terrible to see his father's expression—until the convulsions subsided and there was no more than a periodic twitch. Lucien let go and raised his eyes to his father's face, hoping for the best but knowing as soon as he saw Guillaume's eyes, glassy and hard, staring past him, that something was wrong; he shook his father by the shoulders and placed a finger on his neck—searching for a pulse—and then an ear to his mouth, but felt nothing, no trace of breath. He collapsed onto his father's chest, tears blurring his vision, listening for some echo of a heartbeat, some sign that his father—who only minutes before had spoken to him, had reassured him that everything was going to be fine—was still alive, but in the stillness of a dark, empty house, he found only more proof that Guillaume was dead.

Lucien looked at Guillaume and saw no trace of torment; his expression resonated with peace and even determination, as if his ideals hovered like angels in the moonlight, guiding him forward. To see his father like this filled Lucien with rapture as he considered the irrefutable end of his own grief. Without another thought, he stood up with his chin raised—as if to sing his final aria—and spun around to face the pale twilight streaming through the windows. He offered a short bow to his imaginary audience, put the cup to his lips, and drank, swallowing many times before it was emptied.

He heard glass shatter but he could no longer see; he tried to move and could not. The liquid seemed to turn his stomach to ice, an effect that quickly spread into the rest of his body, so that each thump of his freezing heart sounded like the strike of a kettledrum in a vast hall. He had entered a world unlike anything he had ever imagined, and as a blue tint encroached on the edges of his vision, he feared that he would soon behold Lucifer perched on his throne to dictate punishments for the new arrivals. He remained paralyzed for what seemed like an eternity, or even two, and only after he detected the crash of continents and the resulting eruption of mountains did his heart begin to beat; slowly at first and then faster, until the icy torment he had already endured became a forgotten past and like Pyrrhus and Attila he was delivered into the boiling Phlegethon, doomed to flail in a river of lava. His bones and arteries disintegrated into a glutinous mass and he begged for relief from whatever caused this agony, until in his futility he was merged with the sun and then cast out like a beam of light into the remote beyond, and only when this crossed his mind—this nothingness, *néant*—did the pain begin to ebb, as if someone had turned off a spigot. He felt snow falling, melting away one flake at a time in his slowly pulsing blood.

Third Act

Solidarity

35

We Have to Wake Up from the Existence of Our Parents: In This Awakening, We Must Give an Account of the Nearness of That Existence

NEW YORK CITY, 2002. It was just after five o'clock, and the January sun—shifting north after the winter solstice—was about to set. Martin contemplated the ember tones reflecting off the ice patches on the Hudson and allowed his eye to drift up to the arched towers of the George Washington Bridge, grandly backlit in the manner of a Parisian monument. Now into his fourth month of retirement, he did not cultivate a routine, although he didn't resist one, either. Besides taking care of the cats, he let himself be occupied by small tasks, e.g., alphabetizing his records, reading his favorite Schopenhauer passages, trolling eBay for missing pieces in his silverware pattern (Gorham Hanover), or perusing alpine plant catalogs. Some days he went for walks in Fort Tryon Park or—if the weather was bad—took naps in the afternoon, a luxury that still seemed pleasantly unimaginable after so many years in an office. He spoke to his sister on the phone and several times met Jay Wellings for lunch or dinner downtown. He almost never thought about his old job, and his chronic health problems had improved if not disappeared entirely.

With a thought to follow through on his exploration of a

longer-term relationship, he had imposed a moratorium on the shorter kind. Having taken no other steps to make a longer relationship happen, he knew something was holding him back, though whether habit or history—or more likely, some combination—he could not yet say. In the first few months after 9/11, it had seemed "too soon" to date, but he was starting to acknowledge that the expiration had passed on that particular excuse.

"You just hate not being good at something," Suzie said to him when he admitted his failure to answer even a single "LTR" personal ad, as he had resolved to do. "I call it big-brother syndrome."

"I'm not very good at gardening, either," Martin replied, "and I don't have a problem admitting that."

"That's true," she said, "but the difference is that because of other things you've done—hockey, law, whatever; things that don't require so much emotional investment—you can easily see how to get better. You take a class, you practice, you research, you start small and then you improve. It's more logic than emotion."

"So what's different about dating?"

"Actually, nothing!" she insisted before continuing more earnestly. "It's just that you—like many of our gay brethren—missed out on the usual starting-small phase that others take for granted, the kinds of institutionalized opportunities that allow for *healthier* and more stable romantic relationships."

"You're using your Ph.D. voice."

She ignored him. "The point is, at your advanced age it feels kind of ridiculous—especially for such a 'man's man,'" she added slyly, "to own up to your lack of skill in what is effectively an art."

"Okay, that's enough." Martin laughed. "I think I've been schooled enough for today."

"Small steps, big brother—small steps."

...

As MARTIN CONSIDERED his sister's admittedly sensible advice, he remembered something not entirely dissimilar that Leo Metropolis had said to him years earlier. This was the same afternoon he had bought the house, i.e., the day after seeing *Tristan* for the first time and meeting Leo at Café Joséphine. In Martin's memory, at least, the practical side of the transaction had taken just a few minutes; Leo had given him a tour, they had agreed on rough financial terms, and then it was more or less done. Of course there had been the usual thousands of documents to be signed and notarized, but the closing had been relatively painless; as Martin knew from his career, some deals seemed to move forward like that, as though they were meant to be. They decided to celebrate with a drink; in fact, they had been sitting on the same Biedermeier sofa on which Martin sat now, where for the first time he had been mesmerized by the western light oscillating through the glass to illuminate the gilt spines of Leo's book collection. Leo had ultimately left many of these books behind, along with the bookshelves, two deco armchairs, a dining room set, and much of the rest of the furniture that could still be found throughout the house. Martin had kept it all and, despite his initial plans, had even left the wall treatments, including some very ornate damask wallpaper in the back bedrooms, which had initially struck him as dated and "overwrought." As time passed, he grew to appreciate the opulent textures, which began to strike him as more disciplined and crafted than garish, and—as he did now, considering a similar pattern in the upholstery—regularly felt hypnotized by the gold and silver threading contained within, which like certain species of fish surfaced only at twilight. While there was nothing "clean" about the aesthetic, there was a constant yet subdued movement—a sort of visual white noise—that Martin understood to be musical in reference, not unlike, say, the Paris *Tannhäuser* where Venus is about to grind her lover into a pile of dust, or even the songs of "shoegazer" bands he had long admired—e.g., My Bloody Valentine, Ride—that juxtaposed slow, turbulent beauty and ethereal dissonance to similar effect.

On the day in question, Martin had given in to a form of buyer's exuberance that, while not completely unfamiliar to him—given the many deals he had closed in his career—was augmented by an avuncular benevolence he detected in Leo, who as far as Martin could ascertain was close to twenty-five years older than he was. That they were both gay was a dimension here as well and, as Martin knew, hardly unusual given how often gay men left—or were forced to leave—their actual families for those who were more capable or understanding (or in his case, were alive); in this respect he understood that Leo was willing to mentor him in a manner that Martin was happy to accept. "So—you and Arthur," Martin asked, "are you really—"

"Lovers? I don't like the word either, if it's any comfort to you," Leo noted, "but yes, we've been together for quite some time."

"But he's really married to—?"

"Ghislaine? Oh yes—theirs is an old-fashioned alliance, which I think from the beginning dispensed with any pretense of connubial obligation. They occupy separate wings of the old house where they live in Paris—the Hôtel Georges—which is where I also stay for some portion of the year."

Martin nodded. "Were you ever married?"

"Fortunately no—were you?"

Martin sighed. "Unfortunately yes."

"So she didn't know?"

"Well, no—at least not at first."

"Quelle catastrophe." Leo shook his head.

"I learned my lesson, so to speak."

"I take it you rectified the situation?"

"I divorced, if that's what you mean," Martin clarified. "But I haven't found anyone else."

"Le pauvre." Leo smiled but continued more reflectively. "Do you want to?"

"I think so." Martin understood that Leo was indulging him but could not restrain himself in light of the odd exuberance and loneliness he felt. "But I'm not sure I'm made for marriage of any kind—I sometimes think it's beyond me."

"That sounds rather hopeless for someone your age," Leo said. "Not that I'm trying to convince you."

Because to this point he had told no one, not even his sister, about contracting HIV, Martin wanted to confide the true source of his doubts, namely his fear that he would be dead sooner rather than later. So he explained to Leo what had happened, how he had lived for the past few years, how he had resolved to change, and how—the second he saw it—this house seemed to embody such hopes. It was difficult going at first, because all of this had to be extracted from the mental safe-deposit box, but Leo was a receptive audience and reassured him in those places where he halted to find the right words. When, at the end of his story, Martin realized that they were both in tears, he laughed with relief at having finished and disbelief that he could have provoked such a reaction in a great performer.

"I know why I'm crying," he said, "but why are you?"

"Why am I crying?" Leo repeated. "Because, *mon chère,* I'm old enough to remember myself at an age when a death sentence—*comme tu dis*—would have been something to be cherished, and it makes me sad to think how I arrived at such a point, not because I have regrets but because, as you've begun to understand, to live—to truly live, by which of course I mean to love—is to suffer. You've read Pascal, I assume—'the soul is pained by all things it thinks upon'? When I was your age, I never thought it could be true, but the longer I live, the more inexorable it becomes. But—*néanmoins*—as much as we can know this about ourselves, the nature of compassion is to wish that it were not so hard for others, particularly when we see ourselves in them—and it's also true that, as painful as it seems, we get only one chance, as you are also now realizing."

Martin had not read Pascal, but he felt as if Leo were shining onto his thoughts a light that both warmed him and made him want to turn away. "How—how exactly do you see yourself in me?"

Leo barely paused. "I see someone whose ideals have been tested and quite possibly broken, I see someone with a great capacity for work, and I see someone who desperately wants to love and to understand, but who thinks it's—as you say—beyond him to do so."

Martin could not understand how Leo knew such things, and how his words could resonate so strongly. "You don't think it is?"

Leo's eyes flashed. "Didn't you feel it last night at the opera? Wasn't that love coursing through the music and absolving you? And if not, what was it? And if so—and I know you agree with me that it was—doesn't that demonstrate a capacity to give yourself to the irrational side of life, to throw yourself on its mercy?" He softened. "It's not like you don't have courage—you just have to find it when you need it most."

Martin could agree that he had loved things in his life—music in particular—but also knew that this was not exactly what they were discussing. "But for someone else?"

Leo sighed but was undaunted. "Yes, that's perhaps the rarest love of all, but it's also the most damning, because it will often seem like a mirage and be swept away, and when that happens, you long for nothing but death. But—and this is the greatest irony of all—it's really the only way to learn who you are." Leo paused to wipe the sweat off his forehead with a handkerchief as he continued. "When you suffer this kind of loss, you will know it, and until you have, love is hardly beyond you." He turned to Martin and placed a hand on each of his shoulders. "I know this because if it were," he said very gently, "you'd already be dead."

As if prompted by the disappearing sun, Martin's thoughts drifted back to Keith Loris, with whom he had been so infatuated while living in the East Village. While they had started out as friends— "buddies"—it had quickly evolved into something more, as Martin both did and did not want to admit at the time. They went to the same bars and shows and record stores; they talked for hours about their favorite bands and the fallacy of trickle-down Reaganomics and the genius of Walter Benjamin; they walked around the East Village and discussed all the great things that had been done in the past and could still be done in the future. Like Jay, Keith knew a lot about music, but he possessed a serious, brooding quality that fueled Martin's infatuation, although Martin dared not breathe a word of this to anyone besides himself, and then only in the darkest hours, when he fantasized about Keith's eyes smoldering with desire for him.

One night Martin went to see Hüsker Dü at Folk City with Keith and Jay and a few others. He could almost see the air, blue with smoke and suspense, not only for those like Jay and Keith who had already seen the band but also for newcomers like Martin, whose veneer of skepticism belied a hope to be obliterated. At some point they decided to get closer to the stage, and Martin—anxious to impress Keith and the tallest of the three—eagerly led them into the compacted crowd. Though it was now impossible to talk to Keith, Martin continued to make sporadic eye contact, which seemed to establish an unprecedented camaraderie in what would soon be a roiling mosh pit. There were a few scuffles as people fought for space and air; empty beer cans were tossed around, and occasionally a "Hüskers!" or "Fuck Nancy!" chant made its way through the room; it seemed to

Martin that hours passed, and on the verge of suffocation, he began to question with some bitterness why the band was taking so fucking long; but at the same time, he was already looking forward to describing—sharing—every moment of this with Keith afterward.

Finally the band—there were three members: drums, guitar, and bass—appeared onstage and without a single glance at the crowd checked their respective instruments, before the drummer clicked his sticks one two three four and launched them into a maelstrom of sound more intense—faster, louder, angrier—than anything Martin had ever heard or, for that matter, imagined. A landslide of distortion crashed over the audience, which after a moment of slack-jawed paralysis erupted into a writhing mass. In the mosh pit, Martin gave in to the riptide of bodies and forgot about Keith for a few seconds, at least until their eyes again briefly met, conveying not just that this was a great concert by a great band but—and this, far more exhilarating and shocking—a naked longing that could be characterized only as desire. He was terrified to recognize this in Keith, and even more terrified to realize that his eyes surely reflected the same, and so he was grateful when the onslaught of music and flying bodies carried them apart.

Nor did they discuss it later, when they went with Jay and their other friends to Lucy's bar, where Martin felt electrified when his thigh rested against Keith's as they sat next to each other in one of the booths. They staggered back to Martin's apartment—Jay was sleeping at Linda's—and were listening to *Zen Arcade*, comparing the recorded versions of songs with what they had just heard, when Keith turned to him. "So, Vallence—I have a question for you."

"Yeah?" Martin allowed his eyes to travel along the poster-covered wall of the living room before coming to rest on Keith.

Keith considered him for a second. "Have you ever slept with a guy?"

Martin felt a jackhammer in his chest. "You mean like fucking around . . ."

"Yeah—you know—sex."

The room started to spin as Martin considered how to answer this, before he decided just to tell the truth, albeit with some hesitation. "Uh, no—have you?"

Keith shrugged ambiguously. "What do you think of us, Marty?"

"What do I think of us?" Martin was too stunned to manage more.

Keith's voice became harsh. "Like what are we, exactly?"

"Uh, friends?"

"That's it?" The edge to Keith's voice was gone, and he spoke in a soft but insistent tone Martin had never heard him use before.

"I don't know," Martin said but hated the weakness of it. He had dreamed of this since he first saw Keith but felt completely unprepared; to give in, it seemed, would be the end of his longing, and as with any part of his body, he could not after so many years imagine himself without it. "I want to be—closer to you," he ventured, his voice hoarse. He could barely believe that he had used a stupid word like *closer*, but it was nevertheless a relief to have made the point.

Keith nodded and did not laugh. "But not like friends . . ."

"No, not like friends," Martin admitted and knew that he had finally crossed a certain line for the first time in his life.

Keith shrugged. "So what do you want to do?"

It was too late to go back, and Martin felt possessed by a new urgency to make himself clear. "I guess kiss you."

"You guess?" Keith put his hand on Martin's shoulder, and for a delirious second Martin thought that he was going to lean into him, that it was actually going to happen the way it always had in his dreams, but then he pulled back. "I'm sorry, Marty—I can't."

Martin froze.

Keith's expression was distant, if not inconsiderate. "I can't— you know—fuck around with a guy I'm friends with . . ."

"But . . ." Martin struggled to express the fear and betrayal he felt as his teeth began to chatter and his knee bounced up and down.

Keith's demeanor had completely changed. "Relax, Vallence, it's not the end of the world," he said as he pulled at his scruffy beard, as if pondering a painting. "I've been with guys, so I know what it's like—"

"You have? Since when?"

"When I first moved to New York—you know, there's a certain class of men who will pay a lot of money to get their cock sucked by a twenty-year-old Harvard dropout."

"You hustled?" Martin's disbelief, as he considered it, was soon replaced by a certain perspective that made the fact that Keith had done this no less plausible than, say, sitting in an apartment in the East Village at four in the morning, surrounded by empty beer cans, posters of SST bands, and cigarette butts.

"I hope you're not disappointed in me," Keith said, in a somewhat mocking tone that Martin did not appreciate.

"Fuck you, Loris."

"It was only a few times." Keith shrugged as his eyes returned to a soft familiarity, which despite everything still tugged at Martin. "I was kind of curious, you know, to see what it was like."

Martin felt mildly appeased by this, despite the continuing turmoil in his stomach. "So what was it like?"

Keith looked through Martin. "You'll try it sometime, and then you'll know."

"Right," said Martin, again angry.

"I don't mean hustling, Marty—I mean sex with a guy."

"I don't want to have sex with a guy," Martin said, as his annoyance gave way to paranoia. "You can't tell anyone about this."

"What's to tell?" Keith responded. "Look, Vallence, don't be a fucking girl. We're still friends—I just wanted to clear the air."

"Yeah, we're still friends," Martin agreed, but knew he no longer meant it, because he now hated Keith more than anyone he had ever known.

The next night, when they ran into each other at Lucy's and Keith wordlessly offered him a beer, if a part of Martin felt nothing but dismay at the oily humiliation oozing through him, he found it wasn't too hard to put that part in a box and toss it into the mental attic. Besides, he reasoned, Keith wasn't egging him on; neither of them referred to the incident, and after a sufficient number of drinks, he felt the weight in his stomach dilute, until he was barely disturbed at all, as if it truly had been a nightmare with no connection to the waking world.

BACK IN HIS house—Leo's house—Martin stared at the mutating clouds as if the sky were a map. Dante brushed past his leg as Beatrice—just emerging from the shadowed perimeters—skirted by like a wisp. Although he rarely saw her for more than a few seconds at a time, just the night before, as he was going to sleep, she had jumped up on the edge of the bed and Martin had reached for her, so that his fingers had for the first time passed through the silver halo to her plush coat. It lasted only a second, during which he detected the frantic beat of her heart, before she grew claustrophobic and in her characteristic low crouch slipped away. Later, in an even more remarkable development, he had woken up to see her disappearing over the hilly terrain of pillows and blankets, while a slight coolness on his face led him to suspect that she had just placed a single delicate lick on the tip of his large nose.

Over the years, Martin had often remembered this episode with Keith, but this time for once he felt free from the shame and embarrassment that had haunted him. His pain, it seemed, had evolved into something more wistful than wounded—something he could even smile at—and made his past feel more resolved, so that he was no longer agitated by a gnawing, debilitating sense of wishing things were different when they so obviously could not be. He poured himself another drink and settled into the couch, where he imagined driving over the glittering bridge to states he had never seen.

36

The Heart Is a Lonely Hunter

NEW YORK CITY, 1989. Though almost seven years had passed since Maria's graduation from Juilliard, they felt pleasantly distant and unimportant as she—accompanied by Anna Prus—sat down at Linda's wedding reception. It was a period marked by cheap apartments uptown and a series of unremarkable day jobs and equally unremarkable if necessary stints singing in churches and synagogues. If at times she had been frustrated by the failure of things to come together exactly or as quickly as she had hoped, at this second it all seemed to make sense, given that she was pleasantly drunk and that Anna had just confirmed that Bradford Irving, who managed the young artist program at the Met, was about to offer her a contract, meaning that Maria would be singing full-time starting in the fall. They were in a ballroom at the Pierre, idly sipping wine while the rest of the tables filled up. "You sounded lovely today," Anna complimented her, referring to a Brahms piece she had sung at the ceremony, in a small chapel on East Seventy-third Street. "I think you impressed more than a few of the guests."

"That wasn't exactly at the top of my list," Maria remarked, for she knew that Anna was referring to some of her former classmates who had yet to arrive at their table.

"I know"—Anna smiled—"but these things are important, now that you're emerging from your cocoon."

"So it's finally happening," Maria said, and sighed. "I'm trying to enjoy it—just for today—because I know that as soon as I start, it's going to be so much work."

"As you should." Anna remained impassive as she looked around for a waiter. "It's an end and a beginning, which above all calls for *un coup de champagne.*"

"Yes, *un coup de champagne,*" Maria agreed and was distracted by the commotion of the wedding party, which had just entered the room.

Wine followed champagne as Maria stiffly conversed with her tablemates, three Juilliard alums and their husbands. Only one was still singing, and she made a point to tell Maria within five seconds of sitting down how jet-lagged she was after a flight from London, where she had just finished a Handel opera that Maria was sure would have bored her to tears, and so she could express genuine admiration for the accomplishment of performing it. The woman's husband was a fastidious little mouse who taught music history somewhere and said that he didn't appreciate anything later than Bach. The other two, whose voices had never particularly impressed Maria, both had husbands whose striking resemblance made her imagine a grove of trees from which pasty but aggressive bankruptcy lawyers were harvested by young sopranos more interested in marriage than in a career.

"So Washington Heights—is that in New Jersey?" one of them responded with what Maria felt quite sure was a sneer after she mentioned where she lived.

She decided that, under the circumstances, it would be quite appropriate—and even amusing—to play the diva. "No, it's on an island known as Manhattan," she emphasized with an exaggerated sigh. "Perhaps you've heard of it?"

He teased out the exact location, at Broadway and 160th, before he addressed the table at large. "Doesn't it make you wonder why they didn't keep the numbers going all the way upstate? 'Hey, I live on 5,634th Street, how about you?'" He laughed moronically and then addressed Maria. "So what's it like up there?"

"Oh, it's a drug-infested war zone," she replied, but in an airy tone, as though she were describing a Monet painting. "The streets are filled with garbage, it's loud, the police are a joke—it's a third-world country. Except for the mango ices, I hate it."

"Why don't you move?" asked the other one, as if the answer—money—weren't obvious.

"I like to walk to work."

"And what's work?" retorted the first guy, again with the sneer.

"I'm a dispatcher for an uptown car service." Maria decided to play her trump card, mostly for the benefit of the Juilliard alums, because even if their husbands were ignorant, they had heard Maria sing and—as Anna had said—knew that she was on the cusp of something they were not. "It's not interesting," she admitted, "but it gives me time to work on my voice."

"You sounded spectacular at the ceremony," commented one of the women, genuinely enough for Maria to appreciate why Linda had remained friends with her, even if her husband was—to use one of her grandmother's favorite expressions—a horse's ass. "Brahms has always been—"

"I'm curious," the husband interjected over his wife, "how would someone like you get from Washington Heights to—I don't know— the Metropolitan Opera?"

"The subway?" Maria answered, which made everyone—including her inquisitor—laugh. Although Maria knew very well the many different routes a singer could take from anonymity to the stage, she was not about to justify the implication that her life would be a failure if she did not make the ascent, even if in a sizable corner of her heart she believed it herself. "I don't really think about the practical side of things," she mused. "As Anna has always said"— and Maria nodded toward her mentor, who during this entire conversation seemed to be watching a movie screen in the distance—"when a voice is ready, the rest takes care of itself."

"Sounds very Zen," said the husband, as he raised his glass. "Sharon's always dragging me to the opera—right, honey?—and it's always better when we know someone up there on the stage."

Maria could have responded to this in many different ways, but she decided to follow Anna's example and simply smile and nod toward the dance floor, where Linda and Jay now appeared for the first dance.

"We're surrounded by dolts," Maria said to Anna after the other couples at the table left for the dance floor.

Anna nodded. "Try not to be too judgmental. I hate to tell you this, but in your career, you'll find yourself surrounded by more of these civilians, and believe it or not, you will look back at this time with nostalgia."

MARIA WENT TO the bar and was approached by a man—taller than she was and not exactly thin—with short black hair and impassive blue eyes. She met his gaze and did not turn away when he stated her name.

She raised an eyebrow. "Do I know you?"

"It's been a while." He rubbed a hand over a short beard in a gesture that made him seem a little nervous and on the whole less attractive to her.

There was something familiar about him, but she couldn't figure it out. "Uh—sorry."

"Martin Vallence . . ."

"Martin Vallence," she repeated. "Why do I know that name?"

"Pittsburgh," he said in a flat, ambivalent tone that rekindled her interest in him. "Three rivers, Castle Shannon, Terry Bradshaw, the Thunderbolt, Evonne Goolagong, Cedar Village—"

Then she knew. He was the son of the boss, the kid who lived down the street from Kathy Warren. "My God—Martin Vallence!" she cried, genuinely astounded at the unexpected sight of someone from such a distant—and difficult—period of her life.

"You remember?"

"Well, yeah—did you think I was acting?"

"No—well, maybe," he added, somewhat too pensively to be funny. "I figure if you can sing you can act, right?"

"In theory, but no, I remember you from your father's company." She resisted the temptation to add how much she had hated working there during her summers. "So, Martin Vallence, what brings you to the Pierre?"

He did not exactly return her smile. "I was going to ask you the same thing."

"Okay—I'll go first," Maria offered. "I went to music school with Linda—we were roommates for four years at Juilliard."

Martin nodded. "What's funny is that my last memory of you—before today—was after you won that singing competition in Pittsburgh."

"The Heinz Recitals," Maria said curtly. "That was another life."

"My mother was very impressed," Martin remarked, with a trace of sarcasm that might have annoyed her if he hadn't immediately followed with a more earnest response. "I went to boarding school with Jay," he said and cocked an eyebrow at her. "I take it you missed my toast?"

"I was, uh, in the bathroom, I think—you know, smoking crack."

Martin laughed. "Not that I'm an expert or anything, but from where I sat you sounded incredible—I thought the roof was going to cave in."

"Thank you very much," Maria replied as the bartender approached. "Can I get you a drink? It's on me."

She liked that Martin seemed to appreciate the joke but also admired a pervasive coolness in his expression that made his smile more genuine. He ordered a whiskey and after receiving it suggested they moved to a nearby table to talk. "So—you live in the city?"

"Yes, I came here after high school," Maria answered and told him a few things about Juilliard. "I live uptown now—Washington Heights."

"What's that like?"

"It's a challenge." Maria shrugged. "How about you?"

"East Village—I moved there after college. I was roommates with Jay."

"So you live in a slum, too—congratulations," she said. "What do you do down there?"

"I used to be a music writer," he replied, "but now I'm a lawyer."

"You're a lawyer? You don't look like a lawyer."

"I'll take that as a compliment," he said. "I represent rock bands." He pulled a card from his wallet and gave it to her.

He drank the rest of his whiskey and then contemplated her with his tranquil eyes. "There's something I want to tell you . . ."

"Uh-oh," Maria said.

He did not hesitate: "My parents are dead, too."

"What?"

"My parents died, too," he repeated, but so softly that she could barely make out the words above the music. "Only about five months after yours."

Unexpected as this was, Maria found it difficult to speak; a sick and spinning weightlessness reminded her of those first months after the fire, and she couldn't decide if she was too drunk or not drunk enough.

Martin apologized for the abrupt delivery. "I thought it would be unfair not to tell you. I assumed you didn't know."

"No, I didn't," Maria managed as she shook her head. "What—what happened?"

"Car accident. We were driving home from my high school graduation and it was raining and there was construction." He paused for a second as she listened in disbelief. "A truck skidded out and jackknifed right in front of them."

Shocked as much by the story as by its odd proximity to hers, Maria found it difficult to think. There was a part of her that wanted to laugh it off with the flick of her wrist and a suggestion for a stiffer drink, but to do so would have felt too much like a dismissal of her own past, so instead she offered a trembling hand, which he took. "I'm so sorry."

"I'm sorry, too."

"How could something like that happen—to both of us?" she asked, still gripping his hand. "I mean—how do you explain it?"

"How do you explain anything?" he replied with a subtle aggression that made it easy to believe he was a lawyer. "How do you answer questions like 'Why was I born?' or 'Why am I living in 1989 and not 1889?' or 'Why am I in New York City and not East Bumblefuck?'"

"I know why I'm here." Maria laughed uneasily.

"You're lucky." He rotated the glass in his hand for a few

seconds before he looked up at her with eyes that seemed to flicker as they caught the reflection of candlelight. "Whenever I run into something crazy—something that doesn't make logical or *scientific* *sense*—instead of asking myself 'How could that have happened?' I sometimes think the right question is 'How could that *not* have happened?'" He shrugged. "Is that too much legalese for you?"

Maria slowly shook her head. It actually did make sense, particularly as she considered her impending contract with the Met; of course she had worked for it—and the fact of having it made everything she had endured seem to fall into place, at least in retrospect—but getting to this point had been anything but certain, as the other Juilliard alums more than demonstrated. She returned her attention to Martin. "Okay, then—our parents: how could it *not* have happened?"

He considered her. "We're here, aren't we? I mean, you and me—at this moment, at this table, talking?"

"I guess we are," she acknowledged, and though it was a vague answer, she understood what he meant, that this bizarre coincidence or twist of fate—whatever they wanted to call it—was the reason she could consider him with such empathy; more than anyone she had ever met, he understood that part of her life—and vice versa—without having to be told.

He stared through her and smiled. "I think my destiny—at least for now—is to get another drink. Want one?"

"Please." She nodded, and was relieved to be left alone for a few minutes. She watched him lean against the bar in the self-assured posture of one who was very much at home there, and felt a glimmer of something else—clearly not grief—and was amazed at how her mind could occupy two such disparate spaces at once. Although he wasn't exactly her type—for one thing, he was too tall, and for another, she distrusted lawyers of all stripes—she felt more intrigued than threatened by their shared past. If it would have been an exaggeration to say she had given up on men in the past few years—though more than once she had claimed to have had her fill—she could not help but wonder if, despite her avowals to the contrary, she had just been struck by the fabled arrow of love, here at Linda's wedding. It seemed too perfect, pure storybook, to fall in love with Jay's best friend—a boy she had last seen at the company where their fathers worked—but she felt certain that if he were to ask her to marry him, she would say yes, why not?

Back at the table, he handed her a new glass. "To death," he toasted.

Maria was relieved to find no trace of irony in either his tone or his expression. "To death," she repeated but barely sipped her wine before she set it down on the table. "You probably can't tell, but I'm drunk."

"That makes two of us," he replied. "In case you couldn't tell."

She laughed and decided her attraction to him was a bit sacrilegious, but then decided she didn't care. "Do you want to dance?" she asked and nodded at the dance floor, where a bunch of people were doing the twist.

"Not at all." He shook his head. "Do you?"

"Not at all," she admitted. "But I don't want to sit here anymore, either."

"We could go for a little walk," Martin proposed. "I could use a break."

Maria followed him out of the ballroom and into a long hallway, the quiet reverberation of which made her melancholy, and she paused.

Martin wrapped one of her arms around his shoulder as she steadied herself against the wall. "I thought you said nobody could tell when you were drunk."

"I'm just really fucking tired," she murmured, but already the touch of her hand on his and her arm around his back electrified her, even as she felt her eyes start to tear. "And thanks to you I'm really fucking sad, too, even though I just found out about the biggest break of my career."

She had already told him about her acceptance into the young artist program and everything that implied. "Don't blame me," he said with a smile. "I don't trust anyone who thinks happiness is ever more than fleeting."

It was a gesture of resignation that she never failed to find charming in men who attracted her, so that, when he turned to face her, she could not resist placing her hands on his shoulders, only a few inches from a real hug, and then, when he showed no resistance, closing the gap. Nor did she object when, in return, his hand on her back went from a gesture of reassurance to something more, which led her to grip him a little tighter, which he reciprocated, so that she felt inclined to nuzzle a little at his neck, where his beard gave way to an afternoon stubble, which left her no choice but to kiss him.

"I wish we had somewhere to go," she said.

"What about in there?" he suggested, nodding at an adjacent door.

"It looks like a utility room," Maria said. "I bet it's locked."

"Don't be so sure," Martin said and reached over to push down on the lever.

The door gave way, and Maria cried out—a scream, really, but a very controlled one—in surprise and triumph, after which she followed him into a small supply room, so they were alone in the dark. As soon as the door clicked shut, she grabbed hold of him, an action he did not so much resist as envelop as he fell into her and brought them both to the floor, along with a cascade of toilet paper rolls that strangely never seemed to land. She felt nothing, really, except an odd, blissful heat, until she heard sobs and realized that they were her own. This grief—along with the understanding that Martin shared it—increased her desire, so that she pulled at his shirt and kissed him harder than she had ever kissed anyone, until she was sure her teeth had turned to dust and she tasted blood. Completely immune to any pain, real or prospective, she did not stop as he un-hitched his belt and pushed his pants down while she did the same with her dress and underwear, which she left hanging on one ankle, just above a black leather pump she did not bother to remove. She twisted around on her back, and they attacked each other like starv-ing animals. They heaved and flailed, so what they did seemed less and less like fucking than like some strange ritual of initiation Maria both wanted and did not want to stop. She was beneath and above him at the same time, surrounding him as he surrounded her, melting into him as she lost her vision and spun away from this dark room toward some disembodied space. When they were done, she returned to her body and cried new tears of relief and—somehow—resur-rection, as if, it occurred to her, she had just clawed her way out of a coffin.

37

The World Is the Totality of Facts, Not of Things

PARIS, 1870. Waking up in the diffuse light of dawn, Lucien realized he had been asleep only a few hours. Still shaken by the nightmarish visions he had suffered, he could not believe he had not died from the vaccine. The beating of his heart and the heavy, humid air moving into and out of his lungs confirmed he had not, and as he slowly flexed his fingers, he felt oddly relieved; whatever else had happened—and he was not yet prepared to think about the consequences—the grief he had brought with him to Paris a few weeks earlier had been stripped away, exposing a core of resolve where before there had seemed to be nothing but despair. He crawled a few feet over to his father, still supine on the floor. While it was unbearable to think that Guillaume would never again laugh or smile or even distractedly examine a flower, Lucien's sense of loss was tempered by the knowledge that his father had died in a manner of his own choosing, with no doubts and fully aware of the risks; his death was the culmination of decades of work, and Lucien could appreciate why he had done it.

He held his father's hand and was reminded of what this hand had done for him, not only in his childhood but over the past month, when Guillaume's work had inspired him in unexpected ways. He explained all of this in a low, hesitant voice, pausing here and there to allow space for his father to respond, as though engaged in a final conversation. He promised to carry on as they had discussed, in the service of truth and discovery, and as he spoke, he realized that—unlike before, when he had expected to die—he meant it, knowing he needed this kind of structure—and ideally, meaning—in his life going forward; to return to the state in which he had existed following Eduard's death would be disastrous, whether he lived for one day or one century. At the same time, he continued, in the event his father could hear him—and in spite of everything, smiling through his tears—there would be limits to what Guillaume should expect; there was no point in pretending, for example, that Lucien would ever be a scientist, or any kind of scholar, at least in the traditional sense. *"Aime la vérité, mais pardonne l'erreur,"* he offered as he closed his father's eyes, which seemed to confirm the official passage of these famous words from one generation to the next.

. . .

LUCIEN WENT TO the garden, where he cleared a plot and spent several hours digging. After gently rolling up Guillaume's body in a blanket, he brought it downstairs to clean and dress. He retrieved his mother's wedding ring, which, along with his father's, he placed on a chain around Guillaume's neck. As Lucien carried his father outside, he began to consider for the first time what it might be like to live for two hundred years, and how long it would take before he knew if the vaccine was working. Though he still tended to believe that he had merely survived, and would continue to age like anyone else, he felt a tremor of fear about confronting such a vast unknown. Not willing to reflect too deeply on what in either case could not be undone, he allowed his fear to pass through—or at least around—him, as if he, too, were an island in the Seine. As he kissed Guillaume's cheeks and put him into the earth, under the indifferent posture of the trees and flowers, there was a part of him that envied his father his perfect death, but this, too, he refused to consider for more than a second, knowing that he could no longer imagine his own.

AFTER SPENDING MOST of the next twenty-four hours in a deep, exhausted sleep, Lucien emerged from the apartment and realized the Île was almost entirely deserted. Closer to the Île de la Cité, he found a small militia of servants left behind by the nobility to guard the mansions; from one of these men he learned that the emperor had been deposed and a new republic formed. As shocking as this news was—Lucien could not remember a time when Louis-Napoléon had not ruled France—of more immediate concern was the news that Prussia, still intent on destroying the new French government, had sent troops said already to be within striking distance of Paris, which meant Lucien would not be able to leave. Venturing into the city, he saw bands of men parading up and down the boulevards, guns and knives in hand; he went to the train station, where all passenger cars had been replaced by cargo trains filled with wheat and other foodstuffs rushed in from the provinces, and finally to the Bois de Boulogne, where like something out of a strange dream, he saw herds of cattle wandering aimlessly through the flower beds and stands of forest.

Less than a week later, the Germans arrived and promptly formed a giant noose around Paris; wires were cut, so that nothing penetrated this barrier except a few hot-air balloons, released from the highest hills of Montmartre. Bombs rained down, and the cafés and theaters went dark; statues were covered in burlap sacks, and even the arcades remained empty after a shower of glass fell on a group of pedestrians and sliced them to pieces.

As the months passed, Lucien became demoralized, not only on account of those wounded and killed or otherwise suffering from the siege but also his sense that the city was giving in to a collective longing for death, the very thing he had turned his back on. In the lapping waters of the Seine, he heard the hushed whispers of the condemned and starving, begging for a dose of the poison hemlock that continued to grow in Guillaume's garden. He took to wandering the streets, mostly at night, where even in a starving city, some of the shadowed doorways and twisting passages in the old sections of the Left Bank led to underground cafés and dance halls. When the city seemed most deserted, Lucien heard strains of music but could not always determine if they came from under his feet or from in his head. Strings and harps seemed to cascade down over the darkened streets from the black sky above, and he heard a soft, maternal voice warning him to be careful.

On one such night—in an underground club off the Boulevard St.-Germain, not far from his old theater—he recognized his old friend Gérard Beyle in a group of men, all wearing the red armbands of the Communards. They greeted each other warmly, and Lucien invited Gérard to visit the Île. The next day he learned that Gérard's two children had died during a flu epidemic more than five years earlier, after which his wife had left. Lucien relayed some of what had happened to him over the same period, and for a while they sat in silence, which seemed to make the tragedies they had just described feel very far away. Succumbing to nostalgia and affection, Lucien reminisced about their former jobs at the St.-Germain and the years they had spent carousing around Paris, and remarked how strange it was to realize that he now was older than Gérard had been at the time. While Gérard was willing to indulge him in these memories, and even smiled a few times as he recalled certain details that Lucien had forgotten, he was less willing to romanticize this period of his past, explaining that it had been marked by a cynical disbelief in everything.

"You were so wise," Lucien protested. "Everything you said about love was true."

"Perhaps." Gérard shrugged. "But while love was everything to you then—what were you, sixteen or seventeen?—it was already past for me." He paused and considered Lucien with a grimace. "You've suffered—we both have—but let me play the elder again and say that if you can't find something to believe in—and I'm not saying it has to be the communes, but hopefully it won't be the monarchy, or even the republic—your life will be very long and tedious."

ONE AFTERNOON IN March, Lucien noticed a pause in the shelling, followed by a series of triumphant cries and shouts. He ran outside and crossed the bridge to the Île de la Cité, where thousands had congregated, kissing and hugging, so that the city appeared to have been conquered by a bedraggled army of hobos. Looking out over the masses, Lucien realized that not a tricolored flag could be seen in a frothing sea of red: the city—just as Gérard had predicted—had been taken over by the radicals of the commune. Lucien found a spot in an alcove of one of the fountains at the Place St.-Michel from which he could watch and cheer. As far as revolutions went—and like every Frenchman, Lucien had been extensively schooled in both the concept and the reality—this one was not so bad. As night fell, lines of old women paraded past, sweeping brooms in time to a band of brass players, who in turn were followed by painters and sculptors who had fabricated a giant float out of old scrap metal and paper flowers. There were dancers and singers in sequin suits and laborers and factory workers, while prostitutes celebrated the new age by offering their services for this one night only at a 50 percent discount.

As the morning light crept into the eastern sky, Lucien remained asleep in the fountain, oblivious to the thud of soldiers—the French national army—marching through the city gates. He woke up to witness the soldiers advancing into the sleeping crowds, where they plunged bayonets into those at their feet and fired bullets that ripped off the heads of those who stood up groggily to protest. He watched helplessly until the wave passed, after which he crawled down from his hiding spot; as he edged along from doorway to doorway to make his way back to the Île, he continued to hear the harsh whisper of flames and gunshots, interspersed with screams and the shattering of glass, all of which—like the splintering crack of a human bone—did not need to be experienced to be recognized as grotesque sounds of war.

Near the river, he turned a corner just in time to see Gérard and several of his comrades trying to block the Pont d'Hiver against an advancing column. The soldiers took the bridge without engaging the communists so much as marching right over them. Lucien sprinted ahead, arriving just as the soldiers reached the other side, leaving Gérard wounded and gasping; blood seeped from all over his body. Lucien placed his hands under his old friend's arms and as bullets flew dragged him out of harm's way to a sheltered spot under a stone balustrade. His mind raced as he tried to decide what to do; he repressed an urge to protest the injustice, to stand up like a vengeful deity and wipe his city—his country—from the face of the earth, to protest this last shred of belief—the one he had always held in the fundamentally good nature of his fellow countrymen, the one that would have prevented him from ever believing, had he not seen it himself, that they could kill each other by the thousands—being ripped away, seemingly forever, after everything else he had endured.

He rested Gérard's head in his lap and tried to comfort his friend. Though Gérard seemed too stunned to talk—Lucien was not sure he even recognized him—the pace of his breathing became less frantic, and his moans subsided. As he held him, the rough texture of Gérard's shirt reminded Lucien of the first time they were together at the St.-Germain, and he thanked Gérard for having been so kind to his younger self. He also thanked him for teaching him that the city was a different kind of theater, and finally for these past few weeks, when Gérard had helped Lucien negotiate a loneliness that he suspected could be appreciated only by those whose parents and lovers were already dead.

Gérard lifted his head and looked up with shining eyes. His lips barely moved as he fought to speak just a few words. "Did we win?"

With his free hand, Lucien wiped clear his own eyes and then leaned down. "*Oui, mon chère,* we won," he confirmed, almost but not quite singing the words as he would a lullaby, and knew that like so many lies, this one resonated in the truth.

38

The True Artist Helps the World by Revealing Mystic Truths

NEW YORK CITY, 2002. It was the beginning of May, and Martin's new plants—a mix of dwarf conifers, Japanese maples, and alpine succulents—had arrived that morning in several large boxes from a nursery in Oregon. He'd spent the day, brilliant and warm enough to make the chill of April seem far off, on his deck replanting a collection of concrete troughs—also left behind by Leo—which he had already refurbished with new topsoil, sand, and peat. As he worked—unpacking each plant before carefully placing it in a designated spot and padding it into its new home—he had enjoyed an almost narcotic intoxication he had not experienced since pottery class in high school, or before that when he used to paint goalie masks. In many respects, it had been a perfect day, exactly what he had hoped to achieve when he left his job, and as he settled into a living room chair, from which he could admire his new botanical charges, the wet leaves of which glistened as the sun arced down toward the Palisades, he found it difficult not to contrast the tone of such thoughts with the wounded, bellicose state of the city—and even, or especially, the country at large—since 9/11, and for a second he wished that everyone could afford to take at least a few months off, to cultivate a plot of earth, to be reminded of the certainty that whatever happened, beautiful things could still grow out of almost nothing but air and dirt and water. It was a ridiculously naïve idea, of course—to think that society's problems could be solved through gardening—but he smiled as he remembered discussing it online a few days earlier with a fellow alpine enthusiast and seeker of a long-term relationship. They had been chatting at regular intervals since "meeting" a week earlier;

the only negatives were that this guy lived in Brooklyn—effectively one hundred thousand miles away from Washington Heights, as they had joked—and that he was about to leave the country for three months. But they had agreed to get coffee when he returned, which represented the first concrete step in Martin's "self-improvement program," as he regularly referred to it—with only a trace of irony—in discussions with his sister.

HE SIPPED HIS whiskey, which transformed the encroaching stiffness in his fingers into something almost electric. He flipped over the My Bloody Valentine LP he had on the turntable and thought about Maria Sheehan—he had introduced her to the band—and made a mental note to send her an e-mail. He wondered if he might see her more than once a year now that he had more time, but then considered that her schedule would no doubt remain the limiting factor. He remembered the day he'd met her—or technically, remet her—in New York City, at Jay and Linda's wedding, and how shocked he had been by her transformation into a striking and urbane version of the scowling girl he used to see at his father's company in Pittsburgh. Her voice, of course, was mesmerizing, but there was also the way her lustrous black gown fit so perfectly, as if each reflection of light off the silver threading had been designed to elevate her singing into an effortlessly magnetic performance.

Going to Jay's wedding had not been easy for Martin, not because he didn't wish his friend happiness but because it drew into such sharp relief his own—and at that time, more recent—failures. This disconsolation had made Maria seem like a mysterious and regal countess from some forgotten country who could take him away from his troubles; and in a way, that was exactly what she had done, allowing him for those few minutes to believe that what he felt was more than a reactionary desire to love a woman, knowing that doing so would make his life so much easier. It was more than just a fantasy on his part; he had genuinely fallen in love with her, if love was sharing that which cannot be shared, to the extent that the respective deaths of their parents had created some implausible bond of truth and experience. Or at least this was what Martin had told himself at the time, when he was confronted with the strange but miraculous revelation that he wanted her, not as a friend but in the most visceral, physical way possible, as if in the grip of a chemical addiction. He didn't care that he was "in the closet" or having more sex with men than he wanted to admit even to himself, or that this sudden desire did not seem so far removed from the ridiculous notion he had long held about meeting the perfect woman who once and for all would "cure" him of his homosexual tendencies. If it meant a chance to resolve their shared grief, then to make love with Maria had at that second seemed like the most natural thing in the world.

WHEN IT WAS over, if some part of his vision remained—i.e., he could not escape the feeling of having experienced something magical and ineffable with her that went beyond having sex in a utility room at a hotel, even a luxury one like the Pierre—he knew it was not something that could ever be described as love, or at least not the romantic kind. So when she stared up at him unblinking and motionless, he pushed himself off her, still wanting to be near but not to touch. He caught his breath and became aware of the sounds of the hotel: the mechanical click of the air-conditioning, the distant clanging of pans from the kitchen below, the thud of music from the ballroom. Maria sat up and looked at him as she removed her underwear from her foot. "Well—that's what I call fucking," she said.

Martin laughed at the brazen quality of her statement and helped her to regain her balance. They returned to the hallway and parted ways to go to their respective bathrooms, where as Martin looked in the mirror, he admitted that not even Maria Sheehan would ever be "the one" for him, and although he had come to terms with this certainty in the past—or so he believed—he felt inspired, or altered, enough not to want to hide it from Maria or anyone else. He owed this to himself as much as he owed it to her, and the second it was acknowledged, it felt like a fait accompli, so that he looked back at who he had been a minute earlier and wondered why it had taken so long.

He met her back out in the hallway. "I have to tell you something."

"What now?" Maria stepped around him to a mirror, where she reattached to her ear a dangling hoop of an earring.

"Uh, well—I'm gay," Martin said, and laughed at the ease with which it slipped out, newly amazed that two words could ever have caused him so much grief.

Maria gave him an odd look in the mirror. "Really? And here I thought I was a woman."

"I'm serious," Martin insisted. "I don't know what happened, it's just that—"

"Wait." She now turned to face him. "You're really gay? Like—" Maria frowned. "I'm not going to catch anything, am I?"

"You might."

"You better be kidding."

"I am." Martin had in fact recently received a clean bill of health; at this point, he still labored under the impression that a single kiss with another man could leave him infected with any number of gruesome diseases—besides AIDS—which sent him to the doctor with hypochondriacal frequency.

This seemed to satisfy her. "So nobody knows? Not Jay, not Linda? What about your ex-wife?"

"She knew," Martin admitted. "She took me to the cleaners when we got divorced. But nobody else."

"Good for her," Maria remarked, severely. "You could have said something before—before we fucked."

"I'm sorry—it wasn't premeditated," Martin offered. "Or at least not consciously, and I didn't want to wreck it by pretending it was something I would ever want again. Does that make any sense?"

"No—not really—but sort of." Maria placed a hand on the wall as she reached down to adjust her heel. "It's just that I had my own little drunken fantasy."

"What was your fantasy?"

"Oh, just that we would get married and be like best friends with Jay and Linda."

"Is that something you want?"

They were now at the doors to the ballroom, where she stopped and shook her head. "No, I'm never getting married. There—that's my coming out." Maria said this with the perfect amount of conviction and humor, without any self-pity or bitterness. "I decided that a long time ago. I just had a moment of weakness when we met."

"I have that effect on a lot of people," Martin tried to joke.

She smiled wanly. "You wish."

"I could really use another scotch," Martin responded as he held out his arm. "Join me?"

They found a table in view of the dance floor. New drinks in hand, they talked aimlessly about the past; about Pittsburgh, about Juilliard and Maria's nascent singing career, while he mentioned his stint as a music writer and his latest incarnation representing bands in major-label record deals.

"So you were into punk rock, like Jay?" she asked. "Mohawks and safety-pin earrings?"

"Not as a fashion statement, but the music—yes—for a while. More or less. Punk, post-punk, hard-core, post-hard-core, new wave, no wave. There's a lot I was into."

"I saw the Beach Boys once," Maria joked. "And some of my burnout friends in high school were into Pink Floyd."

Martin put down his drink and took Maria's hand. "Do you have plans for later on?"

"Uh, maybe?" she said.

He laughed and shook his head. "Seriously—do you want to go see a band?"

"Really? What kind?"

"A rock band," Martin said and thought about it for a few seconds. "But a good one. My Bloody Valentine. They're very melodic—kind of psychedelic—but also dissonant without being abrasive."

"Melody and dissonance," Maria mused, and Martin was happy to note that she seemed intrigued. Although it was in no way a quid pro quo, after what she had done for him, he wanted to offer a piece of himself, and taking her to a show by a band he loved seemed like a perfect opportunity. "Do you know *Tristan und Isolde*? Richard Wagner?" she asked.

"Uh—well—not really," Martin stuttered and briefly explained that only recently—thanks to Jay—had he started listening to opera with any seriousness. "I wish I knew more."

"That's okay—"

"It's really not," Martin disagreed. "But if you come with me tonight—or even if you don't—I promise to check out *Tristan* as soon as I can."

"You don't 'check out' *Tristan*, big guy," she replied. "You become it."

IT WAS NOT until after one in the morning that the band—two women and two men, equally androgynous in shaggy haircuts and T-shirts—shambled onto the stage. When a few seconds later they launched into their set, Martin reached out to steady himself on the railing; it was not just the volume but a density that seemed to envelop and move the audience as if they were all part of a giant coral reef. He felt the tremulant distortion rush into him, flooding over and then through the walls he had spent so many years constructing. He closed his eyes and saw the city on the backs of his eyelids, the way it looked from an airplane at night, splayed out like neurons pulsing in time with the booming, hypnotic drum beat, and as he strained to decipher the weightless vocal lines, he knew he would never forget this moment, that he would always associate it with a sense of being scrubbed clean of the past. He looked at Maria, and she nodded back, her eyes silver with revelation and—just as he had hoped—a hint of gratitude that he completely understood, for it was the currency of being introduced to music or art that you had never before encountered but that felt like it had arisen from within you. As the band arrived at a frenzied, orchestrated drone that to Martin resonated not so much with sound as with the truth, Maria reached out her left hand, which he in turn held with his right.

39

On Fire

BAYREUTH, 2002. The morning of what was being billed as the performance of her career, Maria dragged herself out of bed, wrapped herself in a hooded cloak, and donned the biggest, darkest sunglasses she could fish out of the bottom of her suitcase. In her dressing room at the theater, after taking a long shower, she barely noticed when a dresser came in to make a final adjustment to her robe and another appeared to tie her long black hair up into a Grecian knot;

as she stared into the mirror and absently continued to warm up her voice, she felt as if she were looking at herself through a deep pool of water.

All preparations came to a halt less than thirty minutes before curtain, when the sound of frantic feet and muffled shouts jarred her from the fragile tranquillity she had worked so hard to attain. She threw open the door and grabbed an intern, an epicene, straw-haired youth not older than seventeen, who in fits and starts explained that the man playing Tristan—a Dane—had toppled off a scaffolding he had climbed in order to retrieve a sword that someone had placed there—nobody knew who or why—with the intention of demonstrating to his cover an irrelevant point about how some props were better made than others. The Dane had lost his footing and fallen from a height of ten feet onto the understudy, who in his attempt to back out of the way had tripped over his feet and landed on his back. The injuries were not minor: the Dane had apparently broken his wrist attempting to brace the impact, and the understudy also claimed to have cracked a rib from absorbing the weight of a 250-plus-pound man falling on him from such a height.

Maria released her captive and listened to the shouts for medical personnel. She went back to her dressing room, where after deciding not to suppress an urge to smash something, she threw against the wall a small glass water bottle, which exploded in a satisfying pop. She knew it was a ridiculous thing to have done, but it somehow felt necessary at this point, and the fact that it actually did calm her down seemed to justify the act. Then she thought of her Tristan—to whom minutes earlier she had been ready to devote her entire being—and wanted to scream at him for being so stupid. And why couldn't he simply ignore the pain? Tenors were such fucking babies! She could have snapped her own wrist in half right there in the dressing room and held on long enough to get through the show. In fact, she had

practically done just that in a Covent Garden *Elektra* a few years earlier, after severely twisting her left knee in a fall over a loose wire
as she made her entrance. As excruciating as it had been—and she
had later required arthroscopic surgery to repair the tendon—she
had put the pain in a mental box for the duration, allowing it to burst
open only after the final curtain came down. Then she pictured him
again—her Tristan—and knew that not everybody had her freakish ability to withstand physical pain, and she wanted to hold him, to
comfort him, to tell him that they would sing together soon, even if
he had to perform with a cast on his wrist and a bandage on his nose
after she had punched him for being so careless.

Her reverie was interrupted by a knock on her door, which she
opened to find a contingent of festival heavyweights: the intendant,
the conductor, the stage director, and a fourth man who looked
vaguely familiar. "Is it true?" Maria demanded, after they had filed
in. "Did those *Dumpfbacken* really fall on each other?"

"Unfortunately, they did," the intendant confirmed and then gave
a brief account of the accident, which more or less conformed to the
intern's version, before getting straight to the point: neither Tristan
was available.

Maria could barely bring herself to speak. "So we're canceling?"

"Not necessarily. We have a replacement."

"Someone I've worked with?"

"No—"

"Or rehearsed with? Even once?"

"No—"

"My fucking God." Maria pounded her palm against the wall. She
desperately wanted to sing, but not with some third-tier crackpot.
"So I get to make my debut with—"

The intendant flashed a thin but indulgent smile and gestured
toward the fourth man. "I presume you know Leo Metropolis."

"Leo Metropolis?" Maria repeated and realized why he looked so familiar: she had met him almost twenty years earlier.

"Maria." Leo smiled, and to hear his voice made her head swim with the memory of her final year at Juilliard, after she had been knocked out by Lucia Popp's Queen of the Night. She could almost taste the accompanying malaise, which made her detest him for a second, until she remembered how he had helped her and considered whether he might be able to do it again. A few seconds passed, and nobody spoke. Maria stared at Leo and tried to reconcile the man who stood in front of her with the one from her memories. She regretted that she had not seen him since, either onstage or off, to give her a better basis of comparison. Although Anna had never heard Leo, Linda had always claimed that Leo was the best Tristan she had ever seen, and Martin Vallence had not only seen him perform but also—in an even stranger coincidence—had bought Leo's house in Washington Heights; lovely as it was, Maria had visited only once, which given her schedule was not exactly surprising. So it wasn't that she hadn't heard about Leo during these years, but that he had simply hovered somewhere just beyond her immediate attention, which made his appearance now feel almost inevitable.

What was almost odder than his presence—and perhaps unfair—was that twenty years seemed to have barely changed him; he was still big and fierce-looking, with intensely angled eyebrows, a high forehead, and the kind of short silver hair that allowed certain men to appear relatively ageless. She would have been surprised if he was sixty, but that made no sense given that he had been singing dramatic roles from at least the late 1960s, when she had to assume he would have been in his late thirties or forties. Then again, there had always been something elusive and eccentric about his career, and it occurred to her that perhaps he had started singing at a younger age than she could have imagined, or than conventional wisdom—especially for Wagnerians—would dictate. She also knew that when she was twenty, most thirty-five-year-old men looked much older to her than the same age difference would appear to her at forty-one; so maybe he was forty in 1981, which would now make him a young-looking sixty or sixty-one, which was not entirely implausible.

In any event, it was his ability—not his age—that ultimately mattered, and for her to claim anything else would have been hypocritical, given her own refusal—like most singers she knew—ever to discuss the topic of age, at least publicly. She opened an unsmashed bottle of mineral water and swished the bubbly liquid around in her mouth; to flatten the carbonation made her feel a little better, a little tougher, that much more in control of the situation as she addressed him. "So—Leo Metropolis—I didn't know you were still singing."

"If the opportunity arises," he said, and nodded slyly.

"And you're ready?" Maria went on a bit dreamily as she tried to rein in her thoughts. "No rehearsal?"

"I'm always ready," he responded with an arrogance that under almost any other circumstances would have irritated her, to say the least, but at this moment left her more unnerved by the thought that it was a challenge she would have issued herself.

The intendant clutched his hands together in front of his chest and made a slight bow. "I'm sorry, but under the circumstances—"

Maria watched his lips move and weighed her options. She could imagine general managers throughout the world getting wind of this and reasoning that if an opera could be pulled off without any rehearsal at all, why not make no rehearsals the rule instead of the exception? She knew on one hand she could balk—she could push them out the door and say no fucking thanks—and count on any number of sympathetic ears; accidents happened, the opening would be pushed back to the next scheduled performance, and the house would have to take the hit. On the other hand, it was the sort of unpredictable event that made Maria love the theater, where accidents could—and did—happen, even at the highest levels; that they were in Bayreuth, with its perfectly manicured flower beds and sepulchral Wagnerism—a place where such rituals were *never* supposed to go wrong—was not lost on her.

Leo stared back with a salacious expression in which she recognized an obsessive desire to sing that mirrored her own, and she felt all of her objections gather like lemmings and run into a chasm of irrelevance. She took a few moments to compose herself and then looked at each of the men in turn. "Gentlemen, despite the short notice, and because I have no reason to believe that something so idiotic could have been planned, and because I have, up to this point, been treated with nothing but respect by everyone here at the theater, I will sing with Mr. Metropolis." She listened to the collective sigh of relief that filled the room and then addressed the last thread of a practical thought related to how her decision might be perceived. "However!" She held up her hand, not wanting to be upstaged by a wave of Leo Metropolis hysteria. "There will be nothing said about this—that is, no announcements—until after the show, because I am looking forward to performing in an opera, not a circus."

THE LIGHTS WENT down, and a hush swept across the sold-out auditorium, quieting the buzz about the mysterious accident, which in the end delayed the curtain by only fifteen minutes. Maria/Isolde took her place on the stage, in the ship's aft quarters. She did not have to rely on great reserves of acting ability to look at Leo/Tristan with an appropriate mistrust, knowing that she planned to poison him in a murder-suicide as vengeance for killing her first betrothed and taking her to marry his uncle, the hated King Mark. That was all to come; as she waited, she gently rocked on her feet and took deep breaths, filling every available space of her body like an accordion, until, in response to the opening notes of the sailor offstage, she sang. The audience ducked to avoid the beam of sound that splayed across the theater like the first bolt of lightning in a night sky. Maria ignored the conductor—who wore the expression of one savoring the first bite of a spectacular crème brûlée—and the collective murmur that went up in recognition that—*wow!*—the American diva was really on this afternoon.

She paused when the lighting shifted to Leo, who with the lithe bearing of a toreador took three steps forward to hear—in case he was deaf—the news from his second in command that Isolde was not happy. She took in the lines of his face and the dark circles under his eyes and was impressed; he looked like a man who had endured his share of suffering, and in no way like someone walking into a role with exactly no rehearsal. None of which, however, prepared her for what happened when, a few seconds later, he began to sing; as soon as Maria heard him, she gripped the lines of the ship and whispered, "Holyfuckingchrist," as if her entire life were a thin sheet of paper about to be tossed into the flames. Here she was at the height of her power, and the legendary Leo Metropolis had just materialized to step on her like a bug.

Filled with fear and doubt, she hated him and whatever or who-ever was responsible for this moment; she leaned precariously over the rail, seasick with futility, until her Brangäne pulled her back into position, where—perhaps aided by the touch of a fellow singer—she began to concentrate. She spent a few seconds analyzing his voice, the way it seemed to weave through the house, around the columns, and under and over the wooden-backed seats. It was big and stento-rian, but not shrill or athletic; his diction was perfect, and she decided he must be German after all, or Viennese. She remembered what he had said to her—not in the dressing room but twenty years earlier—about his belief in performance, and she felt a spark. Maybe—no, what was she fucking thinking?—*definitely* like him, she could not live without opera; in fact, everything she had ever done—and more than that, everything that had ever happened to her—was in preparation for this moment. She now saw Leo less as a challenge than as a fellow acolyte, ready to welcome her into the fold. She stood up and—beaming with reverence—sang with a conviction as intense as the corresponding anger and doubt that had preceded it. Bombs and missiles could have exploded around her and left her unfazed; she could have played hopscotch or walked a tightrope over a deep canyon, all without missing a single note.

THEY SHARED THE love potion, which poured down her throat like hot poison, and then became an open wound of desire that grew more infected with each passing second. When the act ended and she was ripped from Leo's arms, it was an apocalypse: writhing, she had to be passed to her dressing room like a bucket of water by a line of production assistants and there propped onto a couch and spoon-fed sips of tea to keep her throat moist. Outside the theater, the audience ran laps around the gardens, reviving an old German tradition as they considered what they had just witnessed and, even more important, prepared for what was still to come.

In the final minutes of the intermission, Maria galloped to the stage. She hardly noticed when the curtain parted and the music began, as she sat with Leo under the cloak of moonlight. They sang to each other while he removed the pins and combs holding up her long black hair, then wrapped it around his hands, pulling her closer and closer, until Maria was sure that their hearts had been fused. That their love was an illicit betrayal of the king only heightened her sense that every second spent with him was more valuable than an entire lifetime apart, and she knew she would rather die than endure another separation. When the king's man drew his sword and plunged it into Tristan, Maria looked down at her own body with disbelief; the pain she experienced made it impossible not to believe that she, too, had been impaled, and that her blood also ran down the stage. After the curtain closed, she staggered as if newly blinded back to her dressing room, clutching the walls for support.

During Act III, listening from the wings to her mortally wounded Tristan, she had to be restrained from taking the stage to comfort him. At last freed, she rushed out, only to realize as she saw his ashen face and held his limp hand that it was too late; she heard the echo of his dying words. Tristan was dead, and now it would be Isolde's turn: she turned to face the audience one last time and began her final song of love and death, her *Liebestod*. As Isolde prepared to die for Tristan, Maria—now but a dim star on a misty night—expected to follow. What was the point of living? She had given everything to her voice and to the music for which it was made; she felt exonerated from the pain of life, and could not bear the thought of renewing it; she had never felt so exhausted.

She entered the last bars of her aria, and as her heart slowed—the ultimate control of an involuntary muscle—to a final beat, she closed her eyes and savored for the last time the awed silence hovering over the theater. She heard someone else singing, and—like two shafts of light refracted into a single beam—this other voice joined hers in a perfect unison that gradually softened into an exquisite pianissimo. She assumed it was death, because nothing, not even Leo, had ever sounded so sweet and strong, but it was a female voice, and like a maternal hand, it reached into the deep water and clasped Maria's fading consciousness to pull her gently to the surface.

THE CURTAIN CAME down, and Maria lifted her head from where it had fallen on Leo's chest. She stood up and shivered as she tried to find her balance. She watched Leo follow her to his feet; just as unsteady, he seemed exceedingly frail, nothing but costume and makeup as he collapsed against a boulder, breathing hard. Maria tried to catch his attention, but he was inaccessible, his eyes rheumy in the light. Neither moved until a group of stagehands appeared from the wings to help them down to the front of the stage, where they split the curtain and gingerly took their bows. Maria had never seen an audience in such a frenzy, rioting and screaming as they begged not to be dragged back to the dungeon of existence from which they had been so briefly rescued. They buried the stage in red roses for love and black delphiniums for death, and still they called for more. It was easy for her to imagine that soon they would go home to change careers and conceive children, to call long-lost relatives, to divulge their darkest secrets, and to forgive unforgivable sins. It was, she realized, just as Anna had predicted so many years earlier, when she had first spoken to her about their gift, and the potential it held for those who did not share it. Maria had no doubt that those who had seen this performance would never forget how the opera can make and alter history, and how, on this night, history had been made and altered.

40

Fashion Is a Canon for This Dialectic Also

PARIS, 1871. The commune was over. Bodies were retrieved from the rubble, buildings—charred from fire—torn down, and empty lots cleared of debris. The nobility returned from their summer estates, while the architects and bankers surveyed and measured as they began to raise capital to rebuild what had been destroyed. As much as Lucien understood that all of this represented a resurrection of sorts, to witness it repulsed him, as if he and his fellow citizens were maggots eating away at the dead parts of the city to make way for the new, while the constant hammering and scraping together of bricks and stones created a cacophony that invaded his dreams.

As soon as Codruta arrived at the Georges, he went to see her.

"So you're back," she said, as if he had not spent much of the previous year on the sinking ship of the Île while she had weathered the storm in the Loire Valley.

He shook his head as if to say no, he was not back at all, except for the fact that he was sitting here in this room, where despite everything he was soothed by the familiar clink of her spoon against the teacup. It almost made him angry at her, until she offered her condolences about his father and her hope that he would remain in the apartment, at which point he saw her as if he were a child and felt vaguely—nostalgically—enthralled by the gilt trim of the windows and mirrors, which still gleamed in the bronze sun.

"Yes, I'm back," he said, but then reconsidered. "But I'm leaving Paris," he added, and the second the words left his mouth he knew it was true.

She smiled gingerly. "Nonsense."

He continued more gently: "I wanted to say good-bye."

Her hands trembled as she raised the cup to her lips, and it occurred to Lucien that she, too, was afraid, not only for herself, because she was getting rather old, but of everything that had happened to the city that she loved and that to some extent she no longer recognized. He also knew she understood his intent and was only acting now, because she had always refused to argue about anything, and at this moment—most certainly their last together—she wanted to pretend. "You still haven't told me," she said in a low voice that seemed to skip off the surface of her tea, "when I can expect to hear you at the Paris Opéra."

While a part of him wanted nothing more than to please her, to sing for her and all of her important friends and relaunch his career in Paris, and most of all to give voice to the mutating and oddly distorted strains of sound that had been festering in his mind, he knew it could not happen. Though he no longer attributed his inability to sing to a particular grief for Eduard, he was beginning to detect the contours of a much larger and more complex grief—for his youth, for the city, for his parents—that left him too bereft to consider singing, at least for the foreseeable future. Whether he could sing or not, he knew he had to leave Paris; he could not bear to see Codruta die but wanted to remember her, like the city in which they had lived, as alive and glimmering.

He managed to smile graciously, just as she had taught him. "Soon—very soon," he promised with serene confidence, despite knowing that by the next day, he would be gone.

HE WENT TO Vienna, where he wrapped up his affairs before heading south to Rome and then to Civitavecchia, where he boarded the first of two ships en route to New York. He brought with him only a few tangible remnants of his past: letters from Eduard, the *Tristan* manuscript—into which he had placed his father's formula, as if one were the antidote to the other—and a few rings Codruta had given to him over the years. On most nights—weather permitting, and sometimes when it didn't, because the rain and fog offered a different allure—he left his cabin and went above to contemplate the expanse of the passing water from the deck. The ocean, it seemed, was the opposite of a city, and if it lacked in art and genius, its mutating waters invited reflection. He liked to imagine the horizon passing through him in a thin, straight line, as if connecting the future to his past, notwithstanding the certainty, as he would have been the first to admit, that this was really only a hope—or perhaps a distraction—from his true past, which could never have been described as anything but jagged and erratic.

It was strange to remember—as he sometimes did—that he had been a famous singer, and he could even smile as he remembered the joy of offering his voice to the public and how appreciative they had been in return. Yet as he reflected on more distant episodes of his life, he was troubled by the way new details never ceased to surface, always raising doubts and questions; it made him nervous about moving to a new city—which he had chosen with the hope to be as unencumbered by the past as possible—and only the flat, silver plane of the ocean made it possible to believe that anything he had ever done or felt, no matter how brutal or exhilarating, was as distant as the land he had not seen for weeks.

Although just slightly more than a year had passed since he had taken the vaccine, he was now more inclined to think that it had worked. He seemed to shave less and sometimes at night woke up with his pulse almost gone, like he had slipped into a coma. His needs and desires, at least for now, remained admittedly blunted and primitive: when he was tired, he slept; when he was hungry, he ate, although never robustly. Any sensual longing—even the basest forms—had been relegated to the same empty room as his voice. There were men on the ship he knew he might have found attractive, but he could only watch them from behind the glass walls of an aquarium in which there was space for one. At times he fantasized about offering the vaccine to someone else—someone he loved—but there was still too much uncertainty, not to mention the conundrum of risking the life of anyone who might want to take it. After what had happened to his father, he could not imagine offering the formula to another scientist or university or government; he was afraid of not only what they might do with the vaccine but also what they might do to him, knowing that he had taken it and survived.

AS HE WATCHED a whale launch its massive body above the surface and there seem to float for a second before smashing down with a tremendous splash, he was struck by an eternal quality of the ocean and its denizens, so that even the idea of a two-hundred-year life suddenly seemed brief and inconsequential. The passage of time, he was starting to realize, was filled with arbitrary notions of hours, days, and years, all of which might be as useless to him now as they were to a fish or a bird, and while there were countless institutions and traditions built around the fact that people did not live beyond an age of seventy or eighty or ninety, he had already resolved not to give himself to any of them. As the wind ripped through his shirt to dry the sweat from his chest and arms, it helped him to be reminded that no matter how long he lived, it would still be a mere fragment compared to the life of lakes or conifers or even sea turtles. He thought of cities, which as he could now painfully attest also thrived and suffered in cycles that bore remarkably little relation to the life spans of those who created them. When he had first decided to come to New York, it was little more than an intuition, but he now recognized a more concrete hope to find an entity whose existence might be expected to mirror—and likely outlast—his own. He remembered his vow to his father: to discover some truth about the world and his place in it, to justify his life, and to give it meaning for as long as it lasted. There were moments when he wavered and the prospect frightened him, mostly on account of the loneliness it seemed to promise, but he tried to push these fears aside. He was both sorry and not sorry to be alive, for in the rushing air he could imagine melodies, dulcet and pristine, even as he acknowledged that to sing any of them would for the moment be impossible.

41

Cocksucker Blues

NEW YORK CITY, 2002. August had arrived, and even at the highest point in Manhattan it was feverishly hot. Though Martin's garden had held up well, as he stood inside the sliding glass door and squinted out at the hostile sun, none of the plants in his troughs—not even the gracefully weeping blue spruce, the adorable hen and chicks, or the delicate bell-shaped campanula blooms, all of which just weeks earlier had filled him with such contemplative satisfaction—aroused in him anything but vague loathing. It made him question whether any of "the progress" he had made over the past year, the sense of reconciliation and forgiveness—in terms of himself and others—was anything but a charade, given the way life always conspired to deliver new and unexpected forms of misery from which there could be no escape. He knew that others might laugh or scoff at the nature of his particular plight, but he didn't care; the fact remained that Beatrice was extremely sick—she was in the hospital—which made the surrounding life seem garish and futile.

It had started a week earlier, when he noticed that she seemed thinner than usual. "You know, Beatrice, you could stand to eat a bit more," he had commented after she appeared on the edge of his bed, and he tried to decide if she really had lost weight. It was difficult to assess, given that—despite his almost nightly attempts to coax her in, and her increasing willingness to allow him to rest a single fingertip for one or two seconds on her back—he had never picked her up. On this night, she had looked back at him with a mix of coy intensity and dismissal, as if whatever he was saying, she couldn't quite imagine the stupidity of it. "Well, you don't seem sick," he concluded, but began to monitor her more closely.

For several days she appeared for meals, but she never spent more than a few seconds at the plate before walking away uninterested. While this, too, was hardly unprecedented—she had always been finicky—he became more concerned when she turned up her nose at a fresh cocktail shrimp, which just a month before would have delivered her into something closer to a state of ecstasy.

Martin scheduled an appointment with the vet for the next afternoon, but when Beatrice spent the rest of the day and that night under the bed, Martin—after conferring with the vet over the phone—decided to take her to the emergency room. He went into the bedroom to break the news. "Beatrice," he began softly after kneeling down, "I'm sorry, but we need to go to the hospital." She did not respond, leaving him at a loss as to what to do. He spent a few minutes trying to reason with her as she peered back, her eyes dull and metallic like the heads of nails. Food was obviously not going to entice her at this point, and he did not like the idea of chasing her out, in the event it might exacerbate whatever was wrong. "Beatrice—please—you're sick," Martin begged. "Will you come out for me?"

When she would not, Martin retrieved the carrier from the closet and brought it back to the bedroom, the door of which he shut to keep out Dante, whose pacing and moaning seemed to convey an understanding that something perilous was afoot. Martin pulled down the cover from the bed and sat on top of the mattress, as if he were about to go to sleep. "Beatrice," he called and tapped on the bed three times, their usual signal. He held his breath for a few seconds and repeated the taps; finally, somewhat clumsily, she staggered out, jumped up on top of the bed, and took a few tentative steps toward him in her growth-stunted waddle. Martin suppressed his dismay at seeing how much smaller she had become in just two days. Worse, she trembled slightly, just like the first time he had seen her, trapped in the corner of that miserable cage at the vet's office.

Still, out in the light, her eyes seemed brighter, and Martin tried to reassure her. "Beatrice, I know this is going to feel like a betrayal, but you need to see a doctor. I'm sure it's nothing—maybe you have a summer cold." As he finished saying this, he lunged for her with his left hand—still quick from his hockey days—and managed to scoop her up against his body as he placed his other hand on the scruff of her neck to hold her steady. Weak as she was, she could not escape, although she fought and cried as he managed to stand slowly and place her, one leg at a time, into the crate. Martin was relieved to note that she had the strength to scratch, so that a rivulet of blood ran down the inside of his left arm.

After setting her down by the front door, he ran around the corner to the garage to pick up his car. When he returned a few minutes later, Dante was sitting in front of her carrier, licking her paws, and Martin was relieved that Beatrice was no longer crying. "Say good-bye now," he instructed them, "just for a little while."

He drove down Fort Washington to Broadway and crossed east on 155th, past the public-housing towers at the old Polo Grounds. "We don't like Robert Moses, do we?" he asked in an attempt to distract her, but she remained quiet as he entered the Harlem River Drive and started south. "You picked a good time to get sick," he pointed out. "Not only is it August but it's Sunday, so there's no traffic." In less than ten minutes, they arrived at the Animal Medical Center, which—he could not fail to note with a mix of trepidation and hope—was not far from Sloan-Kettering. "You're going to get the best doctors in the world," he declared, an assessment that seemed to be confirmed by the high-tech swoosh of the automatic doors and the army of staff inside.

It was harder to remain optimistic as he stepped into the inalterably dreary scene of a Sunday afternoon at the emergency room, where he passed through a waiting area filled with sad-looking families and their even sadder-looking pets, along with an assortment of chairs, pay phones, and vending machines. After he explained the situation to a receptionist, he was given the intake forms, which he filled out among the ranks of the downtrodden as he now and again placed one of his fingers through the metal grate of her carrier, where Beatrice sat quietly petrified. From behind the reception counter, Martin could hear people sobbing as vets delivered bad news or worse. Someone walked by on a cell phone, weeping. "Don't worry," he whispered to Beatrice. "You're going to be fine."

After fifteen minutes or so, Martin was led to an examination room for a preliminary consultation with a doctor, who shook Beatrice out of the cage and grabbed her by the scruff of the neck. "She's very yellow," he said as he folded back the inside of her ear. "When's the last time she ate?"

"I—I don't know," Martin admitted. "A few days ago?"

"It looks like hepatic lipidosis," the vet explained. "If cats stop eating for any reason, the fatty cells of their tissues can basically overrun the liver and shut it down."

Martin dug his fingernails into his palms. "Why would she stop eating?"

"It could be anything—a cold, a change in food, depression."

"A cold? Depression?" Martin took a second to digest this, restraining the urge to reason away such a ridiculous premise. "Can you help her?"

"We can try," the vet said in an efficient but superficial tone Martin found somewhat more comforting, before he left to complete the paperwork. This gave Martin a few minutes alone with Beatrice, who now cowered under a small sink, which along with the concrete floor and beige tiles reminded him of the nurse's room at his old elementary school in Cedar Village, not that such memories—as he bitterly noted—were going to be of any use.

"Little Beatrice, they're going to fix you up," he nevertheless promised as he kneeled down beside her; as he spoke, he tentatively reached out his hand but withdrew it when she shrank away.

HE RETURNED FOR visiting hours the following day and met with her "team," all of whom agreed that, while the case was severe, the official stance was one of guarded optimism. The plan was to reverse the lipidosis by tube feeding until her liver kicked in and began to function normally, which the doctors assured him was by no means an unprecedented prognosis, particularly given her age. They had already placed her in intensive care, where he found her in an oxygenated chamber with a feeding tube running through her nose, various IVs attached through each of her hind legs, and her head in one of those plastic cones that looked like an Elizabethan collar. "Beatrice? Are you okay?" he whispered through the cage, and in response, she moaned softly and moved her eyes, which despite her obvious weakness the doctor said was a good sign.

The next morning—Tuesday—Martin received a call from one of the doctors, who told him that, for no reason anybody could figure out, Beatrice's sodium levels—her "electrolytes," a word Martin was surprised to learn existed outside television commercials—had dropped overnight to precarious levels. He immediately went in to find her completely unresponsive, even when he called her name. "What happened?" he asked one of the team members.

"Well, she was weaker than we thought," the doctor explained. "But we had a specialist in this morning, and she made some adjustments. Our most recent readings actually show her electrolytes stabilizing, which is good."

On Wednesday, Martin brought her a few clippings from his planter troughs. It pained him to think that, except for her time in a Dumpster in Brooklyn, she had never been outside but had often watched him intently through the window as he worked with his plants. He had considered letting both her and Dante onto the deck but was afraid—especially in her case—that he wouldn't be able to get them back in. He allowed himself to believe that the clippings helped; or at least something was helping, because she seemed a little stronger, and even stood up like a newborn foal when Martin called to her. "Dante can't wait until you're home," he added, fending off any doubt with this show of conviction. "He would have come himself, but you know how carsick he gets."

On Thursday, another doctor called to give the morning report. "She's not out of the woods yet," she said, "but her sodium has stabilized and her most recent blood work looks good, so I think we can remain optimistic."

Martin went to visit filled with hope: the last four days had been excruciating, particularly as he watched Dante look for Beatrice under the bed, in the pantry, among the orchids, and in her other usual hiding spots; although he tried to reassure himself that for animals fear—much less grief—exists only in the most present and literal situations, he could not shake the idea that Beatrice's sickness had upset a certain psychological balance in the house, and that Dante was no more immune than he was.

But when Martin arrived at the hospital, Beatrice was completely unresponsive, practically comatose. In a panic, he tried to find someone from her team but could locate only an oncologist unfamiliar with her case.

"Her blood work does look better," she noted as she examined the charts. "Maybe she's just tired."

Martin sat with her until visiting hours ended at nine and then went home. "She was tired," he numbly repeated to Dante. "It's just going to take a little longer than we expected."

IT WAS NOW Friday morning; the phone rang and Martin jumped to answer: it was a doctor, who relayed a new theory that some sort of primary condition—cancer perhaps—had brought on the lipidosis, but they could confirm this only with a liver biopsy, a process that in itself greatly lowered the prognosis for recovery. "So what should we do?" Martin asked.

"I think you should come in if you can, and we'll talk about it."

Too anxious to drive and wanting to avoid rush-hour traffic, Martin decided to take the subway. As he walked to the station, the sun hovered cruelly overhead: it made him feel not only scrutinized but slightly paranoid, as if he were being punished for crimes he did not commit or, even worse, crimes which he did commit but for which others were now going to pay the price.

At the hospital, he found Beatrice crumpled and dirty in the corner of her intensive-care unit. Her rib cage heaved in and out with each breath, and her eyes were cloudy and distant. There was no question about what to do. He instructed the team to stop treatment; there would be no biopsy. He asked them to remove the feeding tube and the collar before they brought her out of intensive care and into an examination room so that he could say good-bye.

When she was delivered to him, she was destroyed, worse than drowned, even worse than the day before; her coat was greasy and covered with flecks of dander, her mouth and eyes were coated by thick gobs of something white and unidentifiable; her nose bled from where they had removed the feeding tube, and her skin hung off her ribs and spine. She still had IVs in each of her hind legs, one wrapped in blue gauze and one in red. The pads of her feet felt cold, and he wondered why they had wrapped the IVs so tightly. "Beatrice," he managed between deep breaths. "You're covered in snow."

She tried to stand and managed to totter a step or two before she collapsed against the wall. Her eyes remained open but were dull and motionless, even when Martin showed her a golden bauble with several feathers attached to it he had brought to remind her of home. He told her about everything that had happened during the past week; how hot it was outside, how Dante kept looking for her under the bed, and how none of the games they played were as fun without her. He told her that he hadn't been able to sleep without her saying good night to him. She raised her head a little as Martin placed a finger under her shivering chin. "I know," he said, trying to sound less dire, "you don't want to suffer anymore."

Martin, awash in helplessness, could think of nothing but to restore some semblance of dignity to the most undignified thing in the world, i.e., death in a modern hospital. He took a small cloth he had brought with him and started with her face. As best as he could, he gently wiped away the thick saliva from her cheeks, the blood that trickled out of her nose, and the gunk from around her eyes; from there he moved down to her neck, chafed from the collar, and then to her shoulders and down her side, where each one of her raspy and labored breaths continued to make her stomach rise and fall with a shudder. As he cleaned her polydactyl paws, he remembered how his mother had told him that they were supposed to be good luck, and for a second he hated Jane for it. But this was fleeting, because he knew that Jane had been right about Beatrice, which was why it was so difficult to think of losing her. There was a tap against the window, and Martin nodded before he turned back to her. "Beatrice," he whispered, "I have to call the doctor in now, okay?"

The vet came in armed with a hypodermic full of barbiturate, which he inserted into the IV of one her hind legs as Martin kneeled down and placed one of his big hands over her tiny stomach and a finger under her head. "You're going to sleep now," he managed as the vet plunged the syringe into the IV and Martin looked into her dark green eyes for the last time and saw a flicker of the aurora borealis, and then nothing at all, and he knew that she was dead. He felt baffled by her lifeless form as he picked her up and held her for the first and last time while great drops splashed out of his eyes against the floor. He considered her mitten-paws, which he caressed between his thumb and index finger, and thought about the cold and arbitrary side of nature, its complete disregard for fairness or worth in the choice of life or death. With this certainty came a rush of hatred for life, if it meant having to die in a clinical hell so far from anything of comfort you had ever known, nor did he hesitate to acknowledge an even deeper hatred for those he felt confident would belittle this display of grief from a very large and once athletic man for a very tiny cat, probably just one of thousands that were dying all over the world at this exact second; he recalled a piece in the *Times* lamenting the money spent on pets with so many disasters in the world, as if one were the cause of the other, and he hated the logical part of himself that agreed with all of them, and the accompanying sense of shame he felt at his incapacity to love anyone more than Beatrice.

But as this crippled truth washed over him, it felt as pure as anything he had ever known, and he swore that as long as Beatrice was dead—and her tiny, limp body, fifty times smaller than his own, proved that she was—he would not forget her, which was the only faith he would ever believe in. He tenderly placed her back onto the stainless-steel table and covered her with a hospital blue plastic padded blanket, so that only her head poked out from underneath. He thought of the many nights when she, in effect, had done the same for him, watching over him as he had drifted off to sleep. She had been so small, so fragile, and so ephemeral, really a most insignificant piece of the universe, and in this regard—he realized as he considered the futility he had experienced trying to save her—no different from him. Yet she had been aware and unstinting in her awareness, for was it not true, he next realized, that, as much as he had provided for her—in the most obvious and practical of ways—she had also cared for him?

He touched her one last time and tried to close her eyelids, which did not work. He felt her paw and then opened the door. *"Requiescat in pace,* Beatrice," he whispered through the glass pane and, looking back, feared he would never leave the room behind.

OUTSIDE, HE SLOWLY walked west under an alabaster sky marked by the blue perimeter of an infected blister; it more than festered, it felt permanent, and he tried and failed to imagine a time when it had not been one hundred degrees, when he could take more than two steps without feeling the sting of sweat in his eyes, or the spongy wet elastic of his boxer shorts as they expanded and contracted around his waist. He looked at his arms, where the scratches were starting to heal, and he regretted that, soon enough, every sign of Beatrice would be forever relegated to his dreams and memories. In a daze, he stumbled across Central Park. He considered taking a cab, but the thought of stopping and starting made him nauseated; he again opted for the subway but decided to get something to drink when he realized his throat was dry and raw.

He was about halfway down the block on Seventy-fourth Street when he edged between the bumpers of two parked cars on the south side of the street with the intention to jaywalk to the north side on the hypotenuse to avoid the extra distance to the corner—was there anyone, he wondered, who didn't count every step in this heat?—and looked in the wrong direction as he stepped into the street. As soon as he realized what he had done—i.e., walked in front of a roaring taxicab only nanoseconds away from occupying the same space as his body—the mistake surprised him: he had lived in New York City for "only" twenty years. In his defense, he reconsidered, as he coldly observed the white glare of the approaching windshield, a tendency toward the delusional was understandable in his state. Mitigating or not, this excuse, along with the fact that he had been partially correct—to the extent that it was a one-way street—and that nine times out of ten it would have been of no consequence, did not alter the apparent verdict, which despite his lack of bad intention, or any intention at all, was imminent death. He listened to the distorted roar of the car's transmission and knew it was too late—and way too hot—to escape. He braced himself and sighed; his life seemed so far away before this moment, yet he no longer feared death. As with everyone, he supposed, life had lasted for a little while and now it would end; uncountable others were being born at this very second, and in not very long they, too, would be gone, participants in the same tedious soap opera that Martin would not be sorry to miss.

Then the thought of leaving Dante pained him, despite the fact that Martin had provided for him in his will. He was filled with longing; to go to Sydney, to fall in love, to do something noble for the thousands of underprivileged groups in society—the elderly, the sick, the poor, the transgendered teens, the stray dogs and cats—to go back uptown and mourn with Dante, to watch *L'Atalante*, listen to music, read books, and chatter at the birds, just as they had done until Beatrice had gotten sick. He did not, he decided after all, want to abandon his garden, which would take at least three years to acquire the lush quality he liked to envision when choosing his plants. He did not want to miss a second date he had scheduled with his plant-loving friend, because they were planning to visit the beech trees at Wave Hill in the Bronx, said to be some of the most magnificent in the city. He wanted to confess to someone the extent of his grief for

Beatrice—not on a second date, perhaps, but possibly on a third—
and be that much more understood and absolved, which now struck
him as an eminently reasonable goal in life. To die, he realized, could
mean so many things, and the literal reality of it had not eliminated
his desire for something new, a metaphorical death of the present.
But with no choice, he regretfully closed his eyes and waited for the
inevitable. Yet for all of his preparation, it was not going to happen;
instead—and he could barely believe it—the car went right past him,
missing by inches, leaving him as unscathed as a hologram. He looked
up, more stunned than thankful; he had evidently willed it. For now,
death was a great shark in the open sea, and more forgiving prey was
apparently at hand.

42

Mrs. Stevens Hears the Mermaids Singing

NEW YORK CITY, 2002. On her way out of the apart-
ment, Anna paused in front of a mirror in her foyer, where she ran a
hand over her silver hair, tied up in a simple bun, and briefly examined her khaki pants and zippered black lamb's-wool cardigan. She
had sustained this uniform for enough years that those who knew her
at Juilliard took it for granted, while to her former students she appeared most miraculous, as if she had somehow not aged while they
had succumbed to the effects of a thousand intercontinental flights
and opening night banquets. Whenever she met one of her exhausted
protégés, she felt grateful to have worked when widespread jet travel
was still a novelty, when singers weren't expected to perform in Los
Angeles one night and Paris the next.

She heard the clock strike four; it was beyond time to go. She yelled good-bye to the domestic, double-checked her handbag for keys, and—most important—picked up the brown string-tie folder with the *Tristan* manuscript inside. As she waited for the elevator, she assessed her chronic health problems—tendonitis in the left ankle, arthritic knee, leaky bladder—and was happy that they all seemed to be in check, if not remission, this particular afternoon. In the lobby she smiled at the doorman, a ruddy-cheeked Irishman who jumped up from his desk to hold the door, and once outside allowed herself a few seconds to adjust to the blast of hot, muggy air she knew would be her companion outside. As she put on her sunglasses, a large white frame of two oblong ovals she had worn well before Jackie made them famous, Charlie asked if she wanted him to call her a cab, but she waved him off, explaining she would get one on Columbus.

She stepped out from under the portico and turned right, where she noted a distant honk and a car speeding by—as usual, much too fast—and then the murmured conversation, first distant and then close, of a pair of women headed in the opposite direction. Her thoughts were interrupted by a squeal of tires and the sound of a something heavy thumping over the curb, and before she could even turn it was upon her. She instinctively jumped to the side, an impressive leap that showcased her strength and agility even at eighty-two, but Death, who clearly enjoyed this kind of spectacle—and was very comfortable in the heat—had already arranged for the taxi to buck up and down like a mechanical bull, so that it caught Anna at just the right angle under the fender and catapulted her backward into the air.

She began her flight, a long and—she could only hope—not un-graceful arc, an almost horizontal dive, during which her feet trav-eled up behind her ears and back down again, as her arms—having released her handbag and folder, the latter of which sailed directly toward a man who, as far as she could tell, had caused this calamity, for he stood dumbstruck in the middle of the street—fell freely to her sides and provided the axis to the spinning wheel of her body. Anna allowed her eyes to take in the sculpted frieze of a Beaux Arts building she had always admired, and with the hazy sky beyond, she couldn't help but note with a certain reverence how the city never ceased to be full of surprises.

BECAUSE SHE HAD long prided herself on a forthright ability to confront even the most unpleasant of truths—particularly when it came to her students, whose years of hard work could never obscure the fact that, as much as she loved them, only the smallest percentage would be able to enjoy a real career—she did not try to pretend that this accident could lead to anything but her death. While she permitted herself some sadness at the thought and even allowed for an instinctive fear of the unknown, she felt more reflective than alarmed. As she thought of her life as a whole, she was thankful to have been graced with such good fortune while others had suffered, not that there weren't a few things she would have done differently. She sighed, a breath that mingled with the heavy air flowing past her, and was again amazed at how in the desert of life, happiness, satisfaction, well-being—whatever she might call it—seemed like an oasis at which she was always pleased to arrive but where the water, no matter how deep, always ran through her fingers when raised up to drink.

She thought of the dead friends and relatives she hoped to see in the afterlife (though in limited doses, of course, and with certain subjects still off-limits). And her twins! Perhaps, wherever she was headed, she would find out what had happened to the boy; as for the girl, well, nothing had ever happened to lessen her conviction that it was Maria. Though Anna had never anticipated that one of her children might someday—and not just in a daydream—come back to her, never mind as a singer of such talent and fury, she was proud not to have disclosed her suspicion; she loved Maria and had told her so countless times, had hugged her and warned off the bad spirits with a "ptoy ptoy ptoy" before her performances, had brushed away her tears over the inevitable disappointments delivered by the men she was fated to love. All of this, Anna knew, had taken place through the prism of Maria's career, and Anna had always been careful to maintain a certain distance to prevent her relationship with Maria from extending too far into the maternal; she felt confident—given where Maria was now—that, if given the chance, she would have done the same thing again.

She looked longingly at her folder, which the man in the street had snatched out of the air and now held on his hip. She imagined the manuscript inside, a marvelous tome, bound in a mossy and only slightly matted titian velvet that had barely faded during its long existence, its heavy pages inscribed with elegant staff lines, musical notations, and directions from the composer. To lose it like this was admittedly bothersome: if only she hadn't been hit by a taxi, she lamented, she would surely be in one, en route to Juilliard, a mere eight blocks away, where she had recently made known her intention to donate it, along with the rest of her collection, to the school's library. A part of her had always wanted to give it to another singer, but Maria had preferred the Juilliard idea, which Anna could appreciate; Maria's sometimes startling lack of nostalgia or sentimentality was undoubtedly one reason she seemed destined for the kind of career that Anna suspected might even surpass her own.

She tried to remember if she had placed the address of the school anywhere on the folder, or what stationery she had used to write a short and slightly sarcastic note—Enjoy!—to the librarians, whom she had always found a bit too reverential. As for the man who caught it, unless he possessed an all too rare combination of intelligence and integrity—and how could one be optimistic, after he had drifted like such a hayseed onto the street?—he could just throw it away. It could easily end up on the black market or in a landfill, covered with all sorts of unpleasant stains, odors, acids, and residues that would destroy it well before someone might stumble across it in ten thousand years, on an archaeological dig of Fresh Kills. These regrets felt more wistful than wounded; no matter what happened, she was ready to be released from its relentless, eternal weight, and she understood better than ever why Lawrence Malcolm had lent it to her that afternoon in his antiques shop. She loved *Tristan* and had given herself to it many times, but it now seemed like an unnecessary instruction manual as she considered her own imminent return to the noumenal with something close to relief.

She took a moment to examine the man. Her eyes traveled up his arm, over the madras fabric of his short-sleeve shirt to his collar before finally arriving at his face. Despite wearing an open expression of dismay—which was never becoming on anyone—he was not loutish or unattractive. Perhaps in his forties, with nothing boyish about him, he was tall and broad, not a man who would have been so easily launched into such an airborne arc. He had a closely shorn beard, and his short hair reflected silver in the sun; he wore light khaki pants—like her own—and leather sandals, which she also noted with approval, as he looked somewhat more continental, perhaps even Mediterranean.

And then a disturbing realization: he looked exactly like Lawrence! Her mind began to spin furiously in a way it had not done for many years as she considered whether this man could be Maria's twin brother. Though stunned by the improbability of it, she resisted the impulse to question this deus ex machina. What she felt was not a crushing, panic-stricken regret—Anna was not about to throw open the entire trajectory of her life for reconsideration—but merely a sense of wonder at the infinite threads of life, and her inability ever truly to predict when and where they might or might not be woven together. Sobering as the thought of her death was—and unlike certain other characters throughout history, she did not feel like laughing—she was inspired by the idea of meeting her son like this. She looked into his eyes, and if they did not offer the absolute truth of their relationship, she felt she had achieved a certain understanding with him. She decided to believe he was her son, after all, and was it her imagination or was he even nodding back at her? And if so, wasn't it even better that he now held the manuscript?

INSPIRED BY THE thought of meeting her son like this, she wanted to sing, and with no cause for restraint, took a last, deep breath and delivered her final aria. She opened on a full, sumptuous C-natural before nimbly sliding up the scale to land on an unwavering F-sharp that would have been at home at the nearby Metropolitan Opera. She nailed it, and even better, she knew it. Her thoughts turned to Maria, who was making her debut in Bayreuth, and as Anna sustained her F-sharp, she knew that, just as she could hear Maria, at this second finishing her *Liebestod*, Maria could hear her, and for the last time they embraced.

Professional that she was, Anna projected the novelty of the experience, the way time slowed as Death teased her forward with the most sensuous caress, so that each of these final seconds seemed an eternity, while her life to that point—all eighty-two years—seemed no more than a second. She took a moment to acknowledge the appreciative nods of the many classically trained musicians who in the midst of their unemployed wanderings on the Upper West Side recognized a final performance of one of their own, a fellow obsessive who had spent a lifetime on scales and arpeggios, and who to her eternal credit had not choked or clutched in this farewell.

The sound of her voice made her pause; she knew its allure

stemmed not only from her superb technique but also from its ephemeral nature, which made its brilliance that much brighter. She felt all of
her wants—for this man, for Maria, for the manuscript, for the city, for
the grand opera itself—give way to calm resignation. Her faith both
lost and restored, she stepped back from the canvas of her life and like
a master painter made some minor adjustments, dabbing here and there
in a state of mindless serenity, not unaware of her fast-approaching
death, but not particularly bothered as she entered a last, blissful trance,
confident that her voice was an endless ripple in the sea of time.

43

In Distortion-Free Mirrors

NEW YORK CITY, 2002. The day was perfectly clear,
but as Maria looked back over the harbor at the Twin Towerless skyline, she almost wished that Linda had scheduled Anna's memorial at
night—or better, in the fog—when it might have been easier to ignore such a stark reminder of loss. Still, she was relieved to be on the
water, which at least gave her the opportunity to think for a few minutes, something that, between getting back to New York and helping
Linda plan this event, hadn't happened since long before Bayreuth.
Even—or especially—now, with her thoughts on Anna, the memory
of her Bayreuth Isolde made her smile; it had been a preposterous
night, on which so many disasters had somehow, miraculously, added
up to the best performance of her career. She considered the guests
milling about on the decks below and realized that she was looking forward to singing for Anna, to saying good-bye properly. She saw Leo
Metropolis, whom she had made sure to invite, knowing that he was

in New York. He had mentioned this after the show—before she got the call about Anna—and suggested that they meet, a proposition to which she had been more than amenable; even after the performance, she wished there could have been more time to talk—she wanted to ask how much of their conversation at Juilliard he remembered—but there had been a swarm of patrons and management—all of whom seemed to need reassurance that the performance was in fact as great as Maria knew it had been—to attend to.

Leo, who seemed to detect her thoughts, glanced up and waved at her from a lower deck, where he was talking to Martin Vallence. He looked better than he had in Bayreuth, or at least in the minutes after the show, when he'd seemed so much older than in the dressing room, much less during the performance. At the reception after the opera, he had seemed distracted and forlorn in a way that made her suspect that—despite his incredible voice—he was well into his sixties, if not older. She wanted to ask if he planned to sing again; a part of her doubted it, and even hoped he wouldn't. As she envisioned her own career, she liked to think about painting her voice on the ceiling one last time, so that future audiences might look up and remember a time when they, too, had been young, and the world and its cities had seemed so much bigger and filled with potential, and the great operatic voices had reflected this.

She waved back, and Martin—now also looking up at her—pointed at his briefcase. She still didn't understand exactly how it had happened, but he had witnessed Anna's accident and recovered the *Tristan* score; he had brought it to the service with the intention of giving it to her here, which was the first opportunity for them to meet since her return from Germany. The coincidence might have shocked her more except that her relationship with him had always resonated with an inexplicable sense of fate that—in light of where they both came from, as if they had been pulled here together out of the suburban swamp of their youth—struck her as implicitly urban, permeating the city like stray bullets and shared glances on crowded streets. Perhaps more startling to her—as she considered Martin and Leo together—was how much the two men resembled each other, with the same barrel-chested build, buzzed hairlines, and intense expressions. She did not consider this for long—she was about to sing—except that, as she turned away, she remembered that Martin had made an allusion to this resemblance years earlier, in the context of buying Leo's house, as if one had been a condition of the other.

THE YACHT STOPPED next to the Statue of Liberty, whose long gown seemed to soothe the surrounding bay, which was as flat and reflective as the September sky. The engines were turned off, and Linda led everyone into a ballroom off the main deck, where she gave a short tribute to Anna. This was followed by the musical portion of the program, sung by a selection of Anna's former students. Maria was by far the most accomplished among them and also—not coincidentally—the most daring, to the extent that she was the only one to venture outside the classical repertoire. She had chosen "Sunday Morning" by the Velvet Underground, not only because she felt confident Anna—who claimed to have seen the band once—would have appreciated the gesture but also to acknowledge Martin's role in the events surrounding Anna's death.

As she sang—a cappella, in a soft echo of a voice without a trace of vibrato—Maria's thoughts drifted back to her mother. She smelled the mix of mild soap and tangy perfume that used to hover around Gina before she went out with John on Saturday nights, followed by images of her and her mother madly cutting up construction paper for one of their backyard productions and then—going even further back—being lifted through the air, stuck to Gina's feet as she danced through the hallways of the house in Castle Shannon. She thought of her grandmother Bea—who had died peacefully in her sleep one night, not too long after Maria's graduation from Juilliard—tottering around the house with a drink in one hand and their favorite book of saints and martyrs in the other. For once Maria felt completely embraced by these memories, and she wanted to preserve them, to care for them in the same way her parents and Bea had done for her. She felt a particularly renewed sense of gratitude toward her mother—given the sometimes contentious nature of their relationship—knowing that, even if she hadn't been eloquent or refined, she had instilled in Maria the aspirations that Anna, and ultimately Maria herself, had been able to mold into the most important part of her life.

She was transported to her backyard in Castle Shannon, except it was lush and manicured like a French garden, and as she stood on one of her old stages to sing, she saw Gina, John, her grandmother, Anna, and everyone else she had ever loved—and who had loved her in return—beaming up at her. She remembered what Anna had said to her after the fire about her gift, and Maria knew that it had happened just as Anna had predicted. It made her wonder where she would go now—what her island would look like in ten years—and how long she would have the strength or the desire to maintain it before— as would one day have to happen—she let it go. She felt a pang of sadness as she considered this—which was to say, a life without her voice—but as soon as she saw it, it was gone, and she felt none of the incapacitating detachment that had so often accompanied her memories of Pittsburgh. As she continued to sing, her voice trembled with revelation; she knew that by reconciling her past, she had done the same for her future.

She arrived at the last set of the lyrics, and as she repeated the word *morning* or, as it now occurred to her, *mourning*, she knew that, in the course of singing this simple song, her grief for Anna had opened a passage to this other grief, much deeper and unresolved, at least until now. A seagull passed overhead, and its shadow crossed her face before it disappeared into a speck on the horizon. As she watched it go, Maria filled the final notes of her song with hope and redemption, so sure was she of having found both.

44

La vraie douleur est incompatible avec l'espoir

NEW YORK CITY, 2002. Martin was tempted to laugh when he recognized what Maria was singing, particularly when he realized that Leo—who was standing beside him—did not. But he was far too entranced to do anything but listen; she sang it perfectly, transforming the droning and understated cheer of the original into a melancholy but serene lullaby. He was reminded of how his own musical tastes had changed over the years, from punk to hard core to indie to opera to— lately, in the wake of Beatrice—nothing at all. To hear Maria made him want to abandon this silent, grief-stricken phase—in fact, with the realization, it was already gone—and to resume the explorations that had marked so much of the past year. It had never occurred to him that music could be so much more than a sound track to his memories, that in addition to providing a means of transport, it could also steel him for what he might find and even deliver emotions that had once been beyond him to acknowledge. While Maria—and for that matter, Leo—had long alluded to possessing a faith in performance— and by extension music—Martin had always felt more agnostic. It now seemed he, too, held a certain belief that—as with any intuition—if you could figure out how to listen to these songs, they would take you to places you needed to go, even before you knew why, and once you were there might offer a few small threads of beauty—or even purpose—that on balance could make the difference between wanting to go on and wanting to disappear.

While the vast expanse of the horizon filled him with a certain fear of the unknown—his ability to breathe, it seemed, was also his ability to doubt—he took comfort in knowing that the past year had been valuable. It had changed him in ways he had hoped for, if not exactly anticipated; he was physically healthier—to the extent that his hands and feet no longer ached, and he could sleep through most nights—and less emotionally wounded, this all the more remarkable given that he had been largely oblivious to the condition. To know that he had confronted some of the most painful episodes of his past and survived gave him confidence; it wasn't broad or far-reaching, certainly, but rather struck him as the opposite of the muted despair he now understood—underneath the more superficial measures of success—had marked so much of his life.

Many times in the past few weeks, surrounded by the glass windows of his living room and the views of the city, he had been tempted to think that he could spend his final decades there alone, or at most in the company of a sad succession of cats, sifting through his memories in the continuing attempt to ascertain exactly who he was. But out here on the bay, listening to Maria and with Leo at his side, he knew it was an untenable proposition. It was just as Leo had said: there was only so much you could uncover on your own. If Beatrice had taught him anything, it was the need to reach outside, to search patiently for what he was looking for, whether it was love or faith or anything else that might give his life meaning. He had done this with her, and while it may have been a tentative and crippled form of love, it was for him pure and forgiving, and he had cried the tears to prove it.

He was still only forty-one years old, and the city, splayed out in front of him, beckoned with possibility. He remembered his high school longings for a girlfriend, and how he had always been drawn to the idea of someone molding the spinning mass inside him into something artistic and refined and—most of all—human. What he realized now was that he had presented not just a mound of clay but a wildly off-kilter wheel, so that, no matter how gifted anyone might have been, there was no way to center him. Now, perhaps, the wheel was at least level and spinning in the right direction, and he could almost feel his hands pulling himself up into something to behold.

AT LUNCH BEFORE the service, Martin had described to Leo some of what had happened since 9/11 to him and to the city itself. If not quite sanguine, Leo had been philosophical about the terrorist attacks; as he pointed out, many if not most cities throughout history had suffered far worse mutilations—he specifically mentioned the 1871 Commune, where thousands of Parisians had been killed by their own countrymen in the course of a day or two—and while some of these cities had died and were buried, many had recovered, and still more had been born. They talked about Anna Prus, whom Leo had seen at the height of her career, when—as he assured Martin—she had been most impressive. Martin in turn had described her death, and Leo seemed genuinely astonished, or at least very much intrigued, to learn about the *Tristan* manuscript. Martin offered to show it to him, but Leo demurred, saying that he wanted to wait for Maria; the three of them had already arranged to meet after the service.

Martin returned his attention to Maria's song and soon found himself thinking of Anna. At first the accident had been terrifying to consider, not only because of what it conjured up in terms of Hank and Jane but also because of the thought of an old woman—alone and lonely—getting killed like this, another life ending in a most undignified way, her remains swept up like a pile of garbage. As he reconsidered it now, in the fragmented and dreamlike sunlight reflecting off the water, he felt certain that Anna had not been afraid, that she had possessed an unlikely tranquillity as she flew past, almost as though—he realized with a start—she had arrived at the same conclusions about life and death as he had while awaiting the inevitable, i.e., death in the form of a speeding taxi, but unlike him had made the choice to succumb. Although he continued to resist the idea that she had been looking at him—as opposed to anyone else who happened to be in the vicinity—he did not find it difficult to entertain the notion that she had at least considered him, in the way two people passing each other in a narrow hallway might, with a nod of recognition and understanding that each was now headed in the direction from which the other had just arrived.

45

There Is a Light That Never Goes Out

NEW YORK CITY, 2002. Leo Metropolis ushered Martin and Maria into a small cabin on the upper deck and invited them to sit. They began by talking about the weather, about Bayreuth, about Martin's "retirement" and Maria's facetious desire for the same. Leo complimented Maria on her tribute to Anna and admitted that the significance—if not the beauty—of the song had been lost on him, and as he listened to Martin and Maria discuss its larger meaning, he almost forgot what he was here to do. He remembered what it was like before he had seen anything painful and destructive, when he was young and in love with music, and learning how works of art can sometimes mutate or evolve into other, equally beautiful pieces.

With the cabin infused by the bronze light of the setting sun, Leo raised the topic of the manuscript. Martin abashedly confessed—given how little sense it made—his suspicion, or perhaps hope, that Anna had died in a state of bliss, which led Maria to describe how she had heard a second voice at the end of her *Liebestod* in Bayreuth, and how she had somehow known—even before she got the phone call—that it had been Anna. It pleased Leo to hear this, for it seemed to confirm that in the beckoning aura of the approaching night, there would be a familiar, theatrical sense of possibility, a necessary suspension of belief that would allow his audience to understand his story—just as he had understood theirs—without questioning its plausibility.

Martin opened his briefcase and handed the document to Leo, who—and this was a conscious decision on his part—flipped through the pages not with the reverence of a scholar or the greedy fingers of a dealer but with the easy assurance of one who had handled it hundreds of times. Although he had not expected to have this document at his side and was prepared to tell his story without it, its appearance struck him as a fortuitous break, and one that the performer in him felt obliged to use to his advantage. As Martin and Maria silently watched, he took a breath and began to speak, looking at them each in turn and explaining that he had wanted to talk to them about something for quite some time but that circumstances—along with a certain cowardice on his part that he hoped they would soon understand and forgive—had prevented him from doing so until now. He asked for their indulgence—which they appeared quite willing to give—and begged them not to jump to conclusions; he assured them that he did not want to convince them of anything but only to offer his service and perhaps—in return—ask for their help.

This moment—the beginning of his story—was one he had rehearsed many times, at least in his head, and he welcomed a familiar weightlessness that allowed him to craft every phrase, to fill each syllable with as much love and nuance as he could—at least without singing—as if he were taking the stage for the greatest role in his life. He started quietly, with a more distant, objective tone, not unlike the narrative in his mind when he recalled episodes from his past but could not afford to delve into the accompanying emotion. From his pocket he withdrew an envelope, which he set on top of the manuscript and encouraged them to examine. These notes, he explained, which had been in his possession for a very long time, represented a formula for a vaccine against aging, discovered by a French scientist in the nineteenth century, who coincidentally—and here he nodded at the score—was the father of Lucien Marchand, the French heldentenor who had created the role of Tristan. As Leo said this, he glanced at Maria, who just as he had hoped instinctively nodded—she had obviously heard of the man—while Martin watched pensively beside her.

Leo briefly explained how Lucien had come to possess the score and then offered a few details about his life; he described how Eduard had jumped to his death from the scaffolding of his opera house, and how Lucien had carried his lifeless body through the streets of Vienna to the steps of the palace, as if to indict Franz Joseph, after which he remained in a state of grief-stricken paralysis, unable to sing. He told them what had happened one summer when Lucien returned to Paris, where his father, as per the French emperor's edict, had taken the vaccine, and how Lucien had also taken it, with the unexpected result that Guillaume had died while Lucien had not.

Whether Martin and Maria believed him, Leo knew he had at least captured them—he could feel them wanting to know what had happened to Lucien—and he felt sustained by the artistic alchemy that allowed him to distill so much life into the words and images rolling off his tongue. He told them that Lucien eventually came to New York

City—carrying little more than a *Tristan* manuscript and his father's last words, the formula for the vaccine—where it didn't take long to realize that what he had taken had worked; while those around him aged, he did not (or if he did, it was imperceptible). He lived a solitary life and refused to consider the prospect of sharing his fate with anyone else until he understood it better himself; he changed his name twice, first to Luke Merchant and then to Lawrence Malcolm; he worked as a furniture maker, a shipbuilder, and—finally—a dealer of antiques. He imposed upon himself a spartan discipline and routine; he read thousands of books and studied inventions; he went to museums and gallery exhibitions, he observed the construction of ever-taller buildings and wider bridges in the city; he reflected on his past with as much objectivity as possible, writing and rewriting episodes in notebooks like the ones his father had once used and, over time, grew confident that he, too, was on the cusp of great discoveries about the nature of life, as if he had melded all of his experience into an eternal, golden ring he could offer to those who continued to suffer.

As close as he came to this revelation, as satisfied as he might be on one day, he inevitably lost it the next; as many times as he started the process anew with a thought to improve, he would end up back at the beginning, doubting and afraid. He grew despondent as he arrived at the seemingly futile conclusion that any truth—or at least any truth worth living (or dying) for—was always fleeting, subject to the vagaries of time, while any that lasted was doomed to a fate of the banal, the assumed, the given, the sort of thing—like a geometry formula—that children could appreciate for a second and then discard. Because this new insight contradicted everything he had ever believed about the nature of true understanding, instilled in him by his father, he felt defeated, and worse, it brought into intense relief the maddening loneliness under which he had already labored for so many decades. As he continued to consider his past, it seemed that everyone he had ever touched was about to die, while he, as if made of rock, was doomed to live.

Desperate to escape this numb despair, he returned to the opera. To this point he had avoided it, fearing that it would instill in him a grief-stricken longing that would test—and likely exceed—any bounds of sanity. But on a snowy evening in 1960—almost one hundred years to the day after he had first heard it—succumbing to his deeper intuition, he went to see *Tristan* at the Metropolitan Opera. He knew the second he heard the soft, teasing call of the cellos and winds not only that his fears had been unfounded but also that the music had never ceased to course through him, as if it were his blood, his air, and his food. He emerged resurrected, wanting—or no, needing— to sing, knowing that, without his voice, his body might have been alive but his soul was dead. The truth he had been seeking for so long was not something universal or sublime to be discovered but rather mutable; it was his version of the world—and his alone—to create or, more to the point, to sing, using the language of music, in which he had always felt most at home. So for the second time in his long life he became a singer. He dedicated himself to the opera, with the intent—sure that nobody could ever tell a story such as his—to be the greatest singer who ever lived. He chose a new name—one with which Martin and Maria were already familiar—to reflect this aspiration to tie his past to his future, and here he paused, as if to summon enough strength to smash even the possibility of doubt—the name of Leo Metropolis.

MARIA SEEMED TO brace herself—but with a graceful strength and heightened sense of control that did not fail to remind him of her performance in Bayreuth, which had matched and possibly exceeded his own—while Martin aggressively leaned forward, as if to assault him with questions, a response that also did not lack a certain aesthetic appeal and intellectual rigor. Leo could see both of them working to reconcile their doubts with a desire to believe him, not only because of who he was but also because of everything that such belief implied about the potential of life to deliver the unexpected. And so, as soon as he caught his breath, he asked them to judge him in such terms: he begged them to look at the city in front of them, to consider the skyline, to imagine the streets and the subways, the hypnotic ebb and flow of the people moving in and out of the buildings and elevators, or even the availability—in a certain restaurant on Fifth Avenue—of a *pâté de canard* that brought him back to a Romanian princess he had known in Paris. His life, he maintained, was no less and no more than an attempt to create something transcendent and lasting out of the haphazard and random events that defined so much of it—to order and possess his past, as if he had willed it and not the other way around—just as the city did for the millions who lived there. Or—he added more softly—they might consider Maria's earlier song and Martin's appreciation of the same, or the impossible but undeniable odds that both of their parents had tragically died at such a young age, or even the circumstances that had brought them together on this day. That they had already discussed this idea was apparent to Leo in the way they glanced at each other with expressions that seemed to convey more understanding and determination than shock, although it lasted only a second before they turned back to him with renewed expectation, which he knew stemmed from his failure to explain exactly why he was telling them this story.

On the verge of unveiling this last great secret, he felt exhausted, so that he could barely manage to part his lips to breathe, let alone summon the energy to speak. He grimaced and managed to steady himself; this weariness, he knew, was also an aspect of his performance, a symptom of the self-destructive but sacrificial need to go on at any cost—even the ultimate one—as if the lives of those who listened, those he loved, depended on it. He took their hands and in a hoarse but urgent whisper told them how he had met Anna after her performance—one, he noted, that was almost as miraculous as Maria's in Bayreuth, and perhaps even more unexpected—and inspired by the idea that her voice might help him to regain his own, had invited her to his store. To his pleasant surprise, she had come the following day, and he had impulsively shown her the manuscript and played from it, with a thought to re-create a moment of his youth, to both honor and be absolved from it, and to his astonishment and gratification, she had joined him, singing Isolde to his Tristan.

Maria through her tears quietly confirmed that this was true, and that Anna had never told anyone but her. What she had not told Maria, Leo continued, was that, in the course of singing, they had been gripped in a way that he felt sure they all could understand; and that while he had been physically attracted to women only a handful of times in his very long life, for these minutes, his desire had mirrored her own, and several months later he had received a letter from Anna explaining that she had given birth to twins, one boy and one girl, but that she had given them up for adoption to two families who lived near the city of Pittsburgh, where she was certain they would be given the love and attention she—as an opera singer traveling the world—had not felt capable of delivering. Over their gasps of belief and disbelief, he found the will to tell them that this had occurred almost exactly forty-two years ago, and he hoped they would forgive him for not coming forward until now, because it was only after he realized that he was going to die that he could once again afford to love.

LEO HEARD VOICES and knew it was his *Liebestod,* his song of love and death that had accompanied him through so much of his life, marking the end of one phase and the beginning of the next. Except

while the singing had always been literal and the death metaphorical, this time his death would be most literal, just as the music—he
could almost hear low, tremulant cellos—was dreamlike and distant.
He listened to the words—"How mild and soft is his smile; how gently he opens his eyes! Do you see him? Shining ever brighter . . . how
he ascends, bathed in starlight!"—and he could detect Maria, Anna,
and even his own mother, returning to say good-bye. The words
echoed and were accompanied not only by the surging arpeggios of
harps but also by the rustling of the flags and the soft, overlapping
wake of the boat as it headed toward shore. "Behold how his heart
swells with pride," the voices went on, "how it beats, brave and full,
in his breast! And how from his lips . . . gently issues his sweet breath.
Look, friends . . . do you not feel it and see it?"

He watched with expectant eyes as Martin and Maria briefly con-
ferred and appeared to come to a consensus with regard to his final
request, made only seconds earlier, although the details were already
blurring as images from the past began to cascade over his mind. He
sighed heavily but contentedly, knowing that his will was about to be
done; they were not going to doubt or question but simply lift the burden under which he had labored for so long. Martin ignited a corner
of the brittle paper—the formula—and passed it to Maria as the sheets
caught fire in a whisper and then expanded into a tiny, flickering flame.
Leo felt no regret as he watched the formula disintegrate; this had
been his father's understanding of the world, and only now—through
this transformation—was Leo making it his own. He felt tears of gratitude and forgiveness running down his cheeks as the voices continued: "Do I alone hear this music so wonderfully sweet . . . this blissful
lament from his lips saying all, forgiving all? How it grows within me,
soars on high, and echoes throughout the heavens!"

He tried to raise his arms—he wanted to embrace his children—
but his blood grew thick and slowed, and he could not. Though it

seemed impossible after so many years of longing that he could be possessed by a most irrational instinct to live—an impulse to fight what he craved most of all—he was afraid and for a moment wanted to live a little longer, to know what would happen to Martin and Maria, and he hated the idea of leaving. But he knew that his part in their story was about to end, and in the next second he was consoled by the strong hands he felt on his shoulders, propping him up—this, he knew, would be Martin—and by the graceful manner in which Maria kneeled in front of him, keeping one hand in his while the other held the burning sheets of paper.

Maria sloughed from her fingers the final remnants of the formula, which drifted back and forth toward the floor. Yet still he lived, and to live, it seemed, was to question: would he rise like an angel or be sent to walk the coals of hell? Or—as he had always believed— would he be given to an endless moment of comfort and delivery, as if the gap between the last note of music and the start of the applause, a moment of complete darkness and silence bathed in accomplishment and regret, were extended forever? Trembling with fear and desire, he called out to his children and felt them close by as his eyes turned away from a diffuse light and the voices grew louder.

> *"Growing louder, weaving all about me . . .*
> *. . . are they gentle breezes,*
> *or sweet-smelling clouds?*
> *As they swell and whisper, dare I breathe?*
> *Dare I listen?*
> *Shall I drink them in,*
> *or be engulfed by their fragrance?*
> *In the billowing sea,*
> *their echoing sound . . .*
> *. . . in the surging night*

of the world's life and breath . . .
. . . to drown, to be lost . . .
. . . unknowing, in highest bliss!"

The endless night had arrived; the performance of a lifetime was over. A final shard of scorched paper landed, its flame extinguished, as Leo Metropolis, his children by his side, at last surrendered to the music of the universe.

Acknowledgments

Readers: Meg Muirhead, my brother Michael, Bill Clegg, Matt Hudson, Suzanne O'Neill, and Susan Barnett. *Blogosphere:* Bennett Madison, Choire Sicha, Natasha Vargas-Cooper, Jeff Weinstein, Jennie Portnof, M.Snowe, Megen Gumus, Seth Colter Walls, and Brian Ulicky. *CLOTU:* Dante, Beatrice, Zephyr, Elektra, Syd, Elly, Lucian, and Anjellicle Cats Rescue. *Friends:* Jennifer Baron, Mike Donofrio, Jim Harwood, Brigit Dermott, Matt Kadane, Danielle Nguyen, John Pisani, Thoma Marshall, and Judy Zecher. *Aspen:* Frank Quinn, Susan Gruesser, and Annie Cavlov. *Retreats:* Jonathan Cobb and Kurt Reitz, Phebe and Paul Tanners. *Family:* Ma, Dad, Shawn, Greg, Jan, and Zeppo. *Love, Patience, Inspiration:* Stephen Pickover.

Thanks to my many friends and colleagues at Oxford University Press.

Thanks to Crown and the many great people there who have given every facet of the book so much care and attention.

For more notes, music, photographs, digressions, and links, please visit www.TheMetropolisCase.com.

About the Author

MATTHEW GALLAWAY got his B.A. from Cornell University, where he majored in government, and after working for several environmental groups in Washington, D.C., he attended law school at New York University. (He is fairly certain that he is the only graduate of NYU Law to work as a record-store clerk.) After passing the bar, he played in a rock band (Saturnine) for several years before turning his attention to *The Metropolis Case*. He currently lives in Washington Heights with his partner and three cats.